ECHOES OF HOME

Right from the beginning, even as I was writing *Echoes of a Trumpet*, Ellen kept 'popping up'. I hadn't known about her until my publisher, John Owen Smith, told me the family story in his first 'Riot' book (*One Monday in November*). But then, every so often, Ellen would be pushed to the forefront of my mind again. I tried to ignore her for years, but something kept telling me that she wanted her story told. So here it is…

GW00385029

About the Author:

Jean Newland was born in Four Marks and has lived all her life in Hampshire. Since discovering her close family connection with the legendary 'Trumpeter' she has researched the family from the early days in Selborne to the years spent in Bentley, where her father was born in 1901

For my son Robert

(1964–1998)

Acknowledgement: To my cousin Marian McColl
for all the research done in Tasmania; and to my friends and family
who have never failed in their support

— Illustrations —
Front cover: Hobart town from the new wharf c.1857
Back cover: Washing trough in the memorial garden at the Women's
Factory in Hobart, Tasmania (taken by Marian McColl)
Facing p.9: Ellen in later years with members of her family

Jean Newland.
x

ECHOES OF HOME

Jean Newland

Echoes of Home

First published 2008

Typeset and published by John Owen Smith
19 Kay Crescent, Headley Down, Hampshire GU35 8AH

Tel: 01428 712892 – Fax: 08700 516554
wordsmith@johnowensmith.co.uk
www.johnowensmith.co.uk

ISBN 978-1-873855-56-0

Printed and bound by CPI Antony Rowe, Eastbourne

PROLOGUE

Impression Bay, Van Diemen's Land, 1844

'Bloody hot, ain't it?' The tall, wiry man stared out between the thick iron bars that covered the window.

'It sure is, Bart,' John Ryan said. 'I wonder if we'll be allowed out today. It'd be grand to sit under yonder trees. Can't you just imagine the soft breeze wafting over you?'

'Huh! You bloody Irish are all alike. Always trying to put a poetic slant on things.' Bart Tyrrell aimed a mouthful of spittle out through the bars with practised ease. 'The rest of us have to live in the real world, and we don't much like what we see.'

'Well, and to be sure, who's fault is that,' John asked.

'What do you mean? Whose fault is it? It's the bloody English law that's what.' A sneer turned Bart's face into an evil mask.

'And so the law forced you to knock a man down, take all his money and then shoot him dead, did it?' John raised his eyebrows.

'You don't understand. I was stony broke, had to feed me wife and kids didn't I?'

'I too was destitute, and yes, I admit I did steal to feed my family, but I never killed a man doing it.' Anger began to well up inside him and he moved away. It wouldn't do to lose his temper with anyone, especially someone like Tyrrell, who'd knife a man as soon as look at him. If he could just keep his nose out of trouble for a few more months, then he'd be out of this cursed place. He prayed every night that he would make it. It was a hard thing for any man to do; keeping a cool head on you, when all your instincts were to smash down the gates and make a run for it.

He'd been here at Impression Bay prison for almost a year now. A

5

long, degrading year. Life consisted of rising early and working outdoors in the scorching heat, either digging latrine trenches or building yet another block of cells for the ever-growing prison, then a dinner of bread and water. When they at last came in for the day, it was more bread, a hunk of cheese then bed in one of the tiny cubicles. The prison had improved slightly with the passage of time, but it was still dire in his opinion. Some new Governor had insisted the men's lot be bettered and there had been an effort to do so, but without much success. John shook his head sadly. He'd thought life back in Ireland was bad enough, with no work to be had, only a hovel to live in and a wife who nagged all day – and most of the night too. But to be sent here to this island somewhere on the other side of the world seemed to be harsh beyond all reason.

He was not alone, hundreds of men from all over the British Isles were here, all sent away because the English authority's didn't know what to do with them. Back home the prisons overflowed with miscreants of all kinds, but the worst had been transported. That galled him; he hadn't been particularly sinful, but his judge on the day had been in a foul mood. If he was honest with himself, it hadn't been his first offence, and his mate Thomo had been hasty in knocking that policeman over. The man hadn't been unduly hurt, just a dent in his hat and a speck of dust on his jacket, but his pride had been sorely injured.

John looked back to where Bart stood looking out into the harsh afternoon sunshine. The man was cruel, dangerous, and he hoped fervently that they wouldn't be sent to the same place once they left this prison.

When? That was the question, and where? He had no idea how big this island was. Van Diemen's Land, it was called, but that was all he knew about it. The limited view from the compound showed a rugged coastline away to the right, then a wide bay with high hills beyond. It was the bay, with its startling blue water that had kept his spirits up, and he dreamed of wading into it; the wide sky above him, his body making ripples to break up the clouds reflected there. The stark reality of the dreary prison buildings on the land would be forgotten for a few blissful moments. He knew the other men laughed at him and called him a dreamer, but he didn't care. What was a man without his dreams?

He could let his mind wander at will, seeing again the soft rolling hills of Ireland and smelling the peat fire burning day and night in the grate. He could feel the morning rain and see once more the glorious sunsets away over to the west where the mountains met the Atlantic

Ocean. John sighed. He had long ago accepted that he would never see Ireland again, and it was a high price he'd paid for one night of foolishness.

The clanging of the bell roused him. It was time for their exercise period. As it was the Sabbath they were excused work, but worship in the tiny prison chapel was mandatory morning and evening. Afterwards they could have some free time in the humid, but relatively fresh air before supper.

As the line of men filed past him, John's spirits lifted at the thought of walking across to his favourite position at the wall. The place where he could squint through a narrow gap to gaze at the sea, and no matter that it would be in the full glare of the sun, he would stay for as long as possible drinking in the view before him.

Ellen (centre front) taken with members of her family not long before she died in 1908 at the age of 81 in Zeehan, Tasmania

CHAPTER 1

Selborne, England, April 1847

Eyes squinting against the bright sunlight as she emerged from the tunnel of trees covering the sunken lane, Ellen Newland hurried on her way toward home. Her face set into a grimace as she tried to imagine what kind of reception she'd receive when she told her parents the news. Father would be furious of course, but mother would probably understand because she was that kind of woman, always considering other people's feelings before passing judgement.

The fresh air made Ellen light-headed after being cooped up for so long in the large, dreary house where she lived-in as a kitchen maid and the warm sunshine brought a glow to her already rosy cheeks. In spite of working hard for eight years she had never bettered herself, always being told by the snooty housekeeper that she was too untidy and loud ever to be let anywhere near the gentry.

Well, now they could keep their job, thought Ellen, pushing her bonnet back to reveal locks of dark hair. Soon she would be mistress of her own home. In a few months time she would be twenty-one and old enough to marry whom she chose, without consent from anyone.

And she had chosen. At last she had found someone with whom she could be happy. All right, he might be a lot older than she and a widower, but she was fond of him and he of her; and he owned a smallholding. That, to Ellen, made the future look very secure indeed. It was May now, so it was only five months to her birthday, just time enough for her father to get used to the idea.

At last she rounded the corner by the Church and saw several children playing noisily on the green, known as the Plestor, that fronted it. Ellen smiled, remembering the times she had played there as a child herself.

Suddenly, the children stopped their game of tag and silence descended. Then the vicar appeared from the direction of the Church, and she knew the reason, for as the man approached, the youngsters all ran off as though Old Nick himself was after them. This man of God was far nicer than the previous one, but the village still viewed him with suspicion; the Reverend Cobbold had left an unholy legacy.

As she passed on along the dusty main street of Selborne, with its row of thatched cottages on one side and the butchers and pub on the other, everyone she met greeted her with a smile or a word of welcome, giving Ellen a feeling of comfort. She was glad that she'd been born and brought up here in this small village, deep in the Hampshire countryside, where everyone knew everyone else. She returned the wave from old Mrs Benson who was peering out from her window. And a little way further on she saw Mr Gregg hard at work in his forge, the doors flung wide to let in some cool air, while blowing out a blast of hot at the same time.

Soon the family home came into sight, nestling in the trees close to the foot of the Hanger, a wooded slope of beech and oak trees that rose high above the village. Her parents, although hard-working, were poor, but the small cottage was always warm and welcoming.

Ellen walked up the path and saw her mother struggling to lift a wet sheet from the wooden tub placed outside the cottage door. Every week washing was taken in to provide a little extra money, and in spite of the family pleading with her to stop now that most of them had left home, Mrs Newland continued the weekly ritual of washing, drying and ironing other people's bed linen.

Ellen hurried forward to take one end of the sheet, and soon it was twisted to squeeze out the excess water, then folded neatly ready for mangling.

Ellen's mother pushed back the wisp of hair that had fallen across her face, smiling a welcome. 'How're you, dear? Not been working you too hard have they?'

Pulling a face of disgust, Ellen said, 'Same as always. Want your blood that lot. Is there a pot brewing?'

Ann Newland turned and entered the tiny cottage, then lifted the heavy brown teapot from the trivet by the open fire. ''Course, when isn't there?' She laughed, her eyes lighting with fun.

Sliding along the wooden bench that fronted the scrubbed table, Ellen sat and studied her mother. The once dark hair was now mostly grey and her bright eyes seemed to be lack-lustre, signs Ellen was sure of the hard life her mother had led. But she was a kind and generous mother, loving each of her eleven children in equal measure.

'Where's Harriet?' Ellen asked. Harriet was her youngest sister and at eleven years old would soon be going off to live a life in service, as all the Newland girls had.

'She's off visiting our Jane today and staying until late.' Ann turned now to place a mug tea on the table. She raised her eyebrows. 'You're quiet, is something troubling you?'

Ellen hesitated. 'Not troubling really, ma, but I've something to tell you and pa when he gets in from work and I don't think he's going to like it.'

'And why not? You haven't been in trouble again have you?'

'No, course not. When do I ever have the time nowadays?' They both laughed, but Ellen hated to remember the time when she'd been caught stealing firewood and brought up before the magistrate. It hadn't been fair. At the time her mother was ill, the snow lay thick on the ground and the cottage was freezing, Ellen had been sure that the rich farmer wouldn't miss a few logs. But he had, and insisted the thirteen-year-old Ellen was made to pay for them. She shuddered. Her father had found the money for her fine from somewhere, but it had been a most uncomfortable time. And she'd never been allowed to forget it.

'So, just what have you to tell us then?' her mother pressed for an answer.

Taking a deep breath, Ellen told her, 'I'm hoping to get wed.'

Stillness settled over Ann and she gazed at her daughter steadily. 'Who to? And have you thought it through? I'm sorry to ask you about it dear, but you are so reckless sometimes.'

With good grace, Ellen grinned. 'I know, but this is all right, ma, honestly. He's a bit older than I am, but he has his own cottage. And he says he loves me, and I love him.' She didn't add, "I think", although she did sometimes wonder. 'There, does that reassure you?'

'A little, except you said your father wouldn't like it. Why's that?'

'It's Robert Heath.'

Ellen heard her mother's sharp intake of breath. 'You're right, he's not going to like it.'

After an afternoon of helping her mother with the washing, Ellen sat exhausted at the table while the seemingly tireless woman in front of her cooked a meal. Father was due home any minute and Ellen's stomach clenched in apprehension; he was going to have a lot to say, she was certain.

Her mother glanced round, 'It mightn't be as bad as you think,

11

Ellen. Sometimes your father can surprise everyone by taking a completely different direction to the one you'd expect.'

'Not this time he won't. The bad feeling goes back a long way.' Ellen turned her head toward the door. 'That sounds like him now,' she said as they heard the sound of water being pumped outside.

John Newland always sluiced himself off before entering the home, removing any smell of the farm animals he had tended all day. The latch lifted and both Ellen and Ann waited with baited breath as John entered, shrugging off his work jacket as he came.

His face lit at the sight of his daughter, making Ellen feel even worse. He went to his wife and patted her shoulder, then crossed to Ellen and did the same to her. This was as demonstrative as he ever got. 'How're you,' he asked his daughter. 'You look fair worn out. Been working you too hard up at the house, have they?'

A grin spread across Ellen's face. 'No pa, I've been helping ma all afternoon with the washing and that's worn me out. I don't know how she does it.'

John looked across at his wife, a fond smile curving his lips. 'She doesn't have to do it now, I've told her often enough.'

'You're glad of the extras it buys,' Ann said lightly. 'I've done a mutton stew, how does that sound?'

'Good, I'm starving,' and he leaned over the huge black pot to sniff appreciatively at the contents. 'Cor, dumplings as well, and pearl barley, you're spoiling me today.'

He sat at the table beside Ellen while Ann dished up a large dish full for each of them. 'Everything all right, girl? You're quiet today; I can't usually get a word in edgeways when you're around.'

With a stiff smile, Ellen said, 'I've a lot on my mind, pa that's all. I'll tell you about it in a moment, but eat your meal first.'

'Oh, very mysterious I must say. For you to have a lot on your mind, well that's almost unheard of,' he joshed.

'John, stop pulling the girl's leg,' Ann laughed, but the laughter did not reach her eyes, and Ellen knew that she was worried about his reaction to news of their daughter's proposed wedding.

Once the dishes were cleared away, John turned to Ellen. Stuffing a small amount of tobacco into his clay pipe, he asked her, 'Come on then, girl tell me what this's all about. I can tell by your face's that I'm not going to like what I hear, so spit it out and get it over with.'

Taking a deep shuddering breath, Ellen told him her news, and then waited for the storm that would surely follow.

And follow it did.

'What!' John roared. 'You dare to sit there and tell me that you're

12

going to marry that – that blackguard? Over my dead body you will.' His angry eyes settled on his wife. 'Did you know about this?'

'Not until today.'

'Pa, please listen. It'll be all right, you'll see. He's different now, all that happened many years ago.'

'I'll never forgive him for what he did no matter how many years pass. What in the name of God did you want to get involved with him for? Apart from the fact he's years older than you are and a widower, you knew I wouldn't like it, yet you've gone ahead with it so far as to saying you want to marry him.' Spittle foamed on his lips. 'You'd better not be with child or I'll swing for him, I will.'

Ellen had never seen her father so angry; his face a deep red, thick veins standing out in his neck and eyes almost popping out of his head. In fact his appearance frightened her. He was normally a kindly, placid man, but now he was a monster and she felt terrible at having caused the transformation.

Ann stepped across the kitchen and placed a comforting hand on his shoulder. 'Calm yourself, John, you'll be ill and end up with one of your headaches.'

'I'm not with child,' Ellen said bluntly. 'We've never done anything like that.' Then she stood up. 'I'd better go ma, so you and pa can talk. Tell Harriet I'll see her next time and I'm sorry I missed her.' Then she raced out through the door and ran blindly down the path, tears spurting from her eyes.

Once out in the street, she slowed her steps and wiped her eyes on her sleeve. It was still daylight and she didn't want the prying eyes of the villagers to start speculating on why she might be upset. Perhaps by the time she visited again next month, pa would have calmed down.

'I do understand, John, really I do, but Ellen is a grown woman now and must find her own path in life. I'm sure she didn't realise just how angry it would make you, after all she was only a small child when the trouble happened.' Ann looked sadly at her husband as he sat slumped in the chair by the fire.

'Child or not, she knows the bad feeling that's always existed between the Heath family and us. If Robert Heath was a decent chap I'd say nothing against the marriage, but he's the nastiest of the lot, always has been and always will be. I was nearly hanged because of what he and his brother said about me and I'm not likely to forgive that in a hurry, am I?'

'No, course not, but I don't know what to do. I could always go and see him I suppose; make him realise that by marrying Ellen he'll split the family apart.'

'Ha! That wouldn't do any good, the man's too thick to try and reason with. Of all the men in this county my daughter has to choose from, she has to go and want this one. She must be mad, Ann, that's the only answer.'

'Don't say that about Ellen, I know she's always been headstrong, but that doesn't mean she's not right in the head. And she's not the prettiest of our daughters, is she? I don't think there have been many suitors hanging around.' Ann allowed herself a wry chuckle. 'Not like with Jane or Mary, we had to practically lock those two up.'

'Looks aren't everything. Ellen's got a certain way about her and is spirited enough, things to make some young man a good wife.' He sighed heavily. 'I just don't know what to do. If I thought it'd do any good I'd go and see the father meself. He's old now and although I don't think he ever had much influence over his sons, he might try to get Robert to change his mind. That's if he knows about it, of course.'

Just then the door burst open and in clattered their fifteen-year-old son James, home from his work on the nearby estate. His mother clicked her tongue in exasperation. 'Do you have to make so much noise? And mess,' she added, seeing the mud from his boots all over the floor.

'Sorry ma.' He planted a kiss on her cheek. 'Hello pa. Good day?' He stopped suddenly seeing the look on his father's face and when told of Ellen's news, he sat heavily on the bench. 'Oh! No wonder you're looking angry. What're you going to do?'

John and Ann Newland looked at each other in anguish. What could they do once their daughter reached her twenty-first birthday?

As spring eased itself into summer and the days lengthened, Ellen began to despair. She'd been walking out with Robert for almost a year, but still he wouldn't be pinned down to deciding on a wedding date. 'I don't think you want to marry me at all,' she said petulantly one day as they walked along one of the narrow lanes surrounding Selborne. 'You're just keeping me on a string so that you can look good with a woman on your arm.'

'Don't be so silly, Ellen, of course that's not the way of it. You know my father's in poor health and my mother relies on me to bring home money to keep us all, I can hardly take on a wife as well, can I.'

She pouted. 'Well, it's not fair, I'm almost twenty-one and my sisters were all married by that age. They'll think no one wants me if I wait much longer.'

She heard Robert give a sigh. 'You do say some daft things sometimes, girl.'

'Don't you dare call me daft. I'm no worse than many folk around here. I hate working in service Robert, and I'll make you a good wife. I can cook and sew and clean, you'll have a well-kept house, I promise.'

'I don't doubt that, but you can't tell me that your father is keen on our marrying. You never did tell me what he said when you told him.'

'He was angry, I admit, but he'll get used to the idea. I don't know what the problem is between you. I know bad things happened years ago when I was a child, but surely it could all be forgotten now.'

'What happened in Selborne that day will never be forgotten, Ellen, believe me. It changed the village forever, and many more around the area. All right, brother John and me made the mistake of thinking we saw your father in Headley the following day when they ransacked the workhouse, and he'll never forgive the time he spent in prison because we spoke out.'

'Robert! He was in danger of being hanged, you know he was. Fortunately Mr Fitt spoke up for him and told the court that pa was at home that day, so he only got sentenced for leading the riot in Selborne.'

'Lead it? Huh, all he did was blow that bloody bugle of his. Right racket it was too. Everyone knew Holdaway was the real leader; that was why he was sent off to the other side of the world as punishment.'

A shiver ran up Ellen's spine. 'Poor man, fancy being sent all the way to Australia never to see his family again.' She turned to Robert abruptly. 'The same thing could have happened to pa, and it would've been your fault.'

'All right! All right! I know. But he wasn't, was he? And if you ask me he was lucky to get away with six months in prison and not be sent off like most of the men involved were.'

'My ma had a terrible struggle to feed the family while he was away, you don't get much off the parish however many bellies you have to fill. And she made herself ill going to visit him. And our Bill got frostbite.'

'Don't your family ever forget anything? I'm sick of hearing about it time and time again.'

Ellen bristled. 'How dare you talk like that about my family? We're a darned sight better than your lot anyway.'

Robert rounded on her. 'If you think so little of my family then why are you so keen to marry into it? Eh? Answer me that?'

'Well, I won't then. I'd rather stay single and be an old maid than marry you now.' Then with her back ramrod straight, Ellen stalked off back along the lane, tears of frustration burning her eyes. But she wouldn't look back. Perhaps her father was right; the Heath family were a bad lot.

It was several weeks before she saw him again, and Ellen admitted to herself that she had missed him. Not that she let Robert see that of course. She glanced at him coolly as he stood by the gate waiting for her when she left her parent's cottage after the monthly half-day visit. 'What do you want?' she asked bluntly.

'Just wondered how you were.' Robert shrugged.

'I'm fine, thanks.'

'Good.' He hesitated and then added. 'I've missed you.'

'Have you?'

'Yes. Can we make up our quarrel and walk out together again? Please?'

With her eyes narrowed as though contemplating the question, Ellen stood looking off somewhere into the distance. Should she forgive him? Or should she let him stew for a bit longer? 'Mmm, well all right then. But no more nasty comments about my family.'

'I promise. And no more about mine either.'

Ellen nodded and started walking off toward the village. Robert followed and soon was walking in step with her, then he pulled her arm through his and they strode through Selborne arm in arm for all to see.

Good, now he'll have to name the day, she thought, a wry smile on her face.

As the silence between them lengthened, Ellen searched her brain for a way to open the subject of marriage. Nothing came to mind and in the end it was Robert who spoke first.

'I've been thinking,' he said. 'About us getting wed.'

Her heart soared – at last.

'The trouble is my father. He's in very poor health as you know and to be honest, he's not happy with our union, so I think we'll have to wait awhile until he either dies or changes his mind.'

Ellen's heart plummeted again. 'How long then?'

'Hard to say, he could go on for another year or more.' He turned to look down at her. 'We don't have to wait if that's what you want.'

As his arm tightened around hers, her face flamed. 'Robert Heath, if you mean what I think you mean then you'll be unlucky. There'll be nothing like that until I have a wedding band on my finger.'

With a shrug, Robert told her, 'Please yourself, it doesn't bother me.'

Ellen couldn't help wondering why it didn't bother him. It did most men, in fact that's all most of them ever thought about. A nagging suspicion crept into her mind. Was he seeing someone else? She almost told him there and then that there wouldn't be any wedding but decided to wait a while. It wouldn't do to be too hasty.

Her twenty-first birthday came and went and still there was no sign of Mr Heath senior either dying or changing his mind about the Newland family. Ellen sighed to herself, perhaps she was silly to wait, but as there had been no proposals from anywhere else, there didn't seem much choice.

The winter months dragged by. It was too cold to go for walks and so she saw little of Robert and when she did they talked about everything but getting married.

Visits home were also few and far between as the snow came in drifts, with biting winds that howled across the fields and had even the strongest trees on top of the Hanger bending alarmingly. To Ellen's surprise her parents had hardly mentioned Robert's name for many months. Perhaps they think I've changed my mind, she thought, or was it wishful thinking? Her father wouldn't ask outright if she was still seeing him and Ellen was almost afraid to mention anything about it. Work in the big house became more and more demanding as some of the other staff became too sick to work, with a nasty vomiting illness that laid them low. Ellen fumed inwardly about working all the hours God sent, cleaning fireplaces, just to do the same thing all over again the following day. It'll be different when I've got my own home, she decided. I can do things in my own time and in my own way.

The prospect of marrying seemed to merge vaguely into the future and as soon as she had made her mind up to tell Robert she was no longer prepared to wait, something happened.

One cold, frosty late January morning, Robert called on her to tell her that his father had died in the night of the sickness. Sorry as she was for Robert and his family, secretly she was relieved.

'I'll call round and see you on my half-day to give my sympathies to your family,' she told him.

It was now the end of the month, so they could be married in late February or early March. But when she called at the remote farmhouse to give her condolences, Mrs Heath was less than friendly

17

towards her, making Ellen quake in her shoes. She hadn't realised the woman was so formidable – and she would be sharing the small cottage with her! How would this woman take to having her about? And then Ellen realised with dismay that the house would not be hers to run as she wished. It belonged to the Heath family, and Robert's mother was still very much in charge.

Nonetheless she decided that she really wanted Robert for her husband and after a proper time of mourning, the wedding was arranged.

John Newland said at first that he wouldn't attend, but at his wife's insistence, capitulated. His daughter's happiness would always come first, and if she was determined to marry the man, he would just have to swallow his hatred. But it wouldn't be easy.

CHAPTER 2

The wedding was a rather subdued affair. The parish church of Selborne was sparsely filled, with John and Ann Newland, their son James and daughters, Harriet and Eliza on one side, and Robert's mother and two brothers on the other. Ellen's friend Mary and her husband Thomas were their witnesses, but apart from them, there were only one or two curious villagers hovering just inside the door at the back.

Ellen heard Robert take his vows, her heart singing - and then it was her turn.

For the briefest moment she hesitated, before plunging in and repeating the vicar's words as clearly as she could. Then they crossed to the small table beside the choir to sign the register

There, it was done. She was now a married woman. Mrs Robert Heath.

The solemn group filed out of the church and into the churchyard to stand for an awkward few moments in silence beneath the imposing yew tree.

John Newland cleared his throat. 'You're all welcome to our home for a drink and a bite to eat. If you like....' It obviously cost him a great deal of effort, and his words tailed off at the look on Mrs Heath's face.

The woman puffed out her considerable bosom and said, 'No thank you, we'll make our way home now. Good day to you.' She turned and bustled off down the path, then turned to her sons and new daughter-in-law. 'Come along, the cows won't milk themselves.'

Gripping Robert's hand, Ellen walked away from her family, suddenly filled with apprehension. She glanced back at her parents. The sight of their unhappy faces would stay with her for a very long time, and she wondered when she would see them again.

Robert and one of his brothers helped her up into the shabby cart, then climbed up beside her. Mrs Heath sat on the long bench seat at the front and took the reins, urging the horse forward.

Then they were off, and Ellen realised with a fresh wave of anxiety that a new life was about to begin. What would it be like sharing a home with a man - and his mother?

Robert's two brothers both lived some distance from Farringdon, working on outlying farms, which was a shame as far as Ellen was concerned, as it would be nice to have the two friendly men around. She was used to her own brothers always calling in at home to see their mother, and she wondered if Mrs Heath missed her sons as much as Mrs Newland did.

Soon they were pulling into the lane leading to the small farm, and Ellen grimaced. Why hadn't she noticed before how run down the place was? A few cows stood munching the sparse patch of grass at the front of the property and the yard, when they drove into it was muddy and smelly. Some chickens scattered in terror from the horse's hooves, taking refuge in a derelict barn.

Neither Robert, his mother or brothers seemed in the least concerned with the state of their surroundings, so Ellen put on a good front and pretended not to notice either.

Inside the house, it was no better, with only the barest of furniture and Ellen knew she would have her work cut out to improve things. That was if Mrs Heath would let her.

As the stiff March wind whistled in around the ill-fitting door, Ellen shivered. 'Shall I put some more wood on the fire?' She asked no one in particular.

'That fire is good enough as it is,' Mrs Heath growled. 'Now get yourself out of those fancy clothes and get a meal going.' The woman then plonked herself into the only chair close to the fire and sat back. It seemed obvious that she was glad to have someone else to do everything.

Ellen looked at Robert and he smiled encouragingly. 'I'll show you where things are and give you a hand if you like.'

'Thanks, I'd like that, just 'til I get my bearings.' She searched through the small carpetbag containing all her belongings and took out an old dress and an apron to cover it.

All of a sudden life loomed ahead rather uncertainly.

The meal wasn't a success. The vegetables were undercooked and the mutton tough, but Ellen thought that she'd done well considering the provisions available and the lack of firewood to provide a proper fire under the pot. Robert's mother sat stony-faced, toying with the food on her plate, her lips turned downward in disapproval. 'You'll have to do better than this, we can't work all day on empty bellies, and this isn't fit for pig swill.'

Her hands clasped tightly in her lap, Ellen fought back the tears that threatened. This was her wedding day and should have been a happy occasion, instead she was being criticised and made to feel worthless. She was very glad that Robert's two brothers had left before the meal; the fewer people who saw her distress, the better.

Ellen looked at her new husband to see if any support was coming her way, but he was intent on chewing his meat and appeared not to notice. I suppose he's used to his mother, Ellen thought, and so doesn't hear the sharpness of her tongue.

The meal over, Ellen washed the dishes in a bowl of greasy water. It made her feel sick, but there didn't appear to be any other water on hand. Then she needed the privy. She caught Robert's eye and indicated that she needed to relieve herself.

He grinned and, taking her hand, he led her outside to show her a flimsy lean-to at the back of the house. Inside was a stinking bucket. 'Am I to use that?' she asked in horror.

'Of course, we all do. I'll clean it out tomorrow, but it will have to do for now.' He turned and left her standing in the cold yard, the sickness washing over her once more.

Oh, God, what have I let myself in for, she moaned? Perhaps she should have heeded her father!

If the days were long and difficult, the nights were even worse. Robert clambered on top of her, did what he wanted to do and then rolled off, dropping into a deep sleep straight away. There was no love or affection, no cuddles, just him relieving his sexual needs. It wasn't at all what she had envisaged and most nights she cried herself to sleep, sobbing silently into the straw-stuffed pillow.

After a week of this, Ellen felt her spirits plummet even further. The cottage was filthy and her mother-in-law did nothing to help, but just sat by the fire day in and day out: so much for the pretence of helping on the farm. The woman seemed to be too lazy even to help when she saw Ellen struggling.

The water had to be carried in from the pump in the yard. Not an easy to use pump like her parents had, but a rusty old thing that took all her strength to work. Then there was the question of the fire. As long as Mrs Heath could feel some warmth from it, she would not allow anyone to put on more logs, so the rest of the room was cold. The water for washing and cooking took most of the day to heat, meaning that no sooner had she washed herself and the breakfast dishes, it was time to put on water for vegetables or stew.

It wouldn't have been so bad if Robert had helped, but he didn't. In spite of having the farm to run, he seemed always to be out doing odd jobs for other people. It brought extra money in, Ellen knew so did not comment, but she also knew that he spent quite a lot of his money at the public house in the village and only occasionally brought home fresh food.

The poor cows could often be heard mooing loudly as though in pain, and Ellen convinced herself they were. There were no set times for milking, which she knew was important being a cowman's daughter, and so one evening she broached the subject with her husband. 'Who does the milking?'

'I do, of course, who do you think?'

'Well, it's just that they don't seem to be done regularly.'

'If you're so worried about them, then I suggest you go and do it,' was his blunt reply. Her life back in service at the big house suddenly didn't seem so bad, at least she's had her food cooked and there had been plenty of it. And she'd had a half-decent privy to use.

'Oh, Robert, how can I? I'm busy trying to clean this house and do the cooking and washing.'

He shrugged. 'Please yourself. Now are you coming to bed, or do I have to pull you in?'

Ellen giggled, thinking he was joking, but suddenly his hand reached out and grasped her wrist.

'Ouch! That hurts!' she cried as he twisted it.

'Well get here then, I can't wait no longer.' He pulled her roughly onto the bed and forced his way inside her. When he'd finished and rolled over, Ellen let the tears flow. He had really hurt her and she was sure there would be bruises, but there was no one to tell. No one she could talk to.

A few days earlier, when she'd asked to go and visit her family, he had said quite firmly that her family was here now, not back in Selborne. Now she cried for them as well as herself. Why, oh why hadn't she listened to her father?

As the weeks passed, she fell into a sort of routine, but it was a hard one. The days never seemed long enough to get everything done and the house never looked any cleaner no matter how hard she tried. Robert would walk in, leaving mud from his boots all over the floor and the washing would pile up as Ellen tried to cope with keeping them all in clean clothes. Her mother-in-law would dribble food down the front of her dress and she had a nasty habit of spitting, most of which ended up on her bosom as well. And the woman stank. Ellen was sure that she had never seen her wash since the day of the wedding, and the smell was getting overpowering.

Then one day, a couple of months after her marriage, Ellen rose from her bed feeling decidedly ill. As she lurched from the tiny side room that was the bedroom, she felt the floor coming up to meet her. Mrs Heath was already in her chair, where Ellen was sure she stayed all night, and although she must have seen her daughter-in-law's plight, she did nothing to help.

Almost on her knees, Ellen made it to the door before being sick out in the yard. It took every last ounce of her strength to crawl back inside. Mrs Heath still made no comment and continued to stare into the fire, her face a mask of indifference.

When Robert came in later for his breakfast, Ellen asked him timidly if he could get his own breakfast. 'I feel so ill this morning.'

He sighed heavily and threw her a look of distaste. 'Well, it had better be just this once. I suppose mother's had nothing either?'

Ellen shook her head and turned sadly back to the tiny bedroom, wanting nothing more than to nestle down under the covers and sleep. She could hear voices in the main room and guessed that they were talking about her, but she didn't care. She longed to go home to her own mother who would hold her and smooth her brow, and would most likely have some kind of concoction to ease the sickness.

She must have slept because the next thing she knew was Robert shaking her awake. Not his usual rough shake, but a gentle movement of her shoulder. 'Are you feeling any better?'

Ellen gave a weak smile. 'Yes thanks, a little. How long have I slept?'

'Quite a few hours, so I think it's time you was up and getting some tea, don't you.'

With a moan, Ellen eased herself off the bed, relieved to find she did feel better. As she entered the living room, Robert's mother looked up, something akin to a smile on her lips. 'You look a bit brighter.'

Nearly collapsing in astonishment, Ellen smiled back. 'I'm feeling much better thanks. Let's see what I can do for dinner.' To her surprise there was fresh meat and a newly baked loaf on the side.

'Cook the meat on the griddle and we'll have it with the bread,' Robert suggested. 'That'll be quickest.'

The meat was lean and tender and Ellen was pleased to find that it made a tasty meal without all the bother of chopping it with vegetables and stewing it over the paltry fire.

As she cleared away afterwards, Robert came to stand behind her and putting his hands on her shoulders, he whispered in her ear. 'Do you think you might be with child?'

'Oh! I never thought of that.' Ellen did some calculations. 'Yes, I could be. Oh, Robert how will we manage?'

But to her amazement both Robert and his mother were beaming.

'Shall I drive you to see your parents?' Robert asked.

Shock and joy took hold of Ellen. 'Oh, yes please, it's been so long since I saw them and I'm sure they'd love to know about the baby.'

Life changed beyond all recognition once it became apparent that Ellen was expecting a child. So much so that she almost began to like living on the farm. Mrs Heath had roused herself and helped with the chores and Robert seemed more considerate in bed, as though he didn't want to harm the tiny life growing inside her.

'This'll be my ma's first grandchild so it's really special.' He'd explained one night as he gently stroked her belly. Ellen knew that his brother's had no children and thought how thrilled Mrs Heath must be now that the first one was expected.

'Your mother will love having grandchildren. Mother always says that they bring so much joy, no matter how many she has.'

'Yours is a big family, but my parents only ever had us three boys and my first wife didn't get in the family way even though we were married for nearly twenty years.'

Ellen wrinkled her brow. 'Poor woman.' She took a deep breath, 'How did she die?' It was something she'd always wanted to ask, but never felt the moment was right.

Robert shrugged, almost casually, 'Just got sick and popped off. I don't think she was very strong.'

Ellen found his dismissal of her predecessor rather callous.

Now, as she busied herself getting ready to visit Selborne, all worries drifted away. It would be wonderful to see ma and pa again and maybe one or two of her sisters might be around. The weather was clear and sunny with just a slight breeze and as Robert brought the horse and cart to the door, her excitement mounted. This was the first outing she'd had in over two months.

As the old horse plodded along the country lanes, Ellen chatted away to her husband about her family and asked him about his. This received very little response so she gave up in the end and just sat admiring the glowing hedgerows and delighted in the birds as they darted overhead.

As they passed through the village many friends and acquaintances waved and tears sprang into Ellen's eyes as she suddenly realised how homesick she'd been. Before the cart had stopped she was out of her seat and jumping down onto the road, ignoring Robert's shout to wait.

He grabbed her arm, 'That was stupid; you could have harmed our baby.'

She smiled up into his face. 'I'm fine, Robert, but thanks for caring.'

Then she spun away from him and ran up the path to the cottage, hearing her husband call out behind her; 'I'll wait here, then, shall I?'

Her mother was standing in the doorway drying her hands on the large apron she always wore. Her face lit with pleasure at the sight of her daughter and she held out her arms. Ellen ran into them and buried her face in her mother's shoulder.

They both started speaking at the same time and then fell back laughing. Ellen was almost jumping up and down in excitement. 'Oh it's so good to see you ma.'

'And it's a lovely surprise to see you too, my Ellen. How are you?' Mrs Newland stood back a pace and studied her daughter. 'My, my you've lost a lot of weight, and you look quite peaky. What have they been doing to you?'

'I'm fine ma, honestly. How's pa, and all the family? Are they all well?' Ellen practically fell inside the cottage, feeling it a place of refuge. She would never tell about her life at Farringdon; this was home – and always would be.

'Your father's in good health. He's at work at the moment of course and Harriet is at school, so I'm all alone.'

Ellen's face fell. 'Oh I probably won't see pa. Robert is waiting out in the cart so I can't stay too long.' She hesitated. 'I can't ask him in I suppose?'

Ann Newland shook her head sadly. 'I really don't feel it would be right. If your father ever found out, he might feel betrayed. Perhaps another day when your pa's here. I'm sorry dear.'

With a rueful smile, Ellen sat down at the table. 'I understand, ma. I've got time for a quick cup of tea though.' They both laughed again. Then Ellen wanted to know all the family news; how was her brother James getting on at the stables where he now worked? How was Eliza getting on with her new employer and was Harriet doing well at school?

Her mother grinned. 'Poor Harriet is struggling with her lessons I'm afraid and can't wait to leave school, rather like you were.'

25

'None of us are very bright are we?' Ellen said sadly.

'Never mind, what you lack in learning you more than make up for in other ways. Here's your tea, would you like a slice of cake to go with it?'

'Yes please,' Ellen eagerly accepted the cake, not mentioning that it was something they never had at the farm.

'Why did Robert suddenly decide to bring you?' Ann Newland asked her daughter.

'To tell you our news. Ma, I'm expecting a baby.'

'Oh my dear, I'm so happy for you. You don't look too pleased about it, are you all right?'

'I'm sick every morning and feel terrible the rest of the day, but Mrs Heath is helping out more so it's not too bad. How will I manage with a baby to look after, Ma?'

'The same way the rest of us manage, child. It'll be fine, you'll see. Is Robert pleased? His first wife didn't have any children, did she?'

Ellen shook her head. 'I don't know why. He never mentions her, so I don't know much about her.' She sighed heavily. 'I must be going now, but it's been lovely to see you. Give my love to everyone. Hopefully I can come again soon.' As she stood up her mother moved around the table and hugged her again.

'Look after yourself, and try to put some meat on your bones. I hope you can come again. Perhaps if you tell Robert how much I enjoyed seeing you, he won't mind driving this way soon.'

'I will.' Ellen brushed away a tear. 'Bye ma.' Then she turned and hurried out of the cottage, lest her mother see the tears that now flowed unchecked down her cheeks.

Behind her, Ann also cried. How ill Ellen looked. 'Oh please God, look after her,' she whispered.

Mrs Heath smiled at her daughter-in-law. 'The trip out has done you good, there's some colour in your cheeks.'

'It was wonderful to see ma. May I go again soon? If Robert can spare the time that is,' she added hastily. 'She was thrilled to hear about the baby, even though she has so many grandchildren already, every one is special.' Shyly she added, 'It'll be special for you too, won't it?'

'It will. I feared I'd never live to see a little one running about the place. His first wife was a strange girl and I don't think she had enough strength to carry. Don't know why it means so much, but I am thrilled. It's a new lease of life.'

26

As the weeks and months passed, Ellen grew in girth and felt her strength returning. Better food and less hard work saw to that. Her visits to see her mother had become almost regular – at least once a month, and she looked forward to them, but disappointed that her father was always at work.

As the winter set in the trips to Selborne grew less and less as a biting wind and torrents of sleet lashed the Hampshire countryside. Ellen was fairly content, the farmhouse was warmer this winter than it had been the last and the company was more congenial. Then came news that Robert's younger brother and his wife, who he had married in the summer, were also expecting a child.

Mrs Heath was over the moon. 'By the time your child is here it won't be long before I go off to Alresford to see a second one. My, my who'd have thought it? Two grandchildren in one year.'

Then, one chilly January morning, Mary was born. Ellen couldn't believe how quickly it had happened. She'd woken early with a pulsing pain in her back, then as Robert went to get help, Mrs Heath delivered the baby girl. The midwife arrived just in time to clean up both mother and baby and confirm that all was well.

For the first time since she'd known him, Robert held her hand tenderly and smiled into her eyes with real affection. 'Thank you Ellen, she's beautiful.'

Ellen's heart soared. Perhaps he really did love her after all and it was just that he normally found it hard to show his feelings. 'She's beautiful, isn't she?' and she smiled back, at last more certain of where her heart lay. Later, as she nursed her baby daughter, she whispered, 'I'll take great care of you, little one. Nothing shall ever harm you.' The baby blinked her blue eyes and pursed her tiny lips, then went back to sleep safe in her mother's arms.

The following day there were surprise visitors. Robert was out, but Mrs Heath proudly brought John and Ann Newland in to see their newest grandchild. Ellen knew it must have cost them a great deal in the way of swallowed pride to enter the Heath household, so as well as being thrilled to show Mary off to them, it gave her strength to know how much they cared. She could see by their faces that the state of the farm and house was a shock, but Mr and Mrs Newland were obviously proud of their new granddaughter and concentrated on her, hiding any misgivings they might have about how their daughter was living. Ellen pretended not to notice anything amiss, revelling in the unaccustomed attention. As far as she was concerned, just at this moment everything in her world was perfect.

Unfortunately, it didn't stay that way. When Mary was five weeks old, Mrs Heath left suddenly to go and look after her sick sister in Oxfordshire. 'She's my only kin so it seems only right I go to her, although I shall miss Mary.'

Once more Ellen marvelled at the difference in her mother-in-law. The woman had changed almost beyond recognition since learning about the baby and had been doing more to help about the home since Mary was born, often cradling the baby in her arms and smiling lovingly at her.

Now I'll be on my own, Ellen thought, but felt strong enough to manage Robert, Mary and a few odd jobs about the farm. As long as Robert does his share, we'll be fine, she thought.

But the following day a man called to speak to Robert and before she knew what was happening, arrested him on a charge of stealing. Ellen screamed at the man, 'You can't take my husband away, you can't, we've a baby, how will we manage?'

The man shrugged. 'As best you can, he should have thought of that before he went off stealing other people's belongings.'

Robert struggled in the man's firm grasp. 'I've taken nothing that wasn't owed to me, now have a heart man you can see how upset my wife is.'

The man became more forceful. 'You're coming with me Robert Heath, now let's get going.'

As he was dragged away, Robert called over his shoulder, 'Look after Mary, Ellen. Sell the cattle if you need money.' Then he was gone.

Left all alone, Ellen sat by the fire nursing her baby, tears running down her cheeks. 'What shall we do, Mary? How shall we manage?'

Later she learnt from the man she now knew to be a constable, that Robert had received six months gaol for stealing a man's pocket watch, which according to him he had won fair and square at a game of cards. What on earth was he doing gambling, thought Ellen, had the man no sense?

As the days passed it became obvious that she would have to sell something so that they could eat. The small amount of money she'd found in a tin on the mantle had almost gone. There wasn't much in the house of value, but she was loath to sell the livestock. Robert would need a living to come back to.

Loading up a small handcart with a table and two chairs – the only furniture that had any semblance of being decent - Ellen walked into Alton to the market. With Mary sleeping snugly in a shawl tied around her chest, Ellen stood for hours waiting for someone to buy her wares. But by the time the market finished, with her feet and legs aching unbearably, her goods still sat in the cart unsold. She looked at the furniture sadly, realising now that it was little more than rubbish. Who would have wanted it?

Somehow she made it back to the farm. The cows were waiting at the gate to be milked all gazing at her sternly as she entered the farmyard. Nearly dropping with fatigue, she managed to see to them, then it dawned on her that there was nothing in the house to eat. Mary was fine because she was still on the breast, but that would soon dry up if she didn't eat enough. Ellen could have wept, but comforted herself with a cup of fresh milk. It would have to do for now, but in the morning, she would have to go and see someone about buying some of the cows.

The morning saw her up early, searching around the farmyard for eggs. Surely the scruffy chickens had laid some somewhere, but as Ellen knew, they were not regular layers. Then, in the barn she found two eggs in the scattered straw and hurried indoors to put them in a pot over the fire to lightly boil. At least that was one meal, but what then?

As she ate her eggs, Ellen contemplated as to whom she should offer the cows. She had no idea what they were worth, so would probably be robbed. 'Oh Robert,' she moaned, 'why did you have to do this to us?'

Carrying Mary in her arms, she hurried off toward the village hoping to see someone she knew, however slightly, that might be able to help, but Farringdon was a small farming community and unfortunately very few people liked the Heath family.

Ellen shuddered. Still, nothing ventured, nothing gained, as her father always said.

The village was near deserted with only a few women making their way to the general grocers. Ellen suddenly felt shy, even after living at Farringdon for almost a year, she knew no one to talk to. One woman gave her a curious glance but didn't speak and hurried inside the shop. Perhaps that would be the place to start, Ellen thought.

Several pairs of eyes all turned in her direction as she entered, but no one spoke. Moving slowly toward the counter, Ellen looked into the face of the grocer who didn't seem too unfriendly. Clearing her throat she asked, 'I wonder if you can help me? I need to sell some cows, but don't know how to go about it or who to ask.'

'Well young lady, we don't sell cows in here so I've no need of any, thank you all the same,' the man laughed.

Seeing her discomfort one of the customers took pity on her.

'That'll do Mr Green; can't you see the young woman's in need?' Moving to Ellen's side she pulled back Mary's blanket and smiled. 'And look at this little darling, we can't see her go without, can we?' The woman looked around at the other customers. 'Well, can any of you help?'

A small careworn woman stepped forward. 'My husband might have some off you, if the price is right of course.'

The first woman narrowed her eyes. 'Let us introduce ourselves first, shall we.' She smiled at Ellen. 'I'm Mrs Blake and I live in the village with my husband who's a farrier. This is Mrs Brown, she and her husband have a smallholding down the road towards Alton. I know you're Mrs Heath, but we don't know your baby's name.'

'I'm Ellen Heath, formerly Newland and this is my baby daughter, Mary. She's only a few weeks old.'

'Well, Ellen Heath we'll see what we can do for you. We know your circumstances. Oh don't be shocked, not much goes on around here that we don't know about.' She looked at Mrs Brown. 'What's the going rate for a cow then?'

'Buggered if I know, I'll have to go and ask the old man. You can walk along with me if you've a mind,' she told Ellen.

Not wanting to leave the relative comfort of the shop, Ellen hesitated, but Mrs Blake came to her rescue. 'I'll come with you dear.'

'Thank you. I'll come and buy some provisions when I've got some money,' Ellen told the still grinning grocer. Then she followed Mrs Brown out into the street.

'You one of that John Newland's girls then?' Mrs Brown asked as they made their way along the dusty road.

'Yes, I am. Do you know him?'

'No I don't, and don't want to either from what I've heard.'

Ellen stopped dead in the street, furious to hear her father's name besmirched. 'My father is a good and honest man so don't you dare say anything bad about him.' Her face flamed with colour as she glared at the woman. Then she turned on her heel and started back the way they had just come.

'Hold on dear,' Mrs Blake said, touching her arm gently. 'Think of your baby. I'm sure Mrs Brown didn't mean any harm.'

'Well, she shouldn't go around bad mouthing people she doesn't know.' Ellen's temper was gradually receding.

Mrs Brown shrugged her shoulders and said, 'Come on if your coming.' So off they set once more until they reached a small cottage with a field running along one side.

Mr Brown was rather more friendly than his wife, and ready to discuss a price. 'How many are you thinking of selling?'

'Perhaps two or three to start with, depending on what I can get for them.'

The man rubbed his chin thoughtfully. 'Let's say two and six each.'

Ellen looked at the man to see if there was a hint of shiftiness in his eyes, but could detect none. She glanced at Mrs Blake and noticed the woman chewing her bottom lip while in deep thought. As the silence lengthened, the man eyed the distant horizon as though seeking inspiration. 'Well,' he suddenly said, 'perhaps I can go to three shillings.'

The thought of three shillings sounded a lot to Ellen, but she knew she must be careful, any money she received would have to last a long time. 'Five shillings,' she was surprised to hear herself say. What on earth had made her ask that? He'll be bound to refuse and then she'd have nothing. What a fool she was.

But to her amazement Mr Brown considered the offer. Then he said very slowly, 'Well seeing as it's you, Mrs Heath, I'll agree to pay you five shillings each provided I can have three together.'

With her head whirling, Ellen agreed. Fifteen shillings was indeed a fortune. 'T-thank you Mr Brown. Shall I drive them over to you, or will you collect them?'

'I'll come over for them in the morning and I'll bring the money with me,' Mr Brown touched the peak of his cap.

'Oh, but I wanted to buy food today,' Ellen gasped as hunger pangs cramped her insides.

'Just ask Mr Green for food on the slate, and then pay him tomorrow. He'll be fine about it, won't he Mrs Blake?'

The woman smiled, 'Yes, he'll accept that if you tell him Mr Brown is buying your cows. Off you go now and get yourself and that baby home in the warm with some good food to fill you up.' Then she waved a farewell as she set off up the road, not waiting for Ellen, who said goodbye to Mr and Mrs Brown and plodded in the same direction.

Once back in the shop, Ellen was pleased that there were no other customers present as she tentatively asked the grocer for food, which she could pay for the following day. To her relief he readily agreed and proceeded to fill a small sack with bread, bacon and vegetables, oats and a few apples. 'I'll have some fresh mutton in tomorrow if you'd like some.'

'That'll be very welcome, thank you.' Picking up the sack with difficulty, Ellen smiled at the man and left the shop, well pleased with her morning's work. At least she would be all right for the next few weeks, and then there were always a few more cows to sell if needs be.

The following day, as good as his word, Mr Brown appeared just after breakfast to collect his cows and handed Ellen the fifteen shillings. 'Nice doing business with you. Let me know if you want to sell any more.'

'I will, and thank you.' Ellen skipped indoors, plucked Mary from her small cradle and danced about the room. 'We'll go and pay Mr Green and then I think we'll go and visit Grandma Newland.' Then she added with a laugh, 'that's if the horse will let me harness him.'

To her relief, the old horse stood patiently while she worked out how his harness went, then off they set. Mary wrapped up well from the cold wind, nestled in the back of the cart. Ellen felt happier than she had for many a month; she was free to go and see who she liked, and stay as long as she wished. Perhaps she could stay long enough to see pa.

Although the cold had seeped through into every bone in her body, Ellen jumped joyfully down from the cart, making sure the horse had grass from the verge to nibble, then ran up the path to her parent's cottage. Her mother was surprised to see her. 'My goodness, Ellen. Where did you spring from?' Once everything was explained, Ann Newland grinned at her daughter, pride showing clearly in her eyes. 'You've done well to get yourself enough money to live on and to manage the horse to bring you here. I'm cooking a nice warming broth, so you can stay and have something to eat, can't you?'

'Yes please, I'd like that. Will the horse be all right out there? I don't want him wandering off, it'd be a dreadful long walk home.'

'Just go and check on him, I'll hold Mary.' Ann peered proudly down into the blankets, gently easing it away from the baby's face. 'Oh, you are beautiful, little one. Did you enjoy the ride to see your grandma?'

Ellen eased herself into a new routine. After she'd fed and dressed Mary, she'd have something to eat, go and milk the cows and feed the hens, then as lunchtime approached she'd tidy the cottage while the meal cooked. So busy was she, that the days passed by almost unnoticed, but once a week the horse would be harnessed up and off they'd go to Selborne. Ellen really looked forward to these visits. Often her father would make a quick call home just so that he could see his daughter and granddaughter.

'She's growing into a right pretty girl, aren't you, Mary,' he said one day as she lay in her mother's arms. The warm kitchen emanated homeliness. John Newland turned to Ellen, 'You're doing well girl, running the farm and keeping things ticking over until Robert comes home.'

Ellen smiled at her father; although he would never like Robert, he never said anything against him to her directly, although he could have done seeing as the man had got himself arrested for stealing when he had a young family to care for. 'It's a struggle pa, and I might need to sell off the other three cows soon as the money I made is nearly gone.'

'You make sure you get a good price for them, don't let anyone fob you off.'

'I won't pa.' Ellen sighed then, 'I'm worried about what to do if the money's all gone before Robert comes out of prison. I can manage, but Mary must be fed and if I don't eat, then nor does she.'

Her mother put a comforting hand on her arm. 'You can always come here and stay for a while. We'd love to have you, wouldn't we John?'

'Of course we would.' He confirmed.

This was a comfort to Ellen, knowing that there was somewhere to go if ever she couldn't manage. And after another two weeks had passed, she was calling on Mr Brown again to see if he wanted the three remaining cows.

He eagerly agreed and so Ellen felt rich again with the coins jingling in her pocket. She eagerly stocked up with food from the village store, bought a large sack of logs and made the cottage as homely as possible.

On one visit to her parents, her mother commented on her expanding waistline. 'You're feeding yourself well then?' It was said with a laugh, but Ellen didn't see the funny side.

'When Mrs Heath and Robert were in charge of things there wasn't much worth eating; really frugal they were, so I don't see why I should go without now, especially as I'm feeding Mary.'

'Quite right dear, you need to eat plenty.'

And because Ellen saw no reason to budget tightly, it didn't take long for the money to run out again. One day she eyed the chickens, not sure if they were fit for eating as they were a sorry looking lot who no longer laid eggs and she was sure that there wouldn't be much meat on them anyway. Even so, one morning Ellen took a chopper and chased one of the birds around the farmyard until she cornered it and gritting her teeth, chopped it's head off. That was bad enough, but then it had to be plucked and drawn which was a horribly messy business.

Ellen muttered to herself as she stuffed the feathers into a sack, 'Call myself a country girl? Huh!'

Once it was cooked the chicken looked more emaciated than ever and Ellen ate the whole lot in one meal. This wouldn't do; there was nothing for it but to go and stay at her parents. She didn't want to be a burden to them, but she had Mary to think of.

She would let Mr Green at the shop know where she was in case her mother-in-law should arrive back, although no word had been sent as to when that might be.

CHAPTER 3

It was wonderful to be home again and Ellen relaxed visibly in front of the fire while her mother stood at the sink preparing vegetables. Life had been hard over the last few years, but now she was back in the bosom of her family with ma to look after her. What more could she want?

Her father entered the cottage, jacket slung over his arm. 'Phew, it's hot out there.' Hanging the jacket on the nail behind the door he turned to survey the room and it's occupants. 'You should be helping your mother, Ellen, what are you doing sitting there when there's washing to be fetched off the line? And the baby's things are all over the place. Come on girl, stir your stumps.'

Jumping up guiltily, Ellen rushed outside to get the washing, folding it neatly into the large basket. The cotton sheets were almost stiff where they had dried quickly in the sun and smelt fresh and scented from the summer air.

'Shall I damp these down ma?' she asked as she carried the basket indoors.

'Yes please dear, then I can iron them later. Dinner's nearly ready. I'm sorry it's stew again on such a warm day, but the shop was short because a lot of his stock went off.'

'Aye, we do need some cooler weather,' John observed. 'The barley's ready for cutting already, much too soon and if it rains hard now, it'll be beaten down. I'll check the garden later to see what vegetables I can find us.' He stretched and then sat at the table ready for his meal.

After they had eaten and Ellen sat feeding Mary, her father cleared his throat in the way he did when he had something important to say. 'I think when Robert comes home he should stay here for a while, just until he gets the farm stocked up and that cottage sorted out.'

Ann Newland looked at her husband in horror. 'What? Have that man here? There isn't really room John, apart from anything else, and it would be very uncomfortable for you.'

'If I can stand it for a few weeks, then so can you. Perhaps he could go and sleep at home, then come back here for a meal, or something like that.'

Ellen was shocked. She had never expected her father to suggest such a thing. and for some reason, it made her feel odd. She could not imagine Robert here in the Newland home, no matter how hard she tried.

'How long is it now before he's let out?' her father asked.

'Only a few weeks I think, but I've lost count.'

'Oh Ellen,' her mother scolded. 'You really are the limit. Fancy not knowing when your husband gets out of prison.'

Having the good grace to blush, Ellen bowed her head in shame. 'Time goes so quickly,' she mumbled.

'I dare say we'll know soon enough when he's free, because he'll be bound to come here looking for Ellen and Mary.' John grinned at his wife and Ellen knew that they knew her too well. With a shock, she realised that Robert had never been much in her mind over the months he'd been gone. How awful was that? A wife who never gave her husband a thought; she'd never been to see him, or had a note written.

Seeing the look on her face, her mother took pity on her and reached across to pat her arm. 'Don't worry dear, perhaps things will be better when he gets home.'

Yes, Ellen supposed, perhaps things would be better then.

A few weeks later Robert turned up to see her and Mary. If he was surprised to be asked into the cottage, he hid it well, and Ellen gazed up at him hoping something inside her would awaken. But he was a stranger; there was nothing about him she remembered or recognised, in fact her heart felt heavy in her breast. She forced a smile. 'Hello Robert. How are you? Have they looked after you all right?'

'I'm as well as can be expected. How have you managed? I see the cows are gone.'

'Yes, Mr Brown bought them, but once the money ran out I came here. Shall I come back with you now?'

'Not yet, I need to do some work on the place.' He peered down at his sleeping daughter. 'She's come on a treat.' The smile reached his eyes at last. 'Yes, she's right bonny.' He ran a finger down Mary's plump pink cheek.

'Would you like to stay for something to eat?' Ann asked him. 'My husband has said that you can stay here for a while if you wish.' It was said rather stiffly, but not unkindly.

'That's very civil of you, but a meal would be all I need at the moment, then I'll go back to Farringdon for the night.' Robert's discomfort was obvious.

Ellen wandered out into the garden, hoping he would follow her so that they could talk, and was relieved when his tall figure stooped through the door. Frantically she tried to think what to say. Now that the moment had come her mind went blank.

Robert came to stand beside her. 'I'm sorry I left you without much. I didn't really steal, but it was that man's word against mine. How much did Mr Brown give you for the cows?'

When she told him, he groaned. 'They were worth three times as much as that. I wondered why you'd left because I thought you'd have enough money until I got home.'

'I'm sorry Robert, really I am. I had no idea what they were worth and no one to guide me. Pa didn't say much when I told him, but of course he only milks them, so perhaps he doesn't. Will you be able to get them back?'

'I doubt it, old Brown will hardly be willing to sell them back at the same price. Not that I've got it anyway and until I get a job, I won't have.'

'Here's pa, you'd better come and speak to him.' As Ellen walked back toward the cottage, she could hear Robert's slow footsteps behind her. He obviously wasn't looking forward to meeting her father.

The meal was eaten in silence, everyone concentrating on the food on their plate. Once or twice Ellen or her mother made a comment, but then the hush would descend once more. As soon as they had finished eating, Robert made his excuses and left, and Ellen sighed with relief. As she fed Mary, she wondered, rather guiltily, how on earth she could ever return to the farm. Somewhere inside her, she knew she didn't really want to.

But to her surprise, Robert seemed in no hurry to have her back either. She saw him three or four times a week when he visited her parents, stayed for a meal and sat with Mary on his lap for a few moments, before leaving again. He had made no effort to hug or kiss her and Ellen was perversely peeved; even though she didn't really want him to, it was still painful to be treated in such an offhand way. She thought that perhaps he didn't want her back living with him, but she couldn't stay here forever; her parents would be bound to ask questions about the situation soon.

Then one day Robert announced that he'd found work on another farm. 'As soon as I've enough saved we can buy some more stock and live back at my place,' he told her.

'Oh good,' Ellen replied half-heartedly. She wasn't sure if he sensed her reluctance or not, but he said nothing. She wrestled with her conscience daily, knowing she must return when Robert wished: she was his wife after all.

But one week dragged into another and nothing was mentioned, until her father came in from work one day and repeated some gossip he'd heard at the farm where he worked. 'I thought you ought to know, that husband of yours has been seen most nights in the Fox and Hounds, spending his wages like water and making a play for the women as well.'

Ann Newland looked at her husband, aghast. 'Oh John, are you sure it's true?'

'Well, old Ned doesn't lie, and he saw him for himself.' John gave his daughter a look of sympathy and reached across the table to lay his hand on hers. 'Sorry girl.'

With a shake of her head, Ellen said stoutly, 'I don't care what he does, I'm not going back now.' Tears sprang into her yes. 'Why didn't I listen to you, pa? You said he was no good.'

'Well, these things happen, but what are you going to do? You've Mary to think of now.'

Ellen looked at her mother. 'Can't we stay here? For a while anyway.'

Taking a deep breath, Ann said slowly, 'Of course you can for a while, but Ellen you'll have to find yourself some work and a home before too long. Your father and me are getting on in years now. And it would be difficult to feed you both, there's little enough money to go round as it is.'

Knowing she was right didn't stop Ellen from shouting, 'It's not fair, no one wants me. What am I supposed to do?' Then she cried loudly, her whole body heaving with the sobs.

Sitting down opposite, her mother pulled Ellen's hands from her face. 'Be sensible, dear. You know I'm right. It's time for you to take stock of your life and decide what you're going to do. Other women have found themselves in the same situation and managed.'

Lifting her tear-stained face, Ellen whispered, 'I know, but it's so hard and I feel such a fool.'

A few days later Robert appeared at the cottage door. 'I'm working in the next field for a few days, can you bring me some lunch over?'

Staggered at his cheek, Ellen retorted. 'Oh yes, it's all right for me to bring you lunch, but I'm not good enough to live with.'

He had the grace to look at his feet. 'I will sort things out, but it was being shut up for all those months, I just wanted a bit of fun. Please Ellen.'

'Here, take this bread and cheese. That's all there is and I'll have to go to the shop to get something for pa's lunch, so you'd better be off before he comes in.'

Thanking her, he made his way down the path and Ellen stood seething. She was still raging when her mother came in from the garden a few moments later. 'What's wrong, dear, you're rather red-faced?'

When Ellen told her about Robert, her mother was also extremely angry. 'What a nerve he's got coming here and asking for food.' Her cheeks flamed and for a moment Ellen thought she'd go looking for Robert to give him a piece of her mind, but then she said more calmly, 'Run down to the shop for a small wedge of cheese, please, while I make some more bread.' Sighing heavily, Mrs Newland turned to reach for the flour box.

While Ellen stood in the grocer's shop several women stood whispering on one side and she was sure they were discussing her because of the looks that were thrown in her direction. As she was being served, one spoke. 'Ellen, I hope I'm not speaking out of turn, but that Robert Heath has been seeing another woman in Farringdon.' She hesitated, then added, 'We thought you ought to know.'

'T-thank you. I'm glad you've told me,' Ellen said, throwing the money on the counter and fleeing back to the cottage.

Anger filled her. How dare he!

Well, he needn't think he'd get another thing from her. That was it as far as she was concerned. Ellen had been prepared to try and make a go of her marriage for Mary's sake, but Robert had proved himself to be unfaithful.

Rage and resentment consumed her. He'd be sorry, just see if he didn't. She'd find a way to make him pay for what he'd done.

As she stumbled through the door, Ellen was surprised to see her sister Eliza nursing Mary. Controlling her temper with difficulty, she said, 'Hello, what are you doing here? It's not your day off is it?'

'No, I'm on an errand for Mrs Perkins and she said to take as long as I like. I'm off into Alton in a few minutes.'

'Can I come with you?' Ellen asked.

'If ma doesn't mind looking after Mary, I'd love you to.'

'Off you go. It'll do you good to have a nice long walk,' Ann said as she took Mary from Eliza's arms. 'We'll be fine won't we my little love?'

Placing the cheese for her father's lunch on the table, Ellen took Eliza's hand and hurried out of the cottage.

As they walked briskly along the road toward Alton, Ellen was still seething about Robert. Her mind was in turmoil, but as Eliza prattled on about the place she worked, something her sister said suddenly grabbed her attention.

'What was that?' Ellen asked.

'We're overrun with rats,' Eliza told her, 'and old Mr Potter is setting poison down all over the place to kill them. He's said we must be careful though as if we touch the powder it could make us very ill.'

'What is this powder then?'

'It's called arsenic and you can only buy it in one shop, Mr Potter says.'

'Mmm, I wonder,' Ellen mused aloud.

'Wonder what?'

'Can you keep a secret, Eliza?'

'Of course,' the girl said indignantly.

'Well, I've been told that Robert is seeing another woman, and I thought I'd teach him a lesson. So if I buy some of this arsenic and it makes him ill, it'd serve him right, wouldn't it?'

'Oh, I'm not sure. What if you gave him too much and he died?' Eliza looked somewhat shocked by the idea.

'I can't afford much, so I don't suppose it'd do too much harm. I'll think about it, then we'll ask in the shop in Alton. Which shop is it anyway?'

'The druggists. You know, it's next to the bakery.'

Ellen wrinkled her nose. She rarely visited Alton so her knowledge of the town was not good. 'Show me where it is and then I'll think some more about it.'

Eliza grumbled about having Mrs Perkins shopping to do, but agreed and then chatted about other things, but Ellen scarcely heard, her mind on other things. Dare she do it? Dare she take the risk?

As the young women walked along Alton's main street, Ellen came to a decision. She'd do it; she'd make Robert ill to pay for the way he'd treated her and their daughter, Mary. The poor little girl hardly knew her father.

'We'll get what you want first, then go to the druggist,' Ellen said.

With a huge sigh Eliza agreed, then went into the haberdashers for the silks and cottons Mrs Perkins required. After much deliberation, Eliza decided on what she hoped were the right colours, paid for them and then led Ellen outside.

'Are you sure about buying arsenic?' She asked, placing the paper-wrapped purchases carefully into her basket.

'Yes, I've made up my mind.'

'Right the shop is just along here, and I've to buy some hair oil for cook as well, so I can buy it there.'

'Well, if you've to go in anyway, you can buy the arsenic at the same time.'

Eliza looked doubtful. 'I don't like the idea. I'll feel like a criminal.'

'Don't be daft,' Ellen said, giving her sister a shove into the doorway. 'Just ask for it casually after you've asked for the hair oil.'

Entering the shop slowly, Eliza went to the counter and asked for the Lavender oil so loved by cook and then asked for some arsenic to kill off the rats.'

The druggist looked over the top of his spectacles at her. 'I'm sorry, I'm not allowed to sell that to anyone without a witness.'

'Oh!' Eliza was taken aback. 'Um, well… M-my sister is outside, can she be witness?'

'If you wish.' The man nodded solemnly.

Eliza dashed outside and grabbed Ellen's hand. 'You need to come in and see it signed for.'

With a frown Ellen followed the younger girl inside, where they crossed to the counter again. The man asked again what the arsenic was for and Ellen found the lie came easily. 'It's for the rats, overrun with the things we are.'

'Right, how much do you need?' The druggist asked, pushing his spectacles into place with a bony finger.

'Not a lot, we're told that you only need a small amount. How much is it?' Ellen's heart was in her mouth. Did she have enough money to pay for it after all this?

'Ha'penny an eighth-ounce.'

'That should be plenty,' Ellen told him, handing over the ha'penny that had been the change from her father's cheese. What she would do if ma asked for it, she didn't know.

The shopkeeper lifted a heavy book down from the shelf behind the counter. 'I have to make a note of all poisons sold,' he said, writing briefly on a page already covered with a spiky scrawl. He pushed the book toward Ellen and pointed to where she had to make her mark. Then he folded a small sheet of paper and dropped the powder into it, twisting it tightly to seal it. 'There we are young ladies, now you go careful with that. Don't go poisoning your sweethearts by mistake.' He laughed heartily at his own joke, taking the money for the hair oil from Eliza. He was still chortling as the two girls left the shop and hurried away, eager to be home.

'Phew, that was awful, I didn't expect to have so much bother. Come on it's getting late, let's hurry or ma will be getting worried.' Ellen took her sister's hand again as they made their way back towards Selborne, the tiny packet feeling heavy in her pocket.

For several days the arsenic stayed there. Ellen still wasn't sure how or when she would use it and broke out into a cold sweat every time she thought about it. Then her chance came. Robert called in to say he was working in the fields nearby once again, and could he bother her for a snack at lunchtime.

Ellen knew from the way his eyes slid away from her gaze that he was feeling guilty and guessed that he was still seeing this other woman. Thinking about that made her mind up. He deserved to be punished for being unfaithful to her.

'I'll bring you something about noon,' she told him and smiled behind his back as he walked away. 'I'll teach you a lesson,' she said softly.

Asking her mother if she could make something for Robert's lunch from their meagre larder, she was told that there was some suet pudding left from the day before, and he could make do with that. 'I'll put it to warm then,' Ellen said, thinking how easy it would be to place some arsenic into it.

Wondering if it tasted of anything, but too frightened to try even a tiny amount on her finger, she took a pinch from the paper and sprinkled it over the top. It showed up white so she stirred it into the meat juices with a spoon and then set the pudding to warm beside the fire. At midday, she lifted the basin from the hearth, wrapped it in a clean cloth and set off to find Robert. Her heart was pounding so much she was sure it could be heard for miles around and her mouth was dry with apprehension, but she strode purposefully on.

When she found him, he was with two other men who grinned when they saw her. 'Cor, you're spoilt and no mistake,' one said to Robert. 'Good grub and a handsome wife to serve it.' He winked at Ellen, who glared back, thrust the food into her husband's hand and left hastily, their ribald laughter ringing in her ears.

Nearly choking with fear, she broke into a run. Oh, God, what have I done? Then she sobbed, 'Please forgive me, I know I'm wicked.'

As she ran into the cottage, her mother looked up. 'What ever is wrong, Ellen?'

Ellen bit into her lip hard, and then said, 'It's that Robert and his mates, they all laughed at me. Everyone must know he's seeing some other woman and I'm just a joke.'

'Never mind, dear, don't upset yourself, he's not worth it.' Her mother as kind and caring as usual, soothed Ellen's brow and, placing a bowl of thick soup on the table, said, 'Here sit yourself down and have some of this.'

Through tear-filled eyes, Ellen guiltily thanked her mother – knowing how shocked the woman would be if she knew her daughter's wickedness. Then it hit Ellen hard; what would happen if ma and pa ever found out? It didn't bear thinking about.

They did find out, and in the worst way possible. Early one evening, a few days later, Ann Newland answered a knock at the door and stepped back to admit a constable whose bulk filled the tiny kitchen. He coughed and then asked if a Mrs Ellen Heath lived there.

As her bewildered parents looked on, Ellen felt colour rise in her face, but stayed silent. She would brazen it out; nothing could be proved surely?

The constable gazed at her and then said solemnly, 'Ellen Heath, I'm arresting you on a charge of the attempted murder of Robert Heath.'

As gasps of shock filled her ears Ellen knew she could never admit to her caring family that she had tried to poison Robert. 'I don't understand,' she declared hotly. 'How can I have done such a thing, we don't even live together.'

'You took him a meal on Monday last at about noon, did you not?'

'Well, yes I did, but what's that got to do with anything?'

'That meat pudding contained poison...'

'Now, look here,' Ann cut in, 'the rest of the family all ate that pudding. I made it myself; how could it have had poison in it?'

'Tests done on it show that it contained arsenic, and we have proof that Mrs Heath bought arsenic at the Alton druggists a few weeks ago.'

'That was for killing rats,' Ellen said softly, feeling her world tumble about her. How long could she keep this pretence? Her parent's stricken faces filled her vision and she wanted to scream out loud her innocence. Anything to ease their pain, as well as her own.

'What rats may I ask? Here in your own home?' the man looked at John Newland. 'Have you been plagued by rats sir?'

John threw an agonised look at Ellen and she knew he wouldn't lie. 'Well, no, but that's not to say that my daughter isn't telling the truth. Perhaps someone else asked her to get it.'

'Well?' He asked Ellen.

As her face crumpled and she started to sob, she managed to blurt out that it had all been a horrible mistake and she hadn't meant to kill anyone.

'Ellen!' her father's stern voice brought her upright. 'Tell us the truth about what happened, and why.'

Haltingly, she explained her plan to make Robert ill to get her own back. 'I never thought it would do any real harm, honestly I didn't.'

'It is a criminal offence to administer poison to anyone, whatever the reason may be, and as that's the case, I'm arresting you. You'll be taken to Alton overnight, then on to Winchester for a court hearing.' The constable took a pair of handcuffs from his pocket and moved toward the shivering young woman.

Ellen took fright and fell to the floor in a faint and as her mother stooped beside her, patting her face to bring her round, John jumped to his feet. 'There's no need for those, she won't run away. Can I ask that she stay here for the night? And I'll bring her to Alton tomorrow morning. She's in a bad way as you can see and needs her family around her. And just between you and me, I can see how she was driven to do it, that man has treated her very badly.'

'That's as may be, sir, but the law must be upheld.'

'Of course, we understand that, but she's our daughter and has a young child.'

'Oh, Mary, what will become of her?' Ann cried, holding onto Ellen's arm as she regained her senses. 'You can't take her with you.'

'I will, ma. I must keep my baby with me, I must look after her.'

'But prison is no place for a child; Ellen think carefully,' her mother implored.

'You can sort that out between you, I'm off now. Make sure you bring her in first thing in the morning, sir.' And with that he left, his bulk leaving the kitchen feeling empty.

In the silence that followed, Ellen cast around in her brain for something to say. Sorry, just didn't seem enough, but what else was there?

Her ma spoke first. 'Ellen, I know you've had a terrible time, but what on earth possessed you to do such a thing?' A gentle arm about her daughter's shoulders softened the words.

Turning into her mother's warm embrace, Ellen sobbed as though her heart would break. What was she to do now? How would she cope with prison? 'I've let you all down, I know I have. I'm so sorry that my anger with Robert has brought all this on you.'

'There, there. Let's sit and talk about it, then we'll try to get some sleep.'

'I'll never sleep again. Oh, ma, I've been so wicked. How could I have done such a thing?'

'You never know, you might be let off with a light sentence as you were pushed to the limit,' her pa said. 'We can look after Mary for a few weeks while you're away, and no one else need know where you are.'

Through her tears, Ellen saw her parents smile encouragement. Perhaps it wouldn't be so bad after all.

CHAPTER 4

The small dusty room wasn't quite what she expected. A dank dark cell had seemed more likely. But Ellen shivered just the same, the chilly air seeping through her thin woollen dress and shawl. She'd left Mary with her parents at ma's insistence, but she missed her daughter; missed the warmth of the little body held against her own.

As the day dragged on, she wondered, not for the first time, how long she would be kept here. The man in charge had said she would be sent to Winchester as soon as transport could be arranged. They had brought her some lunch and there was a jug of water on the table, but otherwise she had been left alone.

Wrinkling her nose in distaste, she reluctantly used the bucket in the corner to relieve herself, but then a wry grin came to her lips. It was still better than the outside lav at the farm!

Alone to ponder on her sins, she cursed her own stupid actions. If only. If only. The two words ran round and round in her head. The biggest being: if only she hadn't met Robert Heath in the first place.

A ragged sigh left her lips. No, she had to admit there was no one to blame but herself. There had been no rush to marry him; the fact that her father couldn't stand the man should have been enough to warn her off.

All I can do now is throw myself on the mercy of the court and hope they let me off, Ellen thought, lying back against the metal bedhead and pulling her shawl closer about her.

The darkness outside pressed into the small room and Ellen began to despair of ever getting a light or something to eat. But at last a meal was brought, along with a candle and a change of bucket. In the event it was only bread and cheese, but welcome for all that. And the candle lifted her spirits in some unexplainable way. It also afforded a little extra warmth and after eating her meagre meal, Ellen settled down for the night, praying harder than she had ever prayed in her life, for God to help her and have mercy on her soul.

It was three days before she heard about leaving the small and comparatively comfortable gaol in Alton, and it was not good news. She was being sent to Southampton prison, a larger and more austere building, from what she'd overheard. Her parents were allowed to visit her on that last day and they brought Mary with them. Seeing her small daughter again had Ellen in tears and she begged once more to be allowed to keep the child with her.

No amount of persuasion from her mother could change her mind. 'I need her ma, and she needs me.'

'But prison is no place for such a young child, Ellen. Think how frightened she'll be at being somewhere like that.'

'I've asked about it and they've a special part for mothers with children, it won't be too bad. Anyway, she might forget me if we're apart too long.'

With a shake of her head, Ann gave in. 'If that's what you really want. We'll try to visit soon and bring some clothes for Mary, although goodness knows how you'll manage until then.'

The constable came then and said it was time to leave. 'Sorry Mr and Mrs Newland, but the cart is here to collect Mrs Heath and a couple of other prisoners.'

Hugging her parents tightly, Ellen could only keep repeating the word, 'Sorry,' until they watched as she was helped up onto the covered cart to start on her journey.

'We'll come and visit as soon as we can, girl,' her father said gruffly. 'God speed.'

Watching the sad figures of her parents disappear from sight was the hardest thing she had ever done, and Ellen kept her eyes on the road long after they had left the outskirts of Alton. Holding Mary close to her, she cried, not knowing when she would see them again.

November came and went and still she had no visitors, and Ellen despaired of ever seeing anyone she knew again. The prison, with its bare stone walls and floor was a cold and joyless place to be, but somehow it wasn't as bad as Ellen had expected. Because she had Mary with her, she had been placed in a separate cell for mothers with young children; the food, what there was of it, was just about edible and the children given a blanket each. The stench and noise that had been unbearable at first, soon became a part of everyday life and gradually Ellen stopped noticing them at all.

They were all given dry straw on which to lie and although inadequate, it was better than the bare flagstones. The other women complained of boredom, but Ellen kept herself busy with Mary, either singing or talking softly to her. It would be Mary's first birthday soon and Ellen dreamed about buying her daughter a present, spending hours daydreaming of the things she would like to buy, but knowing it was impossible. The worst part of her time in gaol was waiting to hear when her trial would be. Someone said you could wait for up to a year, but Ellen refused to believe that she would be there that long. Although glad of the company of the other women, she very rarely spoke of anything other than to comment on the food or ask after a sickly child, fearful that if they found out what she had done, they would condemn her without asking her side of the story. Surely these other women had never done anything so wicked? But what they were in prison for she never found out, as they, like her, preferred not to talk about such things.

And then, a week before Christmas, her parents came to see her. Tears of joy ran down Ellen's face as she was ushered into the visitor's room, and Mary held out her arms to Ann, saying, 'Gan, gan,' which brought more tears from Ellen; as well as her mother.

'How're they treating you, girl?' her father asked once they were all seated.

'Not too badly, pa, I think Mary makes the difference. Without her, I'd be in a large cell with a dozen other women who have done goodness knows what.'

Bouncing Mary on her knee, Ann asked, 'Are they feeding you well? I must admit you both look better than I had feared.'

'It could be worse, I suppose,' Ellen said softly, 'but if only they'd tell me when my trial is, the waiting is awful.' She then asked after all the family, especially Eliza. 'Do you think she'll have to appear in court?'

The look that passed between her parents didn't go unnoticed by Ellen. Her father cleared his throat, 'Yes, I'm afraid she will, although what she'll say is anybody's guess. I've told her to tell the truth, but I think she's forgotten what the truth is as she made up so many stories.' He placed a rough hand over hers. 'Sorry, Ellen, but things don't look too good. Robert's got some Winchester lawyer on his case. How he afforded that we don't know, but be prepared for some tough questions when the time comes.'

Ellen shuddered and she closed her eyes. 'I can't believe he'd do that, but I s'pose I've only myself to blame.' Fresh tears forced through her lids and slid down her face. 'I wonder what they'll do with me?' Her eyes flew open, suddenly the enormity of her situation hit home. 'They might hang me!' With fear in her eyes, she stared at her parents, seeing the same fear there on their faces, and she knew they dreaded the same. The thought that she'd brought such pain to these gentle, caring people was almost more than she could bear.

Then the warder appeared and declared time was up and, taking Mary back into her arms, Ellen watched with a heavy heart as her beloved parents slowly left the room, their faces turned toward her and Mary until the last minute. When they had gone, fresh tears flowed and Ellen wondered when this agony would end.

At last the day dawned when she was called into an office and told by a grim-faced woman that her trial was set for the first day in March. It was still several weeks away, but at least now she had something to focus on. By now the women in her cell had changed two or three times, only to be replaced by a new intake, all with crying babies or whining, hungry young children. She wished those who had left well, wherever they were, it must be a relief to see the outside world again.

The weeks dragged, but then the day arrived when she was told that a wagon was waiting to transport her to Winchester Assizes. The journey passed in a haze as Ellen fretted about the coming trial, Mary's grizzling tearing at her nerves. On her arrival she was shown into a cell very like the one she'd left behind in Southampton Gaol.

The following day a warder came for her with the surprising news that her parents were waiting to see her and could stay with her until her name was called.

'Bring your possessions with you, Heath, you won't be coming back here whatever happens,' the warder told her.

Picking up their few belongings, Ellen hoisted Mary onto her hip and set off in the woman's wake. Her belly was churning and her heart thumping as though fit to burst from her chest, but she tried to calm herself for Mary's sake. Then as she was shown into the room where her parents waited, Ellen could control her nerves no longer and started to shiver uncontrollably.

Her mother took Mary into her arms and her father eased her gently into a chair where she slumped visibly. 'I can't face this, I can't! Oh dear God, what can I do?' Her voice rose to a wail and it was only when her own baby started to cry that Ellen knew she must stop or upset Mary further. Her teeth continued to chatter and this she could do nothing about.

'We'll stay for the trial, dear, then we'll see you again afterwards. I'll look after Mary for you.' Her mother stood close and put her free arm about Ellen's shoulders. 'Oh my dear, I just don't know what to say.'

They stayed locked in position as in a tableau; the distraught young woman shaking like a leaf, the parents standing one either side in an effort to comfort her.

Ellen jumped nearly out of her skin when she heard her name called in the corridor outside, but the strength had gone from her limbs and her father had to pull her to her feet and half carry her to the door. There, two gaolers took over and directed John and Ann to a viewing gallery where they could watch proceedings. With them gone, Ellen felt even weaker, the cold taking control of her quivering body, as she was half-dragged into the courtroom.

The trial passed in a haze of words and blurred visions. She was vaguely aware of Robert standing tall, dressed as she not seen him since their wedding day, making wild accusations about her behaviour when they lived at the farm, and saying that he was sure she had been seeing another man. In fact the child she bore might not even be his.

The shock of these words brought Ellen to her feet. 'How could you say that?' she shouted, but was told abruptly by the judge to be quiet, or face more charges.

Then there was Eliza. Poor Eliza, who got so tied up in what she was saying that no one could make any sense of it. She was dismissed without comment, but then the man from the drug shop was there. He pointed out Ellen and stated firmly that she was the woman who had purchased arsenic on the day in question.

Ellen felt that the whole world was against her and looked wildly about the court in the hope of seeing her parents, but wherever they were, it was out of her sight.

Then she was asked to stand and give her version of events. Doing her best to keep her voice level and speak clearly, Ellen told them exactly what had happened, and then how in a moment of madness thought of a way to get back at her husband. 'And in case anyone thinks otherwise I can tell you that my husband is the father of our child. I have never been with another man in all my life.'

'So you do not deny buying the arsenic?' the judge asked, his steely blue eyes boring into her.

'No, I don't, but as I said, I only meant to make him sick. I had no idea the stuff was so strong.'

'Ignorance is no defence, my lord,' Robert's lawyer said. 'There was a determined and wilful attempt to kill my client and so claim his farm and land for her own.'

Fighting down hysteria, Ellen screamed, 'What! Who in their right mind would want that dump? Certainly not me.' Then she slumped down into her seat, exhaustion suddenly overcoming her.

Raised voices came from somewhere, but her mind couldn't register what they were saying, drifting off to somewhere that wasn't a dark and depressing courtroom. She was aware of someone shaking her and telling her to stand up, but it meant nothing and the next thing she knew was that she was on her feet with a burly warder on either side propping her up.

'Do you understand, Mrs Heath?' It was the Judge who spoke.

'W-what?' she muttered.

'Do you understand the charges and plead guilty to them?'

Ellen frowned. What was he on about? Her fuddled brain sought some meaning. Do I understand the charges and plead guilty? Well, yes I suppose I do; I did buy the arsenic and I did give it to Robert.... So she nodded.

'Speak up please so that we might hear you,' the Judge ordered.

'Yes,' said Ellen slowly, and then heard a gasp echo around the high-ceilinged room.

'Very well, then I shall pass judgement. On this day, the first of March, in the year eighteen-forty nine, I find you guilty of attempted murder, the sentence for which is death.'

In the shocked silence that followed, Ellen noticed that the man had put a blank cloth over his wig... Then she fell to the floor in a dead faint.

Her mother's sobs roused her and she reached out automatically to comfort the woman she'd only seen cry on rare occasions. They were in a small, dimly lit room and she was laid on a bed, with something cold across her brow. Her head ached terribly.

As Ellen's mind cleared, she tried to sit up, but fell back as the room swam about her. 'Ma, why are you crying?'

'How can you ask that?' her mother whispered. 'After what I heard today it would make any mother weep.'

Trying to remember what had been said, Ellen looked about her to see who else was in the room. Her father and Eliza both stood behind ma; both ashen faced and still.

She closed her eyes, perhaps everything would come back to her then; but her mind remained blank. When she opened them again, she was alone and realised that she must have slept. How long for, she had no idea and wondered idly where her parents and sister were. Then the door opened and they walked back into the room.

At least her mother had stopped crying. Ellen forced herself up onto one elbow and asked softly, 'Please, tell me what has happened? I seem to have lost my memory.'

51

Sitting himself on the edge of the bed, her father took one of her hands in his work- worn ones. 'Don't you remember what the Judge said, Ellen?'

'No, I vaguely remember being in the courtroom, but that's all.'

John cleared his throat and said haltingly, 'My dear girl, you were found guilty of attempted murder and sentenced to death.'

Her scalp prickled as the Judge's voice echoed in her head. Shock gripped her afresh and her voice rose into a wail, 'I remember now. What shall I do, pa, how can I go and leave my Mary?' Tears cascaded down her cheeks. 'I'm only twenty-three, how can they do such a thing to me?'

Then suddenly, she became calm. I've been wicked and must pay for my sin, if I must die then it's what I deserve, but what about my daughter? How can I leave her? Realising that Mary wasn't in the room, Ellen panicked, 'Where is she, where is Mary?'

'Hush, dear, she's just outside with a kindly warder. We didn't want her to see you upset in case it frightened her.' Ann appeared calmer now too. 'Shall I go and fetch her?'

'Yes, please, ma.'

As the little girl's face lit with pleasure on seeing her mother, all Ellen's resolve disappeared and fresh tears fell unchecked to seep into Mary's woollen shawl.

'We've been told that we must leave now, but we'll come again as soon as we can, dear. Take care of yourself.' With a sob in her voice, Ann Newland turned away, brushing the tears from her eyes before baby Mary could see them.

'I'll try to think about Mary and make arrangements for her, not think about myself. How long before they... You know?'

'We don't know child, but I think we'll be given plenty of notice so that we can come and see you.' Her father hesitated. 'I don't want to raise your hopes, but someone said that they might try and get you a lighter sentence, so hold on to that thought.' He patted her hand and then, uncharacteristically, leaned forward and kissed her cheek. 'Goodbye for now.'

'Bye, pa.' Then her mother and Eliza, who hadn't said a word, both came and hugged her. 'Bye, ma. Bye, Eliza.'

Eliza broke into rasping sobs. 'I'm sorry, Ellen, I really am. I wanted to help, but I made it worse.'

'Shush, never mind, you did your best.' Ellen hugged her sister even tighter. And then they were gone and she was left alone to try and grapple with the fact that she may not have much longer on this earth. Mary gazed up into her face and gave a dimpled smile. 'My beautiful baby, how will I ever leave you?'

Back in Southampton Gaol it was several weeks before anyone came to see her: weeks in which the days merged one into another and time virtually stood still. Unaware of her depressing surroundings, Ellen's only thoughts were for her baby and she cared for Mary as best she could in the confines of a small lonely cell. Food and water were brought regularly, but the warders rarely said more than a few words, and she lived mainly within herself, and concentrated her thoughts on the family and Mary.

One day the door was unlocked at a time when it wasn't normally, and opened to admit a man who looked vaguely familiar to Ellen.

'Good day Mrs Heath. Do you remember me?'

'Not really, although I know I've seen you before.'

'Well, I was council for the defence at your trial. I did my best to keep you alive, but the judge was adamant, I'm afraid. Has a thing about women knowing their place.' The man sniffed as though this belief did not meet with his approval. 'Now, I have been in consultation with the prosecution lawyers to see if I could get your sentence reduced and I'm pleased to tell you that it has been accomplished.'

Ellen's heart leapt, 'You mean, I can go free?'

The man's eyes clouded. 'Well, no it's not as simple as that, I'm afraid. But your sentence has been reduced to transportation for life.'

A deep frown creased Ellen's brow. 'What is that? What does it mean?'

The man cleared his throat nervously. 'It means that you will be shipped off to another country, Australia most probably, and be confined there.'

Something stirred in her memory. The men from Selborne! They had been sent away to the other side of the world as punishment for their part in the riots. And now she would be joining them.

A new thought struck her. 'What about my child? Can I take her with me?'

'I think that is possible. There have been many cases where women have taken their children. Some have even made a good life for themselves I hear.'

'I'll never see my family again though, will I?'

He shook his head. 'Very doubtful indeed.'

'When will I be going?'

'There is no way of knowing that yet, I'm afraid, but you will be given plenty of notice. I expect your parents will want to visit you before then.'

'I hope so. They haven't been for a long time, but I suppose it's hard for pa to get time off from work.' Ellen cuddled Mary close. 'At least I'll have my daughter with me.'

The man stood to leave and Ellen suddenly realised that she hadn't thanked him. 'I'm grateful for what you've done, thank you. I didn't realise anyone was doing anything for me.'

'It's been a pleasure, Mrs Heath and I wish you well in your new life. Goodbye.'

'Goodbye.'

When he'd gone, Ellen laughed and swung Mary up in the air. 'I shan't have to leave you my sweet. Mummy will be able to keep you and take you with her. What an adventure we'll have.' But it was a sobering thought that she would be amongst strangers in a strange land.

Then Mary giggled and clasped her mother round the neck, before planting a very wet kiss on her mother's cheek. Luckily too young to have any idea of what the future held.

A few days later Ellen's parents visited, and they spent a fairly cheerful afternoon playing with Mary. Now that they knew Ellen wasn't going to die, the future didn't seem so bleak, although her father warned her that the journey itself would be difficult. 'You'll be on the ship for many months, and I don't think life will be too pleasant aboard a vessel travelling for so long.'

'I'll have Mary with me,' Ellen declared stoutly, not wanting her parents to see how frightened she was by the prospect of going to live somewhere that few people had heard of.

'Do you think it's wise to take her?' Ann asked, eyeing the tiny girl.

'Other women take their children, so it must be all right. That's what the man said anyway.'

'Didn't you ask his name?' John enquired.

'No, I never thought to. I'm silly I know, but then I've always been like that, haven't I?'

Her parents both chuckled at this, then Ann said, 'Not silly dear, just a bit thoughtless sometimes.'

'Will you be able to come and see me again before I go?'

Her father took in a deep breath. 'It's difficult to get time off from work, the cows don't milk themselves, you know, but I'll do my best. Failing that, your mother could visit with one of your brothers.'

'That would be good, but I would love to see you as well, pa.

How are all my brothers and sisters, anyway?'

The next hour sped by as they chatted about the family, no one daring to think or talk about Ellen's sentence. All too soon it was time for them to leave. 'Is there anything you need me to bring next time, dear?' her mother asked.

'Well, I could do with some kind of bag to carry our clothes in, and perhaps a memento or two, just so that I can hold something and think of home now and again.'

'I'll see what I can do.' Ann Newland bent and kissed her daughter and granddaughter. 'Look after yourself my dear. I'll try to come again soon.'

John stood looking down at his daughter sadness and pain clear in his eyes. His voice was gruff with emotion as he said, 'Goodbye, my dear daughter. If I don't see you before you leave, God Speed and try to live by His commandments.' Then he hugged her close, and Ellen knew that the smell of his tobacco and the feel of his rough jacket would stay in her memory forever.

'Bye,' she called after them. Then came great gasping sobs. 'Oh Mary, how've I come to this? How'll I go on and manage in a new country, with only more prisoners for company? You'll grow up never knowing your grandparents or your aunts and uncles. Oh, please God, help me, for I need someone to.'

She and Mary were then moved back into their cell, and as her life fell back into it's orderly routine Ellen began to be less afraid of the future. The weeks slipped by without word of her fate, and it was easy to make out that it would never happen. Perhaps they've forgotten me, she thought. Perhaps I'll spend the rest of my life here in Southampton gaol. It was a damp and dreary place, but at least she was alive and Mary was thriving. The only thing they missed was fresh air and, standing on tiptoe, Ellen could see the sun shining as it bounced off the building opposite, causing deep shadows in the courtyard below. It looked so inviting; she boldly asked one of the warders if there was any chance of them being allowed outside.

The woman smirked. 'I shouldn't think so.'

'My daughter would benefit from it, she's so pale, poor lamb.'

'Don't you think you should have thought of that before you broke the law and ended up in here?' It wasn't said with malice, but Ellen bowed her head, knowing that the woman wasn't particularly bothered about their fate.

With a sigh, the warder left, leaving behind her a wave of laughter. The other women thought Ellen a fool for even asking.

A little while later, the warder came back. 'You're to come and see one of the Governor's, he has some news for you.'

Following with trepidation, Ellen carried Mary along the dark winding corridors. Not for the first time, she wondered how anyone ever found where they wanted to go in this place. When they arrived, she was shown into an outer office and asked to wait. After what seemed like an age, a man's head appeared round the door. 'Mrs Heath? You can come in now.'

Ellen walked into the inner office and saw that the man had seated himself behind a large desk. 'Sit down, Mrs Heath.' He pointed to a chair opposite. 'Now, I have news of your transportation. In a few weeks, you will be removed from here to Millbank prison where you will await a space on board ship. It will most probably be quite a wait, there are so many prisoners being shipped nowadays.' He peered at her. 'Have you any questions?'

'No, I don't think so.' She thought hard. 'Oh yes, will my parents be able to visit me at Millbank?'

'I should think so, but it will be further for them to travel.'

'Oh!' Ellen realised then that she didn't even know where Millbank was. 'And I will be able to keep my daughter with me at all times, won't I?'

'Yes, of course.' The man's face softened slightly.

'Thank you. I was going to ask if we could go out in the fresh air, but I suppose that's not possible'

'It's not usual to allow prisoners outside, but the journey to the other prison will give you a change of scenery. You may go now, but wait outside for someone to accompany you back to your cell.'

'T-thank you,' Ellen said, knowing she'd never find the way back on her own.

One morning, several weeks later, Ellen was told to collect all her things together as she was leaving. 'Are we off to Millbank now?' she asked.

'Haven't a clue where you're going,' she was told abruptly. This Warder had always been particularly unfriendly. I hope they're a better lot where I'm going, Ellen thought, and picked up the few clothes she and Mary possessed, folding them neatly into a bundle.

Then, with Mary astride her hip, she followed the woman out of the cell, along the corridor and then down a long flight of stairs. And suddenly, there was fresh air on her face. She breathed in deeply, surprised that the air had a sharp edge to it. Perhaps it was autumn already, she thought.

Across the courtyard and into a wooden covered cart Ellen and

Mary were ushered. There were two other women already seated, and the warder climbed in too. Too bad she was coming, one of the nicer ones would have been better company and might even have chatted, Ellen thought, but was determined to enjoy the journey. She hoped they might see something of the countryside as it passed from view behind the cart. But as the door was slammed shut and locked, the only light came from two tiny windows set high in the sides.

Her companions didn't seemed inclined to talk, and soon the swaying of the wagon rocked Mary to sleep, so Ellen rested her head against the wall behind her, closed her eyes and let memories of home wander through her mind. How happy they had all been until a few months ago; now her parents, brothers and sisters must think her a criminal. She prayed though that they wouldn't forget her and hoped that in time they would have fonder memories.

Soon the clopping of her horse's hooves and the rumble of the wagon wheels lulled Ellen to sleep, until suddenly they slowed and the cart lurched over a different surface for a short while. Then they stopped, the door was opened and everyone climbed stiffly down. They were in a cobbled courtyard much like the one left behind in Southampton, but Ellen gazed at the building before her in dismay; this place looked even grimmer.

The building was indeed dire, and the food and people only slightly better. Wondering how long she would be here, Ellen smiled at the woman sitting next to her on the barely covered floor. 'You been here long?' she asked.

The woman shook her head, 'Nah, just a few days. Waitin' to be sent orf t'other side o t'world. And you?'

'Yes, and my little girl with me.'

'She's lovely, ain't she? What's 'er name?'

'Mary and she's getting on for two years old. My name's Ellen, what's yours?'

'Flo. I'm from London, as if yer couldn't tell.' The woman gave a bellowing laugh.

'I'm from Selborne, near Alton,' Ellen told her, 'but we've just been moved from Southampton gaol. This place is awful, but doesn't seem as bad.'

'Blimey, it must 'ave been 'orrible then, it ain't much cop 'ere. The warders ain't too bad though, 'specially to those what 'as kiddies.'

'That's good to know. I do worry about Mary in case she gets sick or anything. Have you any idea how long we'll have to wait?'

'Nah, I've ain't 'eard nuffin' yet.' She sniffed noisily and then wiped her nose on the sleeve of her grubby dress. 'Shouldn't fink it'd be too long though, they likes ter get rid o' us quick. Too many in one place see?'

Ellen nodded then turned her attention to Mary who was getting fretful. 'Do you want a drink? Here let mummy get you some water.' Hitching Mary onto her hip, she crossed to the big wooden bucket and scooped up some of the contents into a tin mug. She then settled back, suddenly tired after the time spent travelling and settling into a new cell. While Mary drank from the cup, dribbling some down her chin, Ellen studied the cell. It was bigger than the one in Southampton, with straw in short supply. 'Looks like Mary will have to sleep on my lap,' she thought unhappily.

As if reading her mind, Flo said, 'Yeh, she will, they don't seem to 'ave any beds. Still it'll keep her warm, gets parky in 'ere at night, it do.'

Ellen shuddered and thought longingly of the small, cramped, but warm cottage in Selborne. Suddenly tears sprung to her eyes, as she realised that never again would she see it, or indeed the village. Everything and everyone she had ever known was now lost to her, and it was all her own fault.

Over the following few days, Flo kept Ellen's spirits up with her bawdy jokes and hilarious stories about her life on the poverty-stricken streets of London, but then one cold November morning one of the warders entered the room and told Flo to pack her things as she was leaving.

'Gawd, where to now?' Flo protested.

'There's a large sailing vessel in the docks at Woolwich and she's about to leave, with you on it.'

Tutting noisily, Flo picked up her few belongings and turned to say goodbye to Ellen and Mary. 'Cheerio, ducks. Never know we might meet up in some other Gawd forsaken place. Look after yerselves. Bye you lot,' she said casually to the other women, none of whom appeared over-friendly.

'Bye Flo, it's been good to have your company,' Ellen called after her, while Mary lifted her hand and waved furiously.

'Ta-ta, Fo,' her little voice cried.

With her companion gone the room felt empty, not just of Flo and her belongings, but empty of her generous nature. 'I wonder who we'll have in with us now?' Ellen hugged Mary to her.

A few weeks later, a warder opened the cell door and beckoned to

Ellen. 'Your parents are here to see you.' Ellen jumped to her feet and picking up Mary, hurried after the retreating man's back.

After greeting them warmly, Ellen relinquished Mary to her grandma's lap where she stayed happily all the while they were there.

'I'm glad you could come too, pa. Did you have a good journey?'

'Not bad, girl, not bad. So, you'll be off soon then?' John said, his voice gruff with emotion. He was never a man to show his feelings easily, but Ellen knew he was upset.

She nodded, 'I think it might be a few weeks, but the warder said to be ready at any time as sometimes they have spaces at the last moment.'

Ann frowned. 'How can that happen then?'

'Sometimes people die before their turn comes, Ma.'

'Oh, I see. What a shame.' Ann looked thoughtful for a moment. 'But I suppose at least they get to stay on English soil.'

An uncomfortable silence followed this ironic view, and then Ellen decided to make it as jolly a visit as possible. 'That's enough talk about dying. Now tell me, how is everyone? Is James still at the stables? And Harriet and Eliza, what have they been up to?'

Ellen knew that they were making a tremendous effort to sound normal as they chatted about home, bringing all the love and best wishes from sisters and brothers, aunts and uncles.

Ann Newland then handed over a small carpetbag. 'Open it, Ellen, there are a few bits and pieces from home in there.'

Eagerly Ellen pulled the bag open and peered inside. 'Oh, look Mary, some ribbons.'

'They're from Jane, then there is a drawing from James that I think is supposed to be the cottage, then there is an embroidered hankie from Eliza and a pressed flower from Harriet. I've put in a spare dress for Mary and one for yourself, although it's rather shabby.' She sighed. 'It was the best we could do. Oh and there are some biscuits as well that I baked this morning.'

'Everything is lovely, ma. Do thank them all and say that I send my love and I'll never forget them.' Gazing at the gifts, Ellen knew that she would treasure everything until the day she died.

All too soon the warder put his head around the door. 'Time for your visitors to leave now, Heath.'

Now that it was here, Ellen knew it was to be difficult, saying goodbye to her parents for the very last time. No one wanted to speak; no one wanted to be the first to utter the unbelievable words. 'Goodbye' sounded too trite, but what else was there?

Then, as Ann rose from her chair to pass Mary to John for a last

59

cuddle, Ellen fell into her arms. 'Please look after yourself, Ma. Think of us often, and pray for us if you can.'

'Of course I'll pray for you my dear child, and you'll be in my thoughts every minute of every day.' Ann held on to her daughter as though never to let go. 'Oh, Ellen,' she gasped. 'My lovely, silly, headstrong, daughter. Look after yourself. And Mary.' As she drew back tears cascaded down her face unchecked.

John coughed, and Ellen knew he was close to tears himself as she took Mary from his arms. He patted her shoulder at first, but then enfolded her in a hug; obviously aware that this was the last time he would be able to do so. 'Goodbye, daughter. Take care. Don't forget your old Ma and Pa now will you?' His eyes were misty.

'Of course I won't, Pa, how could I ever do that? And Mary won't forget you either, I'll make sure of that.'

Then they were gone, hurrying from the room before emotion overcame them.

Her heart felt like a rock in her breast; how would she bear never seeing them again?

CHAPTER 5

A few days later, Ellen was to be ready to leave almost immediately. Barely glancing at her, the warder said, 'Right, Heath, you've got a berth on the St Vincent leaving tomorrow.' Then he was gone.

'That was short and sharp,' one of her companions said. 'You're off at last then?'

'Tomorrow,' Ellen whispered, trying to take in the enormity of what was happening to her.

The time passed all too quickly and soon she was stuffing their few possessions into the carpetbag, and hoisting Mary onto her hip ready to follow a gaoler out of the cell and along the draughty corridor.

As they walked out into the courtyard, the bitter December wind gusted about them, whirling Ellen's skirts about her legs, and chilling her flesh as it penetrated the knitted woollen shawl. Clasping it more tightly about her, she shielded Mary as best she could, but soon the little girl's eyes were streaming and her bonnet bobbed on the back of her head. Gratefully Ellen clambered into the waiting cart where six or seven other women waited silently.

Then, when the back cover had been secured, the cart jerked away and trundled out of the gates on its way to Woolwich docks. Ellen peered through a gap in the cover and noticed poor looking streets, and sometimes, she caught glimpses of a wide river. A sense of excitement welled up in her when she realised that this river must flow into the sea. She'd never seen the sea before but soon they would be sailing across it for months on end and Ellen wondered worriedly how deep it was, and what would they do if the ship sank?

Not long afterwards, the river disappeared from sight and they were entering between huge wooden gates. The cart slowed, jolting over cobblestones and now there were huge warehouses lining the road.

When the cart stopped, no one moved for a moment until the warders who accompanied them shouted for the women to get out. Stiff with cold, Ellen climbed down onto the quay, lifting Mary gently into her arms.

The wind tossed her hair about her head and across her face, so that the first sight she had of the ship was when they were half way across the wide expanse of the quay. The huge vessel loomed above them, her three masts thrusting into the sky. To Ellen's horror she saw that the women were being directed up a flimsy gangway that dipped and swayed as the ship moved at anchor.

She would never make it, she was sure. It was narrow with only a rope along one side to hold on to, but she had her hands full, with Mary held tightly against her hip on one side and the bag in the other. Almost closing her eyes, Ellen followed the woman in front, and prayed.

Within seconds her arms ached and she was terrified of letting go of either the bag or Mary, but gritting her teeth, decided that it would be the bag to go first. If her precious daughter fell into the water far below then she would go after her. They would die together.

But just as she felt all her strength draining away, she was being helped over the side of the ship by a rough looking, but grinning, sailor.

Her face was frozen by the cold into a mask so she couldn't smile back, but hoped the man noticed the look of gratitude in her eyes. Along the deck they were ushered, then were shown down steep wooden stairs. Then there was another flight leading down into the fusty darkness.

In the gloom, all Ellen could see was a mass of people, and the noise was deafening. Voices seem to come at her from all directions, but what any of them was saying wasn't clear.

Gradually her eyes adjusted to the gloom and there before her was row upon row of women lying on straw mattresses with barely six inches between them. She stood uncertainly not sure where to go or what to do, but then a man in a dark blue uniform asked her name.

'I'm Ellen Heath and this is my daughter Mary.'

'Come this way, Heath, we've a special area for women with children.'

Ellen picked her way over the feet of many who lolled about on the floor, apologising every few seconds when someone's foot or hand was trodden on. At last they reached a space where about a dozen women sat with their children and Ellen breathed a sigh of relief; it wasn't quite so crowded here.

'Here's your space,' the man said. 'Sit and wait until you're told to move, we need to do a count.'

Gratefully placing the bag on the floor, Ellen sank down onto the small, lumpy mattress, Mary beside her. No one spoke, but the babble of voices still reached them from the main area and she was grateful not to be in that mass.

Mary stared about her, bewildered by the change in their surroundings, but she didn't cry and seemed quite content as long as her mother was holding her.

It was darker here, but the air was slightly less heavy, and Ellen wondered where on the ship they were; they had taken so many twists and turns that she was disorientated.

Small lamps were held in brackets on the wall, giving off an eerie yellow glow, but gradually Ellen realised that she could see more clearly and studied the faces of the women around her. They looked very much like herself, mostly young and with babies in arms or tiny children like Mary. At least we'll have someone to talk to and the children will be company for each other on the journey, she thought.

After a while the noise abated and they heard the sound of shouting from above, then the ship shuddered and rolled. 'We must be on our way,' a woman close to Ellen whispered.

A wave of excitement mingled with apprehension washed through Ellen. This was it; they were on their way to an unknown land and if only they could see it, England must be slipping away into the distance. Tears welled in her eyes and from the sniffs she could hear, most of her companions were crying as well. Ellen prayed silently, please, dear God, look after us and let us arrive safely.

Slowly the noise returned: some of it from prisoners fighting for space from the sound of it. Ellen glanced at the young woman next to her who was sobbing her heart out. Reaching across, she took one of the woman's hands in her own and said gently, 'Don't cry, you'll upset your baby,'

Lifting her pretty face, the girl swallowed hard and replied, 'Yes, you're right. I'm being silly, it's just that I won't see my family again and baby James here won't ever see his grandparents.'

'You're not being silly, we all feel the same and in the same position. My little girl loves her granny and grandpa, but will never see them again.' She leaned over to look more closely at the baby. 'He's lovely. I have a brother called James, it's a nice name.'

The girl managed a glimmer of a smile. 'My name is Lucy, what's yours?'

'I'm Ellen, and this is Mary.' Ellen smiled at her daughter, who was by now trying to see the baby.

'Let her come closer,' Lucy said, and Mary moved to kneel beside the mattress and peered into the baby's face.

'The baby's name is James, Mary, like your uncle.'

Mary nodded, but said nothing and patted his tiny fingers with her own.

'How old is he?' Ellen asked.

'Only six months. He was born while I was in prison.'

Ellen felt sadness for this pretty young woman who could only be about Harriet's age. 'Mary is nearly two, but I think living in prison has hampered her growth as she's backward in her talking.'

'I'm sure she'll pick up later on,' Lucy said.

Just then two men came along carrying a large pan between them. A woman followed behind with a pile of tin plates in her hands, which she proceeded to hand out. 'Hold your plates out and we'll put your food on it, then afterwards you clean it off and keep it. We'll collect them when we arrive.'

The food looked, and smelled, very much like the prison food, so Ellen managed to eat her stew, breaking off pieces of bread and dipping them in the gravy for Mary. The little girl ate quickly and Ellen realised how hungry her daughter must have been. They had been several hours without food or water. Luckily water was brought to them then, in a huge wooden bucket with a ladle in. 'Help yourselves when you want,' they were told and then left alone.

After they'd all had a drink, another of the women spoke, 'I suppose they won't bother to put a guard in here, we can hardly escape can we?'

'Only if you can swim,' another said.

The first woman gave her a scornful look. 'When you're miles from land, being able to swim is neither here nor there.' Then she lay down and closed her eyes, obviously not wanting any more conversation.

Ellen knew how she felt. Her whole body felt weak and sore, and although she was warmer now, it wasn't a feeling of comfort. She lay down and pulled Mary beside her. 'We'll have a little sleep, shall we? Then when we wake up, ma will tell you a story.'

Mary happily snuggled close to her mother and was soon asleep.

The first few days aboard passed off fairly uneventfully and some of the women began to talk a little, but then one morning, the ship seemed to come alive, heaving first to one side and then the other. Soon everyone was suffering terribly with vomiting. Sea sickness one woman said it was. Whether it was the sea or the ship that caused it, Ellen didn't know, but the vessel pitched and tossed like a leaf in a water butt.

It meant talk was kept to a minimum as they all tried to use the water closets at once. As there were only two for all of them, vomit soon became spewed across the floor and the stench became unbearable, making them sicker than ever. Everyone, including the guards felt miserable and they took it out on the prisoners by being harsh and impatient, even with the children.

Ellen knew that she had never felt more wretched in her life. It was like living in a dark, stinking, moving hell. Every time the ship pitched, her belly went with it, her head swam all the time, and Mary grizzled constantly. Although Ellen felt sorry for her daughter, she was too ill to do much except try to keep her off the putrid floor and wipe her little mouth when she was sick. To make matters worse they were always short of water. The guards slopped so much out as they battled to keep their feet, that there was scarcely half a bucketful by the time it reached them.

Just when she was beginning to think she would never survive long enough to reach the new country, the ship stopped throwing itself about so much and Ellen felt a little better, and soon everyone stopped retching and was able to eat something again. One of the guards told them that the sea was always rough in the Bay of Biscay.

'Bloody hell, I hope we don't have many more of them,' said one of the older women as she dabbed at the floor with a moulting mop. 'There, it's a bit better, and at least it doesn't smell so bad.' She stood back to admire her handy-work.

'Either that or we've got used to it,' another snorted. A rumble of laughter followed this and soon the women began chatting, and the children amusing themselves with pieces of wool or tiny playing blocks. One or two even had wooden dollies that they shared. Mary though was shy and didn't really join in, but she loved to hold baby James hand. She even learned to say his name and never tired of watching him, awake or asleep.

It seemed to be an accepted rule that no one ever asked what crime they had been accused of. Ellen supposed they had all done something similar to her or perhaps had stolen something, but perhaps it was better not to know.

Soon, they were all lulled into a routine and the days began to merge one into another. It was a strange life, Ellen mused, no one was particularly friendly, but there was an obvious affinity. Their talk was all idle chatter; no one wanting to bring up the subject of relations or friends back home in case there was an epidemic of weeping.

Ellen found that the nights were the worst. The huge ship seemed to roll more and the noises from around the vessel were strange and sometimes eerie. Loud creaks and groans mingled with the snores of her companions and occasionally, the heartbreaking sobs of someone missing home and loved ones.

She thought often of her own family. Wondering how they were and what they were doing. She even thought of Robert in a passing moment, wondering if he had married the woman he'd been seeing. A little thing like having a wife already wouldn't stop him she was sure.

Pictures of Selborne drifted through her mind: the hanger in summer with the trees all in full leaf, the dusty village street lined with thatched cottages and flowering hedgerows alive with red campion and wild parsley. Her father in his garden, leaning on his spade while he watched a robin play tug-of-war with a worm. Her mother toiling over the huge wash-tub full of bed linen... Then she would push the memories away, as they became too painful.

Mary blossomed as she started to mix with the other children. One girl in particular seemed to fascinate her. Although older by about three of four years, the girl still had a babyish way about her. Her name was Stella, and her mother's name was Maddie. Soon she and Ellen became more friendly and started to exchange details of their lives. This helped to pass the time, but even so, Ellen still often feared that they were doomed to stay on the ship forever.

Sometimes Lucy joined in these conversations, but more often she lay on her bed, eyes closed. One day Maddie nodded in her direction. 'I don't think she's very strong,' she whispered. 'Can't be very old either, not much more than a child herself.'

Ellen nodded agreement. 'I should think she's about fifteen or sixteen at the most. I wonder how she came to be here.'

Maddie shook her head. 'None of our business.'

'No, you're right, it isn't.' But Ellen couldn't help wondering none the less.

Many days later, Ellen awoke to find herself bathed in sweat. The air was oppressive and it was strangely quiet. She lifted her head to look around and saw that everyone was glistening with perspiration, even the children and Mary stirred then and started to whimper. 'It's all right dear, ma will get you some water.'

But when she reached the bucket it was empty. Ellen peered into the dimness to see if any of the guards were about, but apart from the waking women in the next space, no one appeared to be watching them.

Cautiously, Ellen crept toward the stairway, certain that she would be stopped before she got halfway. Apart from a few questioning looks from some of the other prisoners, no one took any notice, and at last she reached the bottom of the stairs. Still no guards appeared, so she tiptoed upward into the semi-darkness.

At the top of the first flight of stairs she stood listening, but even the rigging had stopped its constant grating so, taking a deep breath, Ellen turned and started up the second flight. Above her she could see daylight and long before she had reached the doorway, the dazzling sunlight seared her eyes. Covering them with one hand, she edged forward and peered around the open door.

'Is anyone there?' she said, her voice hoarse with dryness. No answer came, but then Ellen saw several sailors further along the deck pulling something heavy through a huge wooden hatchway. And as she watched in fascination, they hoisted it over their heads and started tying it to one of the spars that stuck out at an angle from the mast.

Over the next few minutes the sailors had the sail attached and with the use of ropes had it rising high over the ship. The men then scrambled up the mast and along the spars to secure it. It looked rather dangerous to Ellen, but the sailors seemed sure-footed enough.

Just then, Ellen jumped nervously as someone spoke at her elbow. 'What do you think you're doing?' The voice was harsh, but as she turned, Ellen recognised one of the guards.

With one hand to her throat and the other shielding her eyes, she said, 'I was looking for someone to bring water, as the bucket's empty. We're all thirsty and the children need a cool wash.'

The man pushed past her, saying, 'I'll bring some, just you get back below where you belong, otherwise I'll be in trouble.'

Ellen hurried down the stairs after him, the inside of the ship now seeming even darker, but it was a relief to be out of the sun. Even those few moments in its strong rays had made her skin tingle.

The guard collected the empty bucket and a few moments later arrived back with what was, for once, a full one. '

'Why is the ship so still?' Ellen asked him.

'We've hit the doldrums,' the man said, then explained. 'It's an area in the ocean where there's no wind, so we'll only be making slow progress even with every sail up.'

'It's bloody hot too,' Maddie pointed out. 'Is it always like this?'

'Yeh, nearly always. It might go on for days, or even weeks.'

'All we can do is hope that it doesn't last too long,' Maddie said glumly as the guard went on his way to fill the rest of the buckets.

'I hope they have enough water otherwise we'll all die of thirst.' Ellen worried her bottom lip as she gave Mary a drink and then ran a damp cloth round her face. She wanted to do the same for herself, but took only a sip of the tepid water.

It grew hotter and hotter down in the bottom of the ship, and after many complaints, the guards opened small hatchways high up in the hull. No one could have climbed through them so Ellen wondered why they were so reluctant to open them; not that they let in much fresh air anyway and everyone lay still as the sweat soaked them from head to foot.

At first it was very quiet apart from the fretful children having the occasional grizzle, but then about three days later, one of the women from the next area called out, 'Can't you keep that bleeding kid quiet?'

It was Maddie's Stella who was crying at the time so she answered the question with another one. 'Are you hot and uncomfortable?'

'Course I bleeding am,' was the response.

'Well, just think how much worse it is for the children, then.' Maddie said, not unreasonably.

'Can't think why you wanted to bring the little blighters. Fancy dragging a kid half way round the world, you must be mad, or stupid.'

Ellen saw the colour rise in Maddie's cheeks and leaned across to put a restraining hand on her arm. 'Don't rise to the bait, Maddie,' she whispered.

Maddie clenched her teeth, and stayed silent, but the woman was looking for trouble and started shouting obscenities at the women with children, saying some dreadful things about unfit mothers. Until one of the women, who had a baby, scrambled to her feet and walked across to thump the perpetrator full in the face. 'Shut your rotten mouth,' she screamed.

Then all hell let loose.

As Ellen cowered against the side of the ship and held Mary close to her, the world exploded around her, with woman fighting woman, with hair, teeth and blood flying everywhere. She held on to Stella as Maddie tried to separate some of the worst offenders, but the heat began to take it's toll and one by one the women became exhausted, until everything died down again. Then, too late to do anything, one of the guards arrived.

'What's been going on here? You'd better get this place cleaned up, and quick,' he said and walked off again.

Maddie puffed out her breath. 'Silly bugger, surely he heard all the noise. How are we going to clean this lot up, I wonder? He isn't about to bring us a bucket of hot soapy water is he?'

Somehow they managed to clear the worst of the mess, but it took what little water there had been in the bucket, and then they all lay, exhausted and thirsty again until one of the guards appeared with half a bucket of water. 'It's going to be rationed now, so go easy on it otherwise we'll run out long before we reach port.

Maddie stood up. 'Come on children, here's little drink.' She knelt then and ladled a small amount into every waiting mouth, and then the babies were dripped some from a piece of linen. 'We'll have some ourselves when they've finished.' Maddie looked around her at the other mothers. 'All agreed?'

Everyone did agree and Ellen lifted little James and took him for a drink. 'I think he's too young to have water really, but Lucy doesn't seem to have much milk,' she told Maddie.

'No, the poor young thing looks pretty undernourished to me. Here, take her a drop and see if that bucks her up.'

Soon, calmness settled over everyone, and most slept.

Afterwards, Ellen couldn't remember how many days they spent in the torturous heat, but it went on and on, with tempers flaring every so often, but fortunately nothing like the first time. Many women suffered though with sickness and diarrhoea

Lucy caused concern to Ellen and Maddie as she lay listless and uncaring on her pallet. James was looked after between them, but without his mother's milk he began to weaken visibly. 'What can we do?' Ellen asked in desperation one day, as the baby lay propped up against a straw pillow, his little face shrivelled and pale.

'I don't know, but Lucy seems to have all the fight gone out of her so it's no use trying to get her to feed him extra.'

'I don't think she's got any milk left, look at her breasts. They're more like an old woman's than a young girl. I suppose she's not had enough to eat and drink to keep her strength up.' Ellen lifted her own sleeves and studied the loose material. 'We've all lost a lot of weight.'

'Hardly surprising on what we get fed,' Maddie grumbled.

One of the other women who had been listening to the conversation, said then, 'Look, I haven't got much milk, but my babe can eat some solids now, do you think James would feed from me?'

'We could try him,' said Maddie doubtfully. 'Are you sure?'

'Of course I'm sure. I wouldn't have offered otherwise, would I?'

'That's very good of you. Sarah, isn't it?' Ellen asked.

'That's me. Pass him over and we'll try.' Sarah held out her arms and took the baby into them. At first James didn't seem to like being with someone other then his mother, but once he felt some of the liquid, he sucked noisily, until Sarah took him off and changed to the other nipple. 'My goodness, you were hungry weren't you?' she cooed.

'Look Lucy, James has had a good meal from Sarah,' Ellen said. But Lucy just smiled weakly and closed her eyes again.

'I don't think she's going to be with us much longer,' Maddie whispered sadly. 'I suppose we should tell the guards, otherwise they might blame us if anything happens to her.'

'Do you really think she's that ill?' Ellen looked closely at Lucy.

'Yes, I do. I'll tell whoever comes with the food, it won't be long now, judging by my belly rumbling.'

'Your belly's always rumbling.'

Two sailors carrying a stretcher came for Lucy that evening, and insisted that James go with her.

Maddie tried to reason with them. 'Look, the poor little mite isn't going to get any nourishment from her, let him stay so Sarah can feed him.'

'Sorry, missus, he has to stay with his mother, it's the rules.'

'But he'll die,' Sarah wailed.

'That's as may be, but the doctor said he was to stay with her.'

'Where is the doctor? We didn't even know there was one on board.' Maddie was aghast. 'After all we've been through, and he's never shown his face.'

'Too busy looking after really sick people,' the sailor snorted.

'At least we know there is one now, so we can yell for him if we need him.' Ellen said, then added to the sailors, 'Look after Lucy. Tell the doctor we've done all we can for her.'

The men nodded and then left with their pitifully light load. That was the last time they ever saw Lucy – or James.

One of the guards told them later the next day that they had both died and that there would be a burial at sea the following morning, which they would all attend.

'That was one of the most harrowing things I've ever had the misfortune to witness,' Maddie said, as the women all settled back below decks after the burial at sea.

Everyone nodded, but no one spoke and Ellen guessed that they were all too upset to put into words what they were feeling. She felt as though someone had wrenched her insides out and kept seeing in her mind's eye again the sight of the two cloth-covered bodies sliding into the sea. One so tiny, it barely made a splash. The funeral service for Lucy and James had been done with dignity; the Captain mentioning how sad it was when young lives had been cut short, and Ellen was grateful to the man for his sensitivity.

She looked across at the empty mattress; her eyes misted with tears and she wondered if Lucy had a family back home in England. And if so, would they ever know what had happened to her and her baby. Mary kept going to the bed and patting it as though confused as to where her little playmate was. How could you tell a child not yet two years old what had happened?

One person they'd met that morning was the doctor. He'd stood beside the Captain watching sadly, and Ellen noticed that he studied some of the prisoners carefully. He had a kindly face and she wished now that they'd thought about there being a doctor on board before Lucy became so ill, but no one had told them. Then as the sound of footfalls reached her ears, she looked up and the man was standing close by.

Unable to stop herself, Ellen scrambled to her feet and went to him. 'Please, sir, can you tell me if our friend would have been saved if we'd asked for you earlier?'

'It's very unlikely as the poor young woman was very undernourished and also had an illness of long standing.'

'And the baby?' Maddie asked.

'I'm not so sure about him, but of course without his mother's milk, he stood no chance.'

'Didn't the guard tell you that Sarah was willing to feed him?'

'Yes, he did, but I'm afraid there are ethical difficulties with that.'

'There's always bloody difficulties of one kind or another,' Maddie exploded. 'The rest of us are fair to middling, if that's what you're visiting for.'

The doctor smiled. 'I came to see if the smell was as bad as I've been told.' He wrinkled his nose. 'I am alarmed to discover that it is actually worse. I will get something done about that then you may all feel a little better. Hopefully we shall be going ahead very soon as the Captain tells me that the wind is picking up.' He glanced round at everyone. 'Just remember that if anyone of you is taken ill, to send for me, Doctor Samuel Donnelly.'

As he left, Maddie said, 'Bloody too late now; for Lucy and James anyway.'

'It will be better if the smell eases off though.' Ellen tried to be optimistic.

'Yeh, and not before time. Why didn't anyone check that before?'

No one knew, and they all slipped back into quiet contemplation again.

When Ellen slept that night, she dreamed about Lucy and James swimming back to England, and felt happy for them; they could be buried in a village churchyard now. Then she recalled her view of the sea as they stood on deck under the searing sun. It had been silver and glass-like, not at all how she'd seen it once in a book, all green and blue with white-tipped waves. She awoke with a shiver. It was much cooler and she could feel the movement of the ship as it forced it's way through water once more. Perhaps they would arrive at their destination soon now.

But several more weeks passed before one of the guards told them that land had been sighted.

'When can we see it?' Everyone clamoured forward, so that the man backed away, holding his hands up in front of him.

'It'll be a few days yet, but once we're secure in harbour, you'll be taken off.'

'Where to?' One woman asked what they were all thinking.

'The woman's prison in Hobart.'

'What's it like?' Maddie asked.

'Don't ask me, I've never been in a woman's prison.'

'What's the country like?' Ellen wanted to know. 'Is it green and pretty like England?'

One of the older women broke in then. 'Depends on whereabouts in England you live, love. The streets of London ain't particularly green. Where I come from the only green you see is the slime in the gutter.'

Everyone moaned at her to shut up, but Maddie said 'There are parks in London, haven't you ever seen them?'

'Nah,' said the woman, 'we was too busy working to look for a park.'

As the banter went on, the noise rose to fever pitch, so glad were they that the long sea voyage was nearly over.

'Now then, quieten down will you, otherwise I'll have the Captain after me. You're supposed to be prisoners, not on a jolly outing.' But Ellen noticed that he was smiling as he left them.

'It must be hard for them, mustn't it?' she asked Maddie.

'Who?'

'The guards. They spend months at sea looking after prisoners and have to leave their homes and families. It can't be easy.'

'Perhaps it's the only job they're capable of,' Maddie mused.

'Yes, I hadn't thought of that, but even so, it's not a very nice job is it?'

'If you're determined to feel sorry for them, then do, but don't go on about it.' But Maddie grinned to soften the words. 'It'll be great to get off this ship, I know that.'

The babble of voices rose again, showing that they all felt relief now that the end of the journey was in sight.

Four days later, the St Vincent docked in Hobart harbour, but it was the following day before the first of the prisoners where brought up on deck ready to disembark. The women with children were in that group, and as Ellen scanned the surrounding countryside, she breathed a sigh of relief. From the area she could see, it was green and pleasant. Then as she was about to walk down the wooden gangway, she looked up and saw something that took her breath away – a mountain.

It towered over the town like an avenging Angel, dark and forbidding. She felt a nudge from behind as Maddie urged her on, so hitching Mary further onto her hip, she made her way down the swaying plank, this time not at all fazed by the movement.

As she stepped onto firm land though, it was a different matter and she felt rather strange, finding it hard to even put one foot in front of the other. Then she noticed that all the others seemed to be in the same predicament.

Then they all lined up and were instructed to follow a rather formidable woman along the quay and out into a street. It was dry and dusty, and Ellen noticed that some of the trees were bare while others had brown and gold leaves on them. She was puzzled, surely it wasn't autumn yet?

Her eyes kept being drawn back to the mountain and it sent shivers down her spine, It was so close to the town and looked like it might fall on top of it at any minute. As she sensed Maddie alongside her, she voiced her concerns. 'I don't like that do you?'

'What, that big hill? What's wrong with it?'

'It feels as though it's going to fall on us.'

'Don't be daft, I expect it's been there for thousands of years. You'll get used to it in time.'

'I don't want to get used to it.' Ellen stumbled slightly ahead. Didn't anyone else feel as she did? With an effort she kept her head turned away from the mountain and concentrated on the houses bordering the road. They were all small stone buildings with iron roofs and had tiny flower-filled front gardens, and in between were a few shops, a blacksmith's forge and some hotels.

As they turned into another road, a few people stood about

watching their progress and as they neared them a shout went up. 'Here's more of them bloody women.' The man spat in the road. 'Can't they keep their bloody prisoners in their own country? Why should we have them polluting ours?' Several others, men and women joined in a general hubbub of ill feeling, making Ellen feel very unwelcome indeed.

CHAPTER 6

Ellen was surprised to find the woman's prison a hive of activity. It was called the Factory, partly because it sounded better to the locals and partly because the women did make things. They wove their own material and then clothes were made for prisoners to wear. There were many prisons on the island, so they were told; mostly men and they all had to be clothed.

There was only one thing that bothered Ellen to any extent. The women were, for most of the day, working in large groups no matter what part of the manufacturing process they were on, and most of them were less than desirable to be around a young child. Ellen asked to be moved from one such group, but her request was turned down. 'You got yourself here, so you can make the best of it. You've only yourself to blame if your daughter hears things she shouldn't.'

Maddie and Sarah, having children of their own understood and on several occasions Maddie scolded women who used the filthiest language in front of Stella and Mary.

'It's not so bad for me because little Tommy is only a baby, but I wouldn't want him hearing that sort of thing when he's older.' Sarah acknowledged.

'Let's hope we're not still here when he's older,' Ellen said wryly.

Maddie said fervently, 'Amen to that.'

The first few weeks passed quickly as they grew to know their surroundings, got used to the indifferent food, and cemented friendships. The nights were bad for Ellen and Mary because they shared a tiny room with such a narrow bed, that Ellen often feared pushing Mary out. Apart from the bed, there was a small box in which to put belongings. There was no bucket, and no light. Once you were locked in for the night, that was it, and it was difficult to explain to a child that they must wait until morning to have a wee-wee.

'How are you managing?' Ellen asked Maddie one day. 'Stella is bigger than Mary and we only just squeeze into the bed.'

'I usually end up sitting on the floor and nodding off. Bloody cold it is too. I wonder why they don't have bigger cells for those of us with children.'

'How long do you think we'll be here? Someone said that it was just a holding station.' Ellen wrinkled her nose. 'Whatever that means.'

Maddie shook her shoulders in silent mirth. 'It means somewhere to hold prisoners as a temporary measure, but I don't think there's anything temporary about this place.'

'No, it seems solid enough. I wonder if it was built especially for prisoners?'

'I should imagine so. It's not a very big town so probably wouldn't have had a prison this size before they started sending prisoners from England. I feel rather sorry for the people who lived here before, don't you? Fancy having a load of criminal women dumped on your doorstep.'

'There are a lot more than I expected.' Ellen gazed around the huge workroom. 'I wonder what they've all done.'

'Prostitutes mainly from what I've heard.' Maddie sniffed. 'You have to feed your kids somehow.'

Then one morning, Mary's crying woke Ellen. 'What's the matter, dear?' In the darkness, she brushed her daughter's body and stroked one small arm. This quietened the little girl for a while, but then she became restless and Ellen had a moments panic when she realised Mary was going to be sick. Then Mary vomited over them both, and the acrid smell in the room told Ellen that her daughter had probably messed herself as well. 'Oh, my poor little love, what can we do?'

Ellen eased herself off the bed and felt around the wall until she came to the door. She knocked loudly and called out, 'Please help, my baby is sick.' But no help came, although she banged and shouted for what seemed like hours. Finally, the door was opened and Ellen was so frantic by now, that she practically threw herself into the guard's arms. 'My little girl is ill, please help us?'

The guard wrinkled her nose and said, 'Wait a moment, I'll get the doctor.'

The doctor confirmed that Mary was ill enough to be taken to the Dynnyrne Nursery just up the road, and soon, to Ellen's relief, they were on their way by cart. Her daughter's skin was burning hot and the sickness and diarrhoea continued, until Ellen was sure there was nothing left to come out. Mary was listless, and seemed to drift off to sleep for a while, before coming too and crying again, her legs drawn up in pain.

Ellen held her close and rocked her, soothing her brow and making calming noises. She felt so helpless and prayed that once they arrived at the nursery the doctor could give Mary something to ease her distress.

The nursery was slightly better than the prison in that it was lighter and cleaner, and the staff more considerate. Nervously, Ellen waited for the doctor to finish giving Mary a more thorough examination. When he came out of the room, his expression was grim. 'Your daughter has dysentery Mrs Heath. I'm afraid we have rather an epidemic at the moment, but all we can do is give her plenty to drink and keep her cool.'

'Will she be all right?'

'Only time will tell. Some children recover, while others do not.'

Fear had Ellen gasping. 'You mean, she might not get better?' Her hands flew to her face as she tried to contemplate the unthinkable.

The doctor patted her shoulder and said, 'There, there, it might not come to that. We'll do all that we can.'

Ellen prayed harder than she had ever prayed before. Please God, don't take my daughter. Don't take my little Mary. She's all I have left now in the whole world.

Then the following day, Maddie arrived with Stella, then Sarah with baby Tommy.

'We'll all be in here soon,' Maddie said gloomily. 'Nearly all the kiddies are sick.' She smiled at Ellen. 'How's Mary today?'

'Not too good, the doctor says she might recover, but she seems so weak. Oh, Maddie what will I do if I lose her?'

'Ssh. She'll be all right, you can bet on it.' But the sadness in her eyes did not go unnoticed by Ellen.

'I have this feeling of dread, as though something terrible is going to happen, and it can only be to Mary. I can't sleep for worrying about her.' Ellen felt panic rising and fought to keep it under control. Mary needed her; it wouldn't do to break down

All that day and the next, Ellen kept vigil over her daughter. Mary seemed not to know her and it broke her heart to see the tiny body shrinking before her eyes.

Early the following morning, Ellen awoke with a start, not sure how long she had been asleep or what had roused her. Then she looked at Mary – and her heart stopped. Her daughter wasn't breathing…

The screaming went on and on until Ellen could stand it no longer. Who could be making such a hideous noise?

Suddenly the howling stopped and as the silence filled the room, she looked up and in the dim chill of the room saw half a dozen pairs of eyes on her. Becoming aware of the dampness on her face, Ellen scrubbed at her cheeks with both hands.

Realisation dawned; it had been she who cried. With a fresh wave of piercing pain, she glanced down at her baby daughter. 'Mary, wake up. Please! Wake up!' She shook the little girl, but it was no use, the tiny lifeless body flopped about like a rag doll.

She was dimly aware of someone coming to sit next to her on the rickety bed as it dipped under the weight. 'Please, let me take her,' a woman's voice said softly. 'We've called the nurse.'

'No!' cried Ellen. 'Leave her be. She'll recover, you see if she doesn't.' Holding Mary tightly to her, she rocked back and forth, her spine hitting the cold stone wall behind the bed with a dull thud at each movement. 'Come, my little one,' she crooned. 'Wake up for your mummy.'

The rocking went on and the woman looked across at her companions in despair. 'What can we do?' she hissed.

'They couldn't have heard us, and we can't leave her like that,' another said.

'Ellen, can you hear me? It's me, Maddie. Let me look at Mary.' She stroked Ellen's arm encouragingly.

There was no response, so Maddie stood up and moved away to where the other women now clustered together round in a shocked group. Sarah shook her head in sorrow. 'We must call the nurse again, but God knows how they'll ever get Mary away from Ellen.'

Another woman stood up from her bed, her ragged dress causing a draught in the fetid air. 'I'll call 'em if you lot are too scared,' she said loudly, moving to stand by the barred door. 'NURSE!' she yelled, but still no one came. After waiting for several minutes, she started banging on the door, screaming, 'Will you get in here, you filthy rotten bastards.' Then, as tears of anger and frustration began to run down her face, she started shaking the bars, using the whole weight of her body, as though to pull the door from it's hinges.

As her own small daughter cried with fright, Maddie hurried forward, crying, 'Evie! Evie, calm yourself. The nurse will be here in a moment.' As she tried to pry the woman's fingers from the bars, she said more softly, 'I know it's tough, but we've got to try and cope with it. Look at poor Ellen, her little girl dead in her arms. Think about her. Come on, you know we support each other.' Maddie smiled wanly. 'We're all we've got and your little boy is getting better.'

Evie moved away from the door, her energy spent in the madness and fear that had gripped her.

Then two nurses arrived, unlocking the door in a hurry. They crossed to where Ellen still held Mary tightly to her. 'Let me look at Mary, Ellen,' said one, using the prisoners Christian name for the first time.

'No! No, you shan't take my baby. You shan't,' Ellen cried anew, as two women tried to gently take Mary from her arms.

One nurse nodded to the other and then left the room, returning a few moments later with a small enamel bowl in her hands. She took a pad and soaked it in the contents of a blue bottle before holding it over Ellen's nose and mouth. As she slumped back, the nurse said quietly, 'Now let me look at Mary.' She crouched down next to the bed and took one little wrist between her thumb and finger.

Every other woman in the room held their breath, waiting for the nurse to find a pulse - or not. When she shook her head at her companion, they all knew with a dreadful certainty that Mary was gone.

The Chloroform had quietened Ellen and she sat numbly watching as her daughter was lifted from her arms. Inner instinct her told her that Mary really was dead and grief sat heavily within her.

With her baby's body gone, Ellen slumped against the wall, her blood like ice in her veins. A vision of her mother came to mind and she wished with all her heart that she were back in Selborne to feel those loving arms about her. Fresh tears now poured unchecked down her cheeks, but they were silent, hot, angry tears. Anger at all the injustice she'd endured over the years. Anger even at God for taking her daughter...

As the door was locked behind the two nurses carrying the body of a child barely old enough to walk, a profound silence filled the room. Maddie came to sit with her, holding Ellen's head against her ample bosom, and through her unhappiness, Ellen felt grateful for the comfort it gave. The comradeship she'd built up with these women over the past few months was the only thing that would keep her sane through the long months ahead she was sure.

The following day, she was collected from the prison nursery and taken outside to a small corner of a walled courtyard. Still numb with grief, Ellen looked dully about her and saw about a dozen small mounds; each headed by a white wooden cross. A fresh-dug hole yawned beside them, and around it stood several people, two of whom held a small coffin.

Ellen's head swam and her whole body felt as though it was melting; would her legs hold her up, she wondered?

Then a clergyman dressed all in black came and stood by the tiny grave and Ellen felt herself gently pushed forward. She hadn't been aware of anyone next to her, but the two nurses supported, one either side.

The sombre-faced priest gave her a pitying smile before starting to intone the burial service.

Ellen fought to keep a tight reign on herself, fought to keep upright, but her mind refused to take in what was happening. It was when she saw the tiny coffin being lowered into the earth, she finally collapsed, crying out, 'My baby, my baby. Oh Mary... Please God, don't let this be happening. Don't bury her, don't, she won't be able to breath. NO! NO!'

As her heartrending cries filled the air, she became aware of strong arms pulling her to her feet and the comforting presence of another person holding her as her screams subsided into convulsing sobs. When she looked up it was one of the nurses whose face she saw, her eyes filled with compassion as they met Ellen's.

'Come and drop some flowers onto the coffin,' the nurse urged. 'You'll feel better if you say goodbye, and send Mary off with a blessing.'

A small spray of flowers was placed into her hand and through her tears, Ellen watched them fall onto the little box. Her brain refused to accept that Mary was in the coffin. Mary was safe inside, with Maddie watching over her. Surely...

'Come away now, Ellen,' the nurse urged. 'We've been instructed to take you back down the road to the factory.' The woman gave a gentle tug. 'I've got your things.' In her hand was the small carpetbag; a bag that contained everything Ellen had to her name.

"Away in a manger, no crib for a bed..." The words rang out lustily, if a little off key, from the group of women standing in the tiny Chapel. Ellen Heath felt a tear trickle slowly down one cheek as she remembered her own child, dead now these past six months. It would have been Mary's second Christmas and she would have enjoyed the celebrations.

As had been the custom back in England for the last few years, Ellen and the other women had painted paper to hang as chains in the dining hall at the factory and made rough cards for each other. Although they couldn't create the merry Christmas that would be happening in England, the women were determined to enjoy it, in the hope of making up a little for last year when the Yuletide had passed almost unnoticed aboard the St Vincent.

Ellen brushed the tears away. She wasn't alone, several women had lost their small children in the epidemic and they had forged a bond, finding that shared grief helped to lessen the pain. Luckily the spread of dysentery had been halted and no children had died for several months.

Another carol rang out as the priest came to stand in front of them. "O come all ye faithful, joyful and triumphant..." How incongruous that sounded here in this prison Chapel.

Some of the women grinned covertly at one another; the irony not lost on them and Ellen couldn't help overhearing when Maddie nudged Sarah, saying, 'I could make him joyful and triumphant all right, but the poor sod has to be celibate.'

A sound gurgled in Ellen's throat, and for the first time since her daughter's death she found herself giggling. Soon those around her joined in the infectious sound and before too long the women were all collapsing with laughter. To their immense surprise, the priest smiled and stood waiting for the hysteria to stop.

'Here, Maddie,' Sarah spluttered, 'He wouldn't look so happy if he'd heard what you said.'

When they were all quiet, the priest continued, and as though he felt that the women should be allowed to enjoy this special day, his sermon was more spiritual and less fire and brimstone than usual.

Since Mary's death, Ellen had taken time to reflect on her life. She recognised her mistakes and had prayed long and hard for forgiveness. Now all these months later, life was less harsh, although the hours she worked and the treatment were the same. From somewhere an inner peace had come to comfort her and she now took each day as it came. She had even volunteered to help with the Christmas dinner that the Governor had given permission for, and was amazed to see the meat and vegetables stacked on the large kitchen table first thing that morning.

She, Maddie and Sarah, whose children had fortunately recovered from the dysentery, along with six other women, made up the cookery detail. With the normal cook away for the day to be with her family, they set to with enthusiasm to make the most of what they hoped would be a meal to remember. They had left the huge joints of meat roasting over the open fire, while two pots simmered with the vegetables, and several large jam roly-poly were boiling in the muslin wrapping, in a third. By the time the service was over, it should all be cooked, and Ellen for one, felt her mouth water at the feast to come.

At least this will be edible, she thought, not like the muck we usually get dished up. Glancing about the Chapel, there seemed to be more women here than ever and she hoped fervently that there was enough to go round.

As befitted a special occasion, the women and children were being allowed to eat out in the yard at several long trestle tables. Compared to the dark, dingy dining room where they ate every day, it would be a luxury to be in the open air, and a novelty to be eating Christmas dinner in the full heat of a summer day.

Tomorrow it would be back to the normal ten hours working at the loom, making cloth for the prison clothes. Ellen had seen very little of the country to which she'd been transported, but what she had seen reminded her of England. Apart from the mountain that was - who's forbidding mass overshadowed all else.

The meal was a success, apart from the few who'd argued that some had more on their plates than others did. 'These women would argue over whether it was night or day given half the chance,' chuckled Sarah, as she cleaned her plate off by dragging a grubby finger across it.

'Never mind them,' Ellen said, 'Let's get the plates cleared away, then perhaps we can have a sing-song for a while.'

'What a good idea,' said Maddie, scrambling inelegantly to her feet from the rough wooden bench, while seven-year-old Stella, clinging onto her mother's skirt as usual, followed behind. As they washed the dishes, Maddie asked, 'Have you heard about the places we're likely be going to next year?'

Ellen gaped at her. 'What places?'

'We'll all be leaving here soon to go and work out on a farm or some such,' Maddie told her. 'Didn't you know?'

With a shake of her head, Ellen whispered, 'When will we know?'

Her eyes bright with hope, Maddie stared at Sarah and Ellen. 'In a couple of months I heard.'

'Thank the Lord for that.' Sarah pushed back a stray lock of hair that had fallen free from its binding and shifted Tommy more comfortably on her hip. 'This was only ever meant to be a holding station and I wondered how long we'd be here.' Her pretty, but now gaunt, face lit up. 'Hooray, let's hope it all happens soon.'

Her thoughts whirling as she dunked the last of the plates, Ellen wondered where she would be sent. Perhaps she might even be allowed to live with a family again. But then her heart sank; no one would want a convict sleeping in their house. Would they?

Back outside in the sunshine, voices could be heard singing a few of the popular songs from back home, bringing tears and a longing to be back with their loved ones. Through her own tear-misted eyes, Ellen saw that Sarah and Maddie were also crying; how far away it seemed. She knew Maddie was from London and Sarah from Ireland, but no matter where you came from, your heart always remained in one spot. 'Will we ever see England again do you think?' she whispered.

Her friends grimaced, and both shook their heads sadly. There was little chance of that for any of them...

CHAPTER 7

'You're late again, Ryan, I'll have to note it against you.' The impassive face of the chief of police loomed over the desktop.

'Sorry, sir, but there was a ruckus at the prison house and I had to sort it out.' John smiled brightly, but avoided the man eyes.

'Always a ready excuse, haven't you Ryan? Well it doesn't wash with me so get on with your duties. There are three men to take into court this morning, I suppose you can manage that without any problems?' The sarcasm didn't escape John's notice.

'I can do that, sir, and I'm off now.' John fought down the urge to reply in similar vein and hurried out through the side door into what was improbably called, the prisoner's holding room. It was little more than a shack joined onto the police house and courtroom, and with one small window, the heat was stifling under the tin roof. There were two doors, both locked and bolted so that prisoners couldn't make good their escape; not that the flimsy wood from which they were made could have stopped them.

To his dismay, Bart Tyrrell was there along with two other murderous looking thugs. A long heavy chain linked each man and then was fastened to a ring in the wall.

The remembered sneer crossed the man's face. 'Well, well, look who we have here? If it ain't Mr Ryan, the mad Irishman.'

'Hold your tongue, Tyrrell, we're not at Impression Bay now.' John raised his eyebrows questioningly. 'What you up for anyway?'

'It's on the charge sheet.' Bart indicated a sheaf of papers on the table, then grinned. 'That's if you can read, that is.'

'Oh, I can read them, you can be sure of that. Let's see.' John scanned the papers, then grinned. 'You'll have trouble wriggling out of this, Tyrrell, and I should think it'll be the death penalty for you this time.' He grinned as a look of fear flitted across the man's face. 'I always knew you'd come to this, you've been a trouble maker ever since I've known you.'

'Just because they've given you a uniform and a few piffling duties, doesn't make you a better man, Ryan. You're just a crawler, a stinking rotten Irish crawler. With all your blarney, you've never fooled me. You committed a crime same as me and one just as bad, but you talked your way out of it.' He turned to the other two men. 'This is the biggest shyster you'll find this side of the ocean. He ain't got his Ticket of Leave yet, and do you know why? Because even after all the years we've been here, he keeps getting into trouble, that's why. He forgets it's a close community here in Hobart and that word gets about. He keeps losing his job of constable because he can't keep his mouth shut.' The sneer returned. 'Ain't that right, Irish boy?'

The two men eyed John with interest. No doubt thinking that he must a man of some sort of standing to be allowed back into the constabulary time and time again.

'Right, let's get into court, the Judge hasn't got all day,' John said briskly, not wanting Bart to tell the other two any more about him. It was true; trouble always seemed to follow him about. Even when he tried his best, something always went wrong, or someone let him down. He was too trusting for his own good that was his trouble.

He unfastened the chain and led the three men through a door into the courtroom. As courtrooms went, it was decidedly ramshackle, with only a large wooden table in the middle of the dirt floor. Behind this sat a tired-looking elderly man whose impatience could only be ascertained by the drumming of his fingers on the table in front of him.

John Ryan stepped forward and gave the names of his prisoners to the judge. Then he took a pace back to where he could keep an eye on the rogues should they try to make their escape. It had happened to him before and the punishment had been rather out of proportion to the crime in his mind. Stripped of his uniform, he'd been sent to Oyster Cove, another of the colony's penal establishments, on the charge of having let his prisoner escape on receipt of payment. This had been completely untrue, but no one would believe him and John despaired of ever getting his Ticket of Leave, the right to live as a free man. After seven years in this land, he had worked hard for it and thought it should be his right by now.

He now sighed quietly and tried to concentrate on what the Judge was saying, but it was a long, involved case and by the time the man had made his decision, John's legs ached and his head felt as though stuffed with wool.

He'd been right though, Bart Tyrrell and his two accomplices' were to be sent to another prison; one they would never come out of alive. This time John's sigh was one of relief. This place would be better without the likes of these men.

In silence, he led the three men out of the courtroom, handing them over to two armed policemen. They would be taken away by cart to the prison on the peninsular where there was no where to run to, even if they managed to escape.

As he watched the cart move off along the dusty street, John pondered on what made some men so evil. Were they born like it? Or did it happen because of where they lived, or who they lived with? He shook his head and hurried back inside to find out what his next duty was to be.

The Chief grinned unpleasantly as he entered. 'I've got just the job for you, Ryan. Go up to the woman's factory and take some of the lovely ladies along to the new hospital. They need extra cleaners there and have a few volunteers who need to be escorted.'

John groaned inwardly. What in God's name was he to do with a group of women? And how was he supposed to keep them in check single-handed? He knew what some of them were like - hard as nails, and rougher than the men!

He turned, and as he went out through the door the cold wind hit him full force. Although winter held them in it's grip, in general the days were not as cold as they'd been back in Ireland, and John found the concept of winter in May hard to accept.

He hurried along the quiet street, bordered on both sides with wood or stone shingle-roofed buildings that seemed to hug the dirt road. Many were shops or hotels and some private houses, all with smoke rising from squat chimneys. Some of the prison staff lived in this part of Hobart, close to where they worked.

He cursed his luck for the umpteenth time as the high wall of the woman's factory came into view. That was a laugh, he thought, to call it a factory; although he supposed some of the inmates did work at something. He banged his fist on the huge wooden gate and waited for someone to answer.

A grill slid back to reveal a pair of dark unfriendly eyes. 'Yes, what do you want?' asked an equally unfriendly voice.

'Constable Ryan at your service. I've come to take some of your women to the hospital,' John replied in what he hoped was a more congenial way.

'Wait there, I'll get 'em.' The woman turned and gave a loud sniff before moving off out of view. A few moments later her face was at the small square window again. 'Right, there's four of 'em. Got your handcuffs ready?'

'Be Jesus! Of course I haven't got four pairs of handcuffs. I doubt we've got that many in the town.'

He sensed a shrug as the woman declared, 'Well, it's up to you. There's only a small risk of any of them running off. Where would they go? Eh?' A raucous laugh erupted and the smell of the woman's sour breath came at him through the opening.

'I'll risk it,' said John, just wishing to get away. After all, in spite of what he'd heard, surely they couldn't be much worse than some of the brutal beggars he'd dealt with.

The gate swung back, giving him a glimpse of the wide yard inside. It looked bleak and bare, the dull stone showing no hint of warmth. John quickly turned his attention to his charges, and his heart sank. Here were four of the ugliest, untidy and bitter-faced women he had ever set eyes on. His thoughts flashed for a second to the gentle, sweet tempered colleens back home in Ireland. My God what had he been let in for this time. But, as a sheet of paper was thrust into his hand, he forced himself to be civil. 'Come ladies, it's not far. Can I trust you all to be on your best behaviour?'

Four pairs of eyes stared at him, then one spoke. 'Where do you think we'd run off to? This whole bloody Island's one big prison.' She spat on the ground, her sparse brown hair swinging down across her face. Her swearing and general demeanour shocked John, until he remembered that these women were all criminals of some kind or other and probably the dregs of society in England.

One of the others moved forward and spoke. 'We'll be all right, we promise. We just want to get to the hospital and start work.'

Her voice was gentler and had a slight burr to it and John wondered where she came from. She was also slightly better looking than the other three, he decided, with dark curling hair and brown eyes. When she smiled, he found himself smiling back, but remembering his duties, he turned and led the way along the street toward their destination.

After a few steps, he glanced sideways and found her still walking close to him. When she spoke, he wasn't sure if he should answer. It could be seen as fraternisation with a prisoner.

'Where are you from,' she asked. 'By your accent you aren't English, are you?' Her eyes held candid curiosity.

For an instant, John hesitated, then cleared his throat. 'No talking, just keep walking.'

She showed no animosity at being rebuffed and kept apace with him just the same. Then after a few more minutes, she tried again. 'I think you're from Ireland. My friend Sarah here is from Ireland and she sounds a bit like you. Am I right?'

Before John could say anything one of the others grabbed her arm and pulled her back. 'Will you shut up, Ellen. We're not on a bleedin' picnic, nor are we in a position to entice men.'

'You shut your mouth, Evie. I can talk to who I like, and I'm not trying to entice him, I'm just being polite.'

The other women sniggered and John felt his neck grow hot with both annoyance and embarrassment. 'Be quiet, all of you,' he barked, and silence fell. He was relieved then as the hospital loomed ahead. 'Right, we're here now, so in you go.'

'Are you going to wait for us?' asked the young woman he now knew to be called Ellen.

'What would I want to do that for. My duty was to deliver you here, that's all.'

'Oh, but you have the chit, and you've to take us back later,' he was told by one of the group who was taller, had blonde hair and an Irish accent.

'No one said anything about taking you back.' John let out a heavy sigh of annoyance. 'I'd better come inside and check this out.'

His flesh crept uncomfortably as he walked through the door. He hated these places and the antiseptic smell made him feel sick.

Six hours later John breathed a sigh of relief. His prisoners were safely deposited back in the Factory and he could at last relax. On returning to escort them back, he'd had to sit in a sparse, evil smelling room to wait, and what a trial that had been.

Then, as he led them along the street, the women's noisy chatter had assailed his ears. Only Ellen had seemed quieter. Oh, she had talked, but in a more subdued way and although John had pretended to ignore her, he had listened keenly.

He still didn't know why she was here; no mention having been made of that, but he knew she was from somewhere called Selborne in Hampshire, England and although plain to look at, he felt an impish personality bubbling away beneath the surface.

He wondered idly if he would ever see her again, but doubted it.

Ellen couldn't settle. She fidgeted with the material she was supposed to be folding, creasing it deeply, until her exasperated friend hissed loudly to her to pay attention.

'Will you look what you're doing? A fine mess this is in now. What's the matter with you anyway? You've been in a funny mood all morning, in fact now I come to think of it, you've not been right since we went out to work at the hospital yesterday.'

'Sorry, Maddie.' Ellen grinned. 'It was getting a taste of freedom that's all. I'm glad we'll be going again tomorrow.'

Just then Evie came bustling up. 'Here, have you two heard the latest?'

Both women turned to her. 'No, what's that?' asked Ellen.

'I've just heard that we're being moved out of here. Well, a few of us are anyway.' Evie puffed out her huge bosom to show importance at bringing such good news.

Maddie and Ellen gazed open-mouthed at her, then Ellen asked, 'How do you know? You're always making out you know things when you don't. And if this is true, when is it supposed to happen?'

'Well,' Evie leaned forward to whisper conspiratorially, 'I heard we're all going off to a small town somewhere to work on this big estate.' She paused, the corners of her mouth turned down. 'Don't know when yet.'

Maddie narrowed her eyes. 'Are you sure about this?'

'Yes, I heard the Governor talking this morning.'

'Oh, come on, how would you do that? Or are you in his confidence now?' Maddie barely concealed her laugh.

Evie gave a condescending sigh. 'I was at the door, wasn't I? Waiting to go in for me telling off.' Evie was always in trouble, so neither woman doubted this.

'Well, well.' Ellen mused. 'I wonder when we'll be going?' Then her eyes clouded and she gasped, 'Oh, no!'

'What's up with you now?' Maddie asked.

'I won't see him again if we go away, will I?' Ellen explained sadly.

'WHO?' Evie and Maddie asked in unison.

Ellen blushed now and looked at the toes of her well-worn boots. 'That nice young police constable, you know, the one who escorted us to the hospital.'

'Him! Oh for goodness sake, Ellen,' said Maddie in exasperation. 'What would you be wanting with the likes of him? A right rogue if ever I saw one,' she added with a sniff.

Ellen shrugged her shoulders and said, 'Well, I liked him. He's so handsome, and did you notice the twinkle in those blue eyes?'

Before Maddie or Evie could confirm or deny seeing any such thing, Sarah came to join them. 'You'd better get on with some work,' she whispered. 'Old mother Donaldson is on the warpath and she's headed this way.'

Just then a large-framed woman entered the room and glared at the dozen or so occupants. 'Isn't that cloth folded yet? Get a move on will you. I've never known such a bunch of slackers.' As she turned to leave the women heard her mutter, 'I'll be glad when you lot have gone.'

'There, I told you it was true.' Evie tossed her head.

'What's true?' asked Sarah, and her eyes widened as she was told of the forthcoming move.

'I wonder where it is. Still,' she said eyeing the room, 'anywhere is bound to be better than this.'

'Here, here!' her friends all agreed in unison.

It was the following day before they heard anymore, and it was Ellen's handsome constable who enlarged on the news. The women were being sent off to work again in the hospital, and to Ellen's joy it was he who had to accompany them.

As they walked behind him early next morning, Ellen chatted on in her usual way, mentioning that they were to be sent away somewhere.

At this John turned in surprise and said, 'Oh, I wondered who might be going.'

Four pairs of ears pricked up at his words. 'Do you know where it is?' Maddie asked. 'And when?' The women waited silently awaiting his reply.

Taking a deep breath, John Ryan told them what he knew. 'Some of you are to go to Bothwell. It's a small town about twenty-five miles from here. I'm not sure when, but it'll be within the next few weeks I reckon.'

'So why have they given us this work at the hospital if we're leaving?' Ellen wondered aloud.

'You're not all going at the same time,' John said. 'Only a handful of women are to go at a time.'

'So we may not be chosen at all then?' Maddie sounded deflated.

'To be sure, I can't say. I shouldn't really have told you anything, so forget it. Now, get a move on, I've not got all day.'

The rest of the journey was completed in silence, with Ellen failing to take in the colourful gardens along the way as she had on the first outing. It would have been good to get out of the oppressive Factory. Then she brightened; at least she would still see this interesting man nearly every time they walked to work.

As St Mary's hospital filled with patients, the women were needed every day, and soon they began to enjoy the break from the harshness of the Factory.

A couple of months passed without any mention of them being moved, and Maddie became convinced that the matter was forgotten, but Ellen was in no hurry to leave. She could feel herself becoming more and more attracted to John, as he became a part of their daily lives.

She was none too sure if he felt the same; although now and again he would give a cheeky smile that set his moustache quivering. And those eyes! Ellen had never seen eyes so blue, and soon they filled her dreams very night.

She didn't confide in anyone, although she thought Maddie guessed because every so often the woman would give a nudge and giggle as they made their way along the frosty street in the early morning or on their return late in the evening.

'I'm not sure what's worse,' complained Evie, 'cleaning all day or baling the cloth in the stinking shed.'

'Oh, the hospital has to be better,' Ellen told her sternly. 'At least we get to meet other people.'

'Like our young constable I suppose.' Maddie grinned.

Ellen shot her a warning look, but was pleased that her friend shared her secret. If only she could see John on his own for a while, she thought, but she supposed there was little chance of that.

Surprisingly a chance did present itself. Whilst scrubbing the stairs one day, Ellen missed a step and took a heavy fall. One of the doctors examined her, diagnosed a badly sprained ankle, and was adamant that she was sent home to rest. 'Some home - and some rest I'll get there,' she grumbled as she was sent to sit in the waiting area.

Her face lit with pleasure when she saw it was to be John who escorted her. At last they would be alone.

'What have you been up to then?' he asked as Ellen stood up unsteadily, ready to leave.

She smiled warmly. 'Silly me. I missed a step didn't I? Water went one way and me another, you should have seen the mess,' she rattled on, annoyed with herself for wasting precious time by talking rubbish.

John seemed not to notice, but was worried that the walk might be too much. 'Shall I fetch the cart?' he asked. 'It's quite a long walk with a sore foot.

Ellen blushed. She'd never had a man worry about her before and was rather taken with the idea. 'I think I'll be fine just as long as we don't hurry,' she told him artfully.

John smiled and Ellen's heart fluttered. He took her arm and said quietly, 'You can lean on me, I'm sure no one will mind in the circumstances.'

Leaning gratefully against him, her face filled with colour at the closeness. She realised with a shock that she hadn't been touched by any man, other than the doctor, for over two years and had almost forgotten how good it could feel. And this, she admitted to herself, felt very good.

They walked slowly down the street in silence. Ellen wracked her brains for something interesting to say, but her mind stayed stubbornly blank. Then they passed a house whose garden was ablaze with colour. 'Oh, look at that. Isn't it beautiful? In spite of the cold weather, every where's so colourful; It reminds me so much of home,' she added sadly

John nodded agreement. 'Ah yes, it does that. Did you have a garden back home, Ellen?'

'Yes, my father's a keen gardener. He grows mostly vegetables, but there are always a few flowers. Did you have a garden in Ireland?'

'My father has large plot of land where he grows most of what's needed, and keeps a few goats and hens there as well, so it kept all the family pretty well provided for.'

'Is it pretty where you lived?'

'I suppose you could call it that. It's very green and on a clear day you can just see the mountains near the coast.' John sounded wistful.

Ellen shivered and looked up at the nearby Mount Wellington. 'I hope they're not as horrible as that one.'

'Oh, that one's not so bad once you get used to it. Depending on what time of day you look at it, the colours change. Early morning it's brown and gold, then at sunset it takes on a purplish hue as the sun sets behind it.'

Ellen's eyes widened. The man sounded like a poet, and she felt her attraction deepening. Suddenly she wanted this walk to last forever, so content did she feel. He was holding her arm protectively and appeared in no hurry to get her back to the Factory. So maybe, just maybe, he felt the same. She dreamed that they were an ordinary couple out for an afternoon jaunt, but the sight of John's uniform and her own tatty dress, brought her back to earth.

'That does make it seem less daunting,' Ellen said at last, in reference to the mountain.

'You can get used to anything after a while, even living in this place.'

'I wonder what this Bothwell is like. Is it smaller than here I wonder?

She felt John shrug. 'I don't know, but I think it is. One of the other constables rode up that way a few months ago to bring a prisoner back. He said it was way out the back of beyond.' He chuckled then and tilted his head down to look at her. 'Mind you, every where is out the back of beyond on this island. May I ask you something personal, Ellen?'

'I suppose so,' she answered warily. 'What is it?'

'What are you doing here? I mean, what was your crime?'

The moment Ellen had been dreading had come at last and she decided that honesty would be the best policy. 'I tried to poison my husband,' she said bluntly.

After a few seconds hesitation, John asked, 'What did he do to have you doing such a thing?'

'You don't think I'm just wicked then?' Ellen looked up, gratitude in her eyes.

'No, I would never think that about you. You must have had strong reasons to do such a thing. There is a gentleness in your soul which you try hard to disguise. I have no idea why, but it's there none the less.'

'Thank you,' was all she could think to say. It sounded inadequate, but somehow Ellen thought that this man knew what she meant. Then she continued, 'It was a bad marriage from the start. Robert was many years older than I was, and soon after our marriage he was sent to prison, and then when I had our daughter, I couldn't manage and I went back to live with my parents. Then when he came out of gaol, he started carrying on with another women. I begged him to take us back, but he wouldn't have us, even saying Mary wasn't his.' She brushed a tear from her cheek. 'I know I shouldn't have done it, and now I can't think what possessed me.' She sighed heavily. 'It's my parents I feel sorry for most, they have to go on living in the village; have to live with the gossip.'

'A daughter! Did you say you have a daughter? Where is she now?'

The tears flowed more profusely. 'She died just after we arrived here. My lovely little Mary became sick and died.'

John stopped and turned to her, pulling a handkerchief from his pocket. 'Here, dry your eyes. I'm so sorry to hear that, it must have been hard for you to bear?'

Ellen nodded. 'Yes, it was hard, but I was lucky to have some caring friends. The women I met on the journey out here have kept me strong and helped me through. I'll be forever grateful for that.'

As she handed the handkerchief back, John took it and placed a finger under her chin. 'You know Ellen; I've become rather fond of you over these past few weeks. Don't ask me why, because I don't know. I certainly haven't been looking out for a woman as I have a wife at home.' He grinned. 'She isn't as bad as your husband, but bad enough.'

They stood in the middle of the dusty street and stared into each other's eyes. Ellen could think of nothing to say, but wanted the moment to last forever. Her breast swelled with emotion and breathing became difficult. But then John broke the spell by turning and moving off along the road. 'I must get you back or we'll both be in trouble.'

Ellen's lips twitched. She could think of no one that she would rather be in trouble with than this raffish Irishman. Hopefully, they would see much more of each other now. How, she didn't know. But she was sure John would think of something.

The following morning, as he busied himself getting ready for the day, John whistled softly to himself. His dreams had been a jumble of conflicting scenes; sometimes Ellen was there with him, brown eyes dancing with mischief, and at others visions of his wife, Connie came to nag him for some forgotten chore. What a mess he'd got himself into. He wanted to be with Ellen more than anything he'd ever wanted before, but how could that be? They were both still married, and him a Catholic.

As the huge wooden gate opened and the women appeared, his eyes raked the group for her; disappointment hitting hard when it was obvious Ellen wasn't there.

Maddie caught his eye and moved to walk beside him. 'Ellen sends her love. She's got a mighty bruise from her fall yesterday and has to rest, but she'll be back tomorrow.' She winked and dropped slightly behind to walk with Evie. He felt foolishly pleased that she'd sent a message. All he could do was wait patiently until tomorrow.

To his chagrin, the following day he was sent off to collect some prisoners from the docks. Another shipload of men had arrived from England and although John was always interested to see any newcomers, today he cursed his luck. He and eight other constables took themselves off to the quay and waited while the men were checked from the ship and given into their care.

His ears pricked at the sound of many Irish voices and he scanned the group to see if there was anyone he knew, but none of the faces were familiar to him. All the same he kept his ears open for any mention of his hometown, Roscommon.

It took several days to deliver the men to the various prison camps. A few at this one, a few at that. Then at last the remaining men were taken in through the gates of the Impression Bay Penal Colony, and John shivered, memories of his time here rushing to the fore. The place still had a brooding quality and he thanked the Lord that he was no longer within its confines.

Once back in Hobart the constables were dismissed for the rest of the day, but John realised sadly that it was too late to try and see Ellen. Hopefully tomorrow he would have better luck. Throughout the long days he had come to a decision. It was one he hoped Ellen would approve of and after seeing her in the morning he would go to the Governor's office to seek advice.

'Will you at least agree to me asking permission?' John was holding her hand as they stood outside St Mary's the following morning. The other women had hurried inside out of the chill wind that had sprung up, blowing from the direction of the harbour.

'What?' Ellen's eyes widened in amazement.

'Will you?' John asked her again, a wide grin splitting his face.

'How can I? Oh, John I wish it so much, you know that. But I still have a husband back home in England, so how can I marry you?' Her breath came in little gasps and her rosy cheeks glowed even more than usual. 'I suppose there's no harm in asking, but I'm sure they'll never allow it,' Ellen sounded doubtful. Then a warm feeling of pleasure flooded her body and she smiled into his eyes. 'If you're sure, then yes. I'll pray all day that you have success, John. When are you going?'

'Right now. I'll go into the Governor's office on my way back to Collins Street. Look; don't worry about our both being already married. We have been sent here to start a new life and in many peoples lives that means finding a new marriage partner. It happens all the time, believe me.'

Reassured, Ellen smiled, but then a worried frown crossed her face. 'Won't you be in trouble for arriving back late?'

'I'll take that chance. Hopefully, I'll have good news for you this evening when I come to collect you.' With one last squeeze of her hand he turned and hurried away.

Ellen entered the hospital with her head in a whirl. How was she going to do any work today, when her mind refused to concentrate on anything other than Mr John Ryan?

Her companions noticed. Maddie gazed at her quizzically as they scrubbed one of the large wards together. 'You're pretty excited about something, I can tell. You haven't stopped grinning since we got here this morning. What is it? Eh! Go on tell your old mate.'

Ellen knew she would burst if she didn't tell someone, but on the other hand it was supposed to be a secret. What the hell! 'John has gone to seek permission for us to marry,' she whispered.

The bucket of water was sent flying as Maddie reared back in shock. 'Bloody hell. Are you mad, girl? You'll never be allowed to marry. You're supposed to be a secure prisoner for one thing, so how in the devil are you going to explain how you met?' The woman wrung a sodden cloth over the bucket.

'We'll tell the truth. After all, John was acting on orders to escort us.' Ellen sniffed and leaned across to help with the mopping up.

'Those orders said no fraternisation with the prisoners, and you can hardly get to know someone well enough to marry them without at least speaking.' Maddie's eyes conveyed her dread and she shook her head. 'Prepare yourself for trouble, Ellen. I think you and your John are going to get more than you bargained for.'

But Ellen wouldn't be put off. 'We'll see. John will bring news today when he comes to take us back.' And the optimism was still clear on her face.

One look at his face was enough, and Ellen hurried to his side. The sadness in his eyes bored into her and she caught her breath. 'No luck?'

Slowly John shook his head. 'No, my love. I'm sorry, but it was refused out of hand. And,' he added slowly, 'I shan't see you for a few weeks.'

Despair overcame her. 'W-why not?'

John took her hand and said gently, 'I've been given special duties. I'm no longer on escort duty. The bastards have decided to send me out of harms way, as they put it.' He pulled on her arm so that the party of women could set off back to the Factory. 'I'll tell you as we walk. I had to beg to be here, I'm supposed to be somewhere else. The Chief took pity on me, but was adamant it was the last time.'

'What are we to do?' Ellen was distraught. 'John, I can't believe I won't see you every day. Why are they doing this?' Anger was beginning to take the place of sorrow and she stamped her foot. 'I'll go and see our Governor, she's hard as nails, but she might be sympathetic.'

From behind her, Maddie said, 'Ellen, don't push your luck. You know she's a frustrated old spinster, she's hardly likely to let you go and get married is she?'

'I've got to try. I won't let a few old fuddy-duddies' mess up my life again.' Ellen felt all the old remembered rejections come flooding back to her, followed by the deeply buried grief for her baby daughter. This sent her out of control. 'I've never got what I wanted. Not ever,' she screamed, knowing it was untrue and that she sounded like a petulant child.

'Now then, my sweet. Try not to take on so.' John tried to placate her. 'We'll find a way round it, see if we don't. It'll just take a while longer that's all.'

'I don't want it to take longer. I want to get married now. Why should we wait?' Then she rounded on John, all sense of reason gone. 'If you really cared, you'd find a way. You don't care enough to bother though. You don't really love me at all.' Hot tears of anger and pain poured down her face as she broke away and ran off down the street.

By the time she reached the woman's Factory, she was sobbing loudly and in her distress banged her fists on the wooden gate, 'Let me in. Let me in, you bastards.'

The gate swung open and she almost fell inside, before running across to her own little cell where she sat and howled like a wounded animal.

Ellen awoke shivering, darkness pressing about her and the stale air cloying her nostrils. Then the whole ghastly scene came back to her. Dear God, she prayed, what have I done? Why couldn't I hold on to my emotions? Why do I hit out at those who care? John will never want to see me again after today. I've ruined everything. She was filled with self-pity. Nothing ever seemed to go right in her life. It was as though someone had a grudge against her and was determined that she should never find happiness and contentment. She could have found them with John, she knew that, but again fate had taken a hand against her.

Or was it fate? Wasn't it her own stupidity, her own impatience that had spoiled it all? Guilt took the place of self-pity. She had not only hurt herself; she had hurt John too. He had done his best, but she'd thrown it back in his face. No man would ever forgive such a thing.

What would happen to her now? Would she be hauled before the Governor for bad behaviour? Or would they just let her stew for a while. Hunger pangs gnawed at her insides and she wondered idly what the time might be. No sounds came from outside. Perhaps they've thrown away the key and are going to leave me here to rot, she thought disconsolately.

But just at that moment, Ellen really didn't care if they had. All she could do was cry afresh for Mary, her dear, sweet daughter.

CHAPTER 8

'Well, take it, Ryan, it's yours.'

John looked at the man in disbelief. 'T-thank you, sir,' he stuttered, then touched his hat in civility. He stared at the piece of paper in front of him. It was his longed-for Ticket of Leave. The small, insignificant scrap of paper that would allow him more freedom had been granted at last. He could have danced a jig, but thought it highly unsuitable here in the Governor's office.

He must try to see Ellen and tell her this good news. It might also give them another chance of being permitted to marry. He hadn't seen her for a few days as his duties took him across Hobart to another prison where he stood hour after long hour on guard duty at the gate. But she was always in his thoughts and he knew he must see her, must tell her of his Ticket of Leave. Somehow he would have to get to the Factory and try to catch her attention.

Then an idea came to him. He was granted half an hour break for lunch each day, which he usually took in the small inn across the road. A hot drink and something to eat were always welcome after standing all morning in the bitter wind. John shifted his weight from one foot to another, and made up his mind. Today he would go to the hospital and try to speak to her there.

Later, although hunger and thirst nagged at his insides, he set of at a trot toward St Mary's, worried that he could make it there and back in the time. Arriving outside, he wondered how to get in and find her, then decided that the back of the property might be a better option. Grimacing with stitch, John ran round to where he knew the cleaners kept all the buckets and mops. No luck, there wasn't a soul in sight. He looked up at the windows whose glassy stare revealed nothing. Disappointment hit hard; he had been so sure he would see Ellen.

Setting off back to his place of work, John felt determination well within him. He would not give in; he would come again to morrow –

and the next day, and the next. Every day until he saw her. Losing her now was unthinkable; she meant too much to him.

The following day, John set out feeling more optimistic. Yesterday he had felt ill by the time he went off duty from the lack of food or drink and he had no wish to feel like that again and so carried a flask of water and a hunk of bread with him. Walking round to the back of the hospital, John again found it deserted. But studying the windows, he saw a movement at one of them and hurried forward, waving, hoping against hope that it was not someone in charge.

To his relief it was Maddie who returned his wave and pulled up the sash window to lean out, calling, 'Hello there, John. Are you looking for Ellen?'

'I am. Is she there with you?'

'Wait a moment, I'll go and find her.' The window slid back down and he saw Maddie move away. A few moments later, Ellen appeared at the door close to where he stood. She looked pale and half-scared.

John smiled widely and hurried toward her. 'Oh, my Ellen, I've been trying to see you for a week now. Are you all right? You look so pale.' He took her in his arms and held her, not caring who might see.

But Ellen pulled away from his embrace and looked up at him, her brown eyes moist with tears. 'I thought you'd never want to see me again. Not after I was so horrid. Oh John, can you ever forgive me? I've been so miserable.'

'There, there, don't take on so. Of course I want to see you. I understood. Now, I've some good news. I've received my Ticket of Leave.' Ellen looked at him uncomprehendingly and John pulled the paper from his pocket. 'Look,' he said holding it out toward her.

She barely glanced at it. 'What does that mean? You won't be sent away, will you?'

'Bless you no. It means I have more freedom and maybe it'll help us in our bid to be married.'

'Are you sure you still want to marry me after the way I behaved?' Ellen seemed ill at ease.

'I know you were upset, my love. You spoke out of frustration.' John grinned. 'I was feeling the same way myself.'

At last she moved back into his embrace, her face alight with pleasure. 'I don't deserve you, John, I really don't.'

He planted a kiss on her forehead. 'Look, I've to be getting back, but I'll come at the same time tomorrow. Look out for me and perhaps we can have a little longer together.' Another kiss followed the other. 'Bye for now, my love.'

'Goodbye, John. I love you,' Ellen called as he dashed off round the corner of the building.

As he ran the whole way back, John's face was wreathed in smiles, and his lunch lay forgotten in his pocket.

Ellen went straight to find Maddie. 'I can't believe it. John still wants to marry me,' she said in an excited whisper.

'Of course he does. I told you it would work out all right, didn't I?' her friend said without slowing her polishing of the banister rail.

'He's coming again tomorrow.'

'I'm pleased for you, but be careful. You know we're not allowed to speak to anyone never mind have clandestine meetings.'

'I'll risk it. Anything to see him again. I didn't have any hope for the future while I pined in my cell for those two days, but now it's bright again.' Ellen hurried away as one of the nursing staff approached along the upper landing, with rustling starch and squeaky shoes. It was the women cleaner's secret joy; they always knew when the 'enemy' was about.

Ellen kept one eye on the courtyard at the back and only half a mind on her work, which meant that she was shouted at more often than usual the following morning. She didn't care; it was worth it to see John. Then, just when his blue frock-coated figure appeared round the corner of the building, she was called to clean up a mess made by an incontinent patient. She fumed and set too as quickly as possible, hoping no one would check to see if it was done properly or not. As soon as the nurse was out of sight, Ellen threw the wet cloth into her pail, pushed that behind a screen and made a dash for the door. Down the stairs she raced, praying that no one would see her, and out through the back door.

John stood a little away from the building, close to some flowering bushes, and Ellen flew into his arms, almost knocking him off his feet.

'I was beginning to wonder if you could get away,' he said, brushing some stray tendrils of hair back and studying her face minutely.

As she regained her breath, Ellen laughed, 'It was touch and go. I won't be able to stay long and I mustn't be seen or there'll be trouble.'

He pulled her back further into the bushes. 'I can't stay long either, but it's wonderful just to be with you for a few moments.' His eyes gazed into hers and Ellen felt the breath leave her body, her legs became weak and a delicious warmth settled somewhere in her middle.

'I can't believe you want me. It's like a dream. When do you think we can be together?' she asked.

'I'm hoping my Ticket will help us there, but I think it'll be better to wait until we arrive in Bothwell before we try again. Have you heard anymore about going?'

Ellen shook her head and turned down the corners of her mouth. 'No. And I'm not in anyone's good books. That day I ran off, I was left in my cell without food or water for two whole days.'

'Why did they do that to you?'

'It was my own fault. I pushed my way passed a warder and wouldn't speak to anyone, so I was left to stew.'

'My poor girl. I can't wait to get you away from here. Pray that you can come to Bothwell with me, then we can see each other all the time.' He kissed her tenderly. But when his lips moved to her eyes, cheeks and neck, the warmth shifted until it flooded Ellen's body and she sought his mouth with her own. Then his kisses became more demanding and Ellen longed for him to make love to her there and then. His need was evident, matching her own. They could not wait too long. It must be soon.

Two days later, Ellen received word that she was to travel to Bothwell in a week's time. She fidgeted all morning, longing to tell John and hoping against hope that he would be going too. The workload was heavy that day and she despaired of ever getting away to meet him. Maddie kept nudging her to make her concentrate, but Ellen just couldn't keep her mind on anything. 'You've only a few more days here don't forget, then you'll be away.' Her eyes became pensive. 'Only a few days and you'll leave the Factory. I can't wait for my turn to come, so consider yourself fortunate and keep that in mind.' Maddie tried to be firm.

'I know, but I never was very patient and it'll seem like forever, but I'll feel better once I've told John.' Ellen grinned at her friend.

Maddie chuckled. 'I still can't see what you find to like about him, I'm sure. But each to her own I suppose.'

Her brown eyes glittering crossly, Ellen retorted, 'John's a fine looking man, and he's kind. I feel safe with him, safer than I ever did with my husband anyway.' Then as her gaze strayed to the hundredth time to the window, she let out a squeal. 'He's here, he's here. I must go. Maddie, cover for me. Please.'

The woman grinned. 'Of course, off you go. Don't be too long though or you're sure to be missed.'

As she dashed across the grass toward the bushes, Ellen felt her stomach turn a somersault. Somehow she felt that today they're wait would be over. Today, she would be his completely. As the early spring sunshine warmed her back, she looked about her with heightened awareness. How brilliant the flowers: How blue the sky: How sweet the birdsong.

And then she was in his arms and he was kissing her fervently. 'Oh my love, my love,' he murmured.

She pushed him back a little and tilted her face up to his so that she could tell him her news. 'John, I'm to go to Bothwell next week. Do say you can come with me.'

'Just try to stop me.' John grinned, but then added soberly, 'I'll do what I can, but I can't promise, you do understand, don't you?'

When she nodded, he hugged her again and then kissed her. His kisses became urgent and soon they were lost in a world of their own. Slowly they sank to the ground under the beautiful flowering bush; it's heady perfume filling their senses. As their passion mounted Ellen felt her body melt under his caresses, her limbs trembled and her heart sang. With gentle hands he caressed her body and it was all she could do to stop herself from crying out. She raked her fingers through his hair, then held his face between both hands as she kissed him feverishly. Then he was holding her body tight against his, the drab prison dress was pulled away and Ellen felt the fire in him matching her own until at last she was overpowered by the final culmination of their lovemaking. She was really his now, they were as one and she knew that she wanted nothing more than to spend the rest of her life with him. Breathing heavily, she clung to him, never wanting him to leave her again. Her mind whirled with the wonder of it all.

After a few moments he reluctantly eased her away from him and Ellen saw the love shining in his eyes. 'I love you so, Ellen, but I must go. I don't want to, but I must. It won't do for us to be getting into trouble at the moment.' John kissed the tip of her nose. 'I'll see you here tomorrow. Oh, I do love you so much, my Ellen.' He pulled her to her feet and straightened his clothes. 'Keep yourself safe, my love.' One last kiss and he was gone.

When she arrived back at work, starry-eyed and breathless, Maddie looked at her in amazement. 'You took your time, I was sweating on someone noticing you not being here. What have you been up to anyway? As if I need ask.' She lowered her voice. 'Christ, Ellen, calm yourself, you look like the cat that won the cream.

Everyone will know what you've been doing and they'll want to know how, where and who with.'

Her heart still pounding, Ellen went to a sink and ran cold water into her hands, then splashed it over her face. Once it was patted dry, she asked, 'There does that look better?' She smoothed her hair and straightened her dress.

'Slightly. Now just dim the gleam in your eyes and your nearly there.' Maddie shook her head. 'I just hope he's worth it, that's all.'

'Oh, he is, he is. Believe me, he's worth every risk I've ever taken.' How she got through the rest of the day, Ellen never knew. Her heart cried out for him and her body ached for him. Oh, God, I've never felt like this before in my life. Thank you for sending me this man. Thank you.

She rolled over in her tiny bed and rubbed the sleep from her eyes. A smile curved her lips as she recalled that today was the day. Today was the day she was leaving this ghastly place and going to live up-country at a place called Bothwell.

Although Ellen had no idea what it would be like, she didn't care. To her delight, John would be travelling with her and they were hoping to be able to set up home together as soon as everything was sorted out. There was just the small problem of her still being a prisoner, but they were sure that could be overcome. The fact that they were still both legally married to other people was pushed very firmly to the back of her mind.

All she knew was that she was to work in the house of a prosperous landowner and was sure that once she was found acceptable, would be given the freedom to live her life as she pleased. Packing her few belongings into the old carpetbag, Ellen went through to the refectory for breakfast. Hunger was last in her list of priorities, but common sense told her that she needed food to see her through the long journey ahead.

The bread and gruel was hard to swallow, but at last she was saying goodbye to her friends. Hugging Maddie tightly, she said, 'I hope you join me soon. You've been a true friend Maddie and I can't imagine what I'd have done without you. Especially when I lost Mary, you saw me through that.' She held shy little Stella for a moment, and then hugged Sarah and Evie. These women had kept her sane in a strange and frightening world, when the loss of her child could have tipped her into madness. Yes, she owed them all an enormous debt of gratitude.

It was thought that Maddie might join her in a few weeks when another batch of prisoners would be relocated. Sarah and Evie were going further North to somewhere called Launceston to live and work, but who knew, they might meet again one day.

She waited impatiently just inside the wooden gate, eager to see John. They would be spending the day travelling together and would be the longest they had ever spent in each other's company. The excitement was almost too much for her.

At last the gate was swung back to reveal a small horse-drawn cart. As well as John and the driver, two other men sat impassively on the sideways facing seats. Behind her came two other women from the Factory who were also travelling, one of whom Ellen had heard say, was joining her husband who was already in Bothwell. Then she saw John, leaning forwards, his arms outstretched to help her climb aboard and she ran to him. The men tipped their hats, but didn't speak, so she sat herself down next to John and took one last look about her. Hobart town slumbered quietly in the spring sunshine. It wasn't a bad place, she thought. Parts of it were even quite pretty, almost English. Still, she wasn't sorry to be leaving it. Painful memories of the Dynnyrne nursery still had the power to sadden her, but even so she felt the loss of never being able to put an occasional bunch of flowers on Mary's tiny grave.

'I won't forget you, my sweet Mary. No matter where I go or how many other children I might have. I'll never forget you,' she whispered.

'Are you all right, Ellen?' John murmured softly in her ear and put an arm about her shoulders.

She gave him a watery smile. 'Yes, I'm fine. Just saying a last farewell to my daughter.'

'We'll think of her often and celebrate her birthday every year. She'll be forever alive in our hearts and we'll tell all her brothers and sisters about her. What do you think of that?'

'Thank you, I'd like that. You're a good, kind man, John Ryan, and I'm so glad I found you,' Ellen took a deep breath. 'We'll have a great life together, you and me, I can feel it in my bones.'

The cart jolted forward and Ellen grabbed her hat, feeling suddenly much happier and a laugh rose in her throat.

At last the future looked rosier.

CHAPTER 9

The day had begun with clear blue skies, but now the clouds rolled in casting deep shadows amongst the trees, and changing the colours on the sometimes-glimpsed distant hills. The beauty of the surrounding countryside, with strange, colourful birds that darted amongst the trees, and small grey animals that hopped quickly out of sight as the rumbling cart approached, was not lost on Ellen.

Two bright red and green parrots screeched overhead and she cried. 'Oh look at those, John, and look at that tree.' She craned her neck to see the top. 'I've never seen one so tall.' Her enthusiasm affected everyone and soon they were chatting and pointing out new and strange flora and fauna.

The two women were Sophie and Bridget, who were both going to Bothwell and the men were Harry and William. Harry was a policeman too and he would be stationed in Bothwell, but was not a free man yet. William was travelling onto Launceston, further north.

Their talk was of the country they found themselves in: no one wanting to discuss how they came to be there. Content to be away from Hobart they enjoyed the fresh air and open countryside.

After an overnight stop in Hamilton, they journeyed on, the scenery changing imperceptibly from dense trees and bushes to wild open spaces, and in the distance a line of mountains could be seen, dull blue against the faded green of the nearer hills. It was all so different from home, but to Ellen, it still had a charm all it's own.

John nodded. 'It's a splendid country that's for sure. I never thought anything could equal my homeland, but this is close to it.' He pointed toward the river whose course they were now following. 'That's the Clyde.'

One of the men frowned. 'I've heard of that somewhere before.'

John laughed, not unkindly. 'Scotland. That's where the river Clyde is. Well, the original I suppose I should say. There are many

Scottish settlers in these parts so I believe, and a lot of places have been named after their hometowns.'

'I've heard the same. I wonder if there are many in Bothwell? Better introduce myself properly, I suppose. My name's Harry Askew and I come from London originally.'

'Hello Harry, why haven't I seen you in Hobart?' John eyed his constable's uniform.

'Came straight from Oyster Bay I did. Terrible place that is, I was glad to be out of it.'

'I know, I was there for a while myself,' John told him.

'Were you? Then you know what a hellhole it is.' Harry said dryly.

'I didn't know that. Why were you there?' Ellen asked John.

John shrugged it off. 'Oh, just some minor misdemeanour. I'll tell you about it one day.'

Ellen felt that he wasn't being completely honest with her, but decided to leave the matter. Maybe he would tell her one day.

Harry was good company and soon had them all laughing at his Cockney humour and slightly ribald stories. No one asked him what he had done to end up in Van Diemen's Land. They were all criminals in one way or another so it didn't seem to matter much any more. William sat quietly listening; nodding from time to time, and Ellen felt there was something sad lurking behind his eye. Perhaps the man had been dealt a cruel blow such as her when Mary died, she decided.

After a brief stop for a lunch of bread, cheese, fruit and beer, they set out once more, following the river on its journey northwards. Although the Clyde was often out of sight, running between high rocky banks or behind a stand of trees, it would appear again and again, sometimes softly flowing, sometimes a raging torrent. They saw a huge waterfall, where the water fell many feet to the rocks below and the place captivated Ellen. Somehow the rush of water filled her with wonder and excitement.

At least the day had remained dry for which they were all thankful and just as the sun began to dip into broken clouds in the western sky, the driver called, 'It's not far into Bothwell now. Shouldn't be no more than ten minutes or more.'

Ellen was apprehensive; but somehow she knew that now she and John had arrived here, life was going to be perfect.

Many curious eyes watched their arrival in Bothwell. The small town was used to newcomers, but nonetheless, there was always interest in who had come to join them. The cart rolled to a halt outside the Falls of Clyde Hotel and they all stared at the imposing building, then climbed stiffly down from the cart.

A matronly woman of uncertain age came to greet them. 'I'm Mrs Vale, housekeeper here. This is where you women will be working for the time being,' she told them, and ushered them through to the back of the building, but not before Ellen had gazed around the huge hallway. To her it looked both lofty and grand, with panelled walls and a wide staircase, with highly polished banisters that soared up to disappear into the darkness.

John followed with her bag as she hurried along behind Mrs Vale, but as they reached a doorway marked 'Staff Only', he was told to go and report at the police station. 'Men are forbidden to go any further,' Mrs Vale told him loftily, so he handed Ellen her belongings and, with a cheeky wink, left.

Ellen's heart sank. So much for the cosy evenings she had envisaged. Once through the door, her heart sank even further. After the opulence at the front of the hotel, this was bleak. She glanced at her two companions and saw that they weren't impressed either.

Along one side of a dingy corridor were four doors, while on the opposite wall, two candles set into glass holders and one small window gave what little light there was. Along the passageway they marched, their feet echoing on the stone floor, until they reached the last door, which Mrs Vale threw open.

'This is where you three will sleep. You may have a few moments to freshen up, then I want to see you clean, tidy, and presentable, in the parlour.' The woman rapped out the order, turned on her heel and left them to stand open-mouthed.

'Well,' said Ellen. 'Let's see what we've got here.' Cautiously they moved into the room. In the dim light they saw three wooden cots with straw mattresses, one washstand and a cupboard. High on one wall was a small square window. 'No chance of anyone getting through there,' Ellen commented dryly.

'In or out,' said Sophie, who was supposed to be joining her husband here in Bothwell. 'God, it's grim. Not as bad as the Factory, but not far short.'

With a wry grin at her companions, Ellen said, 'Well, we'd better do as she says, or we'll be in trouble before we start.'

Sophie pushed a few stray black locks into the bun on the back of her head. 'I'm not sure my Frank will like me living like this.'

'Won't you be going to live with him?' asked Ellen.

'Not straight away. Might be a couple of weeks yet,' she said quietly.

Quickly they washed the dust of the day from their faces, but their clothing was another matter. They still wore the drab prison frocks that were torn and filthy, showing signs of having seen better days.

'Do you think we should change? Only neither of my dresses are any better than the one I'm wearing.' Ellen said sadly, feeling rather insignificant alongside these two women. Poorly dressed they might be, but they were both taller and prettier than she was. Her lack of height had always been a sore point, and as far as looks went, she'd always felt that she'd been at the end of the queue when they were handed out.

'Nor are mine,' said Sophie, bringing Ellen back from her dispirited thoughts, 'But we'd better make the effort.'

Bridget nodded her head. 'You're right. Then she'll have to take us as she finds us.'

After struggling into their comparatively clean gowns, they hurried back along the corridor in search of the parlour. They found it by following the sound of raised voices. Well back from the grand entrance hall were two doors. One stood open to reveal a cavernous kitchen, the other was closed, but angry words reached them from the room on the other side.

Suddenly the door was flung open, and a young woman dashed past them, her face drenched in tears and her long blonde hair flying about her head. Her sobs could be heard as she fled along the corridor. Then came the sound of a door slamming and all was silent.

Ellen peered tentatively into the room. Mrs Vale stood with her back to the window, her face flushed scarlet. Sophie and Bridget stood so close behind Ellen she could feel their breath on her neck.

'Well, come on in,' Mrs Vale beckoned, and as they moved forward they heard her give an audible gasp. 'My God, what have they sent me this time?' She ground her teeth. 'Didn't they give you some decent clothes in Hobart?'

'No Ma'am,' said Bridget. 'This is practically all we've got to our names.'

Suddenly the woman crossed to a chair and slumped into it. 'How do they think we can run a high class business when they send women dressed as tramps to work here?' Her face softened slightly. 'I suppose you're hungry and thirsty?'

Three heads nodded in unison. Then Ellen cleared her throat. 'Yes, we are,' she said, feeling that a polite answer was called for.

'Very well, I'll send in refreshments then we'll have to find some decent clothing for you.' She waved toward a shabby chaise-lounge that stood along one wall. 'Take a seat.' Then she hauled herself from the chair and left the room.

'What a strange woman,' said Sophie. 'I'm not sure I'm going to like it here.'

'We haven't much choice,' Ellen said. 'We're still prisoners in their book I suppose.'

Her two companions nodded agreement, then they waited in silence until the door opened again to admit a woman carrying a tray on which sat a plate piled high with bread and butter, another with small cakes, a pot of tea and three cups and saucers. With a smile the woman placed the tray on a small table and said, 'Help yourselves,' before she left.

Ellen's eyes nearly popped out of her head. 'My goodness, it's a long time since I had tea, and that much to eat.'

Soon the food had been eaten and the tea drunk and Ellen sat back, rubbing her tummy. 'I think I might like it here after all.'

Bridget grinned. 'I bet we won't get food like that all the time though. That would be too much to ask.'

'Still, you never know your luck,' said Sophie. 'What shall we do now?'

'She said to wait, so that's what we'll do. We can relax for a few moments.' Ellen leaned back and made herself comfortable.

Half an hour passed before Mrs Vale returned carrying three identical cotton dresses over her arm. 'I hope these fit.' She held one up and went to stand beside Sophie, who had risen to her feet and whose face showed that she wasn't exactly thrilled with the plain, grey and white striped gown. 'Hmm, might do you.' Mrs Vale smiled suddenly and her face was transformed. 'Sorry you heard that row earlier, but young Nessie has a lot to learn I'm afraid. Now you three seem more mature and responsible.' She eyed them speculatively. 'I'm the housekeeper here and I oversee the day to day running of the hotel, make sure the rooms are clean and the meals decent. I also rule my staff with a rod of iron.' Again the smile, but Ellen guessed that this woman would take no nonsense.

'Take these and try them on, then return here to me so that I can give you a list of your duties.' Mrs Vale paused for a moment. 'Or would I be right in assuming that you can neither read not write?' Her eyebrows lifted in query.

Ellen spoke up, unashamed of her lack in schooling, 'I can't, Mrs, but I don't know about these two.'

Two pink spots of colour appeared on Mrs Vale's cheeks. 'You will address me as Mrs Vale at all times, is that understood?'

110

'Yes, Mrs Vale,' murmured three voices in unison.

'Go on, go and get changed.' She sighed heavily. 'Otherwise the day will be at an end before you get any work done.'

Ellen felt herself bristle with indignation, but sensibly stayed quiet. Work! When they'd travelled all day to get here. Blooming cheek!

Back in their room, they tried on the new dresses. Ellen found the tiny buttons that ran from waist to neck rather tiresome, and the long tight sleeves restricted her movement. 'How are we supposed to work in this,' she complained. 'I feel as though I'm in a vice.'

'They aren't very elegant either,' Bridget grumbled, pushing back her abundant red hair.

Sophie laughed. 'We're here to work, so you don't expect to be dolled up like a dogs dinner.' Then she grimaced. 'They aren't very becoming though, I must admit.'

With a huge sigh, Ellen opened the door. 'Shall we go. I think it's really unfair to expect us to work tonight after we've spent two days travelling.'

'I agree. I'm so tired I just want to sleep,' Bridget whimpered, eyeing her bed with longing. 'Let's hope we don't have to do anything too energetic.'

They hurried along the corridor and into Mrs Vale's room. She looked up and smiled as they entered. 'Ah, that's better. Now if you would pin your hair up out of the way,' she nodded to Bridget, 'then I'll take you into the dining room.'

What were they going to do in the dining room Ellen wondered, while Bridget struggled with her wayward hair.

Mrs Vale led them across the hallway and in through a pair of double doors, on the other side of which was a huge room furnished with many tables. Then their duties became apparent. Each table had six or seven men seated around it and the noise was ear splitting. Two women, one of whom was Nessie, darted about busily carrying large platters of meat and vegetables.

Mrs Vale lifted a hand and beckoned the other woman over. She was short and stout, and Ellen marvelled at her movements, so swift in someone so portly. She was also much older than the rest of them, looking somewhere in middle age.

'Vera, these are our new workers. Can you take them in hand and show them the ropes. Although serving food shouldn't prove too testing. I suspect they're tired though, so don't expect miracles tonight.'

111

'Any help is better than none, Mrs Vale.' Vera smiled at them. 'Come with me. We'll soon have you sorted.'

As Mrs Vale turned and left, Vera inclined her head for them to follow her. She hurried between tables and took them through a door at the end of the room. As they panted after her, Vera stopped and with a wave of her arm, indicated. 'This is the kitchen,' she said, rather unnecessarily Ellen thought, as it was obvious to them that this was the room they had seen from the opposite side earlier. 'Here, grab one of these each and put them on.' The little woman indicated white aprons hanging from a row of hooks.

Then without waiting to see if they were ready, Vera lifted a huge tray and thrust it into Ellen hands. 'Take that to table ten,' she said and turned to pick up the next tray which went to Sophie.

Ellen coughed and Vera's head snapped round. 'You still here. Table ten, I said. You deaf?'

'No, but how do I know which is table ten?' Ellen was trying very hard to stay calm.

With a sigh, the woman swung the door open and pointed. 'Third up on the left. The tables are all numbered.'

Without waiting for another comment about useless help, Ellen hurried off to the table, but her heart sank as she approached it. Half a dozen men sat, beer mugs overflowing, bawling for her to hurry up. 'A man could bloody starve in this place. Move your arse girl,' one man growled. 'And when we've got our grub, get some more beers in.' As Ellen hesitated, the man brought his hand up and slapped her backside. 'I said, move!' he yelled.

Anger filled Ellen. 'Don't you dare strike me. I'll report you.'

Howls of laughter greeted this as, with cheeks flaming, she placed the plates in front of them.

'You can get your own beers,' she said haughtily, 'because I don't know where it's kept.' With a toss of the head she hurried away back to the kitchen, while behind her a loud chorus of abuse and laughter erupted.

Vera was busy out in the dining room, as was Sophie and Bridget, but the woman who had brought in their afternoon refreshments was carving meat when Ellen walked in.

'Hello dear, they've chucked you in the deep end I see. Don't worry you'll soon get used to it.' She grinned. 'My name's Maura by the way.'

'Hello Maura. What do you do when the men hit you?'

'Tell 'em to take a running jump that's what. They're cattlemen mostly, and aren't here every night thank the Lord. Just that they're in town for a few days and always go mad.'

'They wanted more beer, but I don't know where it's kept,' Ellen told her.

'Let 'em wait, drunken buggers.'

Ellen was amazed that a woman who looked so refined could swear so easily. Her face must have shown her thoughts because Maura roared with laughter and said, 'I've been here fifteen years and believe me I've loved every minute of it. I might have been high born, but this place soon brings you down to earth.' She picked up another tray. 'Can you take that to table four? Fourth table on the right that is. You'll soon get the hang of it. Off you go, before Vera starts panicking.'

As Ellen, Bridget and Sophie dashed about with trays of food; Vera and Nessie spent their time pouring beers. How could these men consume so much? Ellen wondered. She was dropping with fatigue and wondered how much longer it would be before the men left and she could go to her bed. Sophie and Bridget looked worn out too, poor things. They'd all had a long day and would be pleased to see an end to it.

Gradually the dining room began to empty and Ellen grinned at Maura. 'Looks like they'll all be gone soon.'

The woman nodded. 'Yes, but you won't be allowed to go off straight away, there's all the dishes to be washed first, the tables to wash over and the floor swept. Still it shouldn't take too long with all of us.'

Then Vera appeared at the door. 'Right you, start clearing away the plates. Put the leftovers in that bin there. That's the pig-swill in case you're wondering.'

Ellen had been, but didn't relish the thought of going too near the huge bin that stank to high heavens. But she did as she was told and soon, between them, the dining room was clean, neat and tidy. She saw Sophie wipe a tear of fatigue away and felt pretty close to tears herself. Back in the kitchen, Vera was showing Bridget how to clean the huge cooking pots and turned to Sophie and Ellen. 'You two can help, there's still plenty of work to do.'

Taking up a stiff bristled brush, Ellen set to help Bridget, while Sophie was up to her elbows in greasy water with the last of the plates. At last they had a better chance to meet Nessie who was drying things and putting them away.

'Have you been here long?' Ellen asked her.

The girl turned red-rimmed eyes on her. 'Too blasted long. I'm fed up with it and want to go home.'

'Oh, and where's that?'

'Bristol. I want to go home to England and see my parents. I shouldn't have been sent here in the first place, I hadn't done anything wrong.' Nessie angrily threw cutlery into a draw. Ellen nodded sympathetically, but wasn't too sorry for the girl. She'd heard the same thing said so many times before.

Exhausted, she asked no more questions, but leaned her elbows on the edge of the sink to hold herself upright and fought to keep her eyes open. Just as she thought they'd finished, Vera came to stand next to her and Ellen waited for more instructions, but the woman smiled and patted her shoulder.

'Leave that, I'll finish it later. Come and get your supper.'

Ellen couldn't believe her ears. Food! Not sure if she could stay awake long enough to eat anything, she nevertheless went across to the long table where the others were already sitting. Maura doled out what looked like stew and dumplings and Ellen spooned it into her mouth wondering what her first meal in Bothwell would be like. It was tasty and smelled good and before she knew it, her dish was empty.

'Go on you three, off to bed now. We've an early start in the morning. You'll be called at dawn, and will be shown your duties for the day. Goodnight and thank you,' Vera said pleasantly.

As they plodded along the corridor, Sophie said with a yawn, 'I hope it's not always like this otherwise I'll be too tired to give my Frank his conjugals.'

As much a she loved John, Ellen knew that at this precise moment she would no more be able to make love to him than to fly.

They all three slept in their new dresses, not caring what they would look like in the morning.

CHAPTER 10

Leaving the hotel, John hurried along to the Police office to tell them of his arrival. He glanced about him in the gathering gloom and liked what he saw. Bothwell didn't appear to be large, but he noticed another three Hotels and at the end of the street stood a small, but solid looking church. He chuckled to himself and wondered which establishment brought in the most customers. Then there was a forge and general store, two more small shops and a few houses dotted along the main street.

The Police building wasn't large but incorporated the Magistrates office, while opposite, set on a slight rise, was the barracks. John went into the Chief's room and stood to attention, awaiting his instructions.

'Ah, Ryan.' A red-faced barrel of a man addressed him. 'I see from your report that you are of good character.' His beetle brows waggled dangerously. 'I thought we'd start you off with a responsible job, so I'm putting you in charge of the police barracks. Some of the men are on curfew you know, and have only limited duties.' Again the eyebrows did a jig. 'You'll have a set of keys and a list of who should be where, so it's up to you to make sure every man knows his place and is in it. Can't trust some of these convicts you know,' he added conversationally.

Struggling to keep a straight face, John dipped his head in agreement. 'Right you are, sir. Shall I start now?'

'Yes, if you please. It's time to go out on the street and make sure no one's wandering about that shouldn't be. And keep an eye out for those Irishmen who are always out and about. Treated like gentry they are, especially that man Mitchel and his cronies.'

John took the proffered bunch of keys and notepad then bowed his head again before leaving the room. He asked the constable outside where he should take his belongings and was directed to a wooden hut joined on to one end of the barracks.

He was pleasantly surprised by what he found inside. Although small, the room was clean and neat with an iron bedstead along one wall, a wardrobe and a chest of drawers on another and a comfortable chair. There was even a table, on which stood a bowl and water jug. John put his small bundle on the bed. It contained the one change of clothes he possessed, and a drawing of his home village given to him by a young niece before he left. This he propped up against the wall on top of the dresser and his suit he hung carefully on the one supplied hanger.

His spare undergarments were soon consigned to the top draw, and then John poured a small amount of water into the basin to sluice his face. This done, he picked up the book and keys, which he looped over his belt, and set off to put Bothwell to rights.

Several times he passed The Falls of Clyde Hotel and on every occasion he moved close enough to peer through the windows. Ah, he thought, that must be the dining room, and there was his poor Ellen dashing about between tables looking hot and flustered. His heart went out to her. Fancy having to work tonight after a long day spent travelling. The other hotels appeared quieter and John wondered why. That was something he would have to discover.

As he strode about, hands behind his back in what he hoped gave a clear indication of his importance, he met several groups of men. Most appeared to be drovers or cattlemen and whether they should be out at this hour or not he didn't know. The list of names he'd been given meant nothing to him yet, but as long as they caused no trouble, for the time being he'd let them be.

Then two men approached from the direction of a private house. They were in deep conversation, but John caught the accent in their voices as they passed. The hairs on his arms stood up, as the well loved tones of his homeland reached his ears. They didn't acknowledge him, but John resolved to look out for them each evening.

Gradually the streets emptied and he strolled back to the police office. There was only a Sergeant sitting just inside the door so John asked him, 'Is it all right if I go off duty now? It's a long day I've had.'

'I suppose so, but you'll be on call all night. I'll give a shout if I need you. In the gatehouse are you?'

'I'd imagine that's what it's called.' John explained where his room was.

The man grinned. 'That's it, not very grand is it?'

'After some of the places I've had to put up with it's pretty fair, I can tell you.' John tipped his cap and bade the man goodnight. Tomorrow he'd try and speak to Ellen, but for now, he'd fall into bed and dream of her.

Ellen was sure that her head had only just hit the pillow before Bridget was shaking her awake. 'Come on Ellen, you've got two minutes then we're to go to Mrs Vale's office.'

'Two minutes? Why didn't you wake me before?' she said crossly.

'We tried, but you just turned over.' Sophie explained patiently as Ellen moaned.

'You two go on, I'll be with you in a moment. It isn't worth all of us getting into trouble.' Ellen was well aware that if there were trouble to be had, then she would be in it. That was the way things had always been, even before she came to Van Diemen's Land.

'Come on, Heath, where have you been?' Mrs Vale eyed her coldly as she entered the room a few minutes later.

'Sorry, Mrs Vale, I've been in the lav, must have been something I ate.' Ellen lied easily.

'Mmm, well go with the others now and get some work done. The bedrooms don't clean themselves.' The woman pursed her lips and Ellen wasn't sure that she'd been believed. Then in a voice like ice, Mrs Vale called her back. 'What in Heaven's name have you done to that dress?'

Ellen looked down at the offending garment, suddenly noticing the deep creases in the skirt. No answers came to mind, so she looked Mrs Vale in the eye and waited. In her experience, punishment was usually swift and sure.

But to her amazement the woman just sighed and waved her away. 'Go on and get some work done, I'll think of a way to make you pay later.' With those ominous words ringing in her ears, Ellen scuttled off to find the others.

Mrs Vale had her revenge on Ellen for the badly used dress in a simple but effective way. 'You will stand and iron every single item in that pile and they will be pristine. Do you understand?' The woman's eyebrows were raised above the cold stare.

'Yes Mrs Vale,' Ellen said lamely, not at all sure what pristine meant, but she guessed the ironing should be done properly. Her heart sank at the pile of clothes and bedding on the huge table before her. How had Mrs Vale known that ironing was her least favourite chore? And after cleaning bedrooms all the morning, her back ached already.

Maura glanced across at her and Ellen thought she could detect a glimmer of sympathy in her grey eyes. On top of the oven in front of her were three irons and when the first one sizzled as she spat on it, Ellen placed the padded holder over the handle and set to work. The first item was a dress similar to the one she wore and after trying for several minutes without success to remove the creases, Maura came across and stood next to her. 'You need to dampen them, dear. Get me that big jug and fill it with water then I'll show you what to do.' She grinned. 'Not done much ironing have you?'

'Not really. We didn't bother much at home. Our Sunday best clothes were always pressed, but mother had too many of us to do the rest.' Sadness filled Ellen as she recalled the Sunday morning rush to get ready for Church. Her sisters always wanted to be the first and somehow managed to push her into the background. I was always last, she thought. Always. Do they ever think of me now on a Sunday morning I wonder?

Maura brought her back from her reverie with a pat on the arm. 'You all right? You looked really upset there for a minute.'

'Ironing always reminds me of home. Funny that isn't it?'

'I know. It's odd what I think of sometimes. Mind you, I've been here so long that I can hardly recall anything about my previous life.' She dipped her hand in the jug and showed Ellen how to sprinkle the water over the crisp, dry material so that it would smooth under the hot iron.

'Thank you, Maura. I'd forgotten about damping them.' Ellen shook her head. 'I'm hoping to get married again later this year, but I'm hopeless at housework and things. Always have been. Even when I was married back home, my husband's mother moaned about the mess I made in her kitchen. Don't know why, it was filthy, so I'm sure it couldn't have got any worse.' She sighed. 'I keep wondering how I'll manage.'

'A few weeks working here and you'll soon learn a thing or two. I know Mrs Vale is hard, but believe you me, what she doesn't know about keeping a clean house isn't worth knowing. You glean all you can from her and you'll be fine.' Maura turned to go. 'I must be off to get the meat now. Will you be all right?'

'Yes, and thank you again.' Ellen smiled broadly, feeling for the first time since arriving in Bothwell, that life wasn't so bad after all.

It took her all afternoon to get through the pile of laundry, but by the time she'd finished, afternoon tea was ready. Mrs Vale complimented her on the ironing; the dresses were perfect, the sheets crisp. 'You've done well to finish that lot. Now come and have something to eat and drink before we start serving evening meals.'

Ellen entered the parlour to find Bridget, Sophie and Nessie were already sitting along the chaise-lounge, munching on sandwiches and Vera occupied the only other chair. Ellen eyed the plate; they hadn't left her much of a selection. Seeing as there was nowhere to sit, she helped herself to what was left and went to stand beside the small fireplace.

Resentment began to well inside her. She'd been standing all afternoon doing the bloody ironing and now there wasn't even a seat for her. The other women seemed completely unaware of her predicament and carried on chatting as though she wasn't there. After helping herself to a cup of tea Ellen left the room, carrying that and her plate out into the passageway with a view to taking them back to her room. At least she could sit on the bed there.

Then Mrs Vale appeared from around the corner. 'And just where do you think you're going with those?' The bright pink suffused her cheeks.

'To my room, Mrs Vale, as there's nowhere to sit in the parlour.'

'Oh no you don't. Food and drink must not be consumed beyond that door.' She pointed to the corridor entrance.

'I'm sorry, I didn't realise that, Mrs Vale.' Ellen shifted her weight from one foot to another. 'You see, I needed to sit down for a moment and the seats are full in there.' She nodded toward the parlour.

Mrs Vale's temper seemed to subside. 'Very well, let us go and see if we can find you a chair.'

Ellen followed her back into the parlour where the others still sat laughing and talking. Until they saw the formidable figure of Mrs Vale enter, that is.

'Nessie, go and make sure all the tables are properly set in the dining room if you please.' With her arms folded across her ample bosom, Mrs Vale could not be denied.

With a baleful look, Nessie left the room; she obviously didn't see why she'd been singled out to do something.

'There you are, Ellen, a seat. Now sit and finish your food and drink, time is pressing.' Then out she swept.

Sophie turned to Ellen. 'What was that all about? And where have you been all afternoon? Bridget and me have been for a look around Bothwell. It's not a bad place, quite small, but homely looking. And there's a Church.' The girl prattled on, while Ellen fumed. So she'd missed out again. By being late up, she'd been given extra chores and so been denied a trip outside. Maybe she'd have seen John. This thought hurt her to the core. Her first chance to see him in their new home town and she missed it. And all because of her own stupidity. No not even that, it was her own laziness. Well, Ellen Heath, she told herself, from now on you will be a model worker and will be punctual at all times.

Please God, help me to make this work, she prayed.

'Are you all right?' Bridget asked.

Ellen smiled weakly. 'I had to do a huge pile of ironing for being late this morning, so I couldn't come with you. You'll have to show me around tomorrow.'

'Oh, we don't get another day off for a week now,' Sophie said airily.

Ellen felt the world stop around her. 'A week?' she said softly as though her ears deceived her. Then the pain began; all the hurt, frustration and sheer unfairness of it came rushing into her head. The room tilted, and she grabbed at Bridget as she fell into total oblivion.

When Ellen came round, she was laying on her bed, Maura holding her hand, and Bridget peering anxiously over her shoulder. 'Ah, you're back with us,' said Maura. 'You gave us a scare, I can tell you. No, don't try to sit up yet.' She gently pushed Ellen back onto the pillows. 'Vera's bringing some beef tea, that'll revive you.'

'What happened?' Ellen asked, only vaguely aware of everything fading away before her eyes.

'You fainted, my dear. Never mind you're all right now. Mrs Vale said you're to stay here until you feel strong enough to get up, and you're excused duties this evening.' Maura smiled. 'Do you think you could be carrying a child? That's the usual reason for fainting.'

Ellen thought, but dismissed the idea. 'No, I'm sure I'm not. It was the shock of learning we haven't a day off for another week, and that means I can't see my young man.' A tear oozed from the corner of one eye. 'I wanted to see him so much.'

Just then Vera entered the room carrying a small tray on which was a white mug, steam rising from the rim. 'Here you are, this'll put the colour back in your cheeks.'

Ellen was overcome with all their kindness. 'Thank you all so much.' Then taking a sip, she added, 'Mmm, that's lovely. I do feel silly; I've never fainted before. Well, not that I remember anyway.'

'You're not to worry,' said Vera. 'Mrs Vale didn't intend for you to miss a day off and you can have one tomorrow. If you want, Nessie can take a message to your young man to let him know.'

Ellen's head cleared. 'Oh thank you. I'd like that. Only I don't know where he is. We came straight in here and he went off to find the Police Chief's office. How will she find him?'

Maura laughed. 'Don't you worry about that, Bothwell isn't so big, she'll find him without any trouble.' The woman stood up and turned to go. 'Now just you rest and then you'll be all bright-eyed and bushy tailed tomorrow. We can't have the young man disappointed now, can we?'

Vera followed her out of the room and Bridget came to stand by the bed. 'You did frighten me, fainting like that. Still,' she giggled, 'I did catch you in my lap. Right, I'm off for me dinner now. See you later.'

Left alone, Ellen wondered at how dark the room had become. Then she realised that Bridget had taken the candle with her. With a deep sigh, she finished the beef tea and lay down on her side to think of John. She imagined his warm embrace and longed to feel his lips on hers. 'Oh, please, God, let me see him tomorrow,' she whispered into the darkness.

Sophie and Bridget woke Ellen, as they got dressed the following morning. 'Are you coming for breakfast?' Sophie asked.

As she struggled onto one elbow, Ellen said, 'Yes, I think I will, I'm starving. How did things go in the dining room last night?'

Bridget laughed and stood in her petticoat brushing her hair. 'It was great fun, you should have been there. Maura and a customer had a big fight.'

Ellen's eyes opened wide. 'Maura?'

'That's right. She's quite a firebrand on the quiet. This bloke complained about the meat being tough, but Maura insisted it wasn't. Well, one thing led to another, and then she lost her temper and belted him one. You should have seen him shift. I've never seen a man run so scared in my life.'

'But she's only a skinny thing, how could she frighten him like that,' Ellen asked.

'Apparently she's known for her temper around here,' Sophie told her. 'That's why she was sent here in the first place. She killed a man, she did.'

The hairs on Ellen's scalp stood on end. 'Maura! I can't believe it. Mind you, I nearly did the same thing.'

Bridget and Sophie both stood and stared. 'Y-you killed a man?' Bridget asked in a horrified whisper.

'No!' cried Ellen. 'I said nearly, didn't I?'

'Why'd you do that then?' asked Bridget, her hair now pinned neatly into a bun on top of her head.

Ellen paused before saying, 'I had my reasons, believe me. Go on,

I'll be with you in a moment. And save me some breakfast.'

Sadly she wondered if her past would ever be just that, in the past. But then a thought came to her; if Sophie and Bridget were so innocent, what were they doing here? She was determined to find out about them; after all she had a right to know whom she was living with. And, she mused; I must ask Maura what happened to her. They were all prisoners so must all have a tale to tell.

Then she hurriedly dressed, eager to be off to see John. Her spirits rose and the delightful, melting sensation inside her returned, and her body quivered with anticipation.

John was waiting outside the hotel when Ellen came through the door to take her first look at Bothwell. She ran down the steps and into his arms. 'Oh, it's so good to see you. It seems like ages since we parted. How are things, John? What is your position like, and your rooms, are they all right?'

John laughed and held her away from him. 'My darling girl, not so fast, let me answer one question at a time.' He kissed the tip of her nose and smiled into her eyes. 'The position is fine, as is my accommodation. Come on, I'll show you round Bothwell.'

As they walked along the street arm in arm, Ellen looked about her with interest. Bothwell was smaller than she'd expected, but there was a quiet air of calm about the place, with none of the bustle and traffic of Hobart. Her spirits rose. This is where we are to live and I like the look of it. She glanced up toward him and said, 'I feel at home here already. I'm sure everything will work out well for us, aren't you?'

'Yes, I feel the same way. I'll show you where I live later on. I'm in charge of patrolling the streets, but from what I've seen everyone does much as they please.'

'The hotel was pretty noisy a couple of nights ago. The place was full of drovers and cattlemen. I don't know about last night, because I fainted and was allowed to stay in bed.'

'My sweet girl, are you all right now? What caused it?'

'It was the thought of not seeing you for a whole week. I think I would have died if it had been the case.' She raised one eyebrow at him. 'I can't wait to see where you live.'

'Just you be patient, little hussy. You'll see it soon enough. I want to show you the village first.'

As they walked, John told Ellen everything he'd found out about their new home. 'There are some families from Scotland, although they mostly live outside the village on small farms. They came here before it was used as a penal colony and have been settled for over thirty years. Generally the folk here in the village itself are prisoners of one sort or another.'

'Of one sort or another? What's that supposed to mean.' Ellen frowned, unable to think of what the difference might be.

'There are several Irish political prisoners here, although they have quite a bit of freedom to come and go. They're supposed to have passports to travel to other areas, but it's seldom enforced. I can see trouble there if the authorities aren't careful.' His eyes glittered and Ellen was suddenly afraid of what might happen if John got himself tangled up with these men.

'Don't you go getting involved, John. Promise me?'

'What do you mean?'

'I may not know much, but I do know you were in with a rough bunch back in Ireland. Weren't you caught attacking some man's home?'

'Well, yes, but that was different.'

'How different? Look, John, I know I'm a bit backward about a lot of things, but I do know danger when it's lurking.'

'You don't have to worry about them. They keep pretty much to themselves anyway, and wouldn't consort with the likes of me, a common prisoner.' It was said wryly, but Ellen could detect a note of disappointment in his voice.

She smiled brightly and changed the subject. 'So are you going to show me your new home then?'

A wide grin split his face and John stood and held out his hand. 'Let's be going, it'll take all of five minutes to get there.'

When they arrived at the barracks, John bowed Ellen over the threshold of his cosy room. 'Welcome to my humble abode.'

'It's not bad, and it's warmer in here.' Ellen looked about her appreciatively.

'It is good to have a space of my own, to be sure. What's your room like at the hotel then?'

'I have to share with Sophie and Bridget, and it's only a small room. The food is good though and there's plenty of it.' She told him about Mrs Vale, Maura and the others. Then she ginned wickedly. 'What am I doing wasting time talking when all I want to do is kiss you?'

'I wondered when you'd stop jawing and come into my arms.' John sat on the bed and held out his arms. Ellen ran and sat beside him, but was suddenly overcome with shyness.

'What's wrong?'

'This is the first time we've been able to make love on a bed and it feels strange.'

'I would have thought it more appealing than under a bush.'

Ellen felt the colour flood her face and she put both hands to her cheeks to cover them. 'I feel shy, I really do.'

He turned to face her and put a finger under her chin, then lifted her head up to face him. He looked deeply into her eyes. 'My lovely Ellen, don't be shy with me. We were made for each other you know that. Our hearts, minds and bodies are all in tune. So come my sweet and let me love you.' He drew her into his arms and sought her mouth with his and at last Ellen relaxed. Then her body melted and she gave herself up to him, pushing his jacket over his shoulder and unbuttoning his shirt, while he unfastened her dress and slipped his hands inside her camisole top.

At last they could spend some precious time together where there was no hurry and nothing to intrude. Just the two of them in their own private world of love.

Ellen opened her eyes and then closed them again. Sunlight streamed through the small window, filling the room with golden light. She wondered what the time was, but knew there was no rush to leave. John's even breathing told her he was still asleep and she opened her eyes again to gaze at him. He might not be the most handsome man she'd ever met, but there was a certain something about him that attracted her. He was kind and caring, something she'd always before found lacking in men, and he was funny and intelligent. Ellen sighed contentedly and snuggled closer to him. How strange, she thought, that I should be shipped halfway round the world before I found the man of my dreams. And here he is - a man so perfect in every way.

John stirred and awoke with a smile on his lips. 'Ah, it's so good to find you still here in my arms, I was afraid it had all been a dream.'

'Are you going to ask about getting married again soon, John? I want to be with you all the time, not just on my day off.'

'Whoa, my girl, give me chance. I've scarce found my feet in this place, never mind asking for favours.' He placed a finger over her lips. 'I will soon, I promise, then we can be married in the Church along the road and all your new friends can come. Won't it be grand?'

Ellen nodded, only partly convinced. Then she remembered her friend from the woman's factory in Hobart. 'I suppose it would be better to wait until Maddie arrives.' Then she came to a decision. 'Yes, that's what we'll do. Wait until Maddie gets here.' She moved her head to look up at him. 'Is that all right with you?'

He leaned across and kissed the tip of her nose. 'If you're happy then so am I. It won't be long anyway, will it?'

'No. I think she'll be here within a month.' She sought his mouth with hers and for a while again glowed in the ardour of his lovemaking. She could have quite happily stayed in his arms for the rest of her life, so complete did he make her feel; so at one with the world; so very, very happy.

Later, as she dressed, Ellen asked if he'd seen Harry since their arrival.

'Aye, I saw him last night as he staggered into barracks. He seemed happy enough, although his room isn't as good as this. He's moaning about having to share and I think was dropping the hint about moving in here.'

'What!' Ellen was horrified. How could they meet in private if someone else lived here as well?

'Oh, don't worry, I told him it wasn't convenient.'

'Thank goodness for that.' She went to stand before him as he sat on the bed and took his head between her hands. 'I couldn't bear not seeing you now,' she whispered softly.

He clasped her hips and pulled her toward him, his breathing ragged. 'Ellen,' he moaned, 'what have you done to me? You have bewitched me and I crave for you every moment of every day.' Then he drew her onto his lap, to make love to her once more.

Dusk was falling when he walked her back to the hotel, and they said goodnight at the door. 'I'll come round to the back door tomorrow so we can hello, my sweet Ellen.'

'I'm not sure that you'll be allowed to do that,' she told him sadly.

'I can try. For now though, goodnight my sweetheart.' One kiss on her forehead and he'd gone.

Ellen walked through the hotel toward her room in a dream. How wonderful it would be when they were married and could be together all the time. To be able to put her arms about him whenever she felt like it, to kiss him, to... She shuddered; remembering the happy hours they'd spent that afternoon.

As she passed the kitchen door, Nessie caught sight of her and called out. 'Where've you been then? Mrs Vale was looking for you. She's in her parlour and said for you to go straight in when you got back.'

Frowning, Ellen thanked the girl and turned toward the parlour door. She knocked and at Mrs Vale's request to enter, did so.

The woman's face took on its customary florid hue and she eyed Ellen with disdain.

'And where do you think you've been all this time, Heath?'

Nonplussed, Ellen struggled to understand the question and stood looking at Mrs Vale, the frown still on her face. 'I-I'm sorry?'

'You have been absent from these premises for several hours without permission. I want to know what gave you the idea you were free to go wandering off just when you felt like it.'

Her heart sank, and her happiness vanished in a trice. 'But I thought I could have today off,' she stuttered. 'I was told…'

'Not by me you weren't. You do not leave this hotel unless you have reported to me in person and given an account of your expected movements. And you must return before five o'clock. Surely you must realise that a day off does not mean all of that day. Have you not read the notices in your room?'

'W-what notices?' Ellen cringed, realising that she hadn't even seen any. In any case she couldn't read, so it wouldn't have made any difference if she had.

Mrs Vale appeared to soften. 'Heath, I know you view being here as relative freedom, but you are still a prisoner of Her Majesty's government. You are not entirely free to wander at will.'

'I-I'm sorry, Mrs Vale. But you see I can't read, so I'm afraid I really didn't know about all these things. When Vera said I could have today off, I just assumed it meant I was able to go out. And I did want to see my young man so much. And…' She was lost for words as all the old self-loathing returned. She had committed a crime and must be punished for it. She'd been so happy, but now it was all spoilt. Why was life so unfair?

Tears suddenly clouded her vision and she swept them away with her fingers, but before she could turn to leave, Mrs Vale came around the desk and handed her a handkerchief. 'Here, dry your eyes. Look, I know life is hard. It's the same for all of us and must be endured. You'll get used to things as time goes on and after a while everything will take on the guise of normality. Now, go and change. Your help is required in the dining room.'

Ellen hurried to her room, and on entering saw for the first time the pieces of paper pinned to a board on the wall. She wondered if Sophie and Bridget had read them. Or, perhaps they were like her and couldn't read. There was so much she didn't know about the two women she shared with. Then came the frightening thought; was it even safe to be in the same room?

The evening passed in a blur. Although not as busy as her first night at The Falls of Clyde, it kept the waitresses going at a steady pace. As they all sat around the table eating their supper, Ellen decided the time was right to ask questions. She looked Bridget in the eye and asked outright, 'What were you shipped away from England for?'

The normally friendly girl glared and pushed a fork full of food into her mouth. She chewed slowly as the atmosphere in the kitchen became charged. Everyone's eyes were on the red haired young woman from Bath, but no answer came. Instead another mouth-full of food followed the first.

Maura spoke first, 'I think it's only fair we know, don't you?' she said to Bridget. 'After all we have to live and work side by side, so it stands to reason there's going to be curiosity. You know about me and there can't be many worse crimes than murder. Even if it was in self-defence.'

'You know nothing.' Bridget stood suddenly knocking her chair over, before running from the room.

'Oh dear. I seem to have upset her,' Ellen said sadly. 'Should I go after her do you think?'

Vera shook her head. 'No, finish your supper first. It's a shame to let good food go cold over some poor girl who wants to keep her past a secret. We'd all like to do that, but it's damn near impossible. I was a prostitute on the streets of London before I was sent here four years ago. Had to feed my six kids and it was the only work that paid well enough.' She gave a humourless laugh. 'I wouldn't have minded, but the beak what sent me here was one of my best customers.'

As they all laughed, Ellen admired Vera's honesty and looked at Sophie in the hope that she would tell her story, but she sat, eyes downcast, and finished her meal in silence. With a sigh Ellen decided that she'd have to leave it until another day before seeking answers about her companions.

The next few days passed uneventfully, the only bright moments for Ellen being when John called briefly at the back door each morning to give her a quick kiss on the cheek before hurrying off again to his duties. Her curiosity about her roommates increased with each passing day. What dark secrets do they carry, she wondered? Neither Sophie nor Bridget could be drawn on the subject even though Ellen spoke quite openly about her own misdemeanours.

They would change the subject or not answer at all, and Ellen found the latter the more frightening. She often had trouble getting to

127

sleep, afraid of what one or the other might do.

Then at the end of the first week, Mrs Vale called the three women into the parlour. Her face held a smile, which Ellen thought, boded well. She had come to respect the woman who held so much sway in the day to day running of all their lives.

'It is customary to give all new workers an assessment at the end of the first week,' Mrs Vale said now. 'On the whole I have been pleased with your work, your cleanliness and you attitude.' She paused for the merest instant. 'Apart from one of two glitches at the beginning.' Ellen could have sworn the woman gave her a slight wink. 'Now I have been asked to assign you to duties other than here in the hotel.' She turned to Bridget. 'In the light of your hard work and quiet acceptance of rules and regulations it has decided that you will go to the country house of Mr Edwards, the gentleman who owns this hotel. He requires another member of staff in the household and I am sure they will find you of help.'

Then she turned to Sophie. 'You my dear are to travel a short distance to a place called Oatlands where you will be reunited with your husband. He is already there and has a home ready for you.'

Sophie's face lit with pleasure. 'Oh thank you, Mrs Vale. Thank you so much.' She almost curtsied in her excitement and both Bridget and Ellen turned to the young woman and voiced their delight for her. Ellen waited nervously for her own fate to be decided, but Mrs Vale went on speaking to Sophie and Bridget. 'You will both pack immediately and transport will call for you mid-morning.' She came from behind the small table she used as a desk and clasped them both by the hand. 'Thank you for your help this week and I hope your new positions give some stability to your lives. Now, off you go.' She lifted an arm to wave them from the room. Quickly Ellen said her goodbyes and stood forlornly looking after her companions, wondering what fate had in store for her.

CHAPTER 11

Finding herself left alone with Mrs Vale, Ellen was uncomfortably aware of the woman's eyes on her. What was to come now, she wondered? Usually she had done or said something wrong, which meant life would become even harder. Her heart missed a beat when the thought of being moved away from John came into her mind. Please Lord; don't do that to me, she prayed.

After staring at the floor for several moments, she dared to look up and face Mrs Vale. The woman was in fact reading a letter, and from time to time, made a comment to herself or nodded her head. At last she looked at Ellen. 'Right, my dear. Sit down, I want a word with you in private.'

Ellen sat on the edge of the well-used chaise-lounge, her heart hammering, and waited.

'This,' said Mrs Vale, holding up the letter, 'is from the woman's factory in Hobart. It states that you lost your baby daughter about a year ago. Is that correct?'

Tears filled Ellen's eyes. 'Yes,' she croaked. 'Yes, my little Mary died of the dysentery.'

'In light of this it has been decided that you should remain here in Bothwell, close to your young man. You hope to marry I believe, and therefore could have more children. We think that you should be given another chance of happiness.'

Ellen jumped up from the seat and ran forward, tears of joy coursing down her cheeks. 'Thank you, Mrs Vale. Thank you so much. Oh I don't know what to say. And John will be pleased too.' She stood, dashing the tears from her face, completely lost for words.

The older woman smiled widely. 'We all need our chances, Ellen, and you have had precious few since coming to this island. I shall still insist on cleanliness and punctuality mind, but I think you will fair better here than anywhere.' She took a deep breath. 'Right, off you go, and report to Maura. We thought you might like to learn about how a kitchen is run and to learn some cookery.' Then she added with a wicked grin, 'Without any additives, eh?'

Ellen nearly exploded with shock. How did Mrs Vale know about the attempted poisoning of her husband? Of course, she reasoned; my report must follow me about. This woman knew all about her, knew what she'd done, how she'd done it and what had happened to her as a consequence.

Blushing profusely, Ellen said, 'I'll do my best, Mrs Vale. Thank you again.' She turned and left the room before it could all be found to be a mistake, and she was to be returned to a prison somewhere.

Maura welcomed her gladly. 'I'm really pleased you're joining me in here. You said you want to learn housekeeping and where better to start than in the kitchen. It's the heart of every home. Besides, we've a lot in common you and me. Terrible men apart.' She grinned. 'We'll sit and tell all one day, but for now, we've lunch to prepare. Come, I'll show you the storeroom where we keep all the dry foodstuffs. Then it'll be pastry making. Would you like that?'

'Oh, yes. Your pastry is the best I've ever tasted; I'd love to be able to make it like that.'

The first thing Maura impressed on Ellen was cleanliness. 'I believe that dirt harbours germs and insist that food is always be handled with clean hands and nails. Many say it's all nonsense, but then wonder why they get food poisoning so often.'

They worked quietly, Maura pointing out the various do's and don'ts of making light pastry, and just as Ellen was attempting to roll out the cover for the meat pie, they heard a gentle knock at the door leading out into the garden at the back of the hotel. They looked up to see John standing outside.

'Go on, you can see him for a moment. I'll finish this while you're gone.'

Ellen smiled her thanks and skipped off to tell John her good news. He picked her up, his hands about her waist, and swung her around, laughing gaily. 'Oh, Ellen, I'm so glad, that I am. When I heard some of the women were to be sent away, I nearly died. But you're to stay here with me and soon we'll be married. I can't believe our luck; it's turned our way at last.'

'On my day off we can start making arrangements, can't we? I wonder if Maddie's due to arrive yet.'

'I've not heard anything as yet. Quick, give me a kiss to be going on with, then I must be off.'

They held each other close for a few moments and Ellen wished her day off were sooner. She wanted to love him so much it hurt. Gently he pushed her away from him. 'I'll try to see you tomorrow,' he said, his raffish smile as always quickening Ellen's heart. 'Bye for now, my love.'

'Goodbye John. I love you,' she called softly after him. Kissing her hand, she then held it out to blow him the kiss. He saw it and returned the gesture. Turning to go back into the kitchen, Ellen gave a big sigh. The pie was nearly ready to go into the oven and she dreamed of the day she would cook for John. He would be delighted with the splendid fare she placed in front of him, she was certain. Then she recalled an earlier pudding; an earlier man eager for his food and her heart thudded uncomfortably in her breast. How wicked she'd been then. She would never do anything like that to John.

With the passing days, Ellen felt encouraged to ask Maura about Sophie and Bridget. 'Do you know why they were shipped out here, like me?'

She saw Maura's eyes darken, but the woman held her voice steady as she replied. 'I don't know much. Mrs Vale is never one to gossip, but from what I gather, we're better off without them.'

'They were always friendly, and Bridget was kind to me the day I fainted. Most concerned she was.'

'All I know is Mrs Vale was keen for them to be gone. She's quite happy to have you here, but felt the risk was too great with those two.'

'What risk?'

Maura hesitated, kneading the dough on the table in front of her before answering, 'This is to go no further, mind?' she warned. 'That sweet-faced Sophie was charged with killing her two children.'

Ellen grabbed the table edge in shock. 'Oh no! How could she?'

'She always denied it of course, and it does seem hard to grasp. But that's no doubt why she didn't tell you, not after losing your little girl to illness.'

'I can't imagine any woman killing a child. I was wicked to try and poison my husband, but I would have walked over hot coals to save my Mary.' Ellen felt close to tears, her mind trying to grasp what Sophie had done. She looked up. 'And Bridget?'

Maura stood up straight and smoothed down her apron before saying slowly. 'I don't know how much you know about how some women earn their living, especially in the big cities, but Bridget was a prostitute in Bath. Mind you, a feckless husband who'd dragged her from her home in Ireland had dumped her there. She then got into bad company and started thieving from her clients. I do feel sorry for women like her really; she was a victim of circumstance.'

'I can't imagine living like that, I think I'd rather die. I love John and our union is special, but I couldn't do that with strangers.' She shuddered at the thought.

'There's more to Bridget's story though. She started playing off one pimp against another, starting gang warfare. Several men were killed before the law could step in and stop it all.' Maura shook her head. 'Poor girl got in over her head. It just shows what can happen though, doesn't it?'

Ellen said thoughtfully. 'I think I was lucky to live in a small country village. Nothing much ever happened there. Well, apart from the riots, of course.'

Maura's eyes widened in surprise. 'Riots? What riots?'

'About twenty years ago my father was involved in unrest about the tithes. The villagers revolted because they couldn't earn enough to live on, due to the vicar's demands for money. No one liked him anyway and soon most of the village joined in and ransacked the workhouse.' Ellen paused trying to remember what else happened. 'I think some of the men concerned were sent off to Australia.'

'Well I never. Mind you, I don't blame the men. Feeding your family is often difficult and some folk have to do difficult things to manage.' Maura's face took on a determined look. 'Like Vera did. It's amazing what a child with an empty belly can push you to.'

'I was only about eight years old when it happened, but I know there was a lot of resentment because my father didn't get sent away. Well, only for a while in Winchester prison and that was bad enough. My older brothers had to work hard to help keep us all.'

'Why wasn't your father transported then?'

'One of the landowners spoke up for him, and he didn't actually do much; just walked ahead of the mob blowing his trumpet.' Ellen grinned. 'Loved his trumpet, he did,'

'Musical then, was he?'

'I suppose he was in a way, although we rarely heard him play at home. He got it when he was in the army,' said Ellen as though that explained everything.

But Maura seemed to understand. She broke the dough that she had been kneading into portions and slapped them into shape before placing them into four loaf tins. 'Here, help me put these in the oven.' She picked up two and Ellen followed with the others and carried them carefully toward the huge black metal range that took up almost all one wall of the kitchen.

Ellen felt content. She had a good working relationship with

Maura and Vera, and even Nessie was getting chattier.

One thing puzzled her though. Maura was more than happy to talk about other people, but never mentioned her own background. A few days later Ellen decided to be bold and ask her outright what her crime had been.

Her face filling with colour, Maura lowered herself onto a kitchen chair. 'I hardly know how to tell you. You of all people know what it's like to have done something you'll regret for the rest of your life.'

Ellen waited patiently, not wishing to rush the kindly woman.

'It started when I was about nine years old,' Maura said softly. 'I used to help my mother with the household duties. She wasn't a healthy woman and found the house too much to manage most of the time and although I wasn't very old, I did what I could. We lived in Scotland, just north of Edinburgh and my father was absent more often than not. His business in London kept him away I was told, but when he was at home, life was unbearable for both my mother and me. He was a bully and quite often would strike one of us in temper for no reason that we could see.' She stopped and closed her eyes as though to conjure up images from the past. 'One night he entered my bedroom and ordered the nanny out. He climbed into my bed and, and…' Her face crumpled. 'You can imagine what happened. I screamed out for my mother, but she didn't come. No one came. No one.'

Ellen leaned forward and put a hand on Maura's arm. 'How awful. I'm sorry I made you tell me.'

'No, it's all right. I think I'll feel better for the telling. I've told very few people, you see. Only Mrs Vale knows the whole story.'

Feeling honoured to being entrusted with something so personal, Ellen said softly, 'I'm pleased you felt you could tell me.'

A weak smile lightened Maura's face. 'You have a kind and sympathetic nature, Ellen that is why I feel able to talk. My father's disgusting behaviour carried on for many years, until when I was thirteen years old, my mother died. I'm sure she knew what was happening, but never did a thing to stop it. She was too afraid of my father I suppose. I didn't think of that then, just how much I hated them both.' She shook her head. 'How sad it is, to hate your parents.' She looked at Ellen. 'I suppose you think that strange; to hate one's parents?'

'Not when they've treated you so badly, I don't.'

'You're a good girl. The sort of daughter I would have liked to have, only fate conspired against me to ever having a child.'

'Oh, what happened?'

'After my mother's death, my father moved me to his house in London. I had to leave behind all I knew. My nanny, my pony, and the servants, because in a way, they were all the friends I had. There were very few visitors and I was discouraged from mixing with other children.'

Dismay filled Ellen. 'That must have been awful. I can't imagine not having my sisters, brothers and friends around me. You must have been very lonely?'

'I suppose I was, but I knew no other life than the one I had. Anyway, once we moved to London, my father made sure I had plenty of company.' A wry smile twisted her lips. 'He used to invite his rich and powerful friends to dinner parties and guess who was the entertainment afterwards?'

'Oh, the horrible man. How did you bear it?'

'I had no choice. Not for a while anyway. But then one day about two years later, something happened to change everything. I had been unwell for a while and in the end confided to the housekeeper. She took me off to see a doctor and he announced that I was expecting a child.' Maura put a hand to her forehead and gave a ragged sigh. 'As the months passed I felt more and more angry. Then one night I awoke with the most terrible pains in my belly and realised that the baby was coming into the world. I crawled to the housekeeper's room and she ran for my father, but he refused to call a doctor. He had ignored my pleas for help or acknowledged that the child was anything to do with him or his friends. Called me a whore and said I must have been out on the streets. Luckily the woman, for once ignoring my father, helped me back to bed and called one of the maids to help. They stayed with me all night, while I pushed and struggled to get the baby out. By midday the following day, I was exhausted, but still my father refused to call a doctor. In the end, just as I thought I might die, the baby came, but he was already dead. The strain had been too much for him. I was so ill for a long time after that I don't even know what became of him, and the damage it had done to my body meant I could never have another child. After a few weeks, my father was convinced that I was fit enough to continue my services for his friends, but I had made up my mind; there would be no more of it. I was only fifteen, but a woman in fact and I made up my mind that I would refuse, no matter what my father did or said. I went into his study to confront him and we had a furious row, during which, he threatened me with a heavy walking cane. I grabbed it and struck out at him. Once I started, I couldn't stop. I just kept hitting and hitting. Even when his blood spurted over me, I couldn't stop. Someone came into the room and grabbed the stick from me... I don't remember much after that, except that I was hauled into court and charged with murder. No one, apart from the housekeeper stood up for me, and she wasn't believed; no one else came forward to explain what my father had been like. I felt so alone and didn't really care what happened to me. I spent several months in a prison in London and then was sent here where I have found a better life. I don't have the trappings of wealth anymore, but I have a good position and friends. That is all I seek now.'

In the silence that followed, Ellen stared in admiration at the woman before her. How trivial her own crime seemed now compared to what Maura had suffered.

The chief of police tapped his pencil on the blotter in front of him. 'You must enforce these rules, Ryan that is your duty. What don't you understand? What do you think all these men are here for? They appear to walk about the village as though they own it. Your duties are clearly defined; the streets must be clear of prisoners by sundown, which at this time of year is six of the clock. Why then do I see these Irishmen wandering freely about the place and visiting houses they have no right to?'

John looked the chief squarely in the eye. 'To be sure, I cannot be everywhere at once, Sir. I go one way and they pass by another.'

'Don't give me that man. Bothwell only has one main street, how can you miss them? You've been here for three weeks now, so the place must be well known to you.'

'Begging your pardon, Sir, I do know Bothwell like the back of my hand, but somehow these men get past me without my seeing.' John felt his collar warming under the man's glare.

'Too busy minding your own business, I guess. Well, it's got to stop, do you understand?'

John tapped his forehead with one hand in salute. 'I understand, Sir. I will see that it happens no more.'

'Good. Make sure you do, otherwise you could find yourself in very hot water. Go now, I have more important work to do.'

As he backed out of the office, John saw the chief's clerk wink. So that was the way things were, he thought. The chief knew damned well what went on in Bothwell, but he had to be seen to do what was right. A smile spread across John's face. He'd just carry on as usual then.

He hurried round to the back of the hotel to see Ellen, as he did most days, and was thrilled to see her pegging a basket of washing on the line, the wind blowing her hair across her face. He crept up behind her and clasped her round the waist. She let out a scream that was quickly silenced when she saw who it was. Then his lips were on hers and he held her close.

'Hello my beautiful girl,' he said at last.

'Oh John, don't call me that. I'm not beautiful.'

'To me you are.' He smoothed the hair from her brow. 'To me you are the loveliest girl in the world.'

'I wish we could be together more. Have you asked for permission to marry again yet?'

'Not yet. I'm waiting to find the chief in good humour before I mention it.'

'Surely he's not the one to ask, don't you have to see the Governor?'

'I do, but I have to arrange a meeting with him through the chief.' He pulled her back into his arms. 'I'll ask as soon as I can. How many days is it until your day off?'

'Why?' Ellen asked, a sly grin on her face.

'You know why. I can't wait to make love to you again.'

With a sigh, Ellen wrapped her arms about his neck. 'I know, I feel the same, but what can we do?'

'Isn't there a spare room in the hotel? Or what about your room now that the other two have left?'

Shock widened Ellen's eyes. 'John! How could you? That would be a foolish thing to do and would only bring trouble for us both.'

He groaned. 'I know, I know. It was but a thought. I suppose I'll just have to be patient.'

'Anyway, it's only two days until my day off, so it's not long to wait.'

'I'll see you tomorrow anyway. What are you hanging out to dry?'

'These are the kitchen towels, and they won't get dry sitting in the basket, so be off with you.'

John kissed her cheek and turned to leave. 'Bye, my sweet.'

'Bye.' Ellen smiled and returned to her task and he stood watching for a moment as she battled to hold the towels in place long enough to get the pegs in. He shivered. The wind was biting today; time to go and make a cup of tea.

The following morning, John was conspicuous by his absence. When he hadn't appeared by lunchtime, Ellen began to fret. She sat at the table idly fingering the piece of bread on her plate. 'Where can he be?' she asked Maura for the hundredth time.

'Try not to worry, he's probably off doing his duty somewhere and will be back this afternoon. It's your day off tomorrow so you'll see him then, won't you?'

'Yes, I'll see him then.' Colour crept into her cheeks as she thought about what they would do when they met the following day.

Maura grinned. 'You certainly enjoy your day off I must say.'

This brought an even brighter blush to Ellen face. 'Oh dear, does it seem so obvious?'

'Only to those of us who know about such things. Now, eat that bread and cheese, otherwise you'll be hungry all afternoon. Ah, here's Vera. Come and eat, we thought you'd forgotten the time.'

Vera stood just inside the kitchen door, her face drained of colour. 'You'll never guess what I've just been told?'

Ellen and Maura stared at the woman as she came to the table and sat herself down before continuing, 'Word has just come through from Oatlands that there's been a murder. Two of our constables have just gone to arrest someone.'

Relief flooded through Ellen, so that's probably where John was. Her relief was short lived however as Vera went on, 'You'll never guess who they've gone to pick up?' She paused for a moment to give her words more impact.

'Well?' asked Maura. 'Are you going to tell us, or have we to guess?'

'Sophie!'

Ellen's eyes popped. 'Sophie?'

Maura gasped loudly beside her.

'Yes. Apparently she killed her husband.'

'I don't believe it,' Ellen gasped. 'She was looking forward to being with Frank. She kept on about him all the time.'

'That's as maybe, but she's killed him right enough.' Vera sighed. 'And to think we had her sleeping under this roof.'

'I was in the same room,' Ellen was aghast. 'Something must have gone wrong between them, although, didn't you say she'd killed her children?' she asked Maura.

'Supposed to have done, but I could never understand why her husband was here as well. There must have been more to that case than met the eye.'

'Perhaps we'll know more when John gets back.' Ellen felt her insides contract. Although she hadn't got to know Sophie well, she couldn't believe the pretty young woman could do such a thing.

'They're bringing her back here until the magistrate can draw up the papers to send her back to Hobart to stand trial,' Vera told them. 'We'll never know the whole truth I don't suppose.' She nodded sadly and sat down to eat her lunch.

Ellen couldn't help noticing that the shocking news hadn't put the woman off her food!

It was late in the afternoon when the two policemen rode into Bothwell with someone on horseback between them. Ellen and Maura had hurried through to the front window in the dining room when Vera told them of the arrival. Although a smile curved Ellen's lips at the sight of John, her attention was on Sophie's slight figure as she sat slumped in the saddle of a pony, her wrists bound and the reins held firmly by John's companion.

Poor Sophie, what had possessed her to do such a dreadful thing?

Tomorrow was her day off and Ellen decided that it would be worth asking if she could see Sophie for a few moments, if only to let the woman know that they were all concerned for her. Somehow she was convinced that Sophie had not killed her children. But then why had she been charged? It was a mystery, and one that she would be happier knowing the truth about.

Maura looked out of the window, sadness etched on her face. 'I wonder where they'll take her? Into the main prison I suppose, although that's usually only for men.' She sighed, and Ellen told her of her plan for the following day. 'They'll never let you see her, she'll be kept under close arrest.'

'I can try,' said Ellen stubbornly. 'She must feel so alone.'

'Well serve her right if she goes around killing people,' Vera said. 'There can't be one law for one and a different one for another.'

'I know, but I don't think she did kill her children.' Ellen was adamant. 'Don't ask me why, but I don't. There was something about her. She'd never talk about herself and that seemed strange when we'd all been open about our lives.'

The other two women nodded. 'You try to see her,' said Maura. 'Perhaps that'll give her chance to tell you what really happened.'

Then Sophie was escorted away into the prison compound, now walking unsteadily between John and another constable. Ellen felt her heart go out to the young women. She knew what it was like to feel lost and alone.

When Ellen left the hotel the following morning, John was waiting for her. His face lit with pleasure as she ran down the steps and into his arms. He lifted her off the ground and swung her around as usual, before kissing her soundly. 'Oh, John,' Ellen cried breathlessly. 'Do you have to do that? It makes me giddy.' But she laughed to let him know she didn't really mind. 'I want to ask you something?'

'My you have a serious look about you today. What is it you want to know?' He still held her close and sheltered her from the chill wind that blew keenly along the street.

'I want to ask someone if I can visit Sophie.'

'Whatever for? The woman's a murderess.'

'I don't care, I want to see her. After all, I lived with her and got to know her. She must feel so scared. Please. Who can we ask?' Ellen gazed into his eyes and saw his expression soften.

'Very well, I'll go and ask the Chief. I won't make any promises mind.' He took her hand and they hurried down the street to the police office. While Ellen waited anxiously outside, John went in to ask about a meeting, and when, a few moments later, he stuck his head around the door and beckoned to her, she felt her nerves sharpen and her heart missed a beat.

As she stepped inside the office, Ellen was aware of the stout man sitting behind the desk, his face creased into a frown. 'Come in, Mrs Heath.' He pointed to a chair. 'Sit yourself down and tell me why you want to see Mrs Hargreaves.'

Ellen sat, while her head whirled. Mrs Hargreaves? Then she realised that this must be Sophie's surname. 'W-well,' she began slowly. 'I lived and worked with her for a week at the Falls of Clyde hotel and I just thought that perhaps she'd like to see a friend. Oh, I know what she's accused of, but I would really like to see her.'

The chief's brow furrowed in consternation. 'It's not normally allowed for prisoners to have visitors, especially one on such a serious charge.' He studied her for a few moments, then appeared to come to a decision. 'Very well. But you must be accompanied by two police officers and it must be for a few minutes only.'

Ellen breathed a sigh of relief. 'Thank you, sir.' She wanted to jump up and clasp the man's hand, but knew that wasn't appropriate behaviour in the chief's office. Instead she stood and primly bobbed a curtsey to the man, thanking him for his courtesy. Then John took her elbow and led her from the room.

As they hurried across the road to the prison, another constable close on their heels, John asked her, 'Are you sure about this? You could be putting yourself in mortal danger.'

She gave a snort of derision. 'I'm sure everything will be all right. Sophie knows me, and it may help her to talk about things. If she wants to that is.'

'You are funny, I can't make you out sometimes.' John grinned at her. 'I suppose it's because you're such a caring person that I love you.'

Ellen smiled, but said nothing.

And then, as the heavy door clanged back, Ellen remembered another heavy door, one that had been thrown open by the guards who had come to her when Mary died.

She guessed that sound would live with her forever.

Taking a deep breath, she moved into the dim room where Sophie sat quietly on a wooden bench, her hands clasped in her lap. The young woman glanced up as they entered, her eyes lighting at the sight of Ellen, who hurried forward. 'Oh, Sophie, what has happened to you?'

Dashing a tear away, Sophie said, 'Ellen! It's so good to see you. I thought no one would want to know me now.' She patted the seat beside her.

Ellen looked at John questioningly, then at his nod, sat next to her former roommate. 'Are you being looked after, being fed well?'

'Yes reasonably, although the food isn't as good as Maura's cooking of course.'

'Nothing's as tasty as Maura's.' Ellen sat for a moment trying to think of how to get the woman talking about what happened, but then Sophie herself started by taking Ellen's hand.

'Please, try to forgive me for what I've done. I'm sure you've been told by now that I supposedly killed my children. That must have been terrible for you who lost a child through illness.' Her face took on an earnest look. 'I promise you that I did no such thing. Can you believe me?'

'I do believe you, I never thought that you'd done it,' Ellen said. 'I don't know why, but I just couldn't imagine you doing such a thing.'

Sophie gave her an odd look. 'You couldn't?'

'No. I've been in trouble many times in my life and can tell when things don't ring true. Something happened, didn't it, before you were sent here to Van Diemen's Land?'

Sophie nodded. 'No one knows the whole truth. No one, because I didn't dare to tell what really happened. Even here, I had to keep up the pretence.'

'Your husband killed them, didn't he?' Ellen paused looking into Sophie's eyes. 'It was him, wasn't it?'

Sophie gasped. 'How did you guess?'

Ellen shrugged. 'Can you tell us what happened?'

140

John and the other man lowered themselves to the floor, leaning against the rough stone wall, while Sophie sat thoughtfully for a moment, before beginning, 'After our second child, Daniel was born I was terribly ill and needed help. Catherine was only two years old and my mother came for a few weeks to help me, much to Frank's annoyance; he'd never liked her. When I was back on my feet and mother returned home, he took to staying out late at night. Nothing I said could make him see that I wanted him at home with me.' She shook her head sadly. 'He seemed to prefer the company of the men in the alehouse. And he wouldn't work. I'm not sure what happened there, but he came home one day in a temper and said that he was never going back. Soon we had no money, but he still expected me to feed us all. I was at my wit's end. I sold bits and pieces of our possessions, took in washing sometimes and my mother used to send food, but it was a nightmare and I didn't know what to do about it.' Sophie stopped speaking and began wringing her hands as she struggled to control herself. 'One night he came in drunk. Shouting and swearing; demanding a meal. But there was no food in the house. I was hungry and so were the children, but he wouldn't listen. Then he hit me. I was so shocked, he'd never done that before, but it was the first of many beatings I had to endure.' Colour flooding her face, Sophie said. 'I even scavenged for food amongst our neighbours thrown out scraps. Can you imagine the humiliation of doing that?

'But Frank didn't seem to care. I wonder now if he was ill.' Tears filled her eyes. 'He had always been a loving husband and father. Poor little Daniel never knew him like that.' She shook her head again. 'I struggled on for a year until one night, he came in late, the worse for drink as usual. I never knew where he found the money for drink, but he always seemed to manage it somehow. This particular night he beat me black and blue. It was so bad that one of our neighbours intervened. I think my screams were keeping him awake.' A wry laugh escaped her lips. 'But Frank hit him as well. Then when the man ran out, Frank grabbed me by the throat and demanded something to eat.' Tears started coursing down her face unchecked and her shoulders shook violently.

Ellen wrapped an arm about Sophie's thin frame. 'Shhh! Take your time.'

'It's too horrible to remember. I'm not sure I can tell you what happened.'

'Don't worry then, we can come and see you again.'

'No! I'll finish my tale. I must for I don't know how long I'll be here and they might send me to Hobart before I can see you again.'

Silence filled the cell as Sophie struggled to speak. 'I-I said that I had given the children what scraps there had been. H-he threw me back against the wall, grabbed the broom and ran into the bedroom.' Through gasping sobs she told of the next few moments. 'I heard a thumping sound coming from the room. I thought he was trying to scare me, but then he appeared in the doorway.' Sophie cried out then, 'Oh God, please help me.' She turned to Ellen, tears streaming down her face, her voice now little more than a moan. 'The broom handle was dripping in blood.'

Ellen felt her insides constrict, and she hugged Sophie closer and said huskily. 'Oh, my God! How did you bear it? What did you do?'

She felt the young woman's head move slightly as she whispered. 'I ran past him into the room and when I saw what he'd done I just screamed and screamed. I don't remember much after that.'

As she looked across to where John sat, Ellen saw tears in his eyes, while the other constable sat, his head down, staring at the floor. She guessed he too was trying to put the harrowing scene to the back of his mind. Then she was aware of her own tears as they ran down to mingle with Sophie's hair. There was something Ellen didn't understand and she asked, 'But didn't you tell the law what he'd done?'

'I was too scared. He threatened me that he'd kill me too if I told the truth and I had to take the blame. For some reason at that time I didn't want to die. It was only later that I wanted to join my children, but by then I was determined to get my revenge.'

John spoke then, his voice sounding loud in the tiny room, 'Tell me, why was your husband transported as well, if he'd blamed you?'

Sophie lifted her head from Ellen shoulder. 'There was an element of doubt, someone said that the blows were delivered with such force that it couldn't have been me. So the judge sentenced us both. He said that in any case if my husband was there he could have stopped me, so we were both guilty.'

'And you waited all that time to see him again?' Ellen was shocked.

'Yes, it had been over two years since I last saw him, but as time went by I grew more and more certain of what I would do.'

'So you admit to killing him then?' John said quietly.

Ellen felt Sophie's back stiffening. 'Yes,' she said defiantly. 'I killed Frank. And when I get to Hobart, I hope they kill me too, then I shall be at peace with myself, and the Lord. And I shall see my two dear little ones again in heaven.'

'You are brave,' Ellen told her.

142

'No, I'm not brave. I wanted to kill Frank the same way he killed our babies, but in the end I shot him. I took the hunter's gun from the rack, aimed and fired. I thought it wouldn't be so messy, but of course there was a lot of blood.'

Ellen shuddered and she noticed for the first time the splattering of blood down the front of Sophie's gown, and her heart filled with pity. She would probably be given the death sentence, and for what? Seeing that justice was done. Well, that was how she viewed it anyway.

The other policeman stood up. 'I think it's time we were going, John? Mrs Heath? The Chief said a few moments only and we've been here best part of an hour.'

John nodded and held out his hand to Ellen. 'Come, say goodbye.'

Both women stood and hugged each other tightly, their bodies swaying slightly.

'Goodbye, Sophie. God Bless you. I'll never forget you.' Ellen sobbed.

'Thank you for coming to see me, Ellen. I wish you and John a long and happy life, really I do. Goodbye for now, I doubt we'll meet again.'

As John dragged her away, Ellen turned and saw the woman's face contorted with pain. She pushed the image away; she must remember Sophie as the pretty young companion she had shared part of her life with.

Later, as she sat on John's bed, Ellen said, 'I'm sorry, I didn't mean to spoil our day together.'

He nuzzled her ear. 'Just being near you is enough, and it was a very kind thing you did, visiting Sophie.'

Suddenly, Ellen jumped up. 'What's the time? I mustn't be late back.'

Pulling out his pocket watch, John said, 'It's just after five, you'd better go.' He pulled her to her feet and hugged her, before placing her cape around her shoulders and going to open the door.

As they hurried back toward the hotel a carriage bowled by and Ellen caught a glimpse of a young woman with red hair sitting inside. She could have sworn it was Bridget, but dismissed the idea. What would Bridget be doing riding in a grand carriage?

CHAPTER 12

Ellen felt as though she had been back on board ship on the heaving ocean over the past few days. All the sadness and sorrow she had witnessed buried itself in her soul. She knew that compared to some, she hadn't had so bad a life, and began to feel respect for those working alongside her; who knew what they had suffered? Each and every one of them carried the burden of guilt for some crime or another. Some serious, and some probably like her own that had been committed in a moment of madness.

The following morning John came to tell her that Sophie had been found dead in her cell. 'The poor grieving woman used a stocking to hang herself from the bars,' he said as he took Ellen into his arms.

'Oh no! Oh, my God,' she cried. 'How could she?' Ellen felt as though the sky had fallen about her and her heart was heavy, as though turned to stone.

'At least she's at peace now, and God willing, back with her children.' John said quietly.

'Do you think she is?' Ellen lifted her tear stained face to look up at him.

'In my Church it's a mortal sin to take your own life, but there are those with a more lenient stance who say that when the soul is troubled beyond reason, that is the only way out.'

'How can you be sure it won't stop her being back with her children?' she asked anxiously.

'I'm sure God won't hold it against her.' John gently brushed the hair back from her face. 'Now, my love, I must be away as I'm on duty. I'll see you tomorrow.' He kissed her cheek and hurried off, leaving Ellen feeling bereft.

She knew she must tell the others and was worried about how they would receive the news. Mrs Vale seemed like the obvious person to tell, as the woman had been quite sympathetic about Sophie when Ellen had told her the full story the previous day.

'I can't believe it,' was Mrs Vale's response. 'What did the silly girl do that for?'

Ellen bit her lip, not sure how to answer. 'I suppose she couldn't live with what she'd done,' she said tentatively.

A huge sigh emitted from Mrs Vale's mouth. 'Well, I don't know, it's a terrible sin to end your own life. She'll be forever in purgatory, you know that, don't you?'

'Oh no,' Ellen cried. 'I'd hate to think that. Please, Mrs Vale don't you think God will forgive her?'

'No I don't,' was the sharp reply, 'now, go and get on with your work and forget the wicked woman.'

Tears were streaming down Ellen's face when she entered the kitchen.

'What's the matter, dear?' Maura moved to her side and placed an arm about her shoulders.

Once the whole sorry tale had been told, Maura sat Ellen down at the table and placed a hot cup of tea in front of her. 'Now, you drink that, while I tell the others what's happened. And don't take what Mrs Vale says to heart, she doesn't know anymore than the rest of us about such things.'

Feeling slightly comforted, Ellen did as she was told and sipped the scalding liquid until her senses began to settle. She was sure Sophie wouldn't go to hell for what she'd done. Surely God made allowances for people? That's what her father had said and he was a good, Christian man. She could hear his voice now, inside her head: 'Always give others the benefit of the doubt, Ellen and treat them as you would wish to be treated yourself.'

By the time Maura returned to the kitchen with Vera and Nessie in tow, Ellen felt a little recovered and, in her mind at least, sure of Sophie's reunion with her children.

Nessie said very little and even Vera hadn't much to say on the matter except that it was a bloody shame the poor young woman had suffered so.

'Perhaps Mrs Vale was so shocked at the news that she answered without thinking,' Maura said smoothly, and by so saying, poured oil on troubled waters.

Then Vera changed the subject by saying, 'We've a new woman arriving tomorrow. You might know her.' She looked at Ellen. 'Because she's coming from that woman's factory place where you were.'

Ellen's heart did a flip. Could it be Maddie? Was she coming at last? Oh, please God, she prayed, let it be Maddie and little Stella.

And it was. There was much excitement the following afternoon when the cart rolled up outside the hotel and Ellen saw the familiar figure of her friend climb down. Throwing the door open wide, she ran down the steps to greet her. 'Maddie, oh Maddie. I thought you were never coming. It's so lovely to see you.'

The two women hugged, Maddie's big frame almost engulfing Ellen's slighter one. 'And I thought I'd never get here.' Maddie's laugh was balm to Ellen's battered soul. 'My you've put on a bit of weight, but you're looking peaky. What have you been up to?'

Before Ellen could answer, Mrs Vale appeared. 'Heath, what do you think you're doing? It is not your place to welcome visitors, whoever they might be.' She turned her gaze on Maddie and said, 'Come inside, please, I'm sorry for Heath's over exuberant greeting.' In spite of the fact that Mrs Vale sounded stern, Ellen could detect a twinkle in her eye and breathed a sigh of relief and reached out to take one of Stella's hands and lead her inside.

As they piled into the parlour, Mrs Vale indicated the chaise-lounge and asked Maddie to sit down. 'Now Mrs Trueman, you obviously know Mrs Heath and I'll take you through to meet the rest of my staff in a few moments, but I'll tell you something about The Falls of Clyde hotel first. This is a first class establishment and I like it run as such. My standards are high, but if you are willing to work hard, you will find me a fair person.' She turned to Ellen. 'Heath, go and get some refreshment for your friend and the little girl, please.'

Ellen went happily to fetch some tea and sandwiches, eager to tell Maura that her friend was here, safe and well. Now that Maddie was here, John and herself could get married, the small matter of permission completely forgotten. All the pain of the past few days eased a little, just seeing Maddie had brought her life back on track.

Maura seemed to take to Maddie straight away, although Vera appeared reserved and Nessie did her usual thing of cowering in the background. Everyone cooed over the shy Stella, but gradually the girl began to relax and stopped clinging to her mother's skirt. Over the late evening meal after all the dinner guests had left, and Stella was in bed, Maddie filled Ellen in on what had been happening in Hobart. 'We've had a new block of cells built, not that they're much better than the old ones. The yard has been extended ready to take in more inmates, although word is,' she tapped her nose, 'strictly on the quiet, that the transporting of prisoners is going to stop.'

They all gaped at her; then Maura found her voice, 'Does that mean we'll be sent home?'

146

A buzz of excitement rippled round the room and Nessie jumped up as though ready to leave straight away. 'Will we?' she cried. 'Will we be sent home to England?'

Maddie held up a hand. 'No. I'm sorry, but that hasn't been discussed as far as I know. It's only a rumour as yet anyway.'

The jubilation stopped as suddenly as it had started and they sat around with long faces, until Ellen told them of her and John's plan to get married soon. The mood in the room lifted once more; all women loved a wedding.

Later, as Maddie unpacked her few belongings in the room they would share, Ellen recounted the story of Sophie and its sad ending. 'So you see that's why I was looking pale, it was the shock.'

'My poor girl, haven't you had enough sorrow to last you a lifetime?'

'Oh Maddie, if only you knew. I know we're all criminals in the eyes of the law, but most women seem to have just been trying to survive. Some stole to feed their children, like you did, or took to the streets...' she shrugged. 'Why was life so hard back in England? Do you know? I don't think I'd go back now even if I was given the chance.'

'Nor me neither,' said Maddie. 'Life's a sight better here than it ever was back home. I think we're treated pretty well considering.'

'I think it's because there are so many of us. John says that nearly all the inhabitants of Bothwell are convicts.' Ellen leant across the bed and took Maddie's hand. 'And now you're here, I'm as happy as I'll be anywhere. I'll show you round tomorrow, if it's all right with Mrs Vale.'

'She seems to have tamed you somewhat, this Mrs Vale. Or is it John who's brought out the best in you?'

Ellen giggled. 'A bit of both I expect. Was I awful at the factory?'

'No, not really, just trying to kick over the traces like the rest of us.' Maddie stretched and clambered under the covers next to her daughter who was already sound asleep. 'Ah well, I'm ready for my bed. At least it's a proper room with proper beds, I think I'll sleep well tonight.'

'Goodnight, Maddie.' Ellen rolled into her own bed and snuffed out the candle. Feelings of happiness and contentment settled over her as she snuggled down under the bedclothes and fell instantly asleep.

Mrs Vale agreed to Ellen having an hour off to show Maddie the village, and the two women set off along the street towards the police office and the barracks. Hoping to see John, Ellen kept a keen look out for him. 'Would you like to look at the shops? There aren't many, but you need to know who sells what. And what would you like to see, Stella?'

But as always the girl hid behind her mother and wouldn't answer.

'Sounds good to me,' Maddie replied.

'Oh, look, here comes John, and I think he's got Harry with him.'

'Who's Harry?' asked Maddie.

'He travelled here from Hobart with us and is a police constable too.' Ellen explained. 'Hello,' she called as John saw her and a wide smile lit his face.

'Hello there. Ah, it's Maddie isn't it?' he asked.

'That's me. How are you, John?'

'I'm fine. I'm glad you've arrived, now I can ask the Chief to set the wheels in motion about this girl and myself getting married.' Putting his arm about her shoulders, John dropped a kiss on Ellen's cheek.

'How do, I'm Harry, seeing as no one's bothered to introduce us.' The man proffered his hand to Maddie.

'I'm sorry, I was forgetting myself,' John chortled. 'Let me introduce you. Maddie this is Harry. Harry, this is Maddie.' They all laughed and turned to stroll along the road together, Stella bringing up the rear. No one had thought to introduce her.

It didn't take long to walk the length of Bothwell and as they reached the Church, Maddie turned to Ellen and said, 'I think we should soon be getting back, don't you?'

Ellen pulled a face, but had to agree. 'I suppose so. We were told not to be long.' She tilted her face up to John. 'You will see the Chief, won't you?'

'Of course I will, my lovely girl. Just try and stop me.'

Her face beaming with happiness, Ellen said goodbye to the two men and, taking Maddie's arm, hurried her back along to the hotel.

Shaking her head in mock sorrow, Maddie said her goodbyes. 'I expect I'll see you again soon.' Then chuckled as Harry gave her a sly wink.

As the two men watched Ellen and Maddie walk away, Harry said, 'Cor, I'd like to get my arms around her.'

John gazed at him in amazement. 'Maddie! For goodness sake man, she'd eat you alive!'

'I know and wouldn't it be lovely? I mean it, John me old mate,

I've taken a right shine to her. And the little girl, what's her name? She's so quiet you forget she's there.'

Shaking his head, John said with a laugh, 'That's Stella, now come on let's get on with some work or we'll be in trouble and I want to stay on the right side of the Chief.'

A little while later when he entered the Chief's office, John felt his nerves getting the better of him. Why he felt nervous, he didn't know, but his insides were doing a jig.

'Well, Ryan, what do you want? No trouble is there?' The Chief didn't like trouble.

'No sir. I'd wondered if you could do something for me, please sir.'

'Go on man, what is it?' The beetle brows waggled dangerously.

'I want to get permission to be married, sir. I think you have to apply to the Governor's office in Hobart, so I was wondering if you could do that for me, sir.' John felt the heat round his collar and perspiration ran down his neck. 'Please,' he added quickly.

'I see. And who is it you want to marry then? You haven't been here long enough to meet someone surely?' the Chief leaned back in his chair and eyed the young man in front of him with curiosity.

'It's Mrs Heath, sir. The young woman you met the other day when she asked permission to visit Mrs Hargreaves.' John crossed himself. 'May that poor lady rest in peace.'

'You mean that funny little woman from the hotel?' The Chief looked amazed.

John gazed at the man as though seeing him for the first time. Funny little woman? What did he mean? He cleared his throat and said, 'Er, yes sir.'

'Well,' the chief shrugged, 'each to his own I suppose. Right, I'll get a letter off to Hobart in tomorrow's dispatch bag. It shouldn't take too long to hear back. She's of good character I presume. Perhaps Mrs Vale at the hotel can vouch for her?'

'I'm sure she can, sir. Ellen, Mrs Heath that is, is doing very well there.'

'Good. Right, off you go, Ryan, work to do and all that.'

'Yes, sir. Thank you sir.' John backed out of the room, feeling drained. Why did it always feel like dealing with the headmaster when seeing the Chief?

When John called at the back door of the hotel the following morning to give Ellen the news, her squeals of delight could be heard half a street away. Mrs Vale came rushing out to see what was wrong.

'Heath, what is all that noise?'

'I'm sorry Mrs Vale, but John's just asked for permission for us to be married.'

A frown creased Mrs Vale's brow. 'I see. Mmm, well, would you please celebrate more quietly, although why anyone should want to get married at all is beyond me? Never could be bothered myself. Back to work now if you please.'

As the woman turned to go back inside, John asked her quickly, 'The Chief wondered if you would vouch for Ellen, Ma'am?'

Swinging back to face them, a smile crept over the usually stern countenance. 'I'd be honoured, of course. Do tell the Chief that, won't you?'

'Thank you, Mrs Vale.' John doffed his hat.

'Yes, thank you Mrs Vale,' Ellen said excitedly and as the woman hurried away, they hugged and kissed. 'Oh John is it really going to happen? Are we to be married soon?' Excitement filled her so completely that Ellen wished that the wedding could take place there and then.

The next few days passed in a blur for Ellen. All she could do was worry if the longed for permission would arrive, and how soon. Her restless mind wandered to the extent that even Maura had to admonish her for not cleaning properly. 'Where food is concerned, you can't be too careful, you know?'

'I'm sorry, I just can't help worrying.'

'Look, there's nothing to stop you and John getting permission now is there? You're both settled here in Bothwell and have been of good behaviour since arriving, so stop fretting and concentrate on your work. Otherwise we could all be ill and we don't want that if we have a wedding to organise.' Maura moved briskly across to finish the vegetables, leaving Ellen open-mouthed and wide eyed.

Her wedding; she could be planning her wedding in a few days time! Oh thank you God. Then she set about scrubbing the wooden table with great vigour.

Five days later John appeared at the back door, his face alight with joy and Ellen ran into his arms. 'Is it here?'

'Yes, my lovely girl, it's here. We can be married as soon as we like. I'm just off to see the reverend. He'll want to see us both beforehand of course and I'll come and let you know when that's to be.'

'John, we will be happy, won't we?' Suddenly Ellen felt half-afraid of the happiness within her.

'I'm sure we will sweetheart. Now off you go and tell your friends, I'll see you later.'

The urge to turn somersaults was hard to resist, but resist she must. It would be most unladylike to do such a thing. In the privacy of her room she hugged her arms about herself and chuckled delightedly. At last her life was turning round and she had another chance at happiness.

With the wedding now almost upon her, Ellen suddenly realised that she had nothing to wear. Her two old gowns were far too tatty, although she had made them do for the once a week jaunt to Sunday morning service. Then another thought struck her; where were she and John going to live?

As she voiced these concerns to Maddie and Maura, she saw the look of sadness on their faces. 'Well, dear,' said Maura, 'I don't know what you can do. Dresses are very expensive to make so you'll have to make do with what you've got. As regards living arrangements, I suppose you could stay here and meet John each day.'

'Oh no, I want to live with him properly, like man and wife.'

'You can't possibly live in that wooden hut he calls his home,' Maddie told her. 'Try not to worry, I'm sure John has thought about it.'

But when she saw him the following day, it was clear that he hadn't given it any thought at all. 'My lovely girl, I'm sorry, I just didn't think. Don't worry, I'll see what I can do, there must be somewhere we can rent cheaply here in Bothwell. It won't be much mind, because although I receive a small wage now that I'm a free man, it's not very much.' He pulled her into his arms. 'The priest wants to see us this evening, so go and ask Mrs Vale if you can have an hour off.'

'Can't he see us in the daytime?'

'No, he has his parishioners to visit then and they're spread pretty far and wide. The poor man is the only minister in the area. He's a nice man though, Scottish.'

'You won't mind him marrying us though will you? I know you would have liked an Irish priest.'

He laughed. 'No, I'll be civil to him, I promise. Now off you go and see Mrs Vale, and I'll pick you up about six o'clock, so be ready. Bye my sweet.'

Hurrying to ask for time off, Ellen felt her insides heave. The enormity of what she was doing hit her full force and she thought of Robert Heath back home in England. What could she tell the priest if he asked about her married status? She'd have to ask John what he was going to say, she supposed. Rapping the door with her knuckles, she opened it and went into the parlour. Mrs Vale and Maura were bending over the table studying something and looked up in surprise as Ellen walked forward. The paper was quickly turned over and Maura straightened herself, gave a slight grin and left hurriedly, whilst Mrs Vale pushed back some stray hair and fixed a smile on her face. 'Yes, Heath what do you want?'

'Please, Mrs Vale, may I have an hour off this evening to go and see the reverend at the Church? I know it's inconvenient, but it's the only time he can see us.'

'Mmmm,' Mrs Vale seemed to consider the idea. 'Very well, but no more than an hour, understand?'

'Yes, Mrs Vale, thank you very much.' Ellen did a bob and left the room with a feeling of relief, dashing back to the kitchen ready to help Maura with the midday meal.

'Everything all right?' the woman asked.

'Yes thanks. I had to ask for time off to see the vicar.'

'Mrs Vale isn't such an ogre, Ellen, now is she?'

'No, I suppose not once you get to know her. I wonder if I should ask her advice about finding somewhere to live. John doesn't seem to have much idea how to go about such things.'

'You could do worse, at least she'll give you a sympathetic ear.' Maura deftly rolled and folded the pastry she was making for the meat pie. 'In the meantime, could you chop those onions for me please?'

Ellen frowned. It was unlike Maura to be so little concerned for her problems, but then she was busy, she mused, and set about her least favourite task. Onions always made her cry, and she wasn't a pretty sight when she cried.

Just then Maddie came into the kitchen. 'Seen John have you?' she asked Ellen, who nodded. 'What has he said to you for goodness sake?'

Puzzled, Ellen turned to look at her friend. 'What do you mean?'

Just then Maddie saw the onions and laughed. 'Oops, sorry, I thought you were really crying.'

The three women laughed and Ellen felt better. Now everything should work out fine.

True to his word, John arrived at six o'clock to collect her. 'I'm very nervous about what he'll ask us,' Ellen said.

'It's only a formality, they have to do it before they can call the banns.'

'Oh yes, I'd forgotten about them. Does that still apply here?'

'Yes, my love. Don't forget the Church is universal. This is a

Church that has to cover most Anglican religions and the rules are the same here as at home.'

'What do we say when he asks if we're free to marry? I don't want to lie, John, but I can't think of any other way.'

John hugged her arm to his side. 'We'll both say we're widowed, that should do. After all, our spouses aren't here to complain are they?'

'Mine wouldn't if he was, and I don't think he'd care what I did as long as I wasn't around him.'

As they walked into the Church, Ellen shivered. The daylight was beginning to fade outside and here inside it was almost completely dark with only a few lighted candles to lift the gloom. A tall thin man in a black frock coat stood and turned to greet them as they walked up the aisle. He held out his hand in welcome and shook theirs in turn. 'Good evening, I'm Reverend McDonald. Come and sit awhile so that I can explain the wedding vows to you, then we'll run through the order of service.' He led them to the front pew and indicated that they sit.

Ellen felt very self-conscious in her dowdy gown, and clasped her work worn hands tightly in her lap as the man asked a few questions about where they were living and what work they did. She thought that rather pointless in John's case as he was in his uniform, but she supposed it all had to be done according to rule.

'And you are both free to marry I assume?' The reverend gentleman at last asked the question Ellen had been dreading.

John answered without hesitation. 'We are, sir. We were both widowed before we came here.'

One eyebrow lifted just a fraction as the vicar turned his gaze onto Ellen. She tried to keep her voice steady as she answered, 'That's right. My husband died of a fever,' She felt the colour begin to rise and knew she must say something else. 'And then just after I arrived, my little girl died.' She wiped away the tear that had been squeezed from one eye. 'So you see, sir, I am all alone in the world now.'

The Reverend McDonald reached out and took one of her hands. 'Oh, my poor dear lady, I am so sorry. I'm sure God will give this new union his blessing.'

They both thanked him and soon it was all over and they were out in the fresh evening air once more. 'That was inspired, Ellen. Put him right off his burrowing questions.'

'I hate lying, you know that, but I just had to say something. May God forgive me for using my daughter's death for my own ends.' Ellen felt sick and leaned on John's arm as they hurried back to the hotel.

'All will be well, my sweet. Now we have a date set, we can let everyone know. I've asked Harry to stand with me and he's delighted. Are you going to have any maids?'

'No, John. I just want a quiet wedding. We can't afford to do anything special, but as long as I'm with you, that's all I ask.'

'Bless you, Ellen. Sure I'm the luckiest man alive to be marrying such a wonderful girl.'

Ellen laughed then. 'I'm hardly a girl, but thank you. I'm lucky too.' She smiled up into his eyes. 'It's a shame I have to be back to help in the dining room, we could have dropped off at your room for a while.'

'I suppose you do have to go back?'

'Yes I do. Mrs Vale will skin me alive if I don't. I'll see you tomorrow as it's my day off, so we haven't to wait long to kiss and cuddle.'

'I look forward to it, my darling Ellen. See you tomorrow then, sleep tight. I love you.' He kissed her deeply and then watched as she hurried up the steps and in through the front door.

Later that night as she and Maddie prepared for bed, Ellen held up the slightly better of her two dresses. 'Do you think I could do anything with this to make it look better?'

Maddie eyed the gown and grimaced. 'It's very dirty and torn. I suppose you could try washing it, although I wouldn't be surprised if it didn't fall apart.' Yawning widely, she climbed into bed. 'See you in the morning. G'night.' Then she turned over next to her daughter, and fell asleep.

Tears threatened as Ellen rolled into her own bed. Why did everyone seem not to care all of a sudden? She lay on her side and tried to imagine being married to John, but somehow the pictures conjured up in her mind were nothing like the dreams she had been having for the past few weeks. No pretty wedding dress, no lovely new house. It will work out, she told herself, determinedly. It must. I'll make it somehow. But just at the moment, she didn't know how.

At least her day off cheered her up. John was his usual loving self and they enjoyed a passionate and fun afternoon in his cosy room. Ellen looked about her. 'We can't live here can we? There isn't room for one thing, and there's nowhere for washing or cooking.'

'Stop your worrying, my love. It's all in hand, so trust me and come to me once more before you have to go.' John wrapped his arms about her and nuzzled her neck, the one action guaranteed to have the desired effect.

Ellen melted into his arms and gave herself up to the delicious sensations coursing through her. She knew that with John beside her, she could face anything and pushed any worries she might have to the back of her mind.

When she arrived back at the hotel a little later, Maddie gave her a questioning look. 'I must say, that young man certainly brings the roses to your cheeks. I wish I could get some of what he's offering.' Her throaty laugh rang about the kitchen.

'Just for your information, you might get the chance,' Ellen told her archly.

A frown creased Maddie's brow. 'What do you mean?'

'Someone has his eye on you, so you'd better look out.' Holding up her hand, Ellen added, 'It's no use asking me any more, because my lips are sealed. You'll just have to wait and see.'

'You are incorrigible, Ellen Heath. Now you've got me guessing. There aren't that many men it can be, as I've not met anyone since I've been here. Anyway, who would want a woman with a child in tow? I know things are easier now that Stella goes to that little school room each day, but even so…' Then with a look of horror, Maddie asked, 'It is a man, I suppose?'

An explosion of laughter escaped Ellen's lips. 'Of course it's a man. What do you think we're like here in Bothwell?'

'There was plenty of that went on in the women's factory, believe me. I was approached several times.' She raised her eyebrows. 'Weren't you?'

'No, I was not. I'd have punched any woman trying to get off with me, I can tell you.' Ellen was indignant.

Maddie became serious. 'Some of the women were desperate you know. Can't understand it myself, but I suppose if you have urges it must be like an itch you need to scratch.'

Shaking her head, Ellen went to help lay up the tables for the evening meal. She hoped it wouldn't be too busy tonight because tiredness was rapidly overtaking her. An afternoon with John always left her feeling drained. A smile curved her lips. It was definitely worth it though.

Two weeks later she again broached the subject of what to wear on her wedding day. They sat around the huge, well-scrubbed kitchen table eating supper when Ellen said sadly, 'It's only a week now until my wedding and I really don't know what to do, I haven't anything

155

suitable to wear. I don't suppose any of you have a dress I can borrow?'

Nessie giggled. 'I don't think any of mine would go round you.' Ellen shot her a venomous glance.

Maura, Vera and Maddie shrugged and looked vaguely bored and concentrated on their food, to leave Ellen feeling a nuisance for bringing up the subject of the wedding yet again. She sighed and tried to swallow a fork-full of mashed potato, but it stuck in her throat. Was no one interested? Most women she had known always showed excitement at the prospect of a wedding. Perhaps I'm just not interesting enough, she thought and kept quiet for the rest of the meal, listening idly to the chatter that soon started up. That night she tossed and turned, unable to get thoughts of her wedding out of her mind. What could she wear? Where could they go after the service? Who was coming anyway? No one had shown any sympathy for her plight and, Ellen admitted to herself, it hurt. It was spoiling the whole thing by not having anyone to discuss details with. Even Maddie, who usually took an avid interest in everything she did, seemed disinclined to help. Tears ran down across the bridge of her nose and sunk into her pillow before she eventually sank into an uneasy sleep.

In the morning, she awoke to Maddie calling her name. 'Come on, you'll be late for breakfast.'

Ellen forced one eye open, and groaned. It was still dark, what on earth was Maddie getting her up for? She yawned widely and swung her feet to the floor. 'It's still the middle of the night, woman. What are you doing up?'

'We've to go to see Mrs Vale before breakfast. Now, move yourself.' Maddie, with Stella following closely behind, flounced out of the room to leave Ellen struggling into her clothes, before walking unsteadily along the corridor after her.

To her surprise, besides Maddie, Vera, Maura and Nessie also stood in the small parlour, turning to look at her as she entered. Blinking in the light from the oil lamp, Ellen moved forward, dread filling her. What had she done now? Racking her brains, she honestly couldn't think of anything, so stood up straight and awaited her punishment. It was strangely silent in the room and Ellen began to feel even more uneasy. And why, she wondered, were they all looking at her?

Soon all became clear. Mrs Vale, a smile on her face, came round the small table and took her hand, while Ellen did her best not to flinch at the unaccustomed gesture. 'Now, my dear, I understand you are having trouble finding a suitable dress for your wedding on

Saturday?'

The question took Ellen so much by surprise that she stood open-mouthed for a moment before she could recover herself and answer. 'Er, yes, I am. Mine are both so worn that they'd look rather awful.'

'Would that do you?' Mrs Vale pointed to the door behind Ellen, who then turned around. What she saw had her gaping. There, hanging behind the door was a beautiful cream silk gown, which although plain, glowed richly in the lamplight. 'It might need altering here and there, but you are welcome to borrow it for the day,' Mrs Vale was saying.

Ellen was lost for words and looked first from one person and then to another. They were all smiling and Maddie was the first to speak, 'Well, aren't you pleased with it? Thank Mrs Vale, it is she who is lending it to you.'

Ellen felt her jaw move up and down, but no sound came from her mouth. She had never seen such a lovely dress in all her life, how could she possibly borrow it. Someone might spill a drink down it, or it might get torn… Her mind whirled as she tried to speak.

Then Mrs Vale took pity on her and went across to lift the dress from its hanger and hold it against Ellen's front. It smelled faintly of lavender and mothballs, something Ellen hadn't smelt for years. She looked up into Mrs Vale's eyes and was astounded to see tears lurking there.

'I-I don't know what to say. It's the most wonderful dress I've ever seen. Are you sure you want me to wear it? I mean, it might get spoilt or something…' she tailed off, lost for words yet again.

'Try it on,' Mrs Vale said, her usual stern self once more, 'then we can see where it needs altering. Maura is good with a needle and will see to that. Now come on quickly, we haven't all day.'

Maddie moved forward to help Ellen struggle out of her work dress and then slipped the cool silk over her head. 'There, it's a little large, but nothing that can't be put right, eh Maura?'

Maura came to crouch in front of Ellen and studied the dress, pulling it a little this way and then a little the other. 'This'll be fine, I can alter it in no time.' She smiled up at Ellen. 'You silly goose, you didn't really think we'd let you go to church in your own drab dress, did you?'

'I thought no one was bothered about what I was going to wear, and now it's so close to the day I was in despair.' She brightened then, her heart soaring with gratitude. 'Thank you Mrs Vale. I will look after it I promise. Oh, it's so beautiful. I think even I might look a picture in such a gown.' She chuckled. 'And won't John be surprised?'

They all laughed, and Vera said, 'Don't go telling him either, keep it quiet until he sees you on the day.'

Nessie then came to take Ellen's hand, saying shyly, 'I've got a dress as well and, if you'll have me, will stand as your maid.'

'Oh, how lovely, Nessie, yes of course I'll have you.' Ellen hugged the skinny girl, aware of how her bones stuck out from her flesh. Maura winked and shook her head almost imperceptibly, and Ellen wondered what the woman meant. Obviously all would be revealed later.

Then Stella lisped, 'And I'm to be your flower girl, Auntie Ellen.'

So unaccustomed to hearing the child speak, Ellen stared at her for a few seconds before bending down to kiss her cheek.

'I'll be thrilled to have you with me, Stella. Two maids, aren't I a lucky woman?'

Mrs Vale clapped her hands. 'Right now ladies, breakfast, then we have work to do.' She turned to Ellen. 'I'm glad you like the dress, Heath and I hope you enjoy your day whilst wearing it. Someone, help her take it off now please?'

'Thank you again, Mrs Vale. It is good of you to lend something so special.' As the other women filed out of the room, she whispered to Mrs Vale, 'Was it your wedding dress?'

The woman bit hard into her bottom lip before answering, 'Yes. Unfortunately my young man was killed before we were married, so it has never been worn. That is a secret, Heath. I don't want all and sundry knowing my business, understood?'

'Yes, of course,' said Ellen, suddenly feeling great sadness for this hard woman, who had once been young and probably madly in love like herself. How cruel life was sometimes. She guessed that there were probably many women like poor Mrs Vale who had never tasted happiness, and here she was, getting a second chance at it. Soberly Ellen left the room and hurried into the kitchen for breakfast where the others were already tucking into Maura's delicious creamy oats and slices of crisp bread topped with an egg.

Ellen worked hard that day. Knowing that her friends had gone to so much trouble for her brought a warm glow. She knew she was lucky, but still a feeling of annoyance niggled at her for the way they had kept her guessing. I suppose they did that to make the surprise more special, she thought, and it had certainly worked.

As the week progressed, Ellen fretted about the wedding day. Her friends at the hotel had said they would attend the service, but Ellen had no idea what she and John would do after it. And where would

158

they go? When she'd pressed John on the matter, he'd looked affronted and said, 'Don't you trust me at all Ellen Heath? Everything will be fine.'

That was the trouble, she didn't trust him: not completely. He always had a glib answer for everything, but half the time Ellen was sure he was just keeping her quiet. Still she was determined to enjoy the wedding and it thrilled her to think that when they left the church she would be Mrs John Ryan. Ellen Ryan. She liked the sound of that. First she had been Ellen Newland, then Ellen Heath and now another new name. A pang of guilt shot through her when she thought of her family back home. They wouldn't have any idea who Ellen Ryan was. Did they ever think of her? Wonder what she was doing? As always the thoughts saddened her, so she pushed them away, deciding to say a prayer for them all when she stood at the alter speaking her vows.

As his wedding day approached, John began to feel despair. In a few days time he was marrying his wonderful Ellen, but so far his search for somewhere to live had been fruitless. There weren't that many cottages in Bothwell, and those who lived in them were loath to give them up. The Chief had been no help, nor any of the other constables that he'd asked. Everyone shaking their heads and looking at him as though he'd asked for gold. I might as well have done, he thought for all the good it had done. There was nothing for it, he would go and see Mrs Vale. Perhaps they could have Ellen's room at the hotel for a while. Just until something came up. He shivered. The woman always made him feel like a naughty child, and he viewed seeing her with trepidation.

CHAPTER 13

September the fifteenth dawned bright and sunny, and Ellen lay in her bed for a few moments savouring the thought that this was her wedding day. The service wasn't until after lunch and she had to work this morning, but she looked forward to the time when she would go into the parlour to collect the dress. The glorious cream silk gown now fitted her like a glove; it's high neck and long sleeves adorned with rows of tiny buttons and the long flowing skirt hung in soft folds about her legs. The afternoon when Maura had finished the alterations was etched in Ellen's mind. She had stood in the middle of the parlour feeling like a queen, with even Mrs Vale congratulating her on how pretty she looked.

Ellen had felt somewhat amused by this declaration, as she had never considered herself at all pretty. In fact she thought her face rather plain, except perhaps for her eyes, which, she had been told, held in their brown depths, liveliness and vivacity.

She struggled onto one elbow and looked across at where Maddie was stirring and noticed how the sunlight was filtering through the high window to throw a beam of light across the room. Perhaps that was a good omen, Ellen thought, because it had never happened before. But now signs of spring were appearing everywhere, with bushes of yellow blossoms bringing a golden blush to the surrounding hills, and in the village, the gardens were coming alive with flowers that Ellen couldn't put a name to. Her heart filled with joy - what a wonderful day for a wonderful occasion. She slipped out of her bed and went to stand by Maddie's. 'Are you awake yet?' she asked in a hoarse whisper.

'Just about. Is it time for breakfast yet?'

Ellen punched her friend playfully on the arm. 'You! All you ever worry about is your food. Yes it is, so come on, we've a lot to do before lunchtime.'

'Why, is something happening then that I should know about?' But Maddie's laugh belied her pretend innocence.

'I'm going to the kitchen now, don't be long, Maddie, will you?'

'No, I'll be with you in a minute. I just want to check my dress isn't too creased for this afternoon. And make sure Stella's frock still fits. That girl is eating like a horse since we've been here. It must be the country air'

'I thought you did that last night?' Ellen queried.

'It won't hurt to have another look. We can't all be dolled up to the nines.' Maddie made a droll face.

Light-heartedly, Ellen hurried off to see if breakfast was ready; nothing, however important, ever dampened her appetite.

Maura was already standing at the stove stirring the large pot of porridge and turned to smile as Ellen entered. 'You're up bright and early, and looking very perky I must say.'

'It's a lovely day at the moment,' Ellen nodded toward the window, 'do you think the sunshine will last?'

'I should think so and it might be warmer than of late and that can only be a good thing. We don't want us all freezing to death in our finery, do we?'

Becoming serious, Ellen walked across the vast room and touched Maura's arm shyly. 'Thank you for what you've done to alter Mrs Vale's dress. I never thought I'd wear something like that in all my life.' Then she frowned. 'Tell me, if Mrs Vale has never been married why is she called Mrs?'

A slight raising of one eyebrow was the only indication Maura gave as to why Ellen should assume that Mrs Vale had never been married, but she answered in level tones. 'It's a courtesy title. All housekeepers are called Mrs.'

'Oh, I see,' said Ellen, although she didn't. Why should women be called one thing when they were another. She shrugged, deciding that the matter wasn't worth worrying about, and took the proffered bowl of hot oats to the table, where she could sit and dream about the rest of the day.

Harry Askew was standing as John's best man and, to Ellen's astonishment, the Chief had agreed to give her away. They had been at a loss as to who they could ask to take this important stand, until Mrs Vale had suggested the Chief. Ellen had gone to ask him in person and was delighted when he readily said that he would be delighted. And with Nessie and Stella as her maids, the day seemed set fair. All the staff from the Falls of Clyde hotel were going, and so were some of John's colleagues, so the tiny church would be at least half filled, something that Ellen was glad of. She was at one time having visions of an empty church, with just John, herself and the Minister in attendance.

Later that morning, as she took some rubbish out to the waste bin in the back yard, Ellen saw Maddie and Vera holding whispered discussion in the long corridor by the staff bedrooms. She called out a greeting, but when the two women turned and saw her they stopped talking and moved apart, Maddie coming toward Ellen, shaking a duster. 'Haven't you any work to do?' she asked.

A frown creased Ellen's brow. 'Yes, I'm clearing out the rubbish. What were you and Vera talking about?'

Maddie looked out into the garden through the glass-panelled door and said nonchalantly, 'Oh, we were just discussing the weather. Saying what a lovely day you've got for the wedding. I must get on, everything has to be finished before lunch.' She hurried off, calling over her shoulder, 'See you later.'

How strange, thought Ellen. Maddie isn't usually so offhand. Oh well, everyone's so busy today and I suppose I must get a move on. As she stepped back into the kitchen Maura smiled and asked, 'Ellen, can you go and see if room ten is in order, please? I know the bed is made, but I'm not sure about the towels and soap or if the fire is laid.'

Cursing, Ellen went to check. She was sure room ten was all in order as she'd cleaned it herself only yesterday and no one had stayed in it last night. Very few of the rooms were taken in the winter months, so Vera had told her, but once the summer arrived, you had travellers dropping in all the time and the hotel became really busy. When Ellen asked her who came to stay, Vera had remarked rather sourly, that it was mainly salesmen looking to make money from the landowners living around Bothwell. Some of them were fairly wealthy now apparently, what with sheep and cattle farming. This interested Ellen as she'd wondered how people made a living here in this small community.

As she hurried up the stairs, Ellen smiled to herself. Now John and me will be a part of it all, she thought happily.

Seeing that the room was all in order, she hurried back down stairs, but was waylaid in the hallway by Mrs Vale. 'Ah, Heath, can you come and help me sort the laundry?'

Puzzled, Ellen followed the woman back up the stairs and into the linen room. She'd never been asked to do this before, usually Vera or Nessie did it. But as she entered, she saw that there were bales of new sheets and bundles of pillowcases on the floor. 'We've just has a new consignment of bedding and I need to check it in,' said Mrs Vale. 'I thought it would be better for you to have something occupying your mind, otherwise the time will drag.' She gave one of her rare smiles and Ellen settled happily to holding the list while Mrs Vale ticked off so many of this and some of those. How she was helping Ellen didn't know as she could neither read nor write, but Mrs Vale seemed quite happy to have her there so she stood patiently until it was finished. 'There, nearly done.' Mrs Vale consulted the watch pinned to her black blouse. 'Then there will just time for a little lunch before you have to get ready.' As the last sheet was placed neatly on the shelf, the woman opened the door and said, 'Right, let's go down into the parlour now.'

Ellen wondered why they were going to the parlour. Usually lunch was served in the kitchen. But as she entered, there was everyone sitting about with plates of sandwiches on their knees and, on the table a tray of tea things. 'We're just having a light lunch for today,' Maura said as Ellen looked about her in confusion. 'We don't want a heavy meal when we've to stand in church, do we?'

Not being too sure where her next meal was coming from, Ellen was rather dismayed to find only sandwiches, but took some onto her plate and sat on the chair proffered by Mrs Vale. An extra chair had been brought in from the dining room so that everyone had a seat, and somewhere inside her Ellen began to suspect something was afoot.

There had been a lot of whispering going on, and on more than one occasion people had stopped talking when she entered a room. Trying not to show that she noticed anything different, Ellen sat and ate her lunch, but it was difficult because excitement was filling her now that it was almost time to get ready.

Her gaze wandered round to the back of the door where the dress hung. It was so beautiful. Then her eyes filled with tears. If only ma and da could see me in it, she thought sadly.

'Hey, what's with the tears?' Maddie asked, breaking into her reverie.

When she explained, everyone voiced their sorrow at the self-same thing. Nessie spoke quietly from her seat on the chaise-lounge, 'I felt the same when I tried my dress on. It would be lovely if there was a way of sending them all a picture of us, wouldn't it?'

'Unfortunately we don't have an artist amongst us, and even if we did, we could never pose long enough for him to paint us all,' Vera laughed.

This lightened the atmosphere and soon there was a general buzz of chatter in the small, cosy room.

Then Mrs Vale clapped her hands. 'Come on everyone, time for us to get changed.' She sounded so excited that it made Ellen's insides turn over as well, and she felt that Mrs Vale and the others were almost a whole new family. 'Ellen, I think it will be best if you go up and change in my room. Maddie will come with you to help you. There are clean towels and soap at your disposal and we've lit the fire, so off you go.'

Astonished, Ellen stared at the woman before her. Mrs Vale's room was far superior to any of the other staff, as her position warranted.

'What about you, Mrs Vale?' She asked.

'I'll be fine. I can change afterwards, it won't take me long.' The woman was positively beaming, and as Maddie left the room with the dress over her arm, a rather perplexed Ellen followed in her wake.

Eyeing Mrs Vale's room with awe, she whispered, 'I can't believe this, can you? It's a lovely room, very different to ours downstairs.'

Maddie signalled to her to get her dress unbuttoned and then helped pull it up over her head. 'Here, there's warm water in the basin, so get a good wash. We don't want grubby marks on that lovely dress.'

Ellen did as she was told and took great care to wash, paying extra attention to her neck and underarms, while Maddie busied herself smoothing out a camisole to go under the wedding gown. Where had that come from? Ellen wondered, her head beginning to whirl with the wonder of it all. This was going to be a marvellous day; she could sense it. As soon as the slip was on, Maddie lifted the dress from its hanger, looking flushed and out of breath.

'Here we are,' she said quietly. 'My you'll look a picture in this, Ellen. You really will. I hope John appreciates all the hard work.'

'I'm sure he will,' Ellen giggled. 'Oh Maddie, I never thought to have such a day. I assumed it would be a quick visit to the church and then out again.' She pursed her lips. 'Although what we're going to do afterwards, I haven't any idea.'

Maddie grinned. 'Perhaps he'll take you to that teashop along the road. A nice cup of tea and a cream cake, then he'll whisk you off to his room in the barracks.'

'To be honest, I can't think of anything else.'

'Oh well, don't worry about that now. Let's have a look at you.' Maddie pulled the gown into place over Ellen's hips and then stood back to check all was well. 'Let me see to your hair. I think I can do something to improve its usual bird's nest appearance.'

Indignantly, Ellen obeyed and sat impatiently on a small stool while Maddie brushed, pulled and prodded and then, with a satisfied,

'M-mm, that's better,' pulled Ellen to her feet and turned her toward the full-length mirror that fronted the wardrobe.

Staring in disbelief, Ellen stood looking at the stranger before her. 'Oh, thank you Maddie, you've done wonders with my hair.' She put tentative fingers up to touch the shiny curls framing her face and then the ringlets hanging about her shoulders. Her brown eyes glowed. 'And the dress? I don't know what to say. It's like looking at someone else. Someone I once saw in a picture book. A princess I think she was.'

Chuckling, Maddie said, 'Well, come on, princess, we'd better be going. Ah, here's Nessie and Stella. My, you two do look splendid, don't they, Ellen?'

Nessie positively glowed, and for once Stella was smiling happily, the little wicker basket of flowers held proudly in front of her. Ellen stepped forward to give the girls a hug. 'Yes, you both look so pretty, I shall have to watch that John doesn't take the wrong woman as his bride.' They all laughed and then Maddie led the way from the room and down the long curving staircase.

At the foot of the stairs stood the Chief, and Ellen was delighted to see his eyes light appreciatively as she descended toward him. 'My dear Mrs Heath, you look charming. Absolutely charming.'

'Not Mrs Heath for much longer,' Mrs Vale corrected him. 'I think Ellen for today, don't you?'

'Of course. You look lovely, Ellen,' he said. 'And Miss Smith,' the Chief beamed at Nessie, 'what a picture you make. And who have we here? What a charming little girl.' He shook Stella's hand solemnly. 'Now, young ladies it's nearly time for us to go. Are you all right walking, Ellen? Or should I get the small rig?'

'It's such a lovely day, I think it would be nice to walk.' Ellen took his arm, feeling very strange indeed. Here she was little Ellen Newland, born of a poor village family back home in England, walking on the arm of the Chief of Police in Bothwell. It was all she could do to stop the laughter that was bubbling up inside from spilling over.

As they walked along the street, Nessie and Stella following closely behind, people stopped and smiled, with some even emerging from the shops or houses to wish her well. Ellen had never felt so elegant or important in her life. What a day this was. One she would remember for the rest of her life.

Entering the church through the huge oak doors, she was surprised to see so many people sitting in the pews, all dressed finely and smiling widely. Up the aisle they stepped, slowly but steadily, as the organ thundered out a rousing tune, and all the while her eyes were on John where he stood waiting for her at the Alter rail, his face alight with pleasure. And at his side, looking the smartest she'd ever seen him, was Harry.

Ellen's heart fluttered so hard that she hoped she wasn't going to faint. As they stopped alongside, she stole a look at John. How splendid he looked, with his uniform cleaned and pressed, his hair shining in the light from the window behind the Alter, his moustache trimmed to perfection and his blue eyes full of love. The flutter became a pounding, so loud she was sure everyone in the church must hear it.

Then the Chief took her hand from his arm and placed it on John's, and stepped back a pace.

The Reverend McDonald was standing before them, his face sombre, ready to start the service, of which Ellen said later, she remembered very little, except for the moment when the slim gold band was slipped onto her finger.

Soon the service was over and Ellen and John turned to face the congregation as husband and wife. He held her arm tightly beneath his own as they started on the journey back down the aisle, with so many happy faces about them, that Ellen wondered who they could all be. She was sure she hadn't made the acquaintance of so many people in Bothwell in the few weeks since she'd arrived, but it warmed her to know that everyone was wishing both of them good luck for their future together. She glimpsed Maura and Vera, both dabbing at damp eyes with a hankie, and Mrs Vale stood looking proudly as they passed.

On the steps outside the church, someone placed a small bouquet of flowers into Ellen's hands. She smiled her thanks, but had no idea who they came from. Then as they paused to thank people for coming, John whispered in her ear, 'That was the Chief's wife.'

'How kind of her. John isn't this wonderful? I can't imagine who all these people are, but they've made the day very special.'

'They certainly have, my sweet. It's a grand do, I must say. And you look as lovely as I've ever seen you.'

'That's thanks to Maddie and Mrs Vale,' Ellen said softly. 'Shall we go?'

Then, feeling like royalty, the happy couple led the way back along the street toward the hotel. Ellen wasn't sure why they were going back there, until she remembered that she had to return the dress; a thought that saddened her. Never had she felt so good, so blessed. It was a shame the day had to end so soon.

John led her up the steps of the hotel, in through the front door and into the vast hallway. There stood Mrs Vale, who had hurried ahead of them, looking resplendent in dark blue taffeta, her hand extended. 'Welcome home, Ellen and John. Please go into the dining room.'

Ellen blinked at John, then led the way into the room. Her eyes popped at the sight that met them. The tables were laid out with food and flowers decorated the room. Maddie hurried over to the bewildered pair. 'Come on, this way, you have to sit at the top table.' She almost dragged Ellen in her wake as she moved toward the table nearest the window, and showed them to their seats.

'Did you know about this?' John asked his new wife.

'No, did you?'

He shook his head and grinned, 'No, but isn't it grand?'

Ellen was too overcome to answer, and sat numbly watching as the Chief, his wife; Maddie and Harry, Nessie, Stella and Mrs Vale came to sit alongside them. The rest of the crowd, including a load of men in uniform, who she presumed were John's guests, sat themselves at the other tables, until the room was full of noisy, chattering people.

Still too stunned to speak, or even think straight, Ellen felt as though she was in a bubble, terrified that at any moment it would burst, and all this was only a dream.

Food was served, drinks poured and John chatted easily with those around them, but Ellen sat in a stupor, watching as though at someone else's party. The food was delicious and it dawned on Ellen that Maura and Vera must have spent many hours preparing it. Becoming suddenly aware of this, she looked around the crowded room for them, but seeing them both busy serving yet more food, decided to give her thanks later. And Mrs Vale too, because it must have been her who set it all up. Gradually she relaxed and began to join in the talk. Harry was on fine form and Ellen was sure he was trying to talk Maddie into stepping out with him. It seemed like a good idea because she could picture them together, and she kept her fingers crossed that Maddie would agree.

With the food eaten, the tables were cleared and pushed to one side, whilst one of the constables produced a mouth organ and started to play. Then another stood up with a fiddle, and soon jolly music filled the room. The guest started clapping and chanting, 'Dance! Dance! Bride and groom to dance the first dance.'

Shyly Ellen let John pull her to her feet. She had never been much for dancing, but somehow being in John's arms showed her the way until after a while, she begged to be allowed to sit down. Breathless and laughing, they sat and watched, as the room became noisier and noisier. John leaned across and whispered in her ear, 'It won't be long now before we can enjoy our nuptials. I'm so looking forward to getting you alone, Mrs Ryan.'

With a giggle, Ellen said, 'Certainly, anything you say, Mr Ryan. Your wish is my command.'

'I'll hold you to that.' John grinned wickedly.

Feeling exhausted, Ellen wished she could go off to bed. Any bed, just so long as she could rest. But on and on went the dancing and singing, until in the end, her eyes would hardly stay open. She saw Maddie coming toward her and knew she must ask how much longer this was going on. Her friend's face filled with concern and she said to wait a moment, then hurried away, only to return a few moments later with Mrs Vale in tow.

'Now Ellen and John, I can see you are both tired,' said Mrs Vale in a low voice, 'and so if you will follow me, I will show you where you can rest.'

Completely bewildered, they rose from their seats and followed her from the dining room. Up the stairs Mrs Vale went, then turned at the top and handed John a key. 'Room Ten, Mr Ryan. It's yours for the night.' Then with a huge smile on her face, she started back down the stairs.

Stuttering their thanks, they stood for a moment watching Mrs Vale's retreating figure, before Ellen took John's hand and led him to room number ten.

As he entered, John's face was a picture. 'My God. What a room, and look at the size of that bed? They've done us proud Ellen, haven't they?'

'Yes, I'm so overcome, I don't know what to say. To think that we've only been in Bothwell for so short a time, it's amazing.'

'And you're amazing, my sweet. It's you they've taken to their hearts.'

'I don't know why. I was awful when I first arrived. Late on duty, rebellious and slovenly too, if I'm honest.'

'Well, we're here now, my love, and I want you very much. Come into my arms so that we can consummate our marriage.' He chuckled at his own joke.

'Wait John, I must take this dress off and hang it up first.' She saw his look of pique and quickly added. 'This is Mrs Vale's dress. She was good enough to lend it to me, so I must look after it. Once I've removed it, I'm all yours. For all night long, and for all our lives long.'

'Of course, I was being selfish. Don't let me be like that with you, keep me in my place, won't you?'

With the dress on its hanger, Ellen moved across to the large bed and held out her hand. 'I'll make sure your place is always at my side,' she said huskily, as one strap of the chemise was eased from her shoulder, and John bent to kiss her breast.

Then Ellen gave herself up to John's lovemaking, her mind overflowing with memories of the day. How lucky she was; she had a loving husband, good friends and a boss who seemed intent on making her life easier. What more could any woman want? Then, ecstasy overtook her and John transported her to their special place. Life could not get any better, Ellen was sure.

The following morning, Ellen woke to the sound of rain splashing against the window. She had no idea what the time was, but was nestled snugly in John's arms and felt loath to move. As sounds reached the room from downstairs, Ellen remembered that this room was above the dining room and wondered if she should go down and help to clear up from yesterday's party.

She slid from under the sheets, the cold air making her gasp. There was nothing for her to wear except the chemise and there was no way she could appear downstairs in that. Just then there was a knock on the door, and Ellen shot back under the covers, calling softly, 'Come in.'

Maddie's large head appeared round the door, a smile as wide as ever on her face. 'I've brought you tea in bed. Just for today mind, never again.'

'Thank you Maddie, how thoughtful. I was wondering whether to get up and help with the cleaning.' She glanced at her new husband. 'And I don't know if John has to go on duty today or not.'

'I shouldn't worry about that now, just drink your tea and eat your toast, then we'll see later on what you can do.' Giving a cheeky wave, Maddie backed out of the room.

The sound of voices finally penetrating his sleep, John awoke. 'Who was that?' he asked.

'It was Maddie, she's brought us breakfast.'

'Goodness, I never expected anything like this. I think I'm dreaming.' He pinched his arm. 'No I'm definitely here.'

Laughing at his silly joke, Ellen reached across and handed him his tea. 'Are you on duty today?'

'Trying to get rid of me already are you?' John was indignant.

'No, of course not. I just wanted to know. I'm not sure what I'm supposed to be doing. Married women don't usually work, but we need another income, however tiny as well as yours, don't we?'

John frowned. 'I'm sorry my darling girl, I wish I could support us both, but it's only coppers we get.'

'I know, I don't mind, honestly.' Ellen snuggled down next to him to show that her words were meant wholeheartedly.

Placing the tray on the floor, John took her into his arms. 'One day, my love, we'll own our home and some land. We'll have goats for milk and butter, hens for eggs and meat and grow all the vegetables we need. Ah, I can see it now and won't it be grand?'

Ellen liked what she heard and gave a big sigh. 'Yes it'll be grand. I do love you, John.'

'And I love you too. Come let me love you, my dearest wife. It'll be a great way to start our first day of married life together.'

CHAPTER 14

Later, when Ellen had taken the tray back to the kitchen, with only the bedspread to cover her modesty, John lay thinking about what he had to tell her, and so far hadn't had the nerve. He prayed no one downstairs would let on, but cursed himself for not being honest with her. She was such a trusting little thing and he felt terrible for not being straight about things.

He had tried desperately to find them somewhere to live, even to knocking on the doors of the cottages in the village in case anyone knew when one might be coming empty. The Chief had enquired on his behalf too, but without success. No one wanted a penniless convict as a tenant.

In desperation he'd come to see Mrs Vale. He'd sat nervously clutching his cap while the woman sat looking at him and shaking her head. 'You young people nowadays. You don't seem to have things in perspective. I know you wanted to marry Ellen as soon as possible, but surely somewhere to live was important enough to be sorted out first.' She tapped the desk with her pencil and sat deep in thought. Then, 'There is only one solution as far as I can see, and that is for you both to use Ellen's bedroom for a while. Only until something permanent is arranged of course. She can continue working here, but you will have to pay for your meals. If that is agreeable, then you may move in after the wedding.' She'd raised an eyebrow in enquiry.

'Thank you very much, Mrs Vale. I'm sure that will suit Ellen and myself for a short while. I'm still hopeful of finding us a cottage somewhere, but they're scarce as hen's teeth.'

The corner of Mrs Vale's mouth had twitched at the common expression, but John hardly noticed it. At least he and his wife had a roof over their heads for the foreseeable future. But what Ellen would make of it, he dreaded to think.

'What!' Ellen stood, mouth open and stared at Maddie. 'For goodness sake, how can we live here? I share a room with you for one thing. Are we supposed to all bunk in together?' She felt herself shaking with anger. How dare he. Tears welled up then and she dashed them away crossly, not sure if they were caused by temper or hurt.

Turning abruptly, the bedspread held tightly about her, Ellen dashed back up the stairs to room ten.

She saw John's look of surprise, before she slapped him round the face. 'What were you thinking of?' she shouted. 'Do you expect me to live at my place of work, while you carry on as before. I thought we got married to be together, but it doesn't seem to bother you whether we are or not.' She ignored the hand John held out toward her. 'Don't try to get round me, John Ryan. I wouldn't live with you now if you paid me.' Then she ran from the room, down the stairs and along to her old room, to throw herself onto the bed and weep hot tears of frustration.

How long she lay there she neither knew nor cared. Everything was spoiled. All her plans for a life with John, to live happily and maybe have children; even to be able to cook and clean for him would have been fun. But he had ruined it all by asking Mrs Vale if they could stay here.

After a while Ellen stopped crying and lay quietly thinking things over. When she at last opened her eyes, she looked about the room, bewildered. There was something different about it. Slowly she sat up and saw in the gloomy light that things had been changed around. Even the bed was not her own; this was a double. And there was a bigger wardrobe and a dresser with a mirror on top. It looked cleaner and smarter than when she'd last seen it yesterday morning. So who had done all this?

She groaned. Oh no! I've done it again: going off the rails without hearing anyone else's side of the story. Clambering off the bed, she opened the wardrobe and found one of her own dresses hanging there, so quickly put it on, before looking in the mirror to check her hair. Gone was the lovely style Maddie had created for her yesterday and in it's place her usual messy mop. Ellen sat on the bed and pulled pins out from the tangled mess, then brushed it vigorously. She knew she was only putting off the dreaded moment when she had to go and apologise to everyone. Especially John. How could she have hit him, her husband of one day? She supposed he had done his best in an impossible situation. It had been a shock, but the more she thought about it the better it seemed. She would still have a job here, John

172

could go off on duty each morning, and best of all, she would still be able to enjoy Maura's cooking.

She wondered where Maddie and Stella were going to sleep and decided that she must go and see her friend at once. Filled with trepidation, Ellen hurried along the corridor toward the kitchen, pausing outside the door before grasping the handle and going in. Maura was on her own and turned as Ellen entered.

'My, that must have been a deluge of tears you shed. Your eyes are all puffy, come here and bathe them.' She held out a bowl of cold water and a soft cloth.

'I'm so sorry, Maura. What must everyone think of me? I'm so stupid sometimes and just go off ranting and raving without thinking.'

The kindly woman pulled a chair out and pointed at it. 'Now you sit down a moment, dear and listen to me.' As Maura sat opposite, she reached across and took Ellen's hands in her own. 'I must admit that when I first heard of the plan for you and John to live here, I was appalled. Maddie insisted it could work and Mrs Vale was happy about it, but it didn't seem right to me. So I can quite understand why you were angry, I would have reacted in the same way. I know John is doing his best and it's not ideal, but it's only for a short time. Apparently the poor man has been going daft trying to find a place of your own, but there was nothing available. That was why Mrs Vale took pity on him. Mind you, I'm not sure what the owner would say, so I shouldn't tell too many folk if I were you.'

The cold water soothed her eyes and gradually Ellen began to feel better. The fact that Maura understood helped her forgive herself for the outburst. 'I'd better go and see John. Is he still up in room ten?'

'No dear, he was called away about an hour ago. Some trouble with the convicts out on one of the farms. He won't be too long, so don't you fret. You'll make up in no time once he's back.' Just then the door opened and Maddie came in.

Ellen jumped up and ran to her. 'Oh, I'm so sorry for what I said. Can you forgive me? And now I've seen how nice you've made the room, I…' she flung her arms about Maddie's bulk and sobbed.

'You silly goose. Of course I forgive you. But don't go shouting your mouth off like that again. It's not ladylike and makes your face all blotchy.' Ellen couldn't believe how well Maddie had taken her bad behaviour. But then her friend added, 'Seriously, I was annoyed at first, until it dawned on me that John hadn't told you. He really should have done, and explained why he'd had to do it.'

'Do you think he'll forgive me? I hit him,' Ellen told them quietly, ashamed of her terrible temper.

'Bless you, of course he'll forgive you. After all, he only had himself to blame,' Maddie said.

'Come and sit down again, I've made some tea. Then it'll be time to start serving lunch.' Looking at the huge clock hanging on the wall over the cooker, Maura went to examine the contents of the saucepans bubbling away on the hob.

Realising that she'd wasted the whole morning, Ellen asked sheepishly, 'shall I go and clean room ten? Mrs Vale will want it spick and span again ready to rent.'

'I've done it,' Maddie told her. 'Not that you made much mess. Well, only to the bed.'

Colour flooded Ellen's face. 'Don't,' she hissed. 'You are awful, Maddie, but thank you for doing the room anyway.'

A huge sigh left Ellen's lips. Now all she had to do was wait for John's return, and she supposed she'd better go and see Mrs Vale to thank her for everything she'd done yesterday. It had been a marvellous wedding and she didn't want to appear ungrateful. I wonder if I should thank her for the room as well, she mused. Yes, it might be as well, after all Mrs Vale might have put her own job in jeopardy by letting them stay at the hotel.

John hurried across to the police office, his face still stinging from the slap Ellen had given him. He knew he should have told her before she went downstairs, so he only had himself to blame. It was a nuisance that he'd had to come away without going to see her. He knew how much she had set her heart on a home of their own and could understand her tears. His heart bled, thinking of her all alone and crying in her lonely room. He should be with her and once this business was sorted out, he'd hurry back.

Unfortunately the business took him far out into the countryside and he was gone longer than he had imagined he would be. It was late evening before he finished with the paperwork at the police office and could get back to the hotel, but he hurried to the room where he and Ellen were to live. He opened the door quietly and poked his head around it. The room was filled with soft candlelight and Ellen was sitting on the bed sewing. She looked up and saw him and her face broke into an engaging smile.

'Can you forgive me?' they said in unison, then laughed. John hurried into the room and closed the door behind him, and then Ellen sprung up and into his arms. He smothered her face with kisses, until at last she stepped back, breathless.

'Do you want something to eat,' she asked him. 'Maura left you a

174

meal in case you were hungry when you arrived back.'

'I'm starving, had nothing all day since the toast this morning. And we didn't eat much of that, did we?' He pulled her into his arms again and kissed the tip of her nose. 'Mr darling Ellen, I've missed you so today, and I'm sorry for the hurt I caused. I knew I should have explained, but somehow never got round to it.'

'And I'm sorry for hitting you, I don't know what came over me. Did it hurt?' she put her fingers up to his cheek and touched it tenderly.

'It did for a while, my girl, you certainly pack a punch. Now,' he tapped her bottom, 'let's go and get my supper, otherwise I'll fade away before your eyes.' They hurried along the corridor to the kitchen, content in their love for each other now that the first battle had been fought and overcome.

For the next three weeks John walked the streets on his beat, but with half his mind on finding a home. He and Ellen were cosy enough at the hotel and everyone was kind, but it was not like having somewhere of their own.

As he strolled along the main street of Bothwell he would keep an eye on the tiny cottages dotted along its length. If he saw someone standing at the gate he would stop and pass the time of day, asking seemingly innocuous questions about who lived there, how long had they been in Bothwell, and most importantly to him, were they likely to remain?

To his chagrin the occupants of these cottages seemed quite content and in no hurry to move anywhere else. His quest appeared hopeless, until one day, he saw a woman coming through a front door, handkerchief to her eyes and obviously in a distraught state.

John hurried toward her. 'Good afternoon, madam, may I be of any assistance?'

The woman lifted her red rimmed eyes to him and sobbed. ''Tis me old mother, she's passed away. God rest her soul, just gone in her sleep she has.' More tears followed and John moved closer to put a comforting hand on her shoulder.

'There, there, don't take on so. It's very sad I know only too well.' His soft Irish tones washing over her.

'Have you lost your mother too, then?' she asked.

'I did, many years ago now, but I remember the pain as though it were yesterday.'

'I'm so glad you understand. You see I'm alone in the world now and have no one to turn to.' Her look became pleading. 'I don't

175

suppose you could help me? I don't know how to even go about arranging her funeral.'

'To be sure, it's my duty to help the people of this town. Let me take you to the police office where we can make you a cup of tea and then sort out your mother's affairs.' John lifted the latch on the gate and drew the woman through with a conciliatory hand at her elbow. A few moments later they were in the office and John requested some tea for the sorrowing woman, whose name was Mrs Deakin.

Once she was seated, cup in hand, he sat opposite her and placed a sheet of paper in front of him on the desk. He wrote down her answers to his questions discovering that the cottage belonged to the elderly lady who had lived there for about twenty years after it had become hers on the death of her husband. Mrs Deakin was the only surviving child and she had no children of her own, so just as she'd stated she was alone in the world.

'Tell me, madam, where do you live? Is it close by?' John waited with baited breath.

'I live out at Hurrumba, it's a farm about thirty miles north. I'm live-in housekeeper there.'

'I see, so you'll not have need of the cottage then?'

She looked up in surprise. 'Well, no, I don't know what I'll do with that.'

'Never mind that for now. I'll send for the doctor and then we'll visit the undertaker and the Reverend so that everything's in order. Finish your tea first.' John smiled with all the charm he could muster, then went to the outside door to ask the constable there if he could send word for the doctor to meet them at the cottage with the green door.

When he returned, Mrs Deakin was sitting quietly, and in a more composed state. Placing her empty cup on the desk, she looked up and smiled. 'You've been so kind, I'm sorry to take up so much of your time.'

'It's no trouble at all, it's what we're here for. We can't have a good lady like yourself in trouble and not know which way to turn, now can we?'

'Thank you so much. I'll never be able to repay you.'

'There's no need to think of anything like that. Now, if you're ready, we'll go and see if the doctor has come.'

When they arrived back at the cottage, the doctor was just coming along the road. John introduced him to Mrs Deakin and then they all went into the cottage, where on a big bed in one corner lay the old woman. She did indeed look as though she was just asleep and John expected her to open her eyes and look at them accusingly for being in her home. But the doctor confirmed that she was dead, wrote out the death certificate and handed it to Mrs Deakin. 'Old age, I'd say. Been ill lately had she?'

'Not really,' the woman replied, 'but she was over eighty and had gone a bit senile in the last few years.'

This seemed to satisfy the doctor who picked up his bag and walked out without further ado. Before they left, John made sure the place was secure, taking careful note of the cottage as he went, then he took the grieving daughter to the undertakers. There, the funeral was soon arranged, and off they went to visit Reverend McDonald to see what day he could hold the ceremony.

By the time John saw Mrs Deakin on her way an hour later, everything was in order and for him the best part was that she'd said he could rent the cottage for a tiny amount each week. 'It's the least I can do as a reward for all your kindness.' She'd shaken his hand vigorously. 'As soon as the funeral is over, I'll go and clear what I can, then it's yours. Are you married?'

'Yes, just a few weeks ago. My wife will be thrilled to have somewhere of her own as we're lodging at the Falls of Clyde hotel at the moment.' John smiled warmly at the woman. 'Although we're comfortable there it's not the same as your own home. Thank you so much for letting us rent the cottage.' Then, as an afterthought he added, 'Would you like Ellen and me to come to your mother's funeral otherwise it'll be a very solitary affair?'

Her face lit with pleasure. 'That would be very kind of you. Yes please.' Then the tiny cart arrived to take her back to Hurrumba and she climbed aboard, before turning to wave goodbye.

John watched the rig until it was out of sight, feeling more than a little pleased with himself. He couldn't wait to tell Ellen his good news: a place to call home at last.

John waited until they were alone in their room that night before he told Ellen the good news. And her reaction was just as he knew it would be as she flung her arms about him and squealed with glee. 'How wonderful. Oh John, won't it be good, just us on our own in a cosy cottage.'

'It will need a bit doing to it mind, before we can move in. I think the poor old lady hadn't been well for some while as there's mess everywhere and the kitchen is rather smelly.' John tried not to paint too bleak a picture and tell Ellen the truth, that the place was almost derelict. He was sure they could soon clean it up and then it would be grand. 'Now let's get to bed, I've an early start in the morning.'

'When can I see the cottage, John?'

'You'll have to wait until the funeral's over.' He hesitated. 'By the way, I said we'd go to that, as poor Mrs Deakin is all alone in the world.'

'Do we have to? I didn't know the old lady.'

'I promised,' John said gently. 'Please, my love. After all she is letting us have the cottage for next to nothing.'

With a sigh, Ellen climbed into bed. 'In that case I can't refuse, but I'm not looking forward to it.'

'Is there something else I can tempt you with then?' John grinned and climbed in beside her.

With a playful punch Ellen snuggled down under the covers.

Three days later, with the funeral service over and the old lady lain to rest in the cemetery, Ellen and John waved Mrs Deakin off as she walked to the waiting pony and trap. How sad, thought Ellen, the poor woman had buried her mother with only the Reverend McDonald and themselves present at the graveside. It wasn't much to show for a long life and she wondered why none of the neighbours had come to pay their last respects.

But as she and John hurried along the street, the thought of seeing her new home was uppermost in her mind, and as they paused at the front door with it's peeling green paint, she held her breath in anticipation. John produced the heavy metal key and unlocked the door, then with a smile as wide as the sky, pushed it open and with a flourish waved her inside. Ellen's first impression of the gloomy room was the smell. In fact it nearly had her running outside again because it was so bad. She turned to John, who seemed completely oblivious to it, and asked, 'What is that awful smell?'

John sniffed the air. 'It's not so bad, bound to be a bit musty after being shut up for a few days. Mrs Deakin said she'd clean it up for us.'

'Well, I don't think she's done a very good job.' As her eyes became accustomed to the poor light, Ellen could see the unmade bed and the litter strewn across the floor. She inched forward and pulled the covers back on the bed. 'Urrgh! This is disgusting. Look, the sheets are covered in...' she paused, 'something horrible.' The room was small, with only the bed, one armchair and a small chest of drawers filling it. Across the room next to the fireplace was another door and Ellen picked her way across to it. On the other side was a kitchen, with sink, black range and a cupboard. This room too was filthy, with what looked like the remains of food on the stone floor and putrid water in the sink. Opposite was a door that she presumed went out into the garden at the back, as a square of green could be seen through the grimy window.

'It'll take us ages to get this clean.' Ellen was disappointed; she had so looked forward to moving in.

John at last seemed to notice the chaos and said, 'We could ask Maddie to give us a hand.'

'I'd be ashamed for her to see it like this,' Ellen complained, but then saw the wisdom in his words. 'But I suppose I'll have to ask her, we'll never do it on our own.' She turned to leave and noticed the look on John's face. 'I know you've done well to get us this place, but Mrs Deakin has let us down. She can't have been near the place since her mother died.'

'I can see that now. I'm sorry Ellen, I did so want you to like it.' John's appeared so disheartened; she linked her arm through his.

'Don't worry, we'll soon have it spick and span, then it'll be really cosy.'

His face lightened. 'You do like it then?'

'Of course I like it. It was just a shock to see the state it's in. When you see that woman again, I hope you're going to give her a piece of your mind about this.' Ellen wrinkled her nose. 'The old lady must have been living like this for months, poor soul. It doesn't seem as though Mrs Deakin was a very attentive daughter, does it?'

'No it doesn't, and I'm not sure when I'll be seeing her again. I meant to ask her about paying the rent at the funeral today, but it never felt the right moment to discuss money.'

Ellen shook her head and wondered how John was going to pay the rent. And more to the point, did he even know how much it was going to be? She asked him and he smiled. 'Don't you go bothering your head about such things, it'll be fine.' And with that she had to be content.

Later that evening she told Maddie and Maura about the cottage. 'How marvellous,' said Maura. 'Your own home at last. But why the long face?'

Once Ellen had finished describing the state of the place, both women had a look of horror on her face. 'It'll take you ages to get it habitable,' Maddie said crossly. 'I do think John should have checked it first.'

Always ready to defend her husband, Ellen answered, 'I made him show me as soon as the funeral was over. He had no idea the mess would be still there.'

'To be honest, it all sounds a bit fishy to me,' Maura said quietly. 'Does he know for sure that that woman owned the cottage?'

Ellen felt a shock course through her. Something like that had never dawned on her. 'I-I'm not sure, he didn't tell me much.'

Maddie stood up. 'Right, I'm going to see if Harry can find something out for us. I'm sorry Ellen, I don't want to undermine John, but he's gullible and I think this needs looking into more thoroughly.'

'I was hoping you'd help me clean it,' Ellen said lamely.

'Of course I will, but not until we know it's that Deakin woman's place to rent out. When I find her, she'll come and help clean up her mother's filth too. I'm off to bed now, but I'll go and see Harry in the morning.'

As she tumbled into bed, Ellen realised with a jolt that Maddie and Harry seemed to be on very good terms. In spite of everything, a smile played about her lips. How wonderful! John soon arrived after his late turn on duty and as he undressed, Ellen told of Maddie's concerns.

'I wish people wouldn't interfere. I know she's your friend, but anyone would think I was completely incompetent.'

'Maddie doesn't think that at all. It just seems strange that Mrs Deakin didn't ask for any money, or at least arrange when to collect the rent. And why leave her mother's home in such a mess? It doesn't make sense.'

John was quiet for a moment, then said, 'I suppose she's right to be suspicious. Let's hope it turns out all right. Goodnight sweetheart, see you in the morning.' John turned over and fell asleep, leaving Ellen feeling piqued. This was the first time he had gone to sleep without at least a goodnight kiss.

The following morning dragged interminably for Ellen. She cleaned rooms, helped Maura in the kitchen and then cleaned her own room and still Maddie hadn't returned from seeing Harry. The fact that her friend had asked for the morning off especially to find out about the ownership of the cottage made Ellen realise how much she owed Maddie. She was a true friend and no mistake and hoped John wouldn't take the interference too badly. It was meant kindly, Ellen knew, but John was inclined to be quick off the mark, and to take people at face value; much to his cost on more than one occasion.

At last Maddie's kindly face appeared round the door of Ellen's room. 'Phew! What a job that was…' Plonking herself on the newly made bed, she gave Ellen the news she'd been waiting for. 'As far as we can tell, everything's fine. That's the good news. The bad is that

Mrs Deakin has left her employment and gone off without telling anyone where she's going. This means she won't be able to help with the cleaning, but it also means that until she gets in touch, John can't pay any rent.'

'So we'll be living rent free?' Ellen frowned. 'That doesn't sound right to me. I suppose John could always keep some money by in case she shows up again?'

'I think that'll be a good idea. Now, when's your next day off?'

'Tomorrow. Does that mean we can start cleaning up?'

'It certainly does, although I'll have to clear things with Mrs Vale. I think you need to explain the situation to her, because you might need a few things to start you off.'

'What kind of things?'

'I presume you have no bedding, pots and pans, crockery... Need I go on?'

'I hadn't thought of that. I'm rather silly sometimes, aren't I?'

Maddie gave her hearty laugh. 'Only sometimes?'

Ellen felt her face crumbling and tears stung the back of her eyes. I'm such a stupid person, she told herself. Why don't I ever think things through? She lifted her chin, determined not to let Maddie see how upset she was. 'I suppose I thought everything would be there, but of course the old lady didn't have much and what she did have isn't worth keeping is it?' she asked glumly.

'Not from what you've told me, it isn't. I think the best thing to do would be to just clear everything out, then give the place a good clean. It might just be habitable then. Don't know what you're going to do for furniture though, I can't see Mrs Vale giving any away, even for you.'

'What do you mean? Even for me.'

'Oh come on, don't say you haven't realised that you're her pet.'

'She's been very kind, yes, but I think she'd do the same for anyone.'

'No she wouldn't. Think of the wedding dress. That must have meant a great deal to her, but she let Maura chop it about to fit you. What's that if it isn't favouritism?'

Ellen felt colour rise in her face and she bit hard into her bottom lip. 'I had no idea, honestly, Maddie. Do you think anyone else has noticed? I hate to be treated differently to others.'

'Don't let it worry you, no one minds.' Maddie let out a loud guffaw. 'We all love you no matter what you think of yourself. So ponder on what you need for the cottage and we'll make a list.'

'Can you write it please?'

Maddie sucked in a great gulp of air. 'Well, I can try, but my writing's not up to much, nor my spelling. I expect we'll be able to make out what most of it means. It's time for lunch now, so we'll try and find time afterwards. Perhaps Maura can help.' Maddie rose from the bed, leaving a very rumpled coverlet behind and Ellen sighed and quickly smoothed it out, before following her out into the corridor.

She should have been working in the kitchen this past hour, but she'd been so engrossed in her own problems, she'd forgotten. Ellen doubted Maura would want to help now.

But Maura seemed not to have noticed her absence and dished up the lunch, humming to herself. Ellen tried to apologise, 'I'm so sorry Maura, but I was so worried about what Maddie would find out, I completely forgot about work.'

'Don't worry yourself, I can manage.' Then she smiled as Nessie and Vera arrived for lunch. 'Good, you're all here, so sit and eat. We've things to discuss, haven't we Maddie?'

'We have indeed. Ellen and John have the use of a cottage, but it's in a bad way. We're going to help clean it up, but what's needed is furniture. Not much, because the place isn't big enough to swing a cat, but just a few bits and pieces. A bed, a couple of armchairs, a cabinet of some sort and perhaps a table and chairs for the kitchen.' She looked around hopefully. 'Anyone any ideas?'

Vera looked glum and shook her head, while Nessie stared at Ellen in awe. 'Are you going to have your very own home?' she asked.

Ellen nodded and smiled at the girl. 'You shall come to tea as soon as it's finished.'

This seemed to please Nessie enormously and she set to eating her food, without paying any more attention to the conversation going on around her.

Then Vera said, 'I know! What about the stuff from John's room in the barracks?'

With a shake of her head, Ellen told her, 'No, he's already asked. They say it's to stay there for the next constable.'

The kitchen was silent as they all ate and tried to think of ways to acquire some furniture. Maura put her knife and fork down, her face lighting suddenly. 'There's some bits out in the outhouse. They're not up to much, but might do a turn. I'll ask Mrs Vale later.' She sat thinking for a moment. 'I can't remember what's there, but I'm sure there will be something of use.'

Ellen started to fidget. Now it was all coming together, she wanted to get on with it. How was she ever going to wait until tomorrow?

She could tell that John was not too pleased with all the help they were getting. That night, after she'd told him, his voice was flat as he asked, 'And when is all of this to happen?'

'Tomorrow,' she told him. 'Please John, be happy about this. Everyone wants to help us because they like us and want to see us settled. It's not being done to undermine you. After all you work long hours and can't possibly manage everything on your own, now can you?' She smiled and put her arms around his neck, stood on tiptoe and kissed his cheek.

'I know. I should be grateful, and I am really, it's just that I thought I'd be doing all of this for you.'

'You've done the most important part by getting us the cottage. Oh John it's going to be perfect. Once we've finished doing bits to it, it'll be a wonderful home.' She nuzzled his earlobe. 'Just for the two of us, our own love nest.'

He laughed then. 'You're such a lovely girl, and you can always get round me no matter what.' He started to shrug off his jacket. 'Come on then, let's get to our bed and practise for the years ahead in our new home.'

The next day everyone hurried through their chores. Fortunately, not many guests were staying in the hotel and so by mid-morning they were all free to go and see what the outhouse had to offer.

In the dim, dusty and humid interior, Ellen could see nothing but a pile of junk, but as Maddie and Vera waded in and started pulling bits and pieces out, things looked more promising. A rickety table, two wooden chairs – one with a leg missing – and a small washstand, soon stood being inspected by the group of women.

Ellen sniffed. 'Well, nothing looks much good, does it?'

'Hold your horses,' Maddie piped up. 'If we can find the missing leg for that chair and knock a couple of nails into the table, they should do you a turn.' She looked at Ellen with raised eyebrows. 'What do you think?'

'Mmm, I suppose they will. I could varnish them, couldn't I?' she asked.

Maddie nodded. 'I think they'll do, Ellen. And this washstand could be used to store things on if we put a piece of wood across the top, and another here.' She pointed to the struts underneath.

Suddenly Ellen could see it in her mind's eye. 'You're right, it would. So that's the kitchen sorted out, but what about the living room?'

Everyone looked more closely at the contents of the shed, but all that was left were old floorboards, rotten curtains and an assortment of very stained mattresses. 'Ugh! You couldn't use any of those.' Maura said, screwing up her face in disgust. 'I'd like to know why this lot wasn't thrown out years ago.'

'Mind you, the bed in the cottage isn't much better,' Ellen told her. 'So you can imagine why we need to change it.'

'Is it just the mattress?' Maddie asked.

Ellen thought for a few moments. 'I think so. The bedstead looked reasonably strong as far as I can remember. Why?'

'I was wondering if we could find a mattress somewhere and put it on the old bed, that'll save you looking for one piece of furniture.' Maddie was the voice of reason as ever and Ellen could have hugged her.

'What did Mrs Vale say when you asked to have a look through this lot,' Vera wanted to know.

'She said to go ahead and take anything that might be useful, which was very good of her.' Ellen frowned. 'Isn't there anywhere else that furniture is stored?'

Maura shook her head. 'No, the hotels only been here a few years.' Then she stopped and grinned widely. 'I know, what about the other hotels in Bothwell. There are enough of them; perhaps one of them might have things they don't want. Even if they want paying, I'm sure John could find a few coppers from somewhere.'

'What a good idea,' said Ellen, 'but I don't know anyone who lives at any of the others.'

'But I do,' said Maura. 'I'll go and see my friend at the Crown Inn after lunch. It's a smaller place then this, but you never know. It's worth asking anyway.'

As they all went back inside to prepare lunch, Ellen thought how kind they all were, and it warmed her heart to know that such caring people were around.

Lunch over, she and Maddie hurried off to the cottage armed with buckets, mops and a huge bar of carbolic soap that Mrs Vale had kindly donated. 'She never ceases to amaze me,' Maddie said. 'A sterner woman you could never wish to meet, and yet when help is needed, she's there to give it.'

'Yes, it was good of her to say she'd ask the man who does odd-jobs at the hotel to mend the table and chairs, wasn't it?' Ellen swung open the little wooden gate. 'Here we are, Maddie. Hold your nose though.'

Maddie did indeed hold her nose as the acrid stench of the room

184

hit them full force. 'God, what a terrible pong.' With her face screwed up in distaste, Maddie walked around the room, peering into every corner. 'This is going to take longer than one day to clean. Several days I should guess.'

Sadly Ellen had to agree. It would take many hours to even take the worst off, but she was determined to make a start, and rolled her sleeves up in readiness. 'I hope there's a well outside,' she said moving through to the back yard. 'Thank goodness,' she said in relief at the sight of one situated close by. 'I expect we have to share it with the other cottages, but never mind, at least we have water.'

After many attempts, Maddie got the black range to light, although it puffed out smoke for several minutes as though annoyed at being disturbed from it's slumbers. 'You're lucky to have one of these, you know,' Maddie said. 'Some homes only have an open fire to cook on.

'Thank goodness I have it then,' Ellen laughed, 'otherwise we'd starve.' She wasn't sure how she'd cope with this roaring monster, but guessed she'd learn in time. After all, other women used them every day, so it couldn't be so difficult.

While the water heated in the bucket they explored the outside area. There was a long, narrow strip of grass leading off toward the fields beyond. In between was a large mass of dank ground and Ellen wrinkled her nose as they approached. 'That doesn't look very nice.'

'Ah,' said Maddie, nodding her head. 'I think that's the cesspool.'

'The what?'

'It's where you empty the chamber pot. Surely you've heard of a cesspool before?'

'Oh yes. We had one back home, but father called it the pit.' Ellen laughed then, remembering the time her father had tripped up with a full bucket of waste, and it had covered him from head to foot. 'He smelt awful for days after,' she told Maddie after recounting the story.

They both chuckled at the picture this conjured up, then Maddie pulled on Ellen's sleeve. 'Come on let's go and see if the water's hot yet, then we can get on with some cleaning. Although where we're going to start, I don't know.'

Sadly, Ellen followed her friend inside. Where indeed?

Two days, many buckets of hot water and copious amounts of carbolic later, and with much needed help from everyone, the cottage looked presentable at last. Even Nessie with her frail figure had set to enthusiastically and Ellen worried about her as she breathlessly leaned against the door jam after scrubbing the stone hearth.

'Are you all right?' she asked, noticing the girl's pinched features. Nessie smiled. 'I'm fine, just a bit out of breath. I seem to have a permanent stitch these days no matter what I do.'

Ellen shot Maura a worried look and the woman shook her head imperceptibly, but spoke briskly, 'Come on then, we're nearly done, then Ellen and John can move in. Did the man bring those chairs, Ellen?'

'Yes. Aren't they great?' She went outside and ran a hand over the faded chintz. 'I can't wait to see them inside.'

Maura had emerged from the cottage behind her, and agreed. 'Yes, they're not bad considering they've been in a barn for a couple of years. I'll get Maddie to help us move them inside. Ah, here she is, right on cue.'

Maddie pulled a face in mock horror. 'Huh, that's all you want me for, my strong arms.' There was laughter all round, but somewhere in the back of Ellen's mind was the picture of Maura's face when Nessie mentioned the pain in her side, and she resolved to ask as soon as possible what the problem was. But for now the prospect of her home being fit to move into took priority. 'I'm just off to see John. He'll be thrilled that the cottage is ready and we really can't thank you all enough for the help you've given. Once we're settled we'll have a party. Just a little one as a way of showing our appreciation.'

Her friends smiled and waved her away. 'Get along with you, the poor man must be thinking he's never going to get you to himself,' Vera laughed.

Maddie sucked her cheek's in. 'Oh, I don't think not having their own place has dampened any desires,' She lifted her eyebrows. 'Has it Ellen?'

A deep blush crept across Ellen's face and she turned away to go and see her husband. She knew Maddie was only joking, but it still embarrassed her.

After telling John that their home was ready, she left him, grinning ear to ear, to go and let Mrs Vale know. Now that she had her own home her status would be improved greatly and she no longer had to work in the hotel. She was sorry not to be there every day as she had been for the past weeks and wondered how she was going to fill her days. The tiny house wouldn't take long to clean each morning and Ellen sighed; she'd just have to see how things went.

Entering the hotel, she remembered Nessie and went to see Maura first. 'Is Nessie very poorly?'

Maura nodded. 'I'm afraid she's extremely ill, Ellen and we don't think she has long now. The doctors have tried everything, but her

186

illness was too advanced before she said anything about the pain.'

'So why is she still working? Surely she should be resting now. I feel awful letting her help at the cottage too.'

'Don't reproach yourself. Nessie wanted to help and she's thrilled to see it finished.' Maura hesitated. 'Did you not wonder why we chose her to be your bridesmaid?'

Realisation dawned. 'I'm so glad about that, she had a lovely time and looked beautiful.' Tears sprang into Ellen's eyes. 'I'm glad I didn't know the reason though, I'd never have got through the day.'

'That's why we didn't tell you, it might have spoilt it for everyone.'

'Mrs Vale knows I suppose?'

'Yes, and has been very supportive of Nessie. Sometimes it has been necessary to admonish her, just to keep her from guessing the truth, but I have a feeling Nessie has begun to suspect the worst now.'

'I'm off to see Mrs Vale now, I'll see you later and thank you for all your hard work, John and me do appreciate it.' Heaving a huge sigh, Ellen left Maura and went to the parlour where she knew she'd find the kindly woman.

'Come in Mrs Ryan,' Mrs Vale said, a wide smile on her face. She had smiled a lot just lately Ellen had noticed. 'Is the cottage finished?' she asked now.

'Yes, Mrs Vale, and thank you so much for all the help you've given. The furniture from the lean-to and all the cleaning stuff has helped so much.'

'Good, I'm glad to hear it. So you're all set then?' Without waiting for an answer, she added, 'Have you a bed now, only I understand there was a problem.'

Ellen grinned. 'We couldn't find a bed, so we've put an old, but cleaner, mattress onto the old bedstead. It seems all right, if a bit lumpy. And today a man brought two armchairs from the attic of the Crown Inn and they're lovely, only slightly faded.'

'So how are you off for linen?' The plump arms folded across the ample bosom.

'That's the only thing we're lacking now. I've found an old piece of cloth to put over the table, but there is no bed linen, not even a blanket.'

'Well we can't have that, can we? So I've sorted out some things from the store and have two pairs of sheets, two pairs of pillowcases and two blankets you are welcome to.'

Ellen couldn't believe her ears. Proper bedding! 'T-thank you so much, Mrs Vale. I am so grateful, and I'm sure John will be too.'

'They are not in perfect condition of course, but will do you a turn. The sheets have been turned sides to middle and the blankets have a patch or two, but it's better than nothing.'

Not sure how to show her thanks, Ellen teetered on the brink of dashing forward to kiss Mrs Vale's plump cheek, but in the end she just stood awkwardly not sure what to say, until Mrs Vale came to her rescue and told her. 'Off you go now, that husband of yours will be waiting for you. Now, before you go can I ask if you would mind being called to work in the event of us being short handed at any time?'

Glad of a way to show her gratitude, Ellen quickly agreed. 'Of course, Mrs Vale, I'll be only too glad to help out at any time.'

'Thank you, Mrs Ryan, that is most kind of you.'

Ellen inclined her head to the woman and hurriedly backed out of the room, only to bump into Vera outside. In her arms was a parcel wrapped in brown paper. 'Ah, just who I wanted to see. This is from Mrs Vale,' Vera told her, plonking the package into Ellen's arms, she turned to another parcel on the floor behind her. 'And this is from me.'

Ellen took what Vera offered, placing it on top of the other. 'What is it, Vera? You've been so kind already that I don't know what to say.'

'It isn't much. It was my mother's and it's a bit moth-eaten now, but it should do you a turn. I'm off to the kitchen for a drink, you coming?'

'I'm not sure I'm supposed to do that because I'm not working here anymore.'

'Oh, it'll be all right. Maura won't mind and I'm sure no one else will either.' Reassured, Ellen followed her into the kitchen where Maura was just filling the huge brown teapot with boiling water. 'Smelt the tea, did you?' she asked Vera.

'Too right. You know I can sniff it out at a hundred paces. All right if Ellen joins us?'

Maura looked surprised. 'Do you have to ask? Come and sit down dear, you look worn out,' she said to Ellen, who had to agree that she did feel rather weary. Her back ached too and she sank gratefully into one of the kitchen chairs.

'I'll be able to return the kindness soon. You can visit me on your day off and we can have a good chat over a cup of tea.'

'I'd like that, wouldn't you Vera?'

'Too true. Now open your packages, Ellen and let's see what you've got.'

As the paper was pulled back on the first parcel, Ellen was pleased to find the bedding donated by Mrs Vale. 'Isn't it kind of her?'

'Very,' said Vera dryly. 'I'm sure she could have found some a bit newer though.'

'Oh, I don't mind, honestly. I'm glad of everything I get. I'll open yours now.' As Ellen opened the small, but heavy package, her breath caught in her throat. 'Oh, this is lovely. Are you sure you want to part with it?' Ellen looked at Vera, open-mouthed.

'I told you, it was my mother's and it's well worn. Never been too keen on it myself, but you might like it.' Vera sniffed.

'Yes, I do like it. Thank you so much.' Ellen looked down at the glorious riot of colour that was a bedspread, a hand-stitched patchwork quilt. The tiny squares of cotton fabric glowed with reds, blues, greens and yellows. 'It reminds me of the fields and woods back home in summertime. I'll treasure this always, Vera.'

Vera giggled. 'You're welcome, glad you like it.'

Picking up both parcels, Ellen swept a hand across her face and said, 'I'm going back to my home now to make the bed up. Thank you everyone and thanks for the tea, Maura. See you soon. Don't forget to visit, will you?' She looked around the kitchen as Maddie and Nessie entered. 'You too.'

They sent her on her way with best wishes and vowing to call to see her on their next day off, and Ellen left The Falls of Clyde hotel with very mixed feelings.

It was wonderful for her and John to have a home of their own, but she was going to miss the kindness and companionship of her friends.

CHAPTER 15

Opening the door to her home gave Ellen a tingle of delight. John would be home soon and she wanted to make the place look as homely as possible.

Unloading her parcels onto the bed, she stood and looked about her, wondering where to start. The empty grate beckoned and Ellen hurried through to the back to find some firewood. Luckily there was a stack of logs near the back door and in a lean-to she found some kindling, and making a holder of her skirt, she loaded some of each and hurried back inside.

Soon the living room had a fire burning brightly in the grate and Ellen was thrilled to see that it made the room look really cheery. Now for the kitchen range, she thought, then I can cook us some supper. This took considerably longer to achieve because the smoke kept billowing back into the room and the kindling just fizzled out. Ellen looked about her, wondering what she could use to get the fire going, then she saw some old bits of rag behind the bucket under the sink. She stuffed these into the range and lit them and after an initial smoulder they caught light to send flames hungrily licking through the twigs. Kneeling back on her heels, Ellen held out her hands to the blaze and once she could see it had taken, placed some of the smaller logs on top. Well pleased with her efforts, she walked back into the living room to make the bed.

It only took a few moments to put the sheets and pillowcases on and then, carefully smoothing out the creases, she laid the quilt on top. There, it looked perfect, the whole scene was one of domestic bliss, and Ellen sat in one of the fireside chairs to enjoy a few moments of tranquillity in her new home. Her back still ached and she felt extremely tired, but then she had worked hard over the past few days.

It was only a few minutes later when John arrived, a wide smile on his face. 'Hello my darling girl. My, this is grand, so it is. You've done wonders with this place,' he said taking her into his arms and hugging her closely.

Ellen was childishly pleased. 'Do you like it? I've lit the range as well, but I've just realised, we've nothing to cook on it yet. I could make something to drink though.'

'Great, what shall we have?'

'Maura gave me a small box of tea, shall we celebrate with that?'

'Bless the woman. In fact, haven't they all been marvellous. Everyone from the hotel has been so helpful, I don't know how to thank them.'

'They have, John, and I don't know how to thank them either. I couldn't have done this on my own. Aren't we lucky to have such good friends?'

'We are truly blessed my beloved. Now, lets go and get the water on for this tea. Then we shall have to see how much money we've got to buy a few vegetables and perhaps a small piece of meat.'

Side by side they stood in the tiny kitchen and watched as the water heated in an old saucepan, no kettle having been found in the cottage. 'I shall have to go to the store and buy one as soon as we have enough money,' Ellen grinned. 'It'll be hard to cook a meal with only one saucepan. I did think Mrs Vale was going to give us some pots and pans, but I think she forgot and I didn't like to remind her after everything she's done.'

'What are you going to make the tea in?' John said suddenly.

'Oh bother, I didn't think of that. I can't remember what's in this old cupboard.' Ellen crossed to the rather elderly unit leaning against one wall. 'Ah, just what we want.' She held up a teapot - minus its lid. 'There are some cups, plates and saucers here as well. They're rather cracked and dirty, but once they've had a wash they'll be serviceable.' She put them in the sink and poured some of the hot water over them.

Soon, Ellen and John were seated, one either side of the fireplace, cup of tea in hand, enjoying just being together, alone and in their own home at last.

Staring into the flames, Ellen said dreamily, 'This is perfect, isn't it?'

'It certainly is. Harry is trying to find somewhere to live now that he's seen how settled we're going to be.'

'What does Harry want a home for, he's on his own.'

'Not for much longer apparently.'

'What do you mean? Not for much longer.'

'He's going to ask Maddie to marry him as soon as he finds a house.'

191

A squeal left Ellen's lips. 'Maddie? Harry and Maddie! Getting married? Oh the sneaky thing, she never told me he'd asked her.'

'I don't think he has yet, so keep quiet about it.'

How wonderful for Maddie, who'd had such a tough time throughout her life. To be married to a nice man like Harry and have her own home would mean so much to her. Stella would have a father figure too and that was something Maddie had worried about, Ellen knew.

Then John stood up. 'I'd better be going to the store for food, otherwise we'll still be sitting here at bedtime.' He grinned. 'And I can't wait for that either.' He bent and brushed her cheek with his lips. 'I'll see you in a little while, my sweet Ellen.'

She waved him away with a laugh. 'Go on with you, you rogue. Honestly John, you have enough charm to bring the birds down from the trees.'

Shrugging on his jacket, he opened the door and with an elaborate bow, turned and went. Left on her own, Ellen again looked about the room with pleasure and sighed with contentment. Then, reluctantly she rose to her feet and took the cups through to the kitchen, washed them and then attended to the range. It was nicely banked up with logs and would be just right to cook a meal on when John returned.

As she went back into the living room, the pain in her back intensified and she rubbed it firmly with shaking fingers. Damn, she thought, I must have pulled a muscle or something moving the furniture. Making sure the fire was going well, she looked longingly at the bed. Tiredness overtook her and so slipping out of her dress and pulling back the pretty quilt, Ellen climbed onto the bed and sank gratefully into its mattress. As she struggled to stay awake, she noticed that the light was fading outside and decided that after a rest she would go and find some candles. But, try as she might, she couldn't keep her eyes open and soon sleep overwhelmed her.

The next thing she knew everything was in total darkness, and panic took hold as she struggled to remember where she was. Then, realising that she was in the cottage, Ellen grinned into the darkness with relief.

But why was it dark? And where was John? As she tried to sit up, cursing herself for not finding the candles earlier, a sharp pain shot through her back and with vice-like fingers coursed around to her stomach, and as it remained constant, Ellen groaned in agony.

God, what was happening to her? The thought that she must get up and find a candle was uppermost in her mind. Slowly she eased herself to the edge of the bed and swung her feet to the floor, the cold flagstones taking her breath away. As she stood, something wet and sticky ran down her legs, and her body began to tremble uncontrollably. And the searing pain went on. Oh, please God, where's John, why isn't he here with me? What's happening? Tears born of fear and suffering began to run down her face, but she brushed them aside. Knowing she must get to the kitchen, she tried to ignore the pain, and moved forward, her hands in front of her, feeling for one of the armchairs to guide her towards the door. Bent nearly double and sobbing loudly, Ellen managed to find the catch and open the door. She'd expected to find the kitchen warm and glowing with light from the range, but it was cold and dark. Now what? How was she to locate the candles? Leaning against the wall, she willed her brain to work. "Think," she said aloud, "where would they be?" Then she remembered the shelf by the sink. "Yes, I'm sure that's where they are." Her voice echoed eerily in the darkness.

Ellen stumbled across the kitchen floor and came up against the sink. With relief, she fumbled for the shelf and ran her hand along it, fingers flailing, until they touched something metal. The candleholder, thank goodness, she sighed, and felt again for the strikers. There weren't many left, but it would only take one if she were careful. By now her hands were shaking so much, trying to strike the tiny wooden stick was hard enough, but to hold it still to catch the wick was impossible. The first one spluttered out and more tears came, this time of frustration.

Luckily, she succeeded with the second, but when she looked down, her petticoat was stained darkly with blood. Then, with one hand clutching her belly, the other carrying the wavering light, Ellen made her way unsteadily back into the living room. Placing the candle on the mantle-shelf, she went to the chest of drawers, realising that she must get a shawl or freeze to death. This done she hugged it about her and went back to the bed. What she saw broke her heart. The sheets and the lovely patchwork quilt were all soaked with blood. Oh no, they're all ruined, was Ellen's last thought, as she felt herself falling, falling....

Leaving the cottage, John hurried along the street, jingling some coins in his pocket and dreaming about the lovely meal he and Ellen would share later. Once inside the general store, he realised that his few coppers wouldn't buy very much. He selected a few potatoes, some carrots and a turnip, then asked the storekeeper if he could manage to find him meat of some kind, for the remaining pennies. The kindly man produced some off-cuts of salty bacon and John licked his lips in anticipation of a bacon roly-poly, forgetting that their larder didn't yet contain the flour and suet needed to complete the dish.

Thanking the storekeeper, he stepped out onto Bothwell's main street. It was a grand little town and no mistake, and as he hurried homeward, he whistled a tune to show his pleasure. A minute later, he met Harry. 'Hello there, and where are you off to?'

Harry grinned, 'I'm off to see my lady love if you must know.' He hesitated. 'Got time for a quick drink first though if you like.'

'That would be grand, Harry, but I mustn't be long, Ellen is waiting for these.' He held up the paper bag holding his purchases.

'It won't take long, just a swift half, as my old man used to say.' Harry laughed. 'I'm going to pop the question tonight see, and it's making me rather nervous.'

'I remember the feeling well,' John told him. 'Shall we go in here?' he asked as they passed a small hotel. 'So, you and Maddie might be going to tie the knot at last then?'

He and Harry settled themselves at a table, drinks in front of them. 'Yes, it's now or never. Trouble is I'm not sure if she's keen. What do you think?'

John pondered the question. He had never been particularly good with women and knew he would never understand them as long as he lived, but Harry probably wanted to hear something good, so he said, 'I think you'll be fine. She's a fine woman is Maddie and I think she'll make a good wife. And,' he added, 'you'll have a ready made family with little Stella.'

This seemed to satisfy Harry and he relaxed back in his chair, picked up his drink and took a long quaff. Just then a group of men entered the hotel bar and after ordering their drinks came to sit near John and Harry. Within minutes, one man looked across and asked John, 'Are you from Ireland, sir?'

'I am,' said John. 'Who's asking?'

'No offence meant, but I thought I recognised the accent, that was all,' the man said in a friendly way. 'Whereabouts are you from then?'

'Roscommon. Do you know it?'

'To be sure I do. Didn't my old mother, God rest her soul, come from there?'

John shook his head. 'It's a small world isn't it, when you come to think?'

'It certainly is. Let me buy you a drink, just for old times sake.' The man offered.

'I'd love to have a drink with you, but I must away home, the wife is waiting for me.'

There was a general shout of laughter all round, but the man said kindly. 'I'm sure she won't begrudge you one drink with an old pal from back home surely.'

John looked at Harry, who shrugged. 'I don't suppose one more will make any difference.'

As the man went to the bar for more drinks, the rest of the crowd moved across to join John and Harry at their table, and soon a jolly atmosphere filled the room. John apologised for not having any money on him with which to repay the kindness of drinks bought, but no one seemed to mind and the jugs of ale came thick and fast.

Many tales of life in Ireland were recounted and the stories got more and more ridiculous, until, amid much raucous laughter, one of the man's companions insisted that his family were related to Queen Victoria herself.

Suddenly, through a haze, John heard the landlord shouting about wanting to get to his bed. My God, he thought, what can the time be? He looked across at Harry who was red of face and bleary-eyed. 'We should be going, Harry. The girls will wonder where we are.'

'Oh, they'll be fine, John. Stop worrying.'

John stood up and tugged at Harry's sleeve. 'Come on, Maddie won't be expecting you now and you can't ask her to marry you in this state, now can you?' Much ribbing followed this statement as the men all found the idea of getting married quite terrifying. 'Rather you than me, mate,' was the general consensus. With ribald laughter ringing in their ears, John and Harry left the hotel and staggered along the street. Somehow John still maintained a grip on the bag of shopping as he almost carried Harry back to the barracks, watching with a stupid grin on his face as his friend walked unsteadily along to his billet. Then, turning for home, John tried desperately to think of an excuse for being so late. Perhaps Ellen would be in bed, fast asleep. Yes that would be best, he thought in his muddled state. As he approached the cottage, he saw a light and realised that he wasn't going to get off lightly. He moaned then, remembering his promise to Ellen that they would celebrate their new home when they went to bed. Oh, dear God, what am I going to say to her?

Lifting the latch and opening the door slowly, John held his breath and peered into the room. At first he could see nothing amiss, but then saw Ellen lying on the floor, the sight of which sobered him up quicker than ever before.

He ran forward and knelt down beside her prone body and taking one of her cold hands in his, began to chafe it to try and rouse her. When there was no response, John jumped to his feet, panic setting in.

He must get help, but where from this time of night? Oh, my poor Ellen, how long had she been there?

There was only one place John could think to go - the Falls of Clyde Hotel. He turned and ran as fast as he could, out along the street, his feet pounding like the beats of a drum, matched only by his heartbeat. The hotel was in darkness, but he banged on the door with both fists, shouting for help.

At last the door opened a crack, to reveal Vera clad in a nightgown, hair in rags. ''Ere, what's all that noise? Who is it?'

'It's me Vera, John. Please come quickly, Ellen's collapsed on the floor. I think she's dead. Oh, please help me.' His voice cracked with emotion.

'Oh my Gawd,' Vera said. 'Wait there, I'll get Maddie.'

While she was gone, John paced the porch, frantic to get back to Ellen, but within a moment, Maddie appeared and almost bowled him over in her haste. 'What happened?' she gasped as they ran back along the street, Vera in their wake.

'I don't know, I've just found her,' John gasped.

Maddie threw him a questioning look as they arrived, panting at the gate. Quickly John opened the door and ran inside, where he fell to his knees beside the prostrate form of his wife.

Maddie knelt beside him and felt for a pulse. 'She's alive, thank The Lord, but we need medical help.' Turning her head she barked at Vera, 'Go and fetch the doctor. He's staying at the Crown.'

Without a word Vera dashed back outside, leaving a worried John and Maddie to sit looking sadly down at the still form on the floor.

It felt like forever before the doctor arrived. He ordered the bed to be stripped and the patient placed on it, then examined Ellen closely, with the help of Maddie holding the candle.

John stood in a daze, twisting his hands together, and praying. Please Lord; let my lovely Ellen live. He cried out in sorrow as the doctor announced that Ellen had lost the baby she was carrying; a baby neither of them knew she was expecting.

It was very cold in the cottage and Vera set to work to light a fire in the grate, bustling about in her haste. She and Maddie had given him some odd looks, John knew and he guessed they wondered why he hadn't found Ellen sooner. He would have to try and explain, but it would do no good, and it might be too late. He vowed that if he lost his beloved Ellen, not a drop of alcohol would ever pass his lips again.

But he mustn't lose her, he mustn't.

At last the fire took hold and warmth began to permeate the room. The doctor left and Maddie appeared as if by magic, with a cup of tea, which she pushed into John's stiff fingers. 'Here, drink this. You're lucky, the doctor thinks she'll live, although she's lost a lot of blood. It'll be touch and go for several days, so she'll need a close eye kept on her.' Maddie stood up straight. 'Did you hear me, John?'

He nodded. 'Yes, Maddie, thank you. Thank you both for what you've done tonight.' He looked across at Ellen where she lay on the bare mattress, and covered only by her shawl and his topcoat. 'I'll stay with her day and night until she's well again, I promise.' Then he told them what had happened earlier that evening. 'So I blame myself, I should have come straight home.'

To his astonishment, Maddie agreed with him. 'Yes, you should. What's wrong with you men that you can't pass an ale house without going in?' It was said lightly, but John had the feeling that Maddie was very angry with both him and Harry.

Vera stifled a yawn and Maddie said, 'Right, we'll be off to try and get some sleep, but make sure you watch her closely. If there is any change, either send for the doctor, or us. One of us will call in tomorrow.' She came to lean over him and placed a comforting hand on his arm. 'I'm sure she'll be all right, so try not to worry. I'm sorry about the baby, I really am.' Picking up the soiled bedclothes, Maddie led the way out, and John was left sitting in silence, with only the light from the fire and the guttering candle to keep him company.

In the cocoon, warm and safe, Ellen fought against the beckoning light. Her eyelids were heavy and she felt safe in the blackness. Somewhere, as though from far away, a voice penetrated her mind. She knew the voice, acknowledged it even, but any movement was impossible. Her limbs felt constricted by bonds, tight, but not painful, holding her to the bed. Yes, she thought numbly, I'm on a bed, but where?

Slowly her eyes opened, to see John and Maddie's anxious faces hovering over her and gradually realisation sank in. She was in her bed, in the cottage; and she had fainted. That was all she could remember at first, but then memories of the blood soaked petticoat and bedclothes forced themselves upon her.

'What happened?' she whispered, realising that John held her hand. He squeezed it and tried to smile.

'Don't you remember, my sweet girl?' he asked.

Ellen tried to shake her head, but dizziness swept in and she closed her eyes again. 'No,' she managed to say. But somewhere in her subconscious something stirred, some vague recollection. Then her eyes flew open. 'Did I lose a baby?'

She saw Maddie nod and as she turned her gaze on John, she saw tears glistening on his lashes. 'Yes, my lovely girl, you lost our baby, but it was my fault, I should never have left you for so long. I'm so sorry, can you ever forgive me?'

Ellen wrestled with his words, not knowing what he meant. It was she who must ask for forgiveness, for losing something so precious. No words would come, only an aching longing. Tears came then; tears that quickly turned to wracking sobs, not only for the little child born too soon but for her lovely Mary, now dead many months.

I must have been very wicked to have two children taken from me, she cried inwardly. Please God, what have I done to deserve this?

Gradually her tears subsided and she opened her eyes to see Maddie holding a cup. 'Here, you must drink this, Ellen. You've lost a lot of blood.'

She turned her head away, not wanting anything that would revive her. She deserved to die as well as her children. What kind of mother loses two children?

Between them, John and Maddie lifted Ellen into a sitting position, and Maddie tried again with the cup of steaming brew. 'Come along, you mustn't blame yourself, it happens all the time. The poor wee thing probably wasn't strong enough to hold on inside you, and that's not your fault, it's just nature.'

'Are you sure? It wasn't something I did?' Ellen eyed them suspiciously.

Maddie grinned. 'You're a big strong girl, so what could you have done wrong? You didn't even know you were pregnant, did you?'

'No. I wonder if that's why I fainted the other week. Do you think it could have been?' Ellen looked at her husband. 'We did rather a lot of lovemaking, I hope it wasn't that. Or perhaps it was God's punishment for doing it before we were married.'

'Hush sweetheart, I'm sure it wasn't. In any case, God would never be so cruel.' John rubbed the back of her hand gently with his thumb. 'I am the one who must ask for forgiveness. I got caught up in a drinking session and was late home. I swear it will never happen again, my love. I swear.' Looking slightly sheepish, he added, 'I did bring home the food though.'

After a few sips of beef tea, Ellen leaned back exhausted. Then she noticed the crisp white sheets and the warm blanket covering her. 'Where did these come from?'

'The hotel,' Maddie told her. 'Yours were in need of a wash and are being done now. Mrs Vale let me borrow these until your own are dried and ironed.'

'The quilt looked ruined,' Ellen said sadly.

'No, it'll be fine,' said Maddie firmly. 'Now, you settle back and have another sleep. I'll come again later.' She turned to John. 'And mind you stay with her.'

'I will, Maddie, I promise and thank you for all you've done. And the other's at the hotel. I'll thank them when I see them of course.'

With a sound like she was clearing her throat, Maddie walked to the door, gave a wave, and was gone, her firm footsteps resounding on the roadway outside.

'What would we do without her?' John murmured.

Ellen gave no answer; she wanted to sleep. Perhaps sleep could blot out this pain in her heart and bring some peace from the nagging thought that it had been her fault. No matter what anyone said, she was responsible for her children and she had failed them both - miserably.

As he sat watching his wife sleep, John thought long and hard about his life. For too long he had led a bachelor existence, doing what he wanted, when he liked. Even after he married Ellen, he hadn't felt like a husband. He frowned and ran a hand across his face. Why was that, he wondered? Had he been any different back home in Ireland? If he was honest with himself, no he hadn't. His poor Catherine must have been driven mad by his constant gallivanting around, joining first one gang and then another. There always seemed to be something exciting to do in Roscommon, or some new political hot-head to follow.

That was what had got him into the trouble that led to his being here on this island. He'd heard of the band of men who were trying to oust one of the more liberal candidates that was standing at the local elections. The man was sympathetic to the English, and to men who had families they couldn't feed this didn't go down too well. Ireland was in turmoil at the time, with failed crops and rigid rule; many were taking the law into their own hands. Many more had taken what they could carry and left for America, some even leaving starving children behind in the hope that someone would care for them.

No one had, and John recalled seeing children begging on the street, but with his own belly empty all he could do was pass by, eyes firmly fixed on the ground so that he wouldn't see the tiny wasted bodies.

Then, one night, he'd joined a group of friends and they'd gone to teach the candidate a lesson. They'd show him how much they resented his opinions they cheered as they marched along the road toward his house. Not sure of what happened next, John remembered seeing the police running toward them and glancing over his shoulder saw smoke pouring from the man's house. He'd turned to run, but was too slow and was hauled off in handcuffs. Many of his mates had got away and he'd never split on them, but a few were charged, found guilty and shipped off to Van Diemen's Land with him. When he'd asked why they were to be sent so far, he was told that the English prisons were full, and in any case a good life could be had in the prosperous new land.

A wry laugh forced it's way from his throat. If this was what they called a good life, well he'd like to see a bad one. His employment as a police constable was boring and unproductive. There was no way to supplement the few coppers a week he received as payment and he'd relied on the perks of Ellen's job when thinking about the future.

But that must come to an end now. It would take her several weeks to recover and work at the hotel would be impossible, so it was up to him to find a way to make money. He scratched his head, thinking about the jobs he'd had in Ireland. He was fairly adept at several things, including tailoring, but there wasn't much call for that here in Bothwell. No, he'd have to think of something else, some other way to make an honest few coppers.

Slowly the days dragged by, but Ellen didn't notice. All she wanted to do was lie in her bed where she felt safe; safe from all the hurt she had ever suffered. On the day Maddie and Vera had come to change the bed linen, Ellen refused to speak to them, sitting in a chair, eyes fixed firmly on the flickering flames in the grate. Maddie had tried to get her interested in having the pretty quilt back, but still Ellen showed no interest. A plate of food was put into her hands and a cup of beef tea offered, but there was no sign of recognition of her friends. Even John received no more than a cursory glance, and although she knew he was there and was glad of it, Ellen couldn't rouse herself from the stupor she was in. Washing was a half-hearted affair and had it not been for Maddie, she would have lain in her filth for days, uncaring as to her appearance. She knew she was unlovely, so why should she bother about what she looked like? I'm ugly, Ellen thought to herself, why do they keep bothering me to wash and comb my hair. No one will notice, because no one ever looks at me with any interest.

One day, Maddie came as usual with Nessie in tow, bringing the usual bread, cheese and soup. Ellen turned away when her friend approached the bed, unable to look her in the eye and see the reproach she knew would be there. While Nessie was in the kitchen, Maddie leaned close to Ellen and whispered, 'I've brought Nessie to see you, I think it's the last outing she'll be having. Please Ellen, just say a few words to her will you? The poor girl is only just able to stand, but begged to come here to see you, before it's too late and she couldn't make it. Please.'

Somewhere deep inside, Ellen felt a stirring of compassion. Poor Nessie, who'd made such a pretty picture as her bridesmaid only a few weeks before, was failing fast. She looked up as the girl entered and was shocked at her appearance. Already thin, Nessie was now nothing more than skin and bone. Even her blonde hair had lost its shine and lay thin and straggly on her shoulders.

Doing her best to hide her shock, Ellen tried to think of something to say to Nessie and the feelings she had suppressed came to the surface. Fighting for self-control, at last she said, 'Hello, Nessie, it's lovely to see you.'

The girl's thin face lit up. 'Hello Ellen, I'm glad to see you looking better. Maddie told me you were very poorly and needed lots of rest, otherwise I'd have come before. I am sorry about the baby. I may see it soon, because I'm going to heaven and I'm sure your baby will be there as well as your little girl, Mary. All good souls go to heaven that's what Mrs Vale says.'

Tears stung Ellen's eyes and her breath caught in her throat, but she patted the bed. 'Come and sit with me for a while, Nessie. Tell me what's been happening at the hotel.'

The young woman perched herself on the edge of the bed and related some of the goings-on at the Falls of Clyde. Meanwhile Maddie hurried out into the kitchen and put the soup to warm a wide smile on her lips and as John came in through the back door, she inclined her head toward the living room. 'I think you'll see a difference in Ellen now, hopefully she's turned the corner. Try to get her up and about and even outside if you can. Fresh air will do wonders, especially now it's getting warmer.'

John took Maddie's hand and pumped it enthusiastically. 'I'll never be able to thank you enough. I can't imagine what we'd have done these past days without your help, I really can't.'

'Well, it's up to you now. If you can manage, I won't come every day, I'll be needed at the hotel to help nurse Nessie.'

At John's enquiring look, Maddie explained the sad plight of the pretty young girl whose life was almost over, and who had never really had a chance to live at all.

Gradually Ellen regained her strength and although the heartache still sat in her chest like a solid stone, she managed to put on a cheerful face. She wanted to go to church, having been only once in the past few weeks, and that was to Nessie's funeral and so one Sunday morning John with her along the street to the service. The Reverend McDonald smiled his pleasure at seeing them and Ellen felt comforted in the sombre surroundings.

As the prayers were said she thought of her two children who she was sure were now in heaven because they had died free of sin, and she asked the Angels to watch over them for her.

As they walked home from Church, she turned and smiled at John. 'Thank you for taking me, I feel so much better now.'

He turned surprised eyes toward her. 'I'm glad of that, my dear girl. It's lovely to see you smiling again and as it's a beautiful day, shall we go for a walk?'

'Yes, I'd like that. Can we go to the waterfall?'

'It's a long way, are you sure you can manage it?'

'Yes,' came the decisive answer.

A puzzled look on his face, John pulled her arm through his and for a while they walked companionably along the dusty road, then he asked, 'What made you want to come this way?'

Ellen didn't answer straight away, and was obviously deep in thought, but then she said, 'I'm not sure, but something tells me I must do this for my two daughters.'

John stopped suddenly nearly pulling Ellen off her feet. 'Two daughters? Who said anything about the baby being a girl?' He stared down into her face, worry etched in every line of his own.

But she shrugged calmly. 'I just know. Something came to me in Church, something I can't explain. Please John, just humour me.'

After a long hot walk they arrived at the waterfall and Ellen sat down on a rock to watch the water as it cascaded in a torrent below. John scooped up a little from the still pool at the edge and sipped the refreshing liquid, then offered some to Ellen, but she refused with a shake of her head, her eyes never leaving the wonderful sight before her.

Suddenly she reached out and gripped his arm. 'Look John. Aren't they beautiful?'

John looked and saw flashes of light in amongst the reeds at the water's edge. Two dragonflies darted out across the water, their wings shining an iridescent blue in the sunshine, and he glanced at Ellen who watched them enthralled. 'They're very pretty, do you know what they are?'

'Oh yes, I know,' was all Ellen said, before she stood up. 'Let's go home now John, and I'll make us some lunch.' Happiness and certainty filled her; her girls were both safe and well in the arms of Jesus.

Try as he might, John never fathomed out what had made Ellen behave so strangely on that day. He had even discussed it with Harry, but he had even less idea. 'Women are a law unto themselves,' he said. 'As much as we love them, we're never going to understand them.' He grinned. 'Now take Maddie for instance. I've explained time and time again about what happened that night in the bar, but she still doesn't understand that when friends offer a drink it's rude to refuse.'

'I know what you mean, Harry, but even so I do still feel guilty about that night.'

'Well yes, as well you might, but you weren't to know what was going to happen were you?'

'No I wasn't.' Wanting to change the subject, he then asked, 'So, have you persuaded Maddie to marry you yet?'

'Mmm, not really sure. Sometimes she talks as though we're already married and other times she acts all coy.' Harry shook his head in exasperation. 'Buggered if I know to be honest. I suppose she'll make up her mind sooner or later.'

'Listen, Harry, I've been wondering, how can we make some money in this place? You any ideas?'

'Not really, but I think it'll be worth our while to ask around. Someone somewhere must know how to make a few bob.' He sniffed. 'Trouble is nothing much happens here, does it?'

'No, even those Irish prisoners keep their noses clean.'

'Ah well, you think so, do you?' Harry raised his eyebrows.

'What have you heard? Come on tell me.' John was impatient for news.

'I've heard that one of them goes off to visit friends without permission from the Chief. Gone for days sometimes apparently.'

This was not news to John. He already knew of the Mitchel man's excursions: he and several others. But failed to see how that could be used to his advantage.

'Couldn't we blackmail him?' Harry asked.

'Don't be daft man, it's an open secret so he's hardly going to pay for our silence is he? No I'll have to think of something else.' John sighed and rubbed a weary hand across his brow. But what?

'Come in.' The Chief's voice boomed from the other side of the door.

John entered the office with some trepidation; what could he have been called in for?

'Ah Ryan,' the Chief said, 'It has been decided to give you an occupation with a little more responsibility. You've kept yourself out of trouble since arriving in Bothwell, so we are putting you in charge of the prison block.'

John felt his heart sink almost to his stomach. What in God's name was he going to do there? It would be worse than walking the streets all day. 'Um, may I ask why, sir?'

'As I said, you have a clean sheet, have caused no trouble and deserve a better position.' The Chief's brow furrowed. 'Is there a problem with that?'

'No sir, no indeed, I'll be pleased to accept. When shall I start my new duties, sir?'

'Right away, man, no time like the present. Go over there now and see Mcpherson, he knows you're coming and will show you the ropes. He's off back to Hobart tomorrow, so we need someone there we can trust right away.' The hint of a smile twitched at the Chief's lips.

Nodding a slight bow in his direction, John said, 'Thank you, sir, I'll go right away.' He backed out of the room, his mind in a whirl. How am I ever going to cope with being stuck in the prison block all day, every day he wondered dismally?

The tall figure of Constable Mcpherson opened the door and welcomed John inside. 'I'll show you the office and the forms you'll need first, then we'll have a drink,' the man said as he entered a small room just off the main corridor. 'There's nothing much to it really. You can write I take it?'

'Yes, I can, although my spelling's not up to much I'm afraid.'

'Don't worry about that as long as you know what it means,' Mcpherson laughed. 'Don't look so glum man, it's not so bad. There are times like today when you have no prisoners at all, so you can slope off home as long as someone knows where you are. And even when we do have a resident, they're no trouble as a rule. Some even pay for extra's, if you know what I mean?' He tapped the side of his nose.

This cheered John up considerably. The new post was definitely looking more promising.

After a brief review of the forms, he was shown a cabinet where all the files were set in alphabetical order, each prisoner having a file of his own. It all seemed straight forward to John who nodded and said, 'Yes, it all seems fairly simple.'

'Good, then let's be off to the canteen.'

'The canteen?' John queried.

'Yes the canteen, where else did you think we could get a cup of tea?'

Realisation dawned. Tea, of course! John resolved then and there that a few changes would have to be made when he was in charge. How could a man get through the day without a decent drop of the Irish whiskey inside him?

On leaving the canteen half an hour later, Mcpherson gave John the huge ring of keys. 'There you are, Constable Ryan, they're all yours. Good luck.'

'You're off to Hobart I hear?'

'Yes, I'm to run the office in charge of all the new intake.'

'I heard that soon no more prisoners were going to be transported. What will you do then?'

'It's only a rumour, so I'm not worried.'

With a shrug John decided not to pursue the matter, but he was sure Harry had said something about it the other night. 'Well,' he said now, 'all the best then. I hope you get on all right in Hobart.'

'Thanks,' Mcpherson said and the two men shook hands.

As he watched him walked away, John suddenly felt pleased with himself. Promotion was not often forthcoming and he was itching to get home and tell Ellen. 'She'll be over the moon, so she will.'

And she was. 'How clever you are, you'll be Governor of the island before too long.'

'Whoa, steady on, I don't think I'm quite ready for that.'

'Will you be paid extra for this new position?' she asked, looking fondly at her husband.

John wrinkled his nose. 'Only a very small amount, hardly worth anything, but it's better than nothing, I suppose.'

'Of course it is. We'll mange, just you wait and see.' Now that she was fit and strong again she would make up for the loss of his child, and the only way she could think of was to make him as comfortable as possible.

It would soon be Christmas and she had been planning ways of decorating the cottage. She had also begged Mrs Vale for a few days work so that she could buy the food to make John a special dinner on the day.

Her help was needed at the hotel as they were short-staffed.

It still amazed everyone who had been sent from England when Christmas day was spent out in the open air, under a brilliant sky, with warm sunshine caressing their backs.

Ellen had decided that she would pull the kitchen table out onto the grass at the back of the cottage and lay it with a new tablecloth that she had been secretly embroidering and some pretty plates found languishing at the back of the pantry at the hotel.

Maura had insisted she have them, as there were only four left of a set. 'No one is going to need or miss those, you can be sure.'

'I love the pattern.' Ellen had smoothed a hand over the intricate floral design.

'Mmmm, I can't remember ever seeing the whole set, so goodness knows where they came from.'

Standing in her kitchen, Ellen looked about her with pleasure. Gradually, over the past few weeks, she had gathered enough things to make it look really homely. They now had several pots and pans that sat grandly on the shelf that John had put up especially.

The black range no longer frightened her, and usually lit first time, and apart from cooking it was used less now that the hot weather had arrived.

Christmas was going to be extra special this year because on Boxing Day, Maddie and Harry were getting married. Ellen was thrilled for them; they made a handsome couple and seemed to get along very well. Although she found their earthy humour sometimes rather off-putting, she knew they loved one another, and hoped their future together would be long and happy.

All of a sudden life looked altogether brighter and Ellen prayed that the coming year would see her bringing a new life into the world.

That would make her and John's happiness complete.

CHAPTER 16

In was in the gathering dusk of a May evening that Ellen told John that she was expecting another child.

The fire was lit and the room, cosy and warm, safe from the freshening wind that blew outside.

'Oh my precious girl. How do you feel? Are you all right?' John's face was a picture of amazement and Ellen laughed.

'I'm fine, and don't get too excited just in case there's another reason I'm late with my monthly curse.'

He looked up sharply. 'What other reason could there be?'

'Sometimes we women get other things wrong with us, but don't worry, I'm sure it's going to be all right.' She grinned. 'I had some more news today as well.'

'What's that?'

'Maddie and Harry are going to be parents as well.'

'Well I never, the sly old dog, he hasn't said a word.'

'Perhaps Maddie wanted me to be the first to know. Isn't it wonderful, we can keep an eye on each other? She's further on than I am, but didn't say anything until she was certain. Being so big, Maddie wondered if she was imagining it at first.'

John chuckled. 'I'll never understand you women. I'm pleased for them, to be sure, but even more pleased for us.' He rose from his chair and came to kneel in front of her, then taking one of her hands in his; he kissed her fingertips. 'Promise me you'll look after yourself properly this time. No lifting, no carrying. Do you understand?'

'Yes, John, I understand. I don't want to lose this baby either, that would be horrible. You don't think God could do that to me, do you?'

'It's not God, my love, it's nature. Sometimes the babies die because they have something wrong with them. It's no one's fault.'

'Have you become an authority on the subject all of a sudden?' Ellen asked, a twinkle in her eye.

'Well, I did ask a lot of questions when you were so ill the other month. I was worried in case it was something I'd done.'

Ellen reached out to stroke his face with gentle fingers. 'Dear John, you're so caring and I do love you.'

'And I love you too, Mrs Ryan.'

Throughout the winter months, Ellen kept indoors as much as possible and rested. It wasn't that she felt tired, but was so worried about losing her baby that it seemed best.

Maddie agreed, although she was blooming and never rested at all, and still worked at the hotel every day as no more women had been sent from Hobart, not even one to replace Nessie. 'You might look robust, my girl, but it won't hurt you to put your feet up while you can.'

It was Maddie's day off and they sat one either side of the fire as they so often did, drinking tea and eating the little cakes Ellen liked to bake. Outside, the weather was bleak, but sitting in the firelight both women felt sheltered from the winter storm.

'I shan't want to go out after sitting here all afternoon,' Maddie said, then brushing crumbs from her chin, gave her hearty laugh, before leaning forward to say, 'Mmm, guess who was seen the other day? I didn't know her of course, but I was with Vera in the general store and this young woman came in all dressed to the nines.' She looked up. 'Bridget? Used to work at the hotel I gather.'

Ellen's eye widened in surprise. 'Bridget? Goodness gracious, I've caught sight of her from time to time, usually in a carriage. She was sent off to work at the hotel owner's farm, but what happened to her after that we never found out. All dressed up, you say?'

'Yes, Vera says she must have landed on her feet when she went there. By the way, he doesn't own the hotel now, it's a Mr Andrews.'

'I think he moved away so she must be living somewhere else now. Did Bridget speak to Vera?'

'Not really, just smiled and said hello, how are you? But didn't wait for an answer and left the shop. It was a fine gown she was wearing I can tell you.'

'What was it like?'

'It was a soft grey in colour, full skirted, with a pink bodice and a hat to match. Oh yes, and she had a parasol of the same pink too.'

'It sounds lovely. She certainly didn't have anything like that when she lived at the hotel. Like me, she had two rather tattered dresses and that was all. No hats or parasols then.' Ellen sat back and stared into the flames. 'She has done well for herself by the sounds of things, but I wonder if she's happy?'

'Like us you mean?'

'I'm very happy, Maddie, are you?'

With a nod, Maddie said, 'I certainly am. Harry's a really good man. A bit rough round the edges, but lovely with it. He's looking forward to being a father that's for sure. Had no children see, even though he was married back in England, and of course, although he dotes on Stella, it's not quite the same as one of his own.'

'Were you married, Maddie? I don't think I ever asked you before even though we've known each other for so long.'

'I was, to a right pig. Sent me out to work the streets while he lived a life of luxury. Well, it wasn't that good, but it seemed like that to me after standing on cold street corners all night.'

'What happened to him?'

'Got done over one night by some man he'd fleeced. He didn't die, but might as well have done. Left him an idiot it did, so he's in an asylum now.'

'Isn't it strange the way we treat the memory of our lives back in England as though it happened in some other world, some other time.'

'I feel, as though it was, don't you? Aren't we better off here?'

'I suppose we are.' Ellen mused. 'Yes, I'm definitely better off. I met John and we're happily settled so what more could I ask?'

'We certainly landed on our feet, you and me. Well, I must be going; otherwise I'll have Mrs Vale checking her watch. Thanks for the tea and cakes, and if I don't see you before, I'll see you next week. Any messages for anyone?'

'No thanks. I might pop round to see everyone soon. Cheerio for now.'

'Bye,' called Maddie as she bustled out.

The prison in Bothwell so rarely had any inmates that John's idea to make a few extra pennies from them rather faltered.

Then one day a man was brought in who started throwing his weight about as soon as the door closed behind him. His demands for this and that did not go unnoticed by John and once the guards had left, he went in to see what all the fuss was about.

Broderick Henderson explained that he was a wealthy landowner and that he had been brought into Bothwell on a false charge. 'I didn't beat the young Abo, I wouldn't, he's been with me for years. It was his father I guess, nasty bit of work he is. I must see a lawyer as soon as possible, otherwise my farm will go to pot without me there.'

'I'm sorry sir, but the lawyer doesn't come to Bothwell for

another three weeks,' John explained.

Mr Henderson's face suffused with colour. 'Three bloody weeks? Christ, what am I going to do till then?'

John's ears pricked up. 'Well, sir, all I can do is make your stay as pleasant as possible.'

'Pleasant! Pah! The place is cold and damp, how can it ever be anything else?'

'There are ways to overcome the discomfort, sir.'

'Such as?' The man's eyes narrowed, and John knew he must go carefully. Mr Henderson was obviously no fool.

'I could ask the Chief if a small stove could be brought in, or perhaps an extra blanket for the bed.'

'Decent fellow is he, this Chief?'

'He's a fair man in his way, so he is.'

'Mmm, well see what you can do, will you?'

John touched his cap. 'I'll do that, sir. Right away.' As he left the cell, John's face broadened in a wide smile. Now, perhaps he could make enough to treat Ellen to a badly needed new gown.

The Chief didn't want to know. 'I don't care who he is, he's not getting anything to make life comfortable from me. He can wait until his trial like everyone else, then if he's innocent, he'll be able to go home and be comfortable there.'

John had tried a mild protest, but knowing the Chief as he did, realised that Mr Henderson was crying in the wind. So it would be up to himself to see what could be done to ease the man's lot.

'What! He dares to compare me with a common criminal?' Mr Henderson was rampant.

John chose his word carefully, 'Well, sir, of course I can see what might be done privately, but it may mean the outlay of a few pennies.'

'Hrrmph! I suppose if it's the only way. See what you can do man, I've money enough. Here, I've written a list of things I need, so be a good fellow and see to it will you?'

John took the proffered paper and glanced down the line of writing, then nodded. 'I think I can find most of this, sir. It might take a day or two with some things, but I'll do the best I can.'

'Thank you, I'll see you all right constable, have no fear.'

John backed out of the room, his mind working feverishly over what was needed and where to find it. He went first to the prison storeroom and found a small oil stove, two woollen blankets and some toiletries, but just as he was about to leave, the store manager came in and demanded to know what he was doing.

When it was explained who the items were for and that there

might be some profit in it, the man happily agreed to turn a blind eye.

Going next to the canteen, John wandered about the kitchen to see what food might be going spare, but was disappointed to find that the place was clean - and empty. Never mind he'd come back later when the lunches were being prepared; there would something about then he was sure.

But when he returned, there were three men busily preparing a pile of vegetables and tossing them into huge pans that sat on top of the enormous wood burning range. The heat was unbearable and John wondered how the cooks stood it, until he remembered that they too were prisoners serving a sentence. They had no choice in the matter.

Reluctant to share even more of his hard earned cash, John quietly slipped away to rethink his plans. He'd managed to find writing paper, pen and ink in his own office store and Mr Henderson seemed quite happy with the things he'd acquired so far, but food was going to be a problem.

Later as he collected the dishes from his prisoner's cell, and received complaints both about the quantity and quality of the food, an idea formulated in John's mind.

He'd cook some food himself!

His first attempt was a disaster for he badly overcooked the meat, making it tough. John stood looking at the piece of Kangaroo meat for a moment, a hand cupping his chin. Then he prodded it and tried to remember what Ellen did to hers. She cooked it slowly he suddenly realised, not put over a blazing fire as he had done. Throwing it in the bin, he went into the cool room to find another piece. This was smaller and looked a different colour, but he laid it on a flat dish and placed it in the oven, then put the vegetables back into a pan of hot water. They had come out almost as raw as they went in, so he guessed they needed longer too.

Hoping that no one noticed the light on in the canteen, he hovered near the stove, before deciding to go and do his last check of the night while the food was cooking.

Carefully leaving the place in darkness, John set off toward the prison. He looked in on Mr Henderson who complained of being hungry.

'I may be able to help with that very soon, sir,' John told him.

'How's that?'

'I'm just cooking a little something right now, then I'll be back. It'll be a late supper.'

The man grunted. 'Well done. Can't wait to get something decent inside me.'

John hurried back to the kitchen, relishing the smell as he opened the door. If it turned out as good as it smelled, then Mr Henderson was in for a good meal.

It looked great, John thought, as he carefully placed the meat and vegetables onto a large oval platter that he found in a cupboard. Then picking up a bottle of whiskey he'd found lurking in the back of the larder, he made his way back to his impatient prisoner.

Mr Henderson was extremely pleased with his meal. 'My, that was the best piece of meat I've had in many a year. And this is a good drop of the hard stuff too. Can you leave the bottle?'

'Yes, sir, I'll do that. I'm so glad you enjoyed it, sir, the best Irish there is sir. I'll bid you goodnight now.' A broad grin stretched John's face as he hurried back to the kitchen to clear up. It wouldn't do for anyone to suspect anything.

'You're home late,' Ellen greeted him as he came through the door.

'Sorry about that my love. I had a prisoner to make supper for.'

'You? Why did you have to make it?'

'Well, 'tis a long story, but the poor man was hungry so I obliged.'

Ellen giggled. 'I didn't know you could cook.'

'To be honest, my first attempt was not good, but at the second try I produced a decent piece of meat, some potatoes and a few carrots. Really enjoyed himself, he did.'

A frown creased her brow. 'So where did you get this food from?'

'I found it in the canteen larder. There's so much in there I don't think anyone will miss it.'

'How nice to have a full larder,' Ellen sighed. 'All I've got for you is stew.'

'I'm sure it's an excellent stew. Come here and give your husband a kiss, and then you can dish it up.' John held out his arms, and as Ellen ran into them, he gently caressed the swell of her stomach. 'Are you resting enough, my sweet? You look tired.'

'Stop worrying, I'm fine. It's late that's all and I'm ready for my bed.' She planted a kiss on his cheek and then hurried off to the kitchen to fetch the food

Soon John sat back in his armchair, replete. 'That was lovely. I don't know how you do it on what little money I give you, but soon our fortunes may be looking up. How does the thought of a new gown sound?'

Ellen's eyes widened. 'Oh John, that would be wonderful, but how are we going to be able to afford it?'

John tapped the side of his nose. 'You'll see, my love. You'll see.'

As John passed the Chief's office the following morning, a great deal of shouting came from inside, but he hurried by, not wishing to get involved in other peoples squabbles.

Mr Henderson greeted him warmly, and when asked if he slept well, replied, 'Excellent night's sleep thanks to you, my man. A full belly and a tipple do wonders.'

'I'm glad to hear it, sir. Is there anything else you'll be wanting?'

'I suppose breakfast will be a dish of gruel? No chance of anything better is there?'

'I'm afraid there's little chance of me being able to change the meal this morning, sir.'

Mr Henderson shrugged. 'Ah, well, can't grumble after the meal I had last night.'

Later in the day, as John entered the canteen for some lunch, he noticed one of the three cooks had a bruised face. 'Been in a boxing match, have you?' he asked.

'No, I bloody haven't. Got beaten for stealing food, didn't I?'

John looked at him blankly for a moment. 'Good heaven's, well I never.'

'I wouldn't mind, but I didn't take anything. The chief is off his rocker saying that I took his prime piece of steak.'

One of the other cooks came across and grinned at his companion. 'Good was it, that steak?'

'I told you, I didn't bloody take it. Why would I do that when I get all my food through the day?'

'Ah, but I didn't say you ate it, did I?'

'What do you mean?'

With a smirk, the man answered, 'Well, I dare say someone would pay a fair price for something like that.'

John thought the cook was going to explode as the rest of his face turned purple to match the bruises. 'Keep your bloody trap shut, will you? I didn't take the meat, is that clear. Neither to eat nor sell.'

Realising that he was the only member of the constabulary present, John held up a hand and said, 'Now then, men, no fighting. I'm sure there's a perfectly reasonable explanation for what's happened.'

Both men turned and looked at him in amazement. The accused cook pressed his lips firmly together, then muttered, 'If I find out who took that meat, he's a dead man. I don't like being punished for something I haven't done.' Then he sloped off across the kitchen to stir whatever was in one of the large metal pans.

John, thinking a change of subject was needed, asked, 'Can I have the prisoners lunch to take back please? Then I'll return for my own.'

The man nodded curtly and set about slopping spoonfuls of what John thought might be stew onto a plate, then shoved it under his nose. 'Tell 'im that's all there is. Take it or leave it.'

John took the plate and hurried out, and as he crossed the distance from the canteen to the prison, his legs began to shake. Oh dear, he'd better not risk doing that again. Then his nose wrinkled. Why couldn't these men cook a decent stew? His Ellen did much better at only a fraction of the cost.

His prisoner wasn't impressed either. 'For God's sake man, what is that supposed to be?'

'I know, sir, it's disgusting, but it's all there is. And I might not be able to supplement it today as they've a thing going on in the canteen. Apparently someone stole some meat, so they did.'

A great bellowing laugh left Mr Henderson's mouth and his body shook. 'So that's what the row was about. I ate the Chief of police's steak.' More laughter followed until tears streamed down his face, while John stood rooted to the spot, fear filling his mind.

Then Mr Henderson's laughter quietened. 'It's all right, I won't tell anyone, I promise.'

'How did you know, sir?'

'I heard the Chief from here. A right roasting he gave that poor cook.' He nodded toward the high, barred window. 'I know a lot of what goes on outside, as that's right opposite the police office.' He sniffed and looked thoughtful for a moment. 'If I give you the money, I wondered if your wife, if you have one, would buy some food and cook me something.'

'I can ask her, sir. She's a very willing little soul, so I think that would be all right.'

'Good. Get me that book, will you?'

John went and picked up the book, then handed it to Mr Henderson, who turned it over carefully in his hands. With a flick, he lifted the front cover to expose a cavity in which was stuffed a bundle of paper notes. 'I wasn't going to leave it to those scallywags back on the farm. They'd have spent the lot, on booze no doubt. Here, take this.' He peeled a couple of notes off and handed them to John, whose eyes popped at the amount.

'Are you sure, sir. There's a mighty lot of money here.'

'Of course I'm sure. Go on, off with you now and see your good lady.'

'Thank you, sir, I'll do that right away.'

His lunch forgotten, John hurried homeward, feeling like a millionaire.

Exasperation was Ellen's first feeling when confronted with Mr Henderson's idea. 'I'm not good at cooking, John, and I have no idea what he likes to eat.'

'I'm sure he'll enjoy anything you give him. We don't go hungry now do we?' John tried to placate her.

'Well, I'll see what I can do, but won't it look suspicious if we start spending more money in the store?'

'Mmmm, I've thought of that and if they ask, say you've been sent some money from your folks back home.'

'That won't work, no one has money sent. Not in our class anyway, that's for the rich.'

'Ah, well, I'll have to re-think that then. Just buy a little bit extra each day, but not enough to bring attention to it.'

'Me! Why do I have to do it?' Ellen was rather annoyed to think that John had arranged this without first consulting her.

'My sweet girl, it would look odd if I went to buy provisions every day, now wouldn't it?'

With a sigh, she agreed, took the money from John's hand and placed it carefully behind the clock on the mantle. Tomorrow she could go shopping without worrying over the price of the meat. And some more flour and suet wouldn't go amiss either.

And so for the next three weeks, Ellen and John, as well as Mr Henderson ate like lords.

Maddie was the first to say anything. 'These cakes are bigger and better than ever, however do you do it?'

A blush spread across Ellen's cheeks as she explained about the extra money.

'Good God, Ellen, you'll get into trouble if anyone finds out. What on earth possessed you to get involved with such a thing?'

'John thought it was too good an opportunity to miss,' Ellen said lamely.

'Well, I'm sorry, but I think John is being extremely foolish. How does he know he can trust this man? He could be the biggest rogue in the country and could blackmail you forever more.'

With a giggle, Ellen said that would be difficult because they hadn't enough money to pay any blackmailer, then added, 'It's only for a few more days, Maddie, then he'll be gone. Either to prison in Hobart or set free to go back home.'

Maddie shook her head sadly. 'I do worry about you sometimes. You're so gullible. I must be going now; otherwise Harry will be in before I've cooked his dinner. I'll see you next week. Take care.' She heaved herself out of the chair, bent to kiss Ellen's cheek and then made her way to the door. 'Blimey, if I get any bigger I won't be able to get in here.' Then with her customary laugh, she closed the door behind her.

After Maddie had left, Ellen sat for a while, worried by what her friend had said. Would they get into much trouble over the extra food they were supplying for Mr Henderson? She did hope not.

Then her hand went to her cheek where Maddie had planted a kiss. She'd never done that before.

The Chief's punishment was swift and harsh. 'I'm disgusted and disappointed with you, Ryan. I thought you had more sense than to do something like that. Don't you know that it amounted to stealing? And I suppose it was you who stole my steak; someone noticed a light on in the canteen the night it went missing.' His eyebrows did their jig. 'I'm putting you on a charge. No sentence will be metered out unless you break the law again. Is that clear? Just keep out of trouble, if you can. From this minute you are no longer in charge of the prisoners. You can go back on the beat; and this time do your job properly. I want the streets cleared by nine o'clock every evening. No turning away every time some sneaky miscreant passes by.' Puffing from the exertion, he slumped back in his chair. 'Go on, out of my sight.'

'But how did he find out?' Harry asked John later as they enjoyed a quick drink after work.

'I don't know, but I think the store-man might have told someone. The bastard, he had a fair cut too.'

'What about Ellen? You don't want her worrying just now.'

'No and I haven't told her yet. She knows Mr Henderson has gone, so won't expect any more money anyway.'

Harry nudged him. 'Did you make much out of him?'

'Not a lot to be honest. Most of it went on his food. Ellen and I ate better of course, but we haven't become rich overnight. I was hoping to buy her a new gown.'

'Material's expensive, I know. Maddie and me were looking the other day. She's outgrown everything she owns, so I hope the nipper comes soon or else she'll be going around in the buff.' Harry laughed.

John grinned and thought to himself that it would not be a lovely sight. He liked Maddie, but she wasn't exactly elegant.

'Where did Henderson go then?' Harry asked, bringing John back to the present.

'He got let off and went back to his farm. I'm not sure about him; sometimes he showed disregard for others. Maybe he even bought himself freedom.'

'You can never tell with the likes of him,' said Harry. 'Ah well, I must be off, or Maddie will skin the hide off me. See you tomorrow.'

A few days later, Ellen had a fall. Quite how it happened, she didn't know, but one moment she was opening the front door and the next, she was on the floor. Pains shot through her back, and she prayed that no harm had come to this baby. She managed to drag herself into a chair and sat resting until John popped in at lunchtime.

'Oh, my sweet girl. Does it still hurt? Shall I call the doctor? You've two months to go yet, so the baby can't be born yet, it won't survive.'

'I'll be all right, I just needed a rest, that's all. I'm sure baby is fine, he's still kicking, feel.'

John leant forward and placed a hand on her belly. ''So he is, well I never.' Then he seemed lost for words at the wonder of it all.

'Can you do me a favour? I was going to see Maddie this afternoon, but I think I should rest, so perhaps she can come to me if she's no work to do.'

'I'll go and ask her now. Will you be all right on your own, my love?'

'Yes, I'm fine now, honestly.'

John was only gone for a few minutes, and then returned, a sombre look on his face. 'I'm afraid poor Maddie is quite ill, Ellen. The baby started coming, although it's too soon, and something's gone wrong.'

'Oh no! Oh poor Maddie, I must go to her.' Fear clutched at her heart when she recalled the last time they'd seen one another, and Maddie had kissed her. 'Will you walk with me?'

'Of course my sweet. Here, wrap up warm, the wind is bitter today.' John handed her the grey woollen shawl that had travelled across half the world with her.

When they reached the hotel where Maddie, Harry and Stella still lived, they found everyone in a fever of anxiety. 'What's going on?' Ellen asked Maura.

'We're waiting for the doctor to come to Maddie. He was on a call out in the wilds and has only just been contacted.'

'How is she? I came as soon as I could.'

'It's not looking good, Ellen, I'll be honest with you. Maddie is in terrible pain, and poor little Stella is screaming with fear at seeing her mother suffer.'

'Why didn't someone bring the child away?'

'She wouldn't come; we tried everything. Come along, hurry.'

As Ellen made her way to the familiar room at the back of the hotel, she heard Maddie long before she opened the door. Stepping into the room, she saw her friend thrashing about on the bed, sweat beaded her brow and her face was contorted with pain. Stella sat cowering in a corner, her face full of terror, but she had stopped screaming.

Ellen ran forward and took the small girl into her arms. 'Shush, everything will be fine, you'll see. The doctor's coming and he'll make mummy better.' But as her gaze went to Maddie's face, Ellen felt her own rush of fear. She had never seen someone in so much pain, and even as she took one of Maddie's cold damp hands in her own she knew with a terrible certainty that her friend wasn't going to make it.

It seemed like an age before the doctor came, and when he saw his patient he shook his head sadly. 'There is very little I can do for this lady, I'm afraid. There is something wrong with the unborn child, it is too large and can't pass through the birth canal.'

'Can you at least stop the pain?' Harry had come in with the doctor, after pacing up and down outside for the past hour.

'I can give her some powders to lessen it, but there is nothing else I can do.' The doctor delved into his bag and then mixed some white powder in a little water that was spooned into Maddie's mouth.

'Ellen, you must go home and rest,' Maura admonished. 'We'll call you if there's any change.'

'I don't want to leave her like this. I feel so helpless though. After everything she's done for me, I should be able to do something in return.' Then she turned to Stella. 'Would you like to come home with me? We'll bake some of mummy's favourite cakes, shall we?'

The child nodded dumbly and held out a hand. Ellen took it into her own and led her from the room and back to the cottage.

That was the last time Ellen saw her friend alive. John brought the dreadful news later that afternoon and they both tried to console Stella; the strangely quiet little girl that Ellen had never really got to know. She felt guilty now, knowing that she should have made more of an effort, but it had always seemed easier to just let the child tag along in her own silent way. What would happen to her now? She had no relatives here in Van Diemen's Land, only Harry, who had been married to her mother for barely eight months.

As they all sat staring into the fire, a knock came at the door. John roused himself to open it and found Harry standing there, his eyes red from weeping. He stumbled into the room and Ellen stood up and held out her arms. 'I am so sorry, Harry. I can't imagine what we're going to do without Maddie, I really can't.'

'Why? Why my lovely Maddie? She was so good and caring, I can't go on without her,' Harry sobbed.

But then Stella cried out, 'No, you mustn't leave me too. Please, Uncle Harry, don't go.' She flung herself against him and wrapped her arms about his waist.

'I'm not going anywhere, my little lady, so don't you fret. Uncle Harry will look after you.' Harry Askew, the big, bluff Londoner, picked up the small girl and took her out of the cottage, calling over his shoulder, 'Don't worry about Stella, I'll look after her. We're all we've got now, and I know it's what Maddie would have wanted.'

When they'd gone and John closed the door, Ellen felt able to let go of the tight rein she'd had on her grief and sobbed, 'Why did it happen? Dear, Dear Maddie. It's so unfair, just as she was beginning to enjoy life. Oh, John, please hold me.'

Taking her in his arms, John said softly, 'It's not for us to question these things: people are dying all over the world, every day. It's always harder when it's a child or someone we're close to, and I know you were close to Maddie, she's been a good friend to you over the past couple of years, hasn't she?'

'Yes, she has. When Mary died I thought I'd never get over it, but thanks to Maddie I managed to accept it little by little. She made my life bearable. That's why I was so overjoyed when she came here to Bothwell, it made my life complete. We had such jolly times, and when she married Harry it was almost like we were family. And then when we knew we were both expecting babies, well, we laughed, and made such plans. But now our little one won't know her.'

He brushed the hair back from her hot face. 'Come on now, get yourself to bed or else you'll be ill and we can't be having that now can we?'

Ellen let her husband help her onto the bed and cover her before turning to snuff out the candle. He eased himself in beside her and placed one hand on her back. 'Sleep now my love. Perhaps tomorrow you'll feel a little easier.'

The following morning, Ellen went to the hotel, more for something to do than to see anyone in particular. But she sensed that they had expected her and she was taken into Mrs Vale's parlour where the tea tray was already in place on the desk.

As Maura and Vera joined them, Mrs Vale said dryly, 'I shall have to find more staff, we won't be able to manage when the summer comes.' She sighed wearily as though all the happenings of the past few months had taken their toll on her as well. She smiled at Ellen. 'How are you today? You look better than last time you were carrying, I must say.'

'I'm well in myself, but of course I'll miss Maddie dreadfully and can't imagine what it will be like without her.'

'We all took to her, you know,' said Vera, 'she was such a jolly person and her humour was infectious. She was a darned hard worker too.'

Maura nodded. 'It seems so unfair doesn't it. After such a hard life, a body finds a place to call home and settles down, then it all ends so abruptly.'

'We used to say that if one of us had a girl and the other a boy, they'd grow up and get married, but now...?' Ellen let fresh tears fall unheeded. Could life get any bleaker?

Then she was aware of Mrs Vale sitting so quietly and looked up to find the woman with tears dripping from her cheeks and chin to stain the black silk blouse she wore.

For a moment Ellen couldn't think of anything to say, but then she reached over and touched Mrs Vale's plump hand.

'I'm sorry, I don't usually cry in front of other people, but this whole business has upset me. I didn't know Maddie long, but I liked her. She reminded me of my sister in some ways. The jolly laugh, the frank speech and the way she always seemed to be busy. Yes, Margaret was very like that.'

'Where is she now?' Ellen ventured to ask.

'She died ten years ago in a house fire together with my fiancé. My brother and I tried to rescue them, but we were beaten back by the heat. My brother was badly burned and is in a hospital in Cardiff where he'll be for life. There was nothing for me in England after that and so I volunteered to come here and help run the hotel for Mr Ross. He was the owner then,' she explained.

'I often wondered how you came to be here. I didn't think you could possibly be a convict like the rest of us.' Ellen closed her eyes and tried to picture a younger and prettier Mrs Vale. A young woman with her whole life before her: all mapped out just as she and Maddie had. But life was savage, taking twists and turns, throwing everything into confusion. With a deep sigh, she opened her eyes again. 'And you never met anyone else you wanted to marry?'

'No, my dear George was the only one for me. With him gone I knew I had to put my energy into something else.'

'How did you come to still have your wedding dress?'

'That was strange. It was at my friend's house being altered, and after the fire, that was the only item of clothing I possessed, apart from what I was wearing. Everything else went with the house; I was left penniless and homeless.' She sat quietly for a few moments, then sighed heavily. 'Well, I think we should get back to work, otherwise we'll all be maudlin all day.' she said easing herself up from the chair and Maura and Vera stood also.

They both smiled at Ellen, and Maura patted her shoulder. 'Finish your tea, then get home and rest. One of us will pop round later to see if you're all right.'

Ellen lay staring at the ceiling, dry-eyed for the first time since John brought the shocking news about Maddie and her stillborn son. I wonder if they're all together in Heaven now, she wondered. Were Mary and the miscarried baby both with Maddie and her child? If so, then I know my children will be looked after with love and humour.

As her eyelids began to droop, Ellen sensed something at her right shoulder, and then quite clearly she heard Maddie's voice whisper in her ear, 'I will look after them.'

And when John arrived home a short time later, he was relieved to see his wife asleep - a smile on her lips.

CHAPTER 17

The weeks that followed were hard for Ellen. She tried to fill her time cleaning the already spotless cottage, or visiting the hotel to chat with Maura and Vera. There were two new women there now, one a convict, the other a young aboriginal girl, who scuttled about the place, getting her work done in lightening time, but never said a word to anyone. Vera was even of the opinion that she couldn't speak, but Ellen had heard her outside talking to the birds. Smiling to herself, she thought that perhaps the girl preferred their company to that of humans.

Meanwhile John continued walking the beat and life drifted into an ordered and uneventful rhythm, but the loss of her friend still sat heavily in Ellen's breast.

As the winter dragged itself into spring, Mrs Vale surprised everyone by deciding to hold a party. 'What's it in aid of then?' Ellen asked Maura when she told her about it.

Maura frowned. 'I've no idea, it just seems to have come to her. Unless of course there's a reason only she knows of; like a special birthday or something.'

Ellen grinned. 'I have trouble remembering my birthday, and even how old I am. The years seem to have merged all together for me.'

'It does that here. Anyway, I had better get on and organise some food.'

'When is it?'

'A weeks time, on the Saturday, but I need a list of what I have to buy, then there'll be cakes and pies to make.'

'I can help with some of that if you like. Maddie said my cakes were nearly as good as yours are.' Ellen's face clouded at the memory of the last time Maddie had come for tea and commented on the cakes.

Maura smiled. 'Well, you did have a very good teacher, didn't you?'

'The best,' said Ellen suddenly feeling a new affection for the dainty Scots woman.

The next week was spent in a flurry of activity, with everyone doing something to contribute even Blossom, the aboriginal girl, who polished everything until you could see your reflection in it. Silent she might be, but her beaming smile never left her face.

The new convict woman, whose name was Ingrid, was fairly chatty and seemed to single Ellen out, but for some reason she couldn't take to her.

Soon the party day arrived, cool and showery and everyone who was invited made their way to The Falls of Clyde hotel for a late lunch. 'Why is it a lunch instead of an evening party,' John asked as they got themselves ready.

'We have no idea. Vera thinks Mrs Vale is going to spring a surprise on us.'

'Perhaps she's found the perfect man and is going to marry him and ride off to live a life of luxury in Hobart.

'My goodness, John, you're still the romantic Irishman aren't you? It's a wonderful idea, but I can't see it.'

'Why not? Mrs Vale is a handsome woman still, even though at times her tongue could cut through one of the metal prison doors.'

Ellen punched her husband lightly on his arm and tutted. 'Come on, are you ready?'

'That I am, haven't I been waiting these ten minutes while you fix your hair?' John was jesting, but Ellen's mind went back to their wedding day when Maddie had made her hair look the best it ever had, and wished her friend was here now.

John then asked, 'Is Harry bringing Stella today?'

'He is, and isn't it lovely to see how she's blossomed since she's been with him. I don't know how he manages, but he's doing a good job of bringing her up.'

John nodded. 'He is to be sure.' Then he patted his wife's belly and said, 'I hope I can be as good a father to my child.'

'You will be. Now come on or we'll be late.'

John leaned across and gripped her hand. 'It's so good to see you enjoying yourself again, my lovely girl.'

Grinning broadly, Ellen said, 'I never thought I'd be laughing again so soon, but it's a relief.' She squeezed her husband's hand back, and then he pulled her to her feet to dance.

'I like dancing with you, Mrs Ryan, it gives me a chance to hold you tight without anyone thinking wrong of me.'

'I'm getting rather fat for this.' With a giggle, Ellen let him whirl her around the floor, amazed as always at his lightness of foot.

They had enjoyed a delicious lunch and now the tables were pushed back so that everyone could dance to the music ringing out as the fiddler and harmonica player both got into their stride.

Ellen only managed one dance before fatigue overtook her, but she enjoyed watching Harry and Stella dancing, her small feet standing on his, as they did a slow turn around the floor. Ellen was amazed to see Stella laughing fit to burst. Never had she seen the child so happy and only a few weeks after losing her mother too. It was very strange and she determined to have a word with Maura about it.

Everyone agreed that it was the best party Mrs Vale had organised since Ellen and John's wedding reception. It was a special occasion, but no one ever found out what it was for. Mrs Vale kept that secret to herself, but it meant that life was looking far jollier in Bothwell nowadays.

Early December brought hot and humid weather and everyone seemed sapped of strength by it. Just moving from her front door, along the street to the hotel, had Ellen wilting, but after cleaning her own small cottage, she liked to wander the countryside around the village. Under the trees it was cooler and there was always so much to see. Many plants were bursting into flower and tiny new arrivals of both birds and animals kept her enthralled for hours.

As her gaze took in the hazy hills and the curious silver-green of the trees, she tried to recall Selborne, her home in England, but the pictures in her mind were growing dimmer with every passing year. It was more lush and greener than here, Ellen remembered, and the flowers that grew in profusion along the hedgerows were brilliant, but in her memory the names were fading. She had grown to love this land, with its majestic mountains and racing rivers. Why, and how this had happened, she had no idea. There had been so much heartache since she'd arrived, so why did it feel much more like home than the twenty-three years she'd spent growing up in England? Ellen couldn't answer her own question and John laughed when she tried to explain.

These times of solitude became precious to her; she needed to be free from the bustle of village life for a few moments each day to refresh her battered emotions. Now that her baby was almost due, it brought back all the pain of losing Mary and the tiny being that had pushed itself free of her body far too soon.

Sometimes memories of her parents and siblings brought pangs of

224

longing; how were they all? Was Jane married yet? Were William and James still fighting? Oh, how she longed to see them all again; to introduce John to them so that they knew she was well cared for.

No tears were shed through all the reminiscing. She had cried so much over so many things since landing on this island, she thought she'd never cry again. And she felt a new strength inside her, like a band of steel forming a shield against any more pain.

'I can take whatever life throws at me now,' Ellen whispered to the trees one day. 'I am strong, and I have a good man beside me.' She twirled round, her skirt billowing about her and a flock of small, colourful birds took fright and flew off in a screaming cloud. She laughed aloud as they dipped and swooped beneath the canopy of leaves and then settled some way off.

As Ellen turned for home there was only one thing that bothered her. What was John up to?

Before she had time to worry any more about John's possible mis-demeanours, their baby daughter, Ellen May was born. The twelfth of December dawned bright and clear, the oppressive heat gone and in its place a comfortable warm breeze.

Just before setting off for her walk, Ellen decided to wash the kitchen floor. It wasn't really dirty, but she felt full of energy, and soon the water was hot and the soap was making suds in her bucket. As she mopped, a twinge in her back caught her unawares and she stopped for a moment waiting to see if another would follow. When nothing happened she carried on, but then several minutes later another sharp pain had her bending nearly double, and Ellen knew that the time had come.

Feeling perfectly calm, she walked to the hotel to tell Vera, who had arranged a woman to attend the birth. 'I'm getting pains, Vera, is the midwife nearby?'

'No, she's gone off to attend a woman up country somewhere, but don't worry, we have another midwife to hand. Wait there while I fetch her.'

Puzzled, Ellen sat on a small chair in the kitchen and waited, until a few moments later, Vera reappeared with Ingrid.

Ellen felt her insides constrict. She didn't want this woman to see her baby born, but she reasoned with herself, I haven't any choice. So without a word, she led both women to her cottage, where everything was ready.

Before too long, the squalling baby was in her arms, it's tiny red face screwed up as if in anger at being brought out into the big wide world.

Before she could thank Ingrid and Vera, John came bounding in through the door. 'Are you all right, my love? Is our baby fine?'

Vera, grinning from ear to ear, stood back so that the new father could view his wife and new offspring. 'There you are, both in one piece. This one was a dawdle wasn't it Ellen?'

'I wouldn't say that, but it was easier than when I had Mary, I must say.' She turned to Ingrid. 'Thank you so much. I had no idea you were a midwife.'

'Back in England I was, but things are different here. Still, I'm glad of the chance to keep my hand in.'

John pumped firstly Vera's hand and then Ingrids's. 'Thank you ladies, thank you so much. I owe you a debt of gratitude.'

'You're very welcome,' said Vera. 'Right, we'll be off now. Call if you need anything won't you?'

When they'd left, John sat on the edge of the bed and gazed at his daughter. Then he said, 'I want to call her Ellen, after you.'

'But you can't have two of us, it'll be confusing.'

'Then we'll call her May. That's it, she'll be Ellen May.'

'Why May?'

'I remember very clearly that it was May when you told me that she was to be born,' said John as though that explained everything.

Later, Ellen fell to wondering about Ingrid. She had seemed pleasant and caring while helping with the baby's birth. Perhaps I was wrong about her, Ellen thought and decided to make the effort to be friendlier toward the woman in future.

The main street of Bothwell lay thick with dust, and few people ventured out in the heat of the January afternoon. John wished fervently that he could remove his hat and heavy serge jacket as the sweat ran into his eyes and trickled down his back.

Some drovers passed by; their shirtsleeves rolled up almost to the shoulder, showing off their sinewy, sunburned arms. How he envied them their freedom and their devil-may-care attitude to life. Why had he let himself be made a constable when there were better occupations? Maybe because in Hobart there hadn't been much choice. But out here in the countryside…

Perhaps one day he would be able to pursue another way of living, but for the moment Bothwell had to be kept crime free.

There was a whisper that the Irish political prisoners living roundabouts were planning something. Meetings were held more often and a few influential men were now invited to them. One, a wealthy English landowner, was often seen riding into the village in the evening, before disappearing into the home of a known sympathiser. John turned a blind eye; it was none of his business.

That was until a few months later, when one chilly evening in late April, he saw a group of men walking towards the large house and guessed a meeting was on the cards. One of the men turned and saw him watching and asked if he was going to inform on them. When John shrugged and told the man, 'No sir, it's no concern of mine,' he received a slap on the back and praise.

'Good fellow. What's your name my man?'

John cringed at the cut-glass accent, and he didn't like being called 'my man', but he answered in a civil manner, 'John Ryan, sir.'

At the sound of his accent, the man smiled broadly. 'Ah, an Irishman eh?'

'I am sir, from Roscommon.'

'Well, John Ryan, we're pleased to know we're safe with you around to protect us. You do a grand job.'

Touching a finger to his hat, John thanked him and then moved away. He didn't want to be seen talking to the Irish dissidents.

Three or four times that week he saw one of the men, whose name was Mitchel, going into the house. Something important must be being organised, John thought, as that particular gentleman was something of a thorn in the side of the authorities.

He didn't tell Ellen of these sightings as he didn't want to worry her, but he often chatted to Harry about the goings on. He wasn't really interested, but John insisted he take notice. 'There may come a day when we need this information.'

Harry gave a wry laugh. 'Would you really do anything to stop these men taking off.'

John pondered this for a few moments, staring into his glass of ale. 'Probably not, but God knows what the punishment would be.'

'Swift and sure, no doubt,' Harry told him. 'It'd mean certain imprisonment. Would you really want that?'

John shivered. 'No, and Ellen would skin me alive. My life wouldn't be worth living.' Then he grinned. 'It'd be grand to see the Chief's face though.'

'Don't think about such things, man. Keep well out of it. Those men are dangerous; why do you think they were sent here in the first place. Damn trouble makers the lot of them.'

'You don't understand what life was like in Ireland, Harry. Thousands were dying of starvation and children were left abandoned while their parents went in search of food. I saw some pitiful sights I can tell you.'

'Why weren't they growing food? Surely they could manage that.'

'Oh, the fields were thick with wheat, but it was all sent to England to fill their larders, what was left wouldn't feed a sparrow. Then the potato crop caught the blight and the spuds all went to mush in the ground. That was the end really, unless you were lucky, or rich enough, and managed to buy food under the counter. That's why these men tried to stir up trouble; they wanted a fairer deal for Ireland.'

'What were the English parliament doing about all this then?'

'Turning a blind eye to all accounts. Oh, I don't blame the man in the street: he was probably ignorant of what was going on. No, it was the men in the pay of the Crown who were at fault.'

'Not her Majesty? Surely she didn't know what was going on?'

With a shrug, John lifted his glass and tipped it up to drain the last dregs of his ale. 'I haven't any idea, Harry. It all started long before she came to the throne anyway, so no one knows what she might have been told. Well, no one in our station in life anyway.'

'Blimey! So you're better off here then?'

'I certainly am, Harry. I've got Ellen and baby May and we've a quiet, easy way of life, so I'm content.' He looked his friend in the eye. 'I wish you could have found the same, in God's name I do, but you never know what might come along.'

A ragged sigh left Harry's mouth. 'No, I'll look after Stella for as long as she needs me, but I've had my shot at happiness, it'll not come again.'

Solemnly the two men walked from the bar and bade each other goodnight before turning for their homes. John back to Ellen and the cosy cottage, and Harry back to the police house where he'd returned to live with Stella after the death of his wife and son. There was always someone on hand to keep an eye on the little girl, and she was thriving. It didn't seem at all odd to anyone that she was being looked after by a gang of convicts.

As the winter took its grip on the countryside, Ellen was content to stay inside by the fire with May. At six-months-old she cooed and smiled at everyone, including the reverend McDonald at her Christening. The cold water trickling over her head seemed not to cause her any discomfort, as if she knew that she was now a child of the Church.

Ellen had a pang of regret as she remembered that Maddie was to have been May's Godmother, so instead asked Harry to be Godfather.

Although Stella was too young to understand what it meant, she was Godmother, with a very thrilled Mrs Vale as the second.

The hotel even laid on a tea for them on the Sunday of the Christening and Ellen knew that Mrs Vale had done it to show her pleasure at being chosen to stand for May.

Stella took everything in her stride, holding May carefully for part of the service. Sometimes, Ellen would find Stella at the door asking if she could come and play with May. The fact that the baby could neither walk nor talk yet didn't seem to worry the young girl and she would sit and natter away for hours to the fascinated baby.

Harry took his duties as a father very seriously, making sure that Stella always had a clean frock and that her coat and boots were warm enough. He still went for the occasional drink with John, but they never stayed for more than one, both of them remembering the night Ellen had collapsed all alone in the cottage.

One evening, they arrived at the bar for their customary pint, Harry grinned, 'Thanks mate, I will.' Then as they settled with their glasses of ale, he brought up the subject of the Irish Political prisoners. 'There are rumblings again from that lot. Has the Chief mentioned anything?'

'Not a word, but surely something is about to happen. They've been meeting these past few weeks almost every night and that can't be just for fun, knowing them.'

'We'd best keep our eyes and ears open then,' Harry said grimly.

Glancing out of the window, John murmured a reply, 'Aye, we'd better.' But then he changed the subject, not wishing to be drawn into conversations about his countrymen's doings. He had a good idea of what was coming, but decided to tell no one. Not even Ellen. It was a daring plan, and only Mitchel could pull it off as he had the contacts. John had been amazed at how many men sympathised with the cause and were willing to help, even if it meant imprisonment for them.

June saw colder weather creeping in and John was glad that Ellen could stay indoors by the fire every day with May. He still worried about them although they were both blooming. 'John, will you stop treating us as though we were fragile.'

'I can't help it if I'm scared of losing you both.'

'Well, stop it, otherwise you'll make me nervous.'

He kissed the tip of her nose. 'I'm off to work now. Look after yourself, won't you?'

'Yes, John,' he heard her sigh, as she waved him off from the door.

The problems at home were soon forgotten when he reached the police office and was called in by the Chief. The man twiddled the end of his moustache and sat eyeing John nervously. 'You're Irish aren't you?' he asked; rather needlessly, John thought.

'Yes sir, I am.'

'Have you heard any of the whispers going about?'

'And what whispers would they be, sir?'

'About Mitchel making a run for it, that's what.'

'No sir, I've heard nothing like that I can assure you.' John lied.

'Mmm. Assurances from you don't carry much weight Ryan, not after all that trouble over getting extras for the prisoners. Can I believe what you say this time?'

'You can sir, I've had no cause to get involved with the dissidents. They consider themselves to be above me in any case.'

'Oh?' The eyebrows waggled.

'Yes sir, they are from the gentry while I'm from the poor and even in Ireland the two don't mix.'

'Oh, I see. Well, if you do hear anything let me know there's a good chap.'

'I will sir, if I do hear anything.'

'Right, you may go.' The chief wafted an arm in the general direction of the door.

With a slight bow, John left the room and in spite of the cold outside, sweat ran down between his shoulder blades, and he decided that he'd better keep a low profile over the next few days.

Three days later, John arrived home with a new shawl for his wife. 'To keep you warm through the winter,' he explained.

'John, it's lovely, but how did you afford it?'

'Ah well, I helped a man with a problem and he rewarded me with a few coins.'

A deep frown creased Ellen's brow. 'Your help must have been sorely needed to give you enough to buy this.'

'It was one of the fellows who comes into Bothwell for meetings, I just turned a blind eye that's all.'

'Are you sure that's all?' Ellen's voice was sharp.

'I'm sure.' But he avoided looking his wife in the eye. 'Now don't worry your sweet head about it and put your new shawl on so I can admire you in it.'

Ellen was still worried, but draped the soft wool about her shoulders and revelled in the warmth it gave. 'Does it look all right?'

'It suits you well,' John told her, 'and I'm glad I chose the dark red and blue plaid. You always look fine in dark colours.'

Standing on tiptoe, she reached up and planted a kiss on his cheek.

'Is that all the thanks I get?' John teased, putting his arms around her and holding her tight.

With a shiver, Ellen hugged him back and kissed him properly, wishing it was time for bed. But then she realised that John wanted her too and so forgetting the supper they moved across to the bed and made love, until the smell of a burning pan brought Ellen back to reality. Cursing silently, she hurried out into the kitchen to retrieve the boiled-dry cabbage, before returning to her husband's arms. 'Do you want supper or do you want to stay here?' she asked with a grin.

'As much as I love you, Ellen Ryan, I think I'd better have some food, otherwise I'll not last until morning.'

Ellen pulled a face at him, then climbed off the bed and hurried back to the stove. The meat might be rather overdone and the vegetables a bit soggy, but who cared, she thought, having spent an enjoyable hour in the arms of her beloved husband.

After the meal was eaten and cleared away they sat in companionable silence one either side of the fire, until May stirred for her feed. As she sat with the baby at her breast, Ellen could see the firelight reflected in John's eyes. 'What are you thinking about?' she asked.

'I was just wondering what it must be like to leave this island and sail off across the sea to another land.'

This shocked her, as she hadn't expected such an answer. Ellen narrowed her eyes, 'John, what's going on? You tell me that you helped a fellow countryman, and now all this about leaving.'

'Nothing's going on. It was just a daydream.'

'I'm not sure I believe you.' She hated saying it, but that was how she felt.

He turned surprised eyes on her. 'Please don't think of me as a liar, I can't bear it.'

'We'll say no more about it for now, but keep out of trouble, John, promise me?'

'I promise. Now it's time for bed and I think I'd like another cuddle.'

The following day, John paced the street restlessly, with his eyes focused on the road leading into the village. Where were they? Surely it didn't take that long to ride in from the cottage. And the lad should be here before them, but there was no sign of him either.

He looked across to where Harry had some of the constables doing some drill, his voice strident as he ordered the unwilling men into neat rows. They had moaned about this new style of command, resenting the fact that John and Harry were no better than they were, and why should they tell them what to do?

'It's only for a trial period,' they were told, 'just to see if it made any difference to morale.' Harry sniggered behind his hand: if only they knew.

At last John saw two horsemen riding into the main street. They reined in, jumped from their mounts and entered the police house.

Sauntering across the road, John went to stand by the horses and casually took the reins in his hand. He stood scanning the road again, but there was still no sign of the young Mitchel boy. Where the hell was he?

The cold air held a silence, only broken now and again by a sharp word from Harry as the men lost interest in being ordered about and fidgeted.

Suddenly, the sound of running feet could be heard from the police house, and the Chief's voice reached John's ears, calling to halt the two men. He closed his ears and instead handed the reins to their riders, who took off at a mighty gallop, heading on along the road out of Bothwell, the cheers and laughter from passers by ringing in their ears.

The Chief's clerk came panting up to John's side. 'Why didn't you stop them?' he bawled.

With as blank an expression as he could muster, John turned to the man. 'I'm sorry, I didn't realise that I was supposed to stop them.'

'Didn't you hear the Chief call out?'

'No, I'm afraid I didn't. Who were they anyway?'

'For goodness sake man, didn't you recognise John Mitchel, the Irish troublemaker. Blast his eyes, we'll all be in hot water for this.'

'And why would that be then?'

'He's revoked his 'Ticket of Leave' and made off, hoping to escape the island. He's had help, we're sure of that.' The man turned narrowed eyes on John. 'Are you sure you had nothing to do with this? You Irish all stick together.'

'I can assure you it has nothing to do with me. I don't know the man.'

'Bah! I'd better go and tell the Chief. Oh, here he is. I'm sorry sir, no one heard your shout to stop them.'

The chief's face fell and he turned to go back inside, his shoulders slumped. So dejected did he look that John felt quite sorry for the man.

Harry, having abandoned the drill once the danger of someone apprehending the two horsemen passed, walked across, a wide grin on his face. 'All went well, then?'

'Ssh!' John hissed. 'You never know who might hear. If anyone thought we were involved, we'd be skinned alive.'

'I wonder if they'll get away? It's pretty rugged country out there, and it's winter.'

'Don't worry about them, they have friends all over the place who'll help. Good luck to them, I say.'

'Well, you would wish them well, you were paid enough for your help.'

'Harry, how could you suggest such a thing?' John grinned. 'It wasn't much anyway, just enough to buy Ellen a shawl. But I don't know where Mitchel's son is, he was supposed to be here to hold the horses. It was risky me being seen holding them.'

'Must have got held up. Ah, isn't this him now?'

They looked to where a young man walked wearily into the village leading a lame horse. 'Yes', said John. 'I'd better go and give him the good news, then he can get his horse attended to.'

'And I'd better go and let the men know they can go back onto ordinary duty now.' Harry gave a crafty wink. 'I think that worked well, don't you?'

News of the daring escape spread quickly through the small community. Many people prayed the men would get away successfully, even those who had nothing to do with Ireland or it's troubles. But anyone who could outwit the authorities was a hero in everyone's eyes.

The Chief called John into his office later that day, his face black as thunder. 'Are you deaf, Ryan? Didn't you hear me shout the order to stop that man Mitchel?'

'I'm not deaf, sir, but to be sure I heard no shout.'

'Well, I don't believe you. You were in league with that man, I'm certain, now tell me the truth.'

'I don't know Mr Mitchel, and that is God's own truth.' John replied, fingers crossed behind his back.

The Chief's face turned an even deeper shade of purple and John worried for the man's health, but kept his face impassive as the Chief ranted on. 'I will never believe that you had no part in the escape. You Irish all stick together no matter what you may say to the contrary, and if I find out that you've been lying to me, then it'll be the worst for you. Do you hear me now?'

'Yes, I hear you, sir.'

With his lips pursed, the Chief eyed John as though trying to see into his mind, and then he let out a long sigh. 'Heads will roll over this business, and mine is surely on the block. For God's sake man, if you know anything at all about the planning or the name of anyone else involved, then tell me now. I can help to smooth things out with the authorities, no one need ever know where the information came from.'

'I'm sorry, sir, but I can't help you.'

Just then the clerk entered the office holding a sheet of paper in his hand. With barely a glance at John, he said, 'This has just come through, sir. The plan to get Mitchel away on a ship from Hobart has failed. It sailed yesterday morning without him on board, so he's still at large out in the bush. Do you want an armed posse to search the hills?'

'No, there's no point, he'll be long gone, probably up north, so the guards there can look for him. They won't find him; he'll be well hidden by all the cronies he surrounds himself with. And even those who should know better and divulge names refuse to do so, don't they, Ryan?'

John shifted his feet very slightly. 'Are you referring to me, sir?'

'Of course I'm referring to you? Who else is in the room?'

A hint of a smile touched the clerk's lips as he looked at John. 'I'm sure Mr Ryan would tell us if he knew anything. Wouldn't you?'

'I would help if I could, indeed, but there's nothing I know of any importance.'

Sighing heavily again, the Chief sat back in his chair. 'Ryan, you're dismissed for now, but if you so much as stick your nose where it's not wanted, I'll be gunning for you. So just keep yourself out of trouble or your Ticket of Leave will be revoked and you'll see the inside of the prison once more; and you won't be guarding it. Is that clear?'

'Yes, that's clear. Sir.' John added the last word firmly, before turning to march out of the office, sweat pouring down his back. As he trudged homeward to see Ellen, his heart beat loudly in his chest. She must never know of this, it would worry her senseless.

'Are you sure John had nothing to do with it?' asked Maura a few days later when Ellen called in for afternoon tea with her friend.

'He swears not, but I do wonder. Even the Chief doesn't believe him. But I'm sure John wouldn't put his freedom in jeopardy, or that of the Chief if he knew something about it.'

'It all happened so quickly, I gather. No one had any inkling about what was to come. Apparently, the first anyone knew was when the Mitchel man threw his Ticket of Leave back at the Chief and told him he was leaving.' Maura laughed. 'The poor man was so shocked he didn't know what to do.'

'How do you know all this?' asked Ellen.

'He was here with his wife the other evening for dinner. He's a lovely man under all that bluster and I'm sure he hates the job he's been given.'

'I remember when he gave me away on my wedding day, he was marvellous, almost as though he were family. I hope John hasn't been lying to him, I would feel awful after all his kindness.'

'There's not much we can do except leave it to the menfolk to sort out. Now, how are you keeping? Can I hold May for a while?' Ellen had handed over her baby and Maura tickled under the little double chin, bring a snorting laugh from May. 'She is such a happy child, you must be very contented?'

'Yes, we are. John and I are as close as ever, and I think May senses that.' She watched her friend playing with the baby and knew that had things been different, Maura would have been a wonderful mother.

CHAPTER 18

As the year wore on and the days began to lose the sharp grip of winter, Ellen had a strange feeling within her. Was she with child again, she wondered?

When she remembered the silly girl she had been when first coming to live in Bothwell, she groaned with embarrassment. I was so foolish then; thinking the whole world owed me something. A wide smile curved her lips as she sat, hand on stomach, gazing out of the window, wondering if the rain was going to hold off long enough for her to take May for a walk.

The days were getting longer and the weather warmer, but still heavy showers came unexpectedly from the west. Deciding to risk it, she took her smart shawl and pulling it about her shoulders, placed May in the little cart Harry had made and wheeled her into the street.

A few moments later she saw a familiar figure coming toward her. It was the Chief's wife, and Ellen smiled a welcome. Although she hadn't seen much of the woman since her wedding day, the Chief's wife had sent an occasional message to enquire after Ellen's health. As she couldn't write herself, John usually scribbled a reply, but now here the woman was and so they could talk. Ellen wondered if she should offer an invitation to go back to the cottage, but as she drew nearer, her face did not light with a smile and something about her expression put Ellen on her guard.

'Good day to you, Mrs Ryan,' the chief's wife said.

'Hello,' Ellen said, suddenly realising that she didn't know her name. 'It's lovely to see you, and thank you for your kind notes over the past few months.'

'I heard you had a baby girl, is this her?' She eyed the rough cart containing the ever smiling May.

'Yes, she's a lovely baby isn't she? Can I offer you a cup of refreshment, our cottage is only a short way away.'

'No, I'm afraid I haven't time today, and I don't think, in the circumstances that it would be appropriate, do you?'

Ellen frowned. 'I'm sorry, I don't understand. What circumstances?'

The woman fixed Ellen with a steely eye. 'I am on about your husband's collusion with the Irish prisoners, my husband may have lost his position because of it.'

Clapping a hand over her mouth, Ellen could only stand and stare with horror-filled eyes. 'Oh no, surely not. Not John! Oh, he couldn't do such a thing. And the Chief is likely to be leaving?'

'Not from choice I assure you. If Constable Ryan would testify, then it might help matters, but as he refuses to admit any involvement there is little to be done.' The woman then swept on by and hurried away along the street, to leave Ellen staring in disbelief.

Inwardly she groaned, 'Oh, John, what have you done?'

But when she tackled him with it later, he still maintained his innocence, becoming quite angry when pressed on the matter. 'Why is it no one will believe me? Just because I'm Irish, everyone assumes I know what went on. Well, I don't, and I just wish I could be left alone and the matter dropped.'

'But the Chief may lose his position, don't you care?'

'Why should I care about him?'

'Because he showed us such kindness on our wedding day. The man is almost part of the family.'

'Yours maybe, but whatever you may think, he's nothing to me. Ellen, I'm a convict, do you want me to end up back in gaol? There is nothing to tie me to those dissidents, so stop going on about it. If the Chief loses his job then that's his problem, not mine.' And so saying, John strode from the cottage, leaving his wife feeling more confused than ever.

Nothing more was said, although Ellen still felt uncomfortable about the situation. Being determined not to spoil the loving relationship she had with her husband, she kept silent, even when the Chief was shunted unceremoniously off back to Hobart to work in the central office, stripped of any responsibilities.

But things didn't work out well for the constabulary of Bothwell. They were glad to see the back of the Chief, not because he was a hard man, but because he was the voice of authority in the village, and to a man they resented anyone in official office.

There was shock all round when his replacement arrived. The man was a monster, and soon the men were decrying the loss of their former Chief. Orders had to be carried out, at once and without question. The prison was re-arranged, the canteen had its quotas halved, and the men were drilled every morning before they were given a list of duties for the day.

'Cor Blimey, to think I nearly started this a few months ago,' Harry puffed, as he and John marched up and down the street, turning and changing direction at every command. 'The men would've scalped me if I'd kept this up.'

Out of the corner of his eye, John saw Ellen standing at the roadside watching. 'I bet she's thinking, "Serves you right",' he murmured.

'Well, it does,' Harry said sharply. 'You and your bloody friends.'

John's heart sank. Was his best mate now blaming him for everything? He glanced sideways as Harry panted along next to him. 'I'm sorry, I had no idea it would come to this.'

To his relief, his friend grinned. 'Well, what's done is done, so it's no use crying. Perhaps this bloke'll soon get fed up.'

'Quiet you! No talking!' the order rapped out from the new Chief when he saw Harry speak. The rest of the drill passed in silence, but once John and Harry sat with their beers that evening, John tried to placate his mate. 'We've been here a long time now, don't you think it's time we were given a pardon and set free?'

His eyes big as saucers, Harry said, 'Blimey, you don't half come up with some ideas. Who do you think is going to pardon us?'

'The Governor of course. I wonder if you have to apply or if it's granted automatically. I know where I'm going when I get mine.'

'Where have you got this idea from? I've never heard of anyone getting a pardon.'

'Oh yes, there are several families living around here where once the father, or mother, used to be convicts. Now they live in their own house with a plot of land to farm, right cosy it is.'

'Well I'm damned, I never really thought about it.' Harry shook his head slowly from side to side. 'It'd be great wouldn't it?' A far away look came into his eyes. 'Just suit me and Stella, a bit of land to grow stuff and keep a few chickens.'

'Yes, that's what I'm aiming for. Ellen deserves to live somewhere in peace and quiet where she can bring up our children safely.'

'You're safe here in Bothwell, aren't you?'

'Yes, but there isn't much room in that cottage, and if we have any more children, we'll need somewhere bigger.'

'Not straight away. You can stay here for a while yet, can't you?'

Suddenly John realised what it was Harry was afraid of, that he and Ellen would move away, leaving him and Stella here on their own. He patted the man's arm. 'We won't be going anywhere yet, so don't worry. And when we do eventually leave, you can come and live near us.'

A smile spread across Harry's florid face. 'That'll be great.'

Concealing a smile, John wondered what Ellen would make of Harry coming to live near them, wherever they went. She wouldn't mind he was sure, because she was a grand girl, and he had better get home to see her. 'I'm off now, see you in the morning.'

'For more army-style drill I suppose,' Harry sighed.

'You can bet your life on it. Still, it'll keep us fit,' John laughed, ducking as Harry aimed a pretend punch at him.

The new Chief, Horatio Phipps, being an unapproachable man, was left in peace. John was itching to go and ask about his pardon, but quailed at the thought of standing in front of a man who seemed able to look into the depths of your soul, and ask for something he knew had probably been blocked anyway. Best to keep my head down for a while and live as respectable a life as possible, he thought. Perhaps in a few months time things would improve, then he might be in line for his hard-won freedom.

The men were drilled each day until they were ready to drop. It had gone on for weeks now and John and Harry were convinced it was being done out of spite.

'He'll have a mutiny on his hands one of these days, so he will,' John told Ellen on a scorching hot day in early December as they were leaving the cottage. 'We're all worn out before we even start our duties, has the man no heart?'

'Well, if he has, it's well hidden. I'm off to the hotel for an hour, see you later, dear.' Ellen stood on tiptoe and planted a quick kiss on John's cheek. 'And if you're very good, I might have something to tell you.'

He smiled and waved her on her way, but as he walked toward the police house he saw the new Chief standing at the door, not looking a happy man.

'Come here you. Ryan isn't it?'

John came to a halt in front of the man, saluting smartly. 'John Ryan at your service, sir.'

'What in the devil's name did you think you were doing, kissing in public while wearing your uniform?' The cold blue eyes bore into

239

him, leaving John in no doubt about this man's malevolent nature.

'I'm sorry, sir. It won't happen again.'

'If it does, then you will be on a charge. I will not have insubordination in my ranks. Do I make myself clear?'

'Yes, sir.'

'Right, dismiss.' The man turned on his heel, clicking them together before marching back inside.

So that was it, John thought, he was ex-army. But what could have brought him so low as to be sent here to Bothwell, in the middle of nowhere, when it seemed possible that he had been a high-ranking officer? It would be interesting to find out, very interesting indeed.

John was distracted from worrying about the new Chief by Ellen's news that they were to be parents again. December the twelfth was Ellen May's first birthday and her mother thought it appropriate to give John the news on such a special day. Ellen had been bursting to tell him for several weeks, but wanted it to be the right time.

He was delighted and proudly puffed out his chest. 'Aren't we the clever ones? Two children in two years.'

'Mmm,' was Ellen's sardonic reply, 'it's all right for you men to feel good about it, how about giving a thought to us women who have to do all the hard work.' But the sparkle in her eyes and the smile on her lips belied the words.

John pursed his lips. 'It can't be that bad, otherwise why would women go on having babies on after another.'

As her laughter filled the tiny room, Ellen hugged her husband tight. 'Why do you think it's us women who give birth? Men would never stand the pain.' She stood back slightly. 'I've made a cake for May's birthday, would you like a piece now or after your dinner?'

With a sigh, John said, 'As it's my daughter's birthday, I'll have some cake now. Otherwise, we'll have visitors and you'll offer it to them, then there won't be any left for me.'

'Oh, you!' Ellen was still laughing. I'm not expecting any visitors, unless Stella pops in, so there's plenty.

John sat May on his knee and fed her small pieces of cake that dribbled down her chin.

'Not too much, John, she's only just started eating solid food.'

'Ah, she's loving it, aren't you my little pet?'

May gurgled, sending crumbs all over his uniform and he looked up in mock horror. 'Now look what she's done?'

Bringing a cloth, Ellen knelt down in front of them, her heart full of love. How lucky she was to have such a wonderful husband and beautiful baby, and soon another little person to make their lives complete.

To say that John and Chief of Police, Horatio Phipps didn't like each other, was an understatement. It had been hate at first sight, and John knew that if this man had been in charge the day Mitchel escaped, he would now be in prison. He was careful never to mention anything about the events that took place that day to anyone. You could never be sure who might be listening.

He was still trying to think of a way to check up on Phipps, convinced that he had done something shocking to be put in charge of a small police house somewhere like Bothwell. The office was manned at all times by a new clerk who had arrived with the Chief, and John wondered when the man ate or slept, as he seemed always on duty. Deciding to bide his time, John relaxed and enjoyed his family, taking pride in walking along the street on his day off to bask in the glow of adulation directed at his daughter, who smiled at everyone they met.

Life was perfect, he concluded.

Christmas was a merry time. In the morning most of the residents of Bothwell piled into Church to cheerfully sing Carols and listen spellbound to the story of Christ's birth. It didn't matter how often you heard it, Ellen thought, the story still brought a feeling of optimism for the future.

The Ryan family ate lunch outside in the sunshine before walking along to the hotel for a sumptuous tea of cold meat sandwiches and fruitcake.

Mrs Vale held court, but for most of the time she had May sitting on her lap, smiling down at her every few moments.

'That child will be spoiled for life,' Ellen declared, grinning, and more than a little proud that the woman was so enamoured of her daughter. 'It's a shame Mrs Vale didn't have children of her own, isn't it?' she commented to Maura.

'It does seem that way. It still surprises me how she has changed in the last two years. Even I used to go in fear of her when I first came, but slowly, over time, she has mellowed and is now quite human.'

'Maura!' Vera admonished in mock severity. 'You mustn't say such things.' But judging by the laughter that bubbled from her lips, she wholeheartedly agreed.

Later that night as they climbed into bed, Ellen sighed with contentment. 'What a lovely Christmas it's been. Have you enjoyed yourself, John?'

'I certainly have, my love. This year it has been special because we are a complete family now. And by next Christmas, we'll have another baby and Ellen May will be old enough to enjoy it more.' He held his wife in his arms and kissed her gently. 'Let's finish off this lovely day in the best way possible,' he murmured. And as May slept in her warm-lined drawer, her parents made love, then drifted off to sleep to dream of the wonderful day they'd had.

Within weeks the feeling of contentment was rudely shattered. As John signed on for duty one morning, he was called into the Chief's office. His heart lifted; perhaps he was going to get his longed for free pardon at last.

His hopes were dashed immediately he walked into the office to see the Chief's face dark with anger. Gulping, John stood to attention and waited to hear what he was being accused of this time.

'John Ryan, I am putting you on a charge that you knowingly aided and abetted in the escape of a known criminal on the eighth of June last,' the man said without preamble. 'You will be sent to Launceston forthwith to stand trial. Your ticket of leave will be revoked, and you may not contact anyone or discuss the case. Do you understand?'

With his mind numb with shock, and his knees feeling as though they would buckle, John tried to think straight. He stared at the thin-faced man before him, whose hard eyes bore into him. 'I-I don't understand, sir. I knew nothing about it.'

'Silence! You'll have the chance to speak your piece in court.' He nodded to the clerk who opened the door and called two constables into the room. 'Right, take him away.' With a wave of his hand the Chief dismissed them all.

John knew neither of the two men who took him into their charge. They must be new arrivals, he thought. He tried pleading with them. 'I must go and tell my wife what's happening. I have to see her and my child. Please!'

'You heard the Chief, you're to speak to no one, now move.' The man prodded John in the ribs with his pistol.

So it was to be an armed guard they had for him, John mused. But how the hell had this happened? No one knew the truth about his involvement with the Irish dissidents. No one that is, except Harry, and there was no way he would say anything.

As he was led out to the waiting cart, John saw to his horror Ellen being led into the police house; May in her arms. He tried to call out, but she was hurried inside before he could make her hear. Oh my dear God, what is going on? It was as though he was in a nightmare; surely he would wake up any minute to find it all a bad dream.

He was bundled unceremoniously into the cart, handcuffed now to both his companions. He prayed that Ellen would be kindly treated, and that she could keep May with her.

As the cart pulled out into the main street, he saw Harry standing, mouth agape by the roadside. Then like a thunder bolt from the blue, he guessed the truth, for standing next to Harry, a huge smirk on his face, was a man he hated, a man he thought locked up for life long ago. Bart Tyrrell!

Placing May in her cart, Ellen spoke to her daughter. 'What shall we do today? If it's not too hot, we'll go and visit your aunts at the hotel, shall we? I'll just put some more wood on the fire so it's still alight when we get home.' She hurried through to the kitchen, but before she could fill the kettle a furious knocking rattled the front door, so loud it frightened May and made her cry.

Before going to answer it, Ellen picked up her daughter and soothed her. 'There, there, my pet. Who on earth is making such a noise?'

She swung the door back and was confronted by two constables. She smiled thinking they must be friends of John's, but her smile was not returned, in fact they had a menacing look about them.

'W-what do you want?' She gasped.

'Ellen Ryan? You're to accompany us to the Chief of Police.' One of them barked.

Ellen frowned. 'But why, what's the matter?'

'Don't ask questions, just do as you're told.'

'I'll have to bring my baby.'

The man shrugged. 'Please yourself.'

In a daze, Ellen was marched along the street between the two men, May in her arms and the curious eyes of neighbours on her. She was ushered into the Chief's office and wished again that it were the old Chief. He would have smiled and bade her sit down, but she knew there would be no such courtesy from this man, whose steel grey eyes held no warmth whatsoever.

He cleared his throat. 'Ellen Ryan you are charged with knowingly taking payment to conceal the planned escape of political prisoners in June of last year. You will be taken to Hobart Town where you will be imprisoned forthwith. Dismiss.'

The floor seemed to come up and hit Ellen, and it was all she could do to keep a firm hold on her child. She was pulled back upright by the two escort guards who firmly turned her toward the door.

Struggling furiously to free herself, she rounded on the Chief. 'I don't understand. I don't know what you're on about. Where's my husband? He'll tell you. I've never had anything to do with any convicts.'

She saw the man's lip curl and he snarled. 'Never had anything to do with convicts? You married one, woman. Now, get her out of here.' The next thing Ellen knew, she was being hoisted into a cart, and then driven at speed along the main street of Bothwell.

As they passed the hotel, she turned, praying that someone she knew would see her plight, but the place looked deserted. There was no one to see her departure from the village where she had lived for so long, and had come to love.

After many hours in the swaying cart without food or water, John felt sick when they at last stopped. He was dragged out of the cart, across an open area, but in the darkness he couldn't see his surroundings. Then he felt himself falling headlong into somewhere that was blacker than the night outside, to land in a heap on the floor, his bruised body searing with pain.

Where in God's name am I, he thought; it seemed like hell, but without the fire. And where was his lovely Ellen? What had they done with her? His head ached with worry and exhaustion, before he was released into oblivion.

As he struggled to open his eyes, he saw daylight filtering under what he presumed was the door. Then there were noises outside and the door opened.

'John Ryan, come with me,' a voice demanded.

Scrambling to his feet, John swayed as weakness overcame him, but he stumbled outside, blinking rapidly as the harsh sunlight seared his eyes. 'Where am I?' he asked.

'Never mind that, you've to see the Governor and be charged.' The man now at John's elbow was short and squat, but heavily built and the expression on his face gave no comfort to his prisoner.

John tried once more. 'I don't understand what's happening. Why have I been brought here?'

'Stop talking. You'll find out soon enough.' The man shoved John in the back and ordered, 'Walk.'

Having no choice, he obeyed and headed in the direction of a large red brick building that was being indicated by his guard. Up a shallow flight of steps they went, in through a huge wooden door, across an echoing tiled hallway, arriving at last outside a panelled oak door.

'Wait there!' came the order, then the guard knocked, before entering the room, giving John a chance to look about him. It was obviously a building of some importance judging by its size and the number of doors leading off the corridor. And the high ceiling gave it an air of elegance, very similar to the Governors offices in Hobart, large and imposing.

Glancing about him, John suddenly realised that he was alone and his first thought was to run back the way he'd come in the hope of finding the front door. But even as these thoughts were forming, the door opened and he was called inside.

The flood of light from the high windows had John shielding his eyes and it was several moments before he saw, across the vast room, a man sitting behind a desk. The man beckoned, and John walked across the carpeted floor toward him, stopping in front of the desk and standing to attention.

The man picked up a sheet of paper and studied it in detail before looking up and meeting John's eye. 'John Ryan, do you know why you are here?'

'No sir, I have no idea.'

The man leaned back into his chair. 'It states here that you assisted the Irish political prisoner John Mitchel and a friend in their escape from Bothwell. Is this true?'

'No sir, it is not.'

'Were you not on duty that day when he visited the police office?'

'Yes sir, I was.'

'And did you not hold their horses while they were inside?'

'Yes sir, I did. But I had no idea who the men were or what they were about.'

'When the Chief of Police shouted the order to stop the two men from leaving, you ignored him. Isn't that the truth?'

'No sir, I didn't hear him. The two men ran past me and were away before I realised what was happening.'

'You have very glib answers, Ryan. It has been brought to the attention of the authorities that you knew of the intention of Mitchel to escape that day and that you created a diversion for that purpose. Then you ignored an order and let him get clear away.' The man's eyes never left John's face. So close was his scrutiny that sweat began to trickle down John's back, and he felt nausea rising up from his stomach in the stuffy room.

'I assure you sir, nothing like that happened. It was a mistake that's all.'

'So how come you gave your wife the gift of a new shawl costing several shillings, just at the time this escape was being planned? Come clean man, you were paid for your silence.'

'No, no my Ellen knew nothing. I'd saved for the shawl for many months.'

'How did you save it, Ryan? When you have no money to call your own. You can protest all you like, but we have a witness to your deeds and he will stand up in court and swear to it.'

Licking his lips nervously, John asked, 'Who would do such a thing when there is nothing to tell. I'm innocent I tell you. I've done nothing.'

With a slight shake of his head the man turned his gaze to the guard. 'Take him back for now. Solitary.'

As the guard gripped his arm, John tried to follow, but his knees buckled beneath him and he sank to the floor, his strength gone.

He was vaguely aware of strong arms lifting him and of being carried on some kind of stretcher, before finding himself in the dank, dark cell again, alone.

Tears flooded his eyes and he prayed as hard as he could for the safety of his wife and daughter. Please look after them. Please, he whispered into the darkness.

As the cart pulled into Hobart, Ellen recognised one or two buildings. Hugging May close to her, she glanced nervously around, and suddenly, she knew where she was heading: the woman's factory. And sure enough, within minutes she saw the high grey stone wall come into view as they turned into Degraves Street.

She shivered and bile rose in her throat as almost forgotten, painful memories washed through her. This was where little Mary had died so soon after arriving in Van Diemen's Land, and this was where she had first met Maddie, her dear friend.

Instinctively she looked down to check on her sleeping daughter. How could they send her back here with another child? Knowing that her first born lie in the cemetery at Dynnyrne nursery, just a short distance away.

Why, oh why am I here, she cried inwardly. What have I done to deserve this?

Slowly the heavy wooden gate swung back and then she was being helped down from the cart. A woman warder smiled, 'Come this way, Ryan, I'll show you to your quarters.'

246

Ellen thought her ears deceived her. They had never been this welcoming before.

Gazing up at the blue sky through the small window high in the wall, Ellen reflected on her circumstances. Although she was in a cell of her own, this one was not so small and dark as she'd had on her previous stay. As well as her own wooden bed, there was a crib for May and they were allowed out for meals in the huge dining room. Each morning she was escorted to the wash house where she could splash her face with water and clean her daughter, putting a fresh cloth around her tummy to keep the sores at bay.

The fact that May seemed happy kept Ellen sane. Although still frantic with worry about John, she knew she had to stay calm for her daughter's sake, and this in its way, helped her too. Somehow the situation would be resolved she was sure, but as yet she had no idea how, but hoped it would be before her baby was born. The thought of giving birth in this place made her shiver; she wanted better for her children than to be living in a prison.

There had been no word from Bothwell and sadly Ellen assumed that either no one knew where she was or, what was worse, might not care. The riddle of John's arrest still niggled within her. Had he helped those men escape? If not, how did he afford her shawl? She fingered the soft wool as it lay on her bed. It was very fine and must have cost much more than her husband had told her.

'Oh John,' she wailed inwardly, where are you? And how are you?

CHAPTER 19

The days dragged by as John tried to find out what had happened to his wife and daughter. He worried that Ellen might be roughly treated and that it could harm their unborn child. No word was brought to him as to when his trial might be, or if he was going to be able to put his side of the story. What had happened in Bothwell? Had Bart Tyrrell stirred up trouble? Had he got Harry drunk and wheedled some of the details out of him? His head ached from the torrent of thoughts that ran round and round in his mind as he tried to remember exactly what he'd told Harry.

After a while though, he thought that he might have the solution to his problems. If Bart Tyrrell was involved, then he could carry on denying everything. Hadn't the man hated him since the days they were both at the prison in Impression Bay? And wasn't he supposed to be locked up for life at Port Arthur penitentiary? It was a mystery as to how the man was free; John even began to doubt that he'd seen him at all. Perhaps he was an escapee and on the run. That'll be good for my case, John mused.

Autumn moved effortlessly into winter without too much bad weather. He was allowed out into a compound for a while each day to stretch his legs and these times brought some respite from the isolation of his cramped cell. He studied the surrounding countryside and liked what he saw. A man could settle here and bring up his family in peace. There were distant hills, but the area near the prison seemed lush, with green pastures and stands of tall trees. He very rarely conversed with the other prisoners, apart from a casual acknowledgement; being afraid of what he might let slip. It was best not to trust anyone, anymore.

One day in mid-winter, he was called into the office where he'd been charged on his arrival. It was a different man sitting behind the desk, and much to John's relief, this one seemed slightly friendlier. He

248

beckoned John forward, 'Ah Ryan, I have some news for you. Just received notification of your wife having given birth. A boy.'

A gulp of air nearly strangled John as he tried to express his thanks and ask where she was at the same time. In the end, he gasped, 'Thank you sir. Are they both safe and well? Where are they? Oh please sir, are my family all right?'

'Steady on man.' Then the governor frowned. 'Do you mean to tell me you don't know where they are?'

'I don't sir, I've never had word of them since I arrived here many months ago.'

The man shuffled some papers on his desk, then extracted one sheet and started to read it. His frown deepened and the colour rose in his face. 'So you have been here five months now? Have you been informed of your rights and told when your trial will be?

'No sir, I've been told nothing and have been worried sick about my wife and little daughter. Do you know where they are, sir. Please tell me if you do.'

'Certainly, but firstly I must tell you that I am Major Pringle, the new governor in charge here. Your trial is set for next week, and so I shall have to find you council so that your side of the case can be stated.' He tutted noisily. 'This should have been done weeks ago.' He looked up a slight smile on his face. 'Now as to your wife and children, they are in Hobart, in the woman prison, but as the note says, they are in good spirits.'

John doubted that, but said nothing, at least he knew where they were, and that they were safe and well. 'When will I be able to see them, sir?'

'I'm afraid I cannot answer that at the moment, it depends on the trial. I have to find a list of charges and who might be called at witnesses. Leave it with me and I'll hurry things along. Dismiss.'

Backing from the room, John let a ragged sigh leave his lips. Thank you Lord; perhaps the waiting would soon be over.

In Hobart, Ellen cradled her new son in her arms and stroked the fine downy hair on his head. He was bonny and May loved him, cooing over him at every opportunity.

The Governor had been very good about letting her stay here in the factory prison to give birth, instead of going to Dynnyrne where Ellen knew she couldn't cope with having a baby in the same place as where Mary died. It had been an uncomplicated birth, and over so quickly, Ellen wondered if she'd been making a fuss the last two times.

She had decided to call her new son William after one of her brothers' back home in England and hoped that John wouldn't mind. A warder came in then with a smile on her face. 'Ryan, I have news of your husband.'

Her face alight with joy, Ellen could only stare at the woman. Then she found her voice. 'Where is he? Is he safe?'

'He's up at Launceston and is fine as far as I know. His trial is next week so you should have more news of him then.'

'Where is this place, Launceston, is it far away?'

'It's many miles I'm told, although I've never been there myself.'

'So is he in prison?'

The woman nodded. 'I'm sorry that's all I know.'

When she'd gone, Ellen sat gazing at her two children. 'Your daddy is safe, thank goodness. Maybe it won't be too long before we see him again.'

The day following the news of his imminent trial, John received a visit from a lawyer, a Mr Sommerton. The man was puzzled as to why nothing had been done before and promised that he would do everything in his power to rectify the matter. 'Now, let me make some notes. You are accused of helping some political prisoners escape, is that right?'

'That is the charge I believe, but there's no truth in it.'

'Give an account of the time the prisoners escaped, then what followed.'

John recounted the day that John Mitchel and his companion rode from Bothwell. 'The chief was in a right old temper because they had gone, and I hadn't heard him call out to stop them.'

'Why didn't you hear him, have you any idea?'

Pondering on this for several minutes, John wracked his brains for an excuse. 'The only thing I can think of is that the constables were doing drill that morning and with the orders being shouted across the road, the Chief's voice must have blended in somehow.' It sounded a feeble excuse, but it was all he could think of.

The lawyer kept writing. 'Right, what happened after that?'

With a shrug, John said that after the Chief had torn him off a strip for not hearing him, the matter was dropped. 'Although to be honest, I don't think he believed me.'

'Why not?'

'With me being Irish, you see, he thought I must know the men, but of course they were in a different class to me. Educated men they were, and wouldn't have given me the time of day.'

250

This seemed to satisfy the man and there was silence for a while as he wrote this all down. 'So the next thing you know was that you were being arrested?'

With a nod of his head, John told him about the day he was hauled off from Bothwell.

'Can you think of any reason why someone would cast blame on you?'

'No! Why would someone tell lies about me? I'm just an honest, hard working constable, who has his ticket of leave and could be in line for a free pardon any time soon. I would hardly risk being torn away from my wife and children now would I?' John's clear blue eyes held all the innocence he could muster.

This seemed to make perfect sense to Mr Sommerton and he sat for a moment reading a sheet of paper. 'Now can you tell me, do you know a man called Bart Tyrrell?'

John swallowed hard. 'Yes I know him, the good for nothing rogue.'

'Where do you know him from?'

Knowing this was his chance to put the trouble all at Bart Tyrrell's door, John recounted the time spent in the Impression Bay penitentiary and the time in Hobart that Bart Tyrrell was hauled away for a life sentence when he'd killed a man.

'So this man shouldn't have been at large then?'

'Well, it was a shock when I saw him standing at the roadside in Bothwell as I was driven away, I can tell you.'

'You saw him?'

'Yes, he was standing next to my mate Harry Askew. Now Harry is a good chum, but he's slightly fanciful with the truth when he's had a few beers, if you know what I mean?'

Mr Sommerton smiled. 'Yes, I know what you mean. Did you ever discuss the matter of the escaped prisoners with him?'

John appeared to think hard about this. 'I may have done. I thought it was brave and daring to do what they did and probably said as much, but that didn't mean I helped them.'

Seemingly satisfied with this explanation, the lawyer put his papers into a black leather case and stood to leave. 'I'll see you next Tuesday, Mr Ryan. Try not to worry, I think there is a good chance of all charges being dropped. How anyone could take the word of a convicted killer is beyond me.' He shook hands and walked from the room, leaving John feeling almost elated. Better not to celebrate yet, he thought, just in case things go wrong, but it did sound hopeful.

The day of the trial arrived and John had to admit to feeling queasy inside. He hated courtrooms, especially when it was him on trial and he prayed this would be the last time he would see the inside of one.

He was cheered to know that Ellen now knew where he was and what was happening. His poor girl must have been frantic all those months with no news. And him not with her when his baby son was born. He wondered, not for the first time, who had managed to delay proceedings - and why. His mind drifted to Horatio Phipps, the new Chief of police in Bothwell. The man hated him he knew, but why would he do such a thing? Perhaps he'd find out in court.

As he was marched into the courtroom John received a shock. Sitting at one side on the long bench seat was Police Chief, Archie Collins, and alongside him, Police Chief, Horatio Phipps. Did these two men know each other? John wondered, and felt a distinct unease at the thought; although he'd had a reasonable working relationship the old chief at Bothwell, he certainly hadn't with the new one.

Then he saw Harry, sitting and looking very apprehensive, while a few feet away sat Bart Tyrrell. The blood drained from John's face at the thought of the ordeal ahead. How was he ever to convince the judge and jury of his innocence with all these men ready to testify against him? The only friendly face he could see was Mr Sommerton's.

Before the judge had outlined the charges, he introduced Mr Sommerton as the defence lawyer and for the prosecution was a gloomy man called Mr Wright.

Sommerton then stood up and called for the first witness to come forward. John held his breath as former Chief of police for Bothwell; Archie Collins came to stand at the wooden rail in front of the judge. After he'd taken the oath, he stood to attention obviously waiting for the questioning to start.

'In your opinion, what kind of police constable was John Ryan?' Was the lawyer's first question.

Without even a glance in John's direction, the Chief said that for most of the time, he was a good, conscientious upholder of the law.

'Only most of the time?'

The well-remembered eyebrows waggled. 'There were one or two occasions when I had to remind him what his duties were.'

'Was one of these occasions the day when the Irish political prisoners escaped?'

The Chief frowned. 'No, not especially. I was annoyed that he hadn't heard my shout, but there was such a din going on outside, that it wasn't really surprising.'

John thought his ears deceived him and he saw that the other lawyer, Mr Wright's face dropped noticeably.

'I see.' Sommerton paused before saying, 'No further questions, M'lord. Please call Police Chief Phipps.'

As the current Police Chief of Bothwell took the stand, John's heart did a somersault. This man was not going to be so charitable, he was sure.

'You are Police Chief, Horatio Phipps?'

'I am.'

'Can you give me your opinion of John Ryan at the time of his employment as a police constable in Bothwell?'

The hard eyes seemed to bore into the lawyer as he answered. 'I have to be honest and say that I do not like the man, but as a policeman, he was first class. Rather sloppy in his appearance on occasions, but otherwise exemplary.'

Again, John couldn't believe his ears.

Mr Wright's face became glummer than ever.

Mr Sommerton pursued his questioning. 'How did you come to hear about his alleged involvement with the Irish dissidents?'

'A man came to my office and claimed that he had proof that John Ryan had helped in their escape.'

'Who was this man? Is he present in this court?'

'He is.'

'Can you name him?'

'Bart Tyrrell.' He nodded in the direction of the benches.

'Did he say how he had found out about these allegations?'

'He did. He said that one Harry Askew, a friend of the prisoner, had told him everything over drinks at one of the hostelries in Bothwell.'

'Did you call in Mr Askew to ask him about this?'

'I did, but not until after John Ryan had been taken off to Launceston. I couldn't take any chances of Ryan running off if the story was true.'

'What did Harry Askew tell you?'

'He said that his friend John Ryan had laughed about the prisoners getting away, but knew nothing of any help he'd given them.'

'Did you ask Mr Tyrrell what he had to say about this?'

'I did. He still swore that Askew had told him what he claimed.'

'What did you do then?'

'I put in a report and sent it to the Governor in Hobart.'

'Did he reply to your report?

'Yes sir. He said that the matter was in hand and he would forward instructions to Launceston that Ryan must stand trial so that the truth of the matter could be concluded.'

'Did you wonder why nothing was heard about any trial after five months had passed?'

'I did, and I wrote to Hobart to query the matter.'

'What reply did you get?'

'The Governor said that he would look into it.'

'Right, thank you Mr Phipps, that will be all.'

Mr Sommerton puffed out his chest and turned to the judge. 'Your honour, I believe a great injustice has been done to John Ryan. He was locked up in Launceston prison and forgotten. No one followed up on his case, a case I might add, that rests on the say-so of a convicted killer, who should not be at large. If your Lordship insists then I will call more witnesses, but I do not think there is enough evidence to deem this necessary.'

The Judge called both lawyers to his table where they held a long and whispered conversation.

Meanwhile John stood, his heart in his mouth, praying. Surely it couldn't be over so soon? After all these months on anguish!

In a daze, John listened to Mr Sommerton's words. 'It seems there was a genuine oversight of your case, I'm afraid. Some office worker in Hobart filed it in the wrong place. Then when Chief Phipps queried it the mistake came to light. In the meantime, Bart Tyrrell has been living as a free man. A matter that has now been rectified, I might add. How he thought he could get away with it is beyond me. Did he think no one would check to see if he was an escapee once his name came up in a court case?'

'How long has he been free?' John asked. 'And how did he escape from Port Arthur?'

'He won't say who it was, but we believe it was someone who worked in the prison, but lived outside. Mr Tyrrell won't escape again, that's for sure.' Mr Sommerton stood and reached across to shake John's hand. 'I'm away now that this is all settled. I'm glad the judge saw it was the right thing to do, and to give you your free pardon to compensate. Hopefully you can now send for your wife and children and settle somewhere in peace.'

John pumped the man's hand so vigorously that the lawyer winced. 'Oh, I'm sorry sir. I'm just so pleased it's all over, and my friend Harry is still my friend. I would've hated for him to stand up in court, the poor man's been though enough over the past months, so he has.'

'He's waiting outside to see you, so I'll send him in, shall I?'

'Yes please, sir, that would be grand.' John stood and with one last shake of Mr Sommerton's hand, let out a huge sigh of relief. It really was all over; he could hardly believe it.

Harry walked into the room looking with uncertainty at John, obviously not sure what kind of welcome he would get. But when he saw the wide smile on his friend's face, he came forward and the two men embraced like brothers. 'It's good to see you mate. Things were a bit hairy for a while, I can tell you. If only I'd known who that man Tyrrell was, I'd never have sat with him.' He grinned in the familiar way. 'Never know who you're sitting down to drink with do you?'

John shook his head. 'You sure don't. I always knew you'd come through for me, Harry. How's Stella doing, by the way? Is she well?'

'She's blooming, and soon, when I get my pardon, we'll come and visit you.'

'Is your pardon coming through soon then?'

'It is, as soon as Hobart can get my paperwork done, I'll be away from Bothwell.'

John frowned. 'Aren't you going to stay there? I'm hoping to go back today and have Ellen and the children brought to me.'

'Ah! You haven't been told then?'

A frisson of fear coursed through John. 'Told about what?'

'The rightful owner of your cottage has come forward. I'm afraid that woman duped you; she didn't own it at all.'

'You mean we've been living rent free all those months?' John's mouth gaped wide. He wondered what else could possibly go wrong in his life. Here he was a free man, but with no home to welcome his wife to. What was he to do now? 'I'll have to come back to Bothwell and collect our things, then set about finding somewhere else to live. I don't believe it, I really don't.'

'Try not to worry, mate. We'll sort something out, you'll see.'

Just then a knock at the door startled them both. Harry turned to see who was there and it was one of the clerks from the court. 'There's a cart here to take you back to Bothwell gentlemen, but Mr Ryan is to report to the Chief of Police's office on arrival.'

'Right, thanks,' Harry said. 'Come on then John, me old friend, let's be off.'

Out in the chilly air, John realised suddenly that he was a free man. Free to do what he liked, when he liked. Wasn't it just the grandest feeling? He put his arms in the air and spun around. 'Harry, I'm free!'

His friend laughed and together they climbed aboard the waiting cart.

On his arrival in Bothwell the following day, John hurried to the police office. He wanted to thank the Chief for supporting him, and also wanted to find out what he should do next.

Chief Phipps sat behind his desk and looked up as John entered, but before John could open his mouth, the man rose to his feet, glaring his usual cold hard stare. 'Ah, Ryan. Your belongings have been taken to the Falls of Clyde hotel, and you will collect them and be out of Bothwell before tomorrow noon. I've been given instructions to lend you a small handcart on which you can load it all. Your time in Bothwell is up, so please leave, I do not want to see you here again. Is that clear?'

'Y-yes, sir,' John stuttered, unable to believe this was the same man who had stood up in court and vouched for him. 'I wanted to thank you, sir, for what you did in Launceston.'

Phipps face filled with colour. 'You don't know how lucky you were, if I'd had my way, you'd have been locked up and the key thrown away.'

'B-but…'John began, but was interrupted.

'That's all, Ryan. On your way.' Then Chief Phipps looked down at the papers on his desk, making it clear that the interview was at an end.

John left the office in confusion and hurried off to the hotel to find his family's belongings. Mrs Vale came into the hallway to meet him, her face showing anxiety. 'Thank the Lord you're safe, we've been so worried these past months, with no word of Ellen and May. Are they safe?'

'They're fine, Mrs Vale, and I'm sorry you've had the worry. I think Ellen was sent off to Hobart without a chance to tell anyone where she was going. I'll tell you as much as I know, but firstly I need to know if all our belongings are here.'

'Yes, everything is safe, so don't worry about that anymore. I'll send for tea and then we can sit in the parlour and try to piece this awful business together. Go on in, I'll not be a moment.'

John sank gratefully onto the chaise-lounge, a feeling of comfort washing over him. It was almost like coming home seeing all the familiar furniture, pictures on the wall, and the battered old desk. Soon his reverie was broken into as the door opened and Mrs Vale entered, closely followed by Maura and Vera.

'Here we are,' Mrs Vale said cheerfully. 'While I pour the tea, you can tell us what happened. We've heard garbled bits and pieces from Harry Askew, but the poor man was too embarrassed to come here because he thought we'd blame him for your arrest.'

John quickly told them what had happened to him, with frequent 'Oh no's' and 'Oh, I say's' punctuating his story.

'So you had no idea where Ellen was then?' Maura asked.

'No, I was worried sick I can tell you. I caught a glimpse of her being taken into the police house just as I was being driven away, but had no idea what happened then.'

Mrs Vale rubbed her brow. 'No one saw her go and it wasn't until we saw Harry that he told us she and May had been put in a cart and taken off, but where to was a mystery.'

'And that nasty man Phipps wouldn't tell us anything,' Vera snapped. 'I asked him very politely, but was told it was nothing to do with me and to mind my own business. I ask you?'

'I have some news for you ladies. Since leaving here for Hobart, my Ellen has had a baby boy.' John sat back and beamed, while the three women all clamoured for information. 'I'm sorry, I don't know anything else, except that they are all fine and to be sure, I must try to get to Hobart and find them, but first I need answers to my questions about the cottage.'

Mrs Vale settled herself comfortably on her chair. 'The first we knew anything about this man was when Harry said he was at the police house looking for whoever lived in the cottage. By listening at the door, Harry discovered that the old lady who'd rented the cottage was supposed to pay rent to an agent, and it was only when it was reported that no rent had been paid for some considerable time that he'd come to investigate. Luckily, when he was told you were in prison, he didn't ask for the back rent, but of course we all ran down there and took your stuff out in case he tried to sell anything,'

A wide grin split John's face. 'He'd not have got much for any of that.' Then he became serious. 'But I can't thank you enough for taking our belongings to safety. It's not much, but it's all we've got, and now I've got to send for my girl and find somewhere to live.'

'Will you stay in Bothwell?' Maura asked.

'I would have loved to and I guess Ellen would too, but Phipps has given me my marching orders, so we must find somewhere else.'

Maura's face paled. 'You mean Ellen and the children can't come back here?'

'I'm afraid not.'

'Oh no,' Vera cried. 'That's not fair. He really is a horrible man.'

Mrs Vale sat silent, but John detected the hint of tears in her eyes. When she spoke, it was with a husky voice. 'Bothwell will never be the same again.' She studied her hands for a moment. 'Do you know why Phipps is so bitter?'

John frowned. 'No, I couldn't work out why he spoke up for me in court, but then was nasty to me today when I arrived.'

'Had no choice did he?'

His frown deepened. 'Why was that?'

'Because Police Chief, Archie Collins blackmailed him.' Mrs Vale puffed out her already considerable chest and laughed wryly. Then she leant forward and told John what had happened. 'He found out that Phipps was sent here convicted of killing two men in his regiment back in England and that he should never have been given such a position of rank. Flogged them, he did. I don't know how Archie Collins found out, but he told him that if he didn't help to get your charges dropped, he'd blow the whistle on him.'

'How do you know all this, Mrs Vale?'

'His wife told me. Mrs Collins and I became good friends after you and Ellen's wedding, and she came to Bothwell with him and so came to see me. Phipps was in a right stew as he thought he'd end up back in some penitentiary. I doubt he would of course, but he couldn't risk it.'

John blew out his breath. 'Well, I never. I always thought there was something bad about the man, but fancy Chief Collins finding out and using it to free me. I'll have to find a way of thanking him, but goodness knows how.'

'I write to Mrs Collins from time to time, so I'll mention it in my next letter about how grateful you are.'

'But why did he do it?'

'He became very attached to Ellen and I think wanted to see that she had another chance of a better life.'

With his head swimming, John tried to make sense of it all. He had a wife and two children, a few sticks of furniture and his freedom, but what was he to do next?

CHAPTER 20

As she sat with baby William at her breast, Ellen received the news that her husband was a free man. 'Oh, thank you God,' she breathed. 'Thank you, now we can all go home.' She closed her eyes and saw her cottage in Bothwell, looking just as it had all those months ago, and the longing to return was strong. She opened her eyes and smiled at May. 'We're going home my love, we're going home.'

Ellen tried to find out if she was free to leave, but several days passed before someone came to see her and inform her of her freedom. 'As your husband now has a free pardon, you may leave whenever you wish.'

Within minutes Ellen had gathered their few possessions together into a bundle and was ready to go. The governor called her to the office and told her that there was a coach leaving later that day for Bothwell, and she could be on it, so Ellen hoisted William onto one hip and took May's little hand in hers and strode purposefully out to the wooden gates.

After what seemed like an eternity the coach ground to a halt and she was climbing in. 'Here, missus, how about payin'?' the coach driver said.

'My husband will pay when we reach Bothwell,' said Ellen airily, and as the man seemed to accept that, she settled herself and her children comfortably inside. How nice this was. She never ridden in a proper coach before and was determined to enjoy it, thinking that she'd earned it anyway after being locked up for so long for no reason.

At the overnight stop, she pleaded to be given a room, saying that the money would be sent back with the coachman on his return. 'My husband is living in Bothwell and will have money. I can't sit in your bar all night with two small children, now can I?'

The landlord shrugged and sent her off to a room and Ellen smiled to herself. How simple life would be from now on.

Harry and John sat in the bar of their favourite hostelry, a large jug of ale each and pondered the future. 'I've got to be out of here by midday tomorrow, but goodness knows where I can go. I thought of going to Hobart, but I expect Ellen will be on her way here if I know anything about her.' John smiled faintly.

Stroking his chin, Harry said slowly, 'I did hear of some place in the North of the Island where land is going for practically nothing to men who have received their free pardon. It's a long way away though; Stella and me wouldn't see much of you, well not until my pardon comes through anyway and then perhaps we could move nearby.'

'Where is this place then, and how did you hear about it?' John was still rather cautious where Harry was concerned.

'There's a notice about it on the board outside the chief's office.'

'Why the devil didn't he tell me about it then? He's an evil bugger, so he is. I've been giving myself a headache with the worry and he could have saved me all that.' He sighed heavily. 'I'll go and read the notice first thing in the morning, but right now, I'm going to enjoy this ale, it's been in pretty short supply where I've been staying.'

'Plots of land for rent or sale to free men,' John read and muttered to himself, 'Sounds good, but I wonder how I can get there.' Looking at the rough map on the poster he saw that it was far away northward. He wandered outside and set off toward the hotel; these were the only people who would be able to help him, he knew, but they had done so much already it seemed a cheek to ask for any more favours.

He found Maura in the kitchen making a meat pudding. When he told her of his dilemma, she stopped chopping the onions and bit her lip. 'I wish I could help John, but I've no money of my own. It's too far for you to walk with the handcart so I don't know what to suggest. Mrs Vale will be back shortly and we'll ask her what she thinks.'

'She'll be back before noon won't she?' John asked anxiously.

'Yes, I should think so. That man hasn't given you much time to sort anything out has he? And how are you to let Ellen know where you are?'

They stood in silence for a few minutes and John wracked his brains for a way out of his problem. Why was it, he wondered, that just when he thought everything was going well, another obstacle came to stand in his way?

They heard the main door close and Mrs Vale came bustling into the kitchen, her mouth set in a grim line. 'Honestly that man is the giddy limit.'

'Who's that?' ask Maura.

'That so-called chief of Police, Phipps. He told me to make sure John here was away from Bothwell by noon otherwise he'd have me on a charge for harbouring a criminal.'

'But he's given me so little time to organise anything,' John said, exasperated. 'And how dare he take out his anger on you. If I could get in touch with Chief Collins in Hobart, I'd make life most uncomfortable for Phipps, so I would.' He scratched his head. 'How I'm to travel is the problem, Mrs Vale, but I will leave; I'll not have you in trouble on my account. It means I won't be here if Ellen comes, but you'll keep an eye on her won't you?'

'Do you need to ask, of course we will. There's a coach that travels as far as Launceston leaving tomorrow morning. I don't know how much further this place is from there.' Maura turned down the corners of her mouth. 'Where can we hide you though, that's the problem?'

'And money for the fare,' John reminded her.

They stood in silence for several minutes, each wracking their brains for an answer.

Just then Vera appeared, puffing and panting from the exertion of polishing the dining room tables. 'What's up, then? Why the long faces?'

John told her of his difficulty.

'Phew! He's a right bastard isn't he?'

Mrs Vale's eyebrows raised visibly at the blasphemy. 'That'll do Vera.'

'Sorry, Mrs Vale, but that man's enough to make a Saint swear.'

'I'll put the kettle on, shall I? A cup of tea always clears the mind.' Maura lifted the huge black kettle from the range and filled it at the kitchen pump.

'How much is the fare from here to Launceston?' asked John.

'I don't know, but I guess it's more than we've got between us. No one earns more than a few coppers a year,' Vera answered. 'And anyway, John, how are you to buy this land and stock it with chickens and the like without money? It only says the land is available.'

'I was hoping I'd think of something.' John told them lamely.

'Didn't they offer you anything to compensate for the delay of your trial?' Mrs Vale asked.

'My lawyer did say something about it, but then nothing else

261

happened so I thought they forgotten it.'

The tea made, they sat around the table pondering on what John could do. Then he realised with a shock; this was the first time he'd ever seen Mrs Vale sitting in the kitchen drinking tea.

The big clock on the wall ticked loudly in the silence, and John watched nervously as the hands crept toward twelve o'clock. His belly lurched with every minute that passed. Please God, he prayed, send me an answer to my prayers.

'I know!' Vera spoke so suddenly that John slopped his tea.

'What?' He held his breath.

'What about old Charlie at the Crown Hotel, he's goes somewhere up north to visit his sister. Can't remember the name of the place, but I've an idea he goes on Tuesday, and that's today.'

'Can you run and ask him, Vera, please,' Mrs Vale stood up looking purposeful. 'Let's just hope he hasn't left yet.'

Vera scuttled off, the sound of her feet drumming on the wooden floor of the hall, leaving three breathless people standing in the middle of the kitchen, their faces full of hope.

Vera was soon back and, gasping for breath, she pointed back the way she's just come. 'H-he's leaving right now, so if you hurry you can catch him. He doesn't mind about taking you, but you'll have to put your stuff on his cart quickly.'

'It's out the back, come on.' Mrs Vale led the way to where the little handcart sat waiting. 'Here's your belongings; I've packed them into several large sacks.'

John gratefully took the sacks and tossed them into his cart, before running round the corner of the hotel. 'I'll let you know how I get on, and give my love to Ellen. Tell her I'll send for her as soon as possible,' he called over his shoulder. 'And thanks for everything you've done.'

As Charlie drew up outside the hotel, John hoisted his cart onto the back of the larger one, and then, with five minutes to spare, he left Bothwell for the last time.

'What! You mean I've missed him?' Ellen was aghast. 'So where's he gone then? And did he say for me to follow?'

'Not really, he left in such a hurry you see,' Maura took one of Ellen's hands in her own. 'Chief Phipps gave him so little time to organise anything that it was rather a panic.'

Tears threatened as Ellen wondered how she was going to pay the coachman, and the innkeeper. 'I was sure he'd be here, and have enough money to pay for my travel and overnight stay. Oh, what am I to do?'

'Mrs Vale will go and have a word with the coachman; he can hardly take what you haven't got, can he?'

Baby William began to wail and Maura took him from Ellen and placed him against her shoulder, patting his back gently until a loud burp told her he was pain free.

Just then Mrs Vale swept into the kitchen. 'My dear Ellen, it's lovely to see you, and is this the new arrival?' She peered at William and cooed, which started him crying again. 'Oh dear, he doesn't seem to like me. Hello May. My you've grown while you've been away, haven't you?'

Ellen smiled in spite of her worry. 'William will be fine when he gets to know you. I'm sorry to plonk myself onto you, but I thought John would be here now that he's been released from prison.'

'Poor man, he's had a dreadful time. Here, sit down and Maura will explain everything while I go and placate the coachman. I presume he expects payment for your travel?'

'Yes,' Ellen answered weakly.

'Leave it with me.' And off she went, in her usual way of giving the impression of a ship in full sail.

After Maura had finished the saga of John's unfortunate circumstances, Ellen felt even more wretched. 'So he's gone off somewhere to buy land and stock with no money, and nowhere for us to live?' Ellen had been devastated by the news about the cottage here in Bothwell. 'I loved living there, and had all of my friends close by. If I follow John, it will mean another fresh start where I know no one.'

'You didn't know anyone here when you first arrived,' Maura reminded her.

'That's true, and of course I wasn't married then either.' She took William and cuddled him, putting her other arm around May. 'And I didn't have you two rascals.' May giggled and hid her face in the folds of her mother's skirt. 'Are Harry and Stella still here?'

'Yes they are and I think perhaps Harry might know where John's gone, because they were together last night. Ah, here comes Vera.' Maura grinned. 'Look who's here, Vera.'

'My, my, what a lovely surprise. Oh, look at you two,' she crouched in front of Ellen and took a hand each of the children. 'May's grown I must say, and isn't this little chap gorgeous?'

'This is William and he's just over a month old now.' Ellen told her proudly.

'Would you like to leave the children here and go to find Harry?' Maura suggested.

'That's a good idea, thanks. I wonder if Mrs Vale has managed to stop the coachman demanding my scalp?' Ellen edged toward the door and listened.

Mrs Vale returned then, a smile of her face. 'That's him settled. It's surprising what an offer of a free meal and a bed for the night will do. I've told him he can stay here, without charge, on two occasions, so that the bill is settled.'

'Oh, Mrs Vale, what would I do without you, but that still leaves the matter of my overnight stay in Hamilton.'

'Never mind about that now. Once the landlord has had a whinge, he'll forget all about it.' Vera observed.

Ellen grimaced. 'I do hope so. I'll be off to find Harry now, I won't be long.'

'No need to hurry,' Mrs Vale said. 'You'll be staying with us for a while, just until John's found a place, so don't worry yourself anymore.'

Feeling overwhelmed, Ellen stood in the middle of the kitchen and shook her head. 'I really don't know how I would have survived here in Bothwell without your kindness. All of you are wonderful, and I'll never be able to repay you.' Then, knowing tears would fall at any moment, she ran from the room and set off to find her husband's friend.

Harry was just coming out of the police office when Ellen saw him. 'Hello, Harry, how are you?'

'Good grief! Ellen! What are you doing here? You're supposed to be in Hobart waiting for John to send for you.'

'What? Did he expect me to stay in the women's prison for months on end while he finds us a place?'

'Prison? But he had no idea you were in prison.'

'Where did he think I was staying? At the best hotel?'

'Er, to be honest, I don't think he thought about it. He just thought you were safe...' Harry finished lamely.

'That's just like him, isn't it? Never thinks about anything properly. Anyway, I came to find you in case you know where he's gone.' Ellen's face flamed as she waited, with arms akimbo, for his answer.

Harry screwed his face into a mask of mock concentration. 'It's somewhere up in the north.' Then he said more brightly, 'I'll show you the poster,'

'If you remember, Harry, I can't read, so that's no good.'

'I can point to the place and tell you the area.'

'Oh very well, let's see.'

As they stood studying the notice on the board, the chief of police appeared. His face registering shock, then anger when he saw Ellen. 'What in the devil's name are you doing here?'

'I'm trying to find out where my husband's gone. Thanks to you, he's set off and no one knows for sure where he's gone.'

'Good. And he'd better stay away as well. If I see him in Bothwell again, I'll have him shot.' The grey eyes blazed with fury as the man turned on his heel and strode away.

Ellen shook from head to toe with anger and would have run after him if Harry hadn't held her back. 'He's not worth it, let him go. He'll get his just desserts soon enough.'

'What do you mean?'

Harry tapped the side of his nose. 'I hear that his days in Bothwell are numbered.' He grinned then, 'So are you coming to see my Stella?'

Calmer now, she linked arms with him and said, 'Of course. How is she?'

'She's doing really well. I'm teaching her to read.'

Later, back at the Falls of Clyde hotel, Ellen was full of Stella's progress. 'She's getting to be a right little lady, and she's so bright. I don't think Maddie ever showed her much attention to be honest. I know I shouldn't say that about my friend, but then I'm not sure of the way Stella came to be born, as Maddie never spoke about it.'

Maura nodded her head knowingly. 'All kinds of things can happen, as we know only too well. Now then, Mrs Vale has given you a small room down the corridor where there's a bed and a crib. I've put your things in there and William looks ready for bed so if you'd like to settle him and unpack, we'll discuss what to do over supper.'

'Are you coming, May.' Ellen held out her hand and the little girl toddled across and took it. 'I think you're ready for bed as well, don't you?'

Once both children were asleep, Ellen hurried back to the kitchen. 'Can I do anything to help? I feel I should earn my keep.'

'There are only two guest staying tonight, so there's nothing much to do now that they've had a meal.' Maura set out the places for the staff's supper.

Suddenly, Ellen realised something. 'Where's Ingrid? I haven't seen her since I got back.'

'She's gone to work in another hotel. Still here in Bothwell, but she and Mrs Vale never saw eye to eye.' Maura gave a wry laugh. 'At it hammer and tongs they were. Too alike in some ways I think. Still, we can manage until the spring, then we'll have to get another woman in.'

'I can help out for a while if you need me.'

'Thanks, Ellen, you never know we might make use of you. You look tired so I'll dish your supper out now, then we can all talk in the morning.'

'Thanks, I do feel worn out, what with all the travelling, then the worry over where John's gone. I don't know, Maura, my life seems to be a never-ending struggle.'

'It'll all be fine in the end, you'll see. Once you find John and settle down on some nice little smallholding, you won't know yourself.'

'Chance'll be a fine thing.' Ellen muttered before tucking into a portion of Maura's mouth-watering meat pie.

Standing uncertainly in the middle of Launceston, John studied his surroundings. Nice town by the look of it, he decided, but it wasn't where the offer of land was. That was still several miles away. Then he had an idea; perhaps the officer in charge of the prison would help. The man had certainly brought the plight of his long-term imprisonment into the open, so might know how to go about applying for land.

He hurried along toward the prison and stopped at the gate to ask for permission to enter, but couldn't remember the name of the man he wanted to see. John tried explaining the position he was in, but to no avail; no one seemed interested. His plan thwarted, he turned and wandered back into the town centre, fishing in his pocket to see if he had a coin big enough to buy something to eat.

If only he hadn't spent his last precious few coppers on ale the other night with Harry, but he hadn't seen past that moment, never realising he'd be travelling on so quickly. Then he berated himself; of course he'd known, hadn't the Police Chief told him to leave. He sighed; why did he never think ahead?

Leaning on the handcart, he watched people hurrying by, knowing he should do something, but was at a loss to know what. Then, a miracle happened; he saw the man he was looking for coming toward him.

Stepping boldly forward he stood to attention and asked, 'Please sir, I don't know if you remember me, but my name is John Ryan, and you helped me with my release from prison here.'

'Yes of course I remember you, Ryan. Glad you gained your freedom, what are you going to do now?'

'That's just the trouble, sir, I don't know.' Then he recounted the story of what happened when he returned to Bothwell.

'Good Heavens! That man Phipps is a right blackguard, I must say. Come with me, I'm just off back to the prison office, and we'll see what we can do.'

This time when they approached the gates, they opened without a word, and John couldn't help grinning to himself. It was always, 'who you knew rather than what you knew,' that counted in this life.

Leaving the handcart outside, he followed the governor into the vast building, along the corridors and across another hallway, before entering the familiar office. 'Sit down Ryan, I'll just send for your file.'

'Thank you, sir,' John dusted his trousers off before sitting on one of the leather covered chairs. He studied the room; amazed that such a marvellous place had been built in, what seemed to him an out of the way town.

A man in police uniform entered the room, a sheaf of papers in his hand, and these he handed to the governor, who spent several moments reading them. Then he looked up and smiled. 'I see you have your free pardon, Ryan, and not before time I might add. This being the case we can offer you a loan to get a home started. You have two children now, is that correct?'

'Yes, sir.' John held his breath, waiting to find out how much he could borrow.

'In that case we can lend you ten Guineas. It must be paid back within two years though, do you think you can manage that?'

John leapt forward from his seat. 'That's very generous, sir, indeed it is.' He wanted to shake the man's hand, but decided against it; he was a governor, after all. But all that money, John couldn't believe it, it was more than he'd ever had in his life.

'I'll make the necessary arrangements, so if you can call back tomorrow, I'll have documents here for you to sign and a money order for the full amount. You don't receive money in hand, I'm afraid, but it can be used to purchase land, building materials and livestock.' He pulled a face. 'Not that you can buy much for ten guineas, but hopefully it will help get you started.'

'Thank you again, sir. I'll see you tomorrow.' John hesitated. 'Will I be able to get past those fellows on the gate? Only they were less than helpful earlier when I came looking for you.'

'I'll see to it that they let you in, never fear. Just say Major Pringle is expecting you.'

Pushing the handcart in front of him, John walked back into Launceston. What was he to do now? He had no money, nowhere to stay, and no way of getting to the place where he knew there was land to be had. Cupping his hands, he drank water from the horse trough, then trudged round to the back of the shops and sat under a tree to await the morning.

Although she missed John, Ellen quickly settled into life at the Falls of Clyde hotel. She worked hard, cared for her children, and enjoyed the company of her friends. She still felt an ache of sadness whenever she passed the cottage that had been her home, and where she had lost their first baby. It all seemed so long ago, but when Maura helped her reckon it all up, it was only four years since she had first arrived in Bothwell. 'Isn't it amazing how much has happened in that time?' she said. 'I feel as though I've been in Van Diemen's Land forever, and life back in England is just a dream.'

'Do you still think about your family back home?' Vera asked one day as they sat cleaning silver at the kitchen table.

'Oh yes, all the time. My parents especially, but I can always see them in my minds eye, just as they were on the day they came to say goodbye at the prison. Of course,' she added wistfully, 'I had my Mary with me then.'

'How many brothers and sisters do you have? Only I never had any because I was a foundling, you see.'

'Oh Vera, I'm so sorry, I never knew that. It must be awful not to have a loving family.'

Vera sniffed. 'Well, what you've never had, you never miss.'

Ellen tried to count on her fingers the number of brothers and sisters she had. 'Let me see, there was William and Mary, they were older as my mother had them from her first husband. Then came Fred, John, Jane, they're all older than I am. Then after me came Arthur, another William, James, Eliza and Harriet.'

'Good Heavens! Your poor mother has eleven children?' Vera was aghast.

'Well, I can't count, but yes, that's all of us.'

Looking puzzled, Vera asked, 'Why are there two William's?'

But Ellen shook her head, not having any answer to that. 'But, I've added another one, haven't I?'

They both laughed and as Maura came into the kitchen, they told her about all Ellen's siblings. 'My, your poor mother.'

'She loved us all in spite of the hard work and although we were very poor, there was always enough food on the table because my father grew vegetables and kept chickens.'

'I expect the older children helped with the little ones as well,' Maura observed.

'Yes, we all helped as much as we could.' Ellen sighed and smiled. Home was so far away and yet in her heart it felt close enough to reach out and touch.

John staggered into the small village, and stopped to look about him. This didn't look too bad and he just hoped there was land enough left for him to buy. He'd managed to reach the town by a series of begged lifts and it had taken him more than a week. He'd worked the odd day here and there to make enough cash to buy food, but had sheltered under hedges and in fields by night. The cold had been appalling, but sheer determination, and the thought of Ellen joining him, had kept him going.

He then moved on along the dusty street, hoping to find somewhere where he could find out about land. Governor Pringle in Launceston had assured him of the validity of the claim, saying that he had sent several families to the area.

Soon John found what he was looking for, the 'Land Registry' office. He walked in and was asked to sit down while his papers were read, and was pleased to be offered a hot drink and some bread and cheese. This was more like it, he decided, much more civilised.

After a while, a man came out of a side room. 'Mr Ryan? Come this way, please. I'm the overseer for this area.'

John followed him into an office so full of papers that he wondered how anything was ever found, but he was asked to take a seat while the man sat behind his desk, elbows resting on top.

'Well, Mr Ryan, this all seems in order, so welcome to our small village of Latrobe.' The overseer stood and leaned across the desk, his hand held out in greeting.

John smiled and also stood to shake the proffered hand. 'Thank you, sir.'

'Now, I'll take you to see Mr Watson, who in turn will take you out to view the plots of land we have left.'

His heart leaped inside him as John contemplated seeing for the first time, the place where he and Ellen would make their home. His smile must have been wide as his companion laughed, pointing out that this was the best part of his work; helping free men find somewhere to settle. 'The new citizens of Van Diemen's Land,' he proclaimed.

Out in the street, John grasped the handles of his trusty cart and waited for Mr Watson, and as a swarthy, middle aged man approached them he was introduced.

'It's not too far, just a few miles away,' Mr Watson told him, and then turned to speak to the overseer, before leading John along the unmade road that led out between a few houses and a shop.

'There's not that much here is there?' John asked Mr Watson.

'Not yet, but give us a few years and we'll have built up a big town, just you see. Everyone coming here is committed to hard work and leading a worthwhile life. We've several families settled already, and with more and more men getting a free pardon, there's no telling how big a community we'll end up with.'

'It all sounds very exciting, to be sure. I can't wait for my wife and children to join me.'

'It won't be long before you have a house built and the land tilled.'

John balked at this. 'You mean, I've to build my own house?'

'Of course, this is virgin land, only the Abo's lived here until recently.' Mr Watson glanced sideways. 'It's all right, we've driven them off, and they're no trouble now.'

'I have no problem with them,' John assured him. 'Is it easy enough to buy the materials for a house?'

'Yes, everything's in Latrobe, and you'll find that all your neighbours will lend a hand. That's how it works here; we all pull together.'

Sighing with relief, John picked up his step with renewed vigour, all tiredness from the long days spent on the road from Launceston forgotten.

Then, as his companion turned off the main road, John saw some small buildings away to his left. They were basic, but not so different from the cottage in Bothwell. His heart lifted; was this to be their new home?

The air was clear and fresh, and the soil looked like Irish soil, rich and dark. He'd be able to grow anything he wanted to here: oats, barley, potatoes and other vegetables. He sang in his head, 'It won't be long now my sweet Ellen. It won't be long now.'

CHAPTER 21

As the weeks dragged on, Ellen began to wonder if perhaps her husband had forgotten her. No word had been received from him and it was now autumn, a good time to travel – if only she knew where to go.

'Just sit tight,' was Maura advice. 'He'll send for you, or even come to collect you as soon as he can.'

'I know, it's just that he's missing so much of the children's growing and they'll be wondering who he is when they do see him. May was only just over a year old when she last saw him, so I'm sure he'll be a stranger to her.'

'She'll soon get used to him, so don't fret. Is Stella coming today?'

'Yes, she'll be here in a moment. I can't believe how helpful she is for such a little girl.' Although now eleven years old, Stella was still small for her age, but bright and willing to do whatever was asked of her.

Maura smiled. 'Yes, she is a help, especially with May.'

May looked up at the mention of her friend's name. She loved Stella and the feeling seemed to be mutual as they spent hours together, May toddling after Stella as she busied herself with clearing the tables or peeling vegetables.

'They'll miss one another when we go.' Ellen said.

'That's true, but they soon forget.' She looked round. 'Didn't Harry say he was going to join you though?'

'At one time he did, but I'm not sure now.'

'Why?'

'Haven't you seen him with Ingrid?'

'No, I haven't. Is it serious do you think?'

Ellen nodded. 'I think so, and Stella likes her too, so I think they might all stay in Bothwell.'

Maura shook her head. 'Well I never did,' was all she said.

Ellen grimaced. 'I must admit that when I first saw them together I was angry because I wondered how he could find someone else so soon after losing Maddie. Then I realised it's been nearly two years since she died, so I suppose it was only natural.'

'They do make an odd couple on the face of it, but then we don't know what they might have in common.'

With a frown creasing her brow, Ellen stood up from the kitchen table and prepared to go and start on the bedrooms. The hotel was filling up now and most of the rooms were occupied, so there was plenty of work to be done. 'I'll just check on William then I'll go up and start room number two, the occupant should be gone for the day by now.'

William lay in a wooden draw balanced between two chairs just outside the back door, in the shade, and seeing that he was fast asleep, Ellen hurried away to begin the days work. When she arrived in room two she found that the man had left papers strewn all over the bed. Tutting loudly, she bent to pick them up, deciding to place them on the chest of drawers. Underneath the papers Ellen found a brown leather wallet and was about to put it aside when she noticed its bulk. 'Blimey,' she thought, 'there must be a lot of money in there,' and couldn't resist opening it to look. Her eyes nearly popped out of her head when she saw the thick wad of bank notes. Although she had no idea how much was there, she knew it must be a great deal and stood for a moment, wondering what to do with it. It would have been so easy to just pop it into her pocket, but she knew that the owner would most likely be back for it at any time and if he knew where he'd left it, then she would be found out. Sighing deeply, Ellen placed it on top of the papers, knowing honesty was always the best policy. But she couldn't help wondering just what she could have done with so much money. She and John could probably have had a grand house, and a carriage, and servants... Ellen laughed out loud at her own silly daydreams, when suddenly the door burst open and a man came dashing in.

Seeing the wallet on the dresser, he sighed with relief. 'Oh, thank goodness it's here, I've been worried sick.' He looked at Ellen thoughtfully and said, 'Did you see it?'

'Yes, sir, it was on the bed under the papers. I hope you don't mind me moving them, but I wanted to make the bed.'

'No, I don't mind at all, and I must say I applaud your honesty as there is a lot of money in here.' He held up the wallet. 'It's to pay for stock, that are to be taken to the north for the new settlers there.'

'That's where my husband is now,' Ellen told him.

He smiled. 'Well then, he might be glad of a few sheep or cattle.' As he crossed to the door, he said, 'Thank you again,' then was gone.

Ellen let out a long ragged breath. What a good thing she hadn't taken any money, it might have meant John wouldn't have any livestock to buy.

Meanwhile, John was making good progress. The area he was in was called New Ground, which exactly described what it was. His was one of several smallholdings that dotted the open landscape and he was making friends with all his neighbours.

'This is a grand place, I must say,' he said to Mr Watson one day while in Latrobe buying more materials for his house.

'Yes, I think we're very fortunate to have been granted this tract of land. Everything grows so quickly and the climate is excellent.'

'It's a balmy day, to be sure and I'm certain my Ellen will love it. I've only got the roof to go on, and we're starting that tomorrow, then a few sticks of furniture and I'll be ready to go and collect her.'

'Do you need much?' Mr Watson asked.

'Not a lot really. We've two armchairs, a small chest of drawers, a table and two wooden chairs, all battered and worn, but we'll make do with them for now. We've bedding and pots and pans, but there may be other things we'll need once my wife arrives.'

'Didn't you say that you have two children?'

'I have. Oh, my goodness!' John slapped his forehead with an open hand. 'I haven't thought of where they'll sleep, have I?' He groaned, 'And I've just realised that we need a stove or fire of some sort to cook on.'

'Well, there's quite a selection in the store here. Over the back there, see?'

'Can you work out for me how much I've left of my loan, please? Then I can go and sort something out.'

'Certainly, I'll go and get your paperwork. What have you there?'

'I've three dozen planks to make shingles for the roof, I need more than that of course, but my handcart will only carry so many.'

'Do you know how to do that?'

'No, but my neighbour is giving me a hand as he's done his own. I was going to thatch the roof like back home, but there aren't the reeds here. Still, he assures me its snug, so hopefully it'll be all right.'

Mr Watson laughed. 'Yes, it's fine, all the buildings here are done like it. Right, I'll away now and check on your balance.'

While he was gone, John wandered across to look at the cast iron stoves. When he asked the price he knew very well that he couldn't afford one. He sighed and thought of his poor Ellen cooking on an open fire again. She'll manage though, she always did.

Mr Watson arrived back. 'You've two guineas left.'

'Ah well, I'll buy some more wood to make the children's beds. The stove will have to wait.'

'Have you bought seed yet?'

'Indeed I have, and they're sown, and there's shoots showing already. I've some hens so I'd better get some feed for them, then I'll be away. Thanks for your help, sir.'

'Glad to oblige. See you soon, Mr Ryan.'

John tipped his hat, and revelled in the fact that he was now called 'Mr'. As he walked home, the handcart laden down, he tried to work out how long it would take him to finish the house. It was basic, just two rooms, but he was sure it would be cosy. He hoped and prayed that Ellen would like it, and that they could settle down to a good life here. A few days to finish the roof, he reckoned, then he could ask his neighbour to keep and eye on his newly sprouting vegetables and the chickens, then he'd set off for Bothwell to collect Ellen and the children. He'd have to be careful when he arrived in case Phipps was on the lookout, but it was a risk he'd have to take. The thought of seeing his wife, little May and the new baby spurred him along and soon New Ground came into view. Already it looked like home. He breathed in the fresh air, that was close enough to the coast to bring in a salty tang, and happiness flooded through him. Ah, yes, home.

Ellen pulled all the sheets from the huge copper with the aid of a wooden stick, then plunged them into the tin bath full of cold water. She gave them a good trouncing to get rid of as much soap as possible, then lifted them, one at a time, up onto the ledge at the front of the mangle. It was hot and tiring work, but she carried on diligently, memories of her mother uppermost in her mind, until they were all done and ready to be hung on the line. Piling them into the wicker basket, she heaved it up until it rested on her hip and made her way to the door that led into the garden.

Just as she was about to cross the doorstep, she saw the figure of a man bending over William's makeshift crib. 'Hey! What are you doing?' she shouted, dropping the laundry basket and running forward.

Then the man straightened and turned round. Ellen gasped and shouted in delight, 'John! Oh, John, where have you sprung from?' Her eyes were like saucers and her mouth stayed open.

He laughed. 'Yes, 'tis me my sweet. Is this bonny baby here our son?'

Nodding, Ellen said breathlessly, 'Yes, this is William.'

'That's a grand name to be sure.' He opened his arms then and Ellen ran into them, her arms going round his neck.

They hugged for several minutes, just happy to be together again. Then Ellen felt a tug at her skirt and looking down saw May staring at them, a puzzled look on her face. 'Here, my love, here's your daddy. He's come to take us home.' She glanced at her husband. 'Well, I presume he has.'

'I have indeed. Hello May.' He knelt down in front of the little girl and tried to take her hand, but May pulled back, unsure of this strange man.

'She'll be fine once she gets to know you. Don't forget, she was only a baby when she last saw you.'

John stood up again and went to retrieve the laundry, which luckily had stayed in the basket. 'Do you need a hand with these?'

'Yes please, they're so heavy when wet. How my mother managed on her own all those years I'll never know.'

As they pegged the sheets on the line, John told Ellen that he would have to keep out of sight as Phipps would probably try to cause trouble if he knew of the visit. 'I'll tell you all about our new home once we've finished this and you've given your poor old starving and weary husband food and drink. His eyes twinkled in the old familiar way and Ellen caught her breath, glad to see that although thinner, he was still as handsome as ever.

Inside, the hotel kitchen was soon buzzing as news of John's arrival spread. Mrs Vale held court while Maura busied herself making a meal and a large pot of tea, while Ellen sat, entranced, while he told them what had happened to him in the four months since he'd fled Bothwell in such a hurry.

'So you think this place is going to suit you, then?' Mrs Vale asked.

''Tis a grand place, to be sure. The soil is good, I've planted some vegetables already, and the climate is fair. I've a few chickens and I've built a house for us.'

'Is there a town close by?' Vera wanted to know.

'It's little more than a village at the moment, but I've heard that it will become a large town as the sea comes inland at that point and ships will bring supplies. Within a year, so I believe, a thriving community will living there.'

'I can hardly believe it all,' Ellen clapped her hands. 'A whole

275

new township, and we'll be part of it.' She lifted May onto her lap. 'Won't it be lovely? There will be loads of other children to play with and…'She looked up, her face alight. 'Perhaps even a school.'

'I'm sure there will be,' John told them, 'because there are already a lot of children about. The neighbours are all good, helpful folk too and have helped me build the house, so it's all ready for us.'

Ellen almost bounced out her seat in excitement. 'I can hardly wait.' But then she sank back in her seat. 'Oh dear, John, how are we to get there? We've no money for a cart or the coach.'

John bit his lip. 'That is the problem at the moment, but I'll think of something.'

'Well, never mind for now, let's eat. I'm sure John is ravenous after spending many days on the road, and I've a nice tankard of ale for him to wash it down with.' Maura placed a plate piled high with food in front of him.

He picked up his knife and fork and set about it with gusto, while the others ate in a more sedate way. Then the bell sounded from the front hall and Mrs Vale, who had taken to eating in the kitchen nowadays, rose from the table and went to see who wanted attention.

Several minutes later she returned with a wide smile on her face. 'I think I may have the answer to your problem,' she said, then sat to finish her meal, while Ellen stared firstly at her and then at John.

With the last mouthful of food cleared from her plate, Mrs Vale looked up and smiled again. 'Do you recall finding a gentleman's wallet yesterday?' she asked Ellen.

'Yes, he'd left it under all his papers on the bed, but I'd put it on the dresser, so it wasn't really lost.'

'Well, whatever the circumstances, he is extremely grateful. He seems to think that some people might not have been as honest as you were and so he has asked me to pass on a small reward.' She held out a paper note.

Ellen felt her face flame. 'Oh, no I couldn't possibly take anything.'

'He insists,' Mrs Vale told her. 'And that is not all. He travels on to Launceston tomorrow and has offered you the chance of riding in the coach with him, as his guests.'

Now both John and Ellen sat open-mouthed, before John suddenly realised what this meant. 'Oh, what a grand chap. I must see him and thank him.'

'I should wait until he comes in for his meal this evening,' Mrs Vale told him, 'otherwise you might be seen and I don't trust Phipps one little bit.'

'He's still here then?' John asked.

'He is, and as unpleasant as ever. There was talk of him being moved on, but it's never happened.' Mrs Vale sniffed.

'Are you going to see Harry, while you're here?' Vera wanted to know.

'I don't think I'll risk it. To be sure, Harry is a grand chap in many ways, but I'm not sure he could keep his mouth shut about me being here.'

Mrs Vale agreed. 'The fewer people who know of your visit, the better.'

Just then a wailing could be heard coming from outside the backdoor, and Ellen jumped to her feet. 'Poor William, it's way passed his feed time and I'd forgotten him. Come on John, you can meet your son properly now he's awake.'

As she carried her son to her room to feed him, Ellen couldn't help smiling. Her life felt complete now that John was back. They would be leaving here tomorrow and travelling to a new home - one where they would be safe from the likes of Horatio Phipps. They could live the life they chose; not one forced on them by circumstances. With William settled to her breast, she daydreamed about what it would be like. She'd miss Bothwell very much, and the wonderful friends she'd made here, but there would be new friends she was sure, and once the farm was up and running, she could tend it and perhaps John could find employment so that they would have a better standard of life.

John came into the room then, with May holding his hand. 'This little girl is pleased to have her daddy back, so she is, and is quite happy to be in his company.' He sat on the bed next to his wife, and May scrambled onto his lap. 'We're going to have our hands full, to be sure, but I think everything will be fine.'

'It will, John, everything will be so good.' She grinned then, her old mischievous grin. 'It'll be a tight squeeze in here tonight, but I'm sure we'll manage.'

'My, my, Mrs Ryan, you haven't changed a bit.'

As the coach didn't leave until just before noon, Ellen decided to go and visit various people who had helped her in the time she'd lived in Bothwell. Her first stop was to see the reverend McDonald, who shook her hand vigorously when she told him the news. 'May God bless both of you and keep you safe. I hope your new life goes well for you.'

Then she went into the hotel where Ingrid was now working. The woman was surprised to see her as they had never been particularly friendly, but she smiled and wished them well. 'Please pass on our best wished to Harry and Stella. We haven't told him John is here, as John thought he might get excited about seeing him again and think they could spend a pleasant hour or two in their favourite hostelry. I'm sure he'll understand, but we can't risk Phipps finding out he's here. Give Stella a big hug from me and May. Are you and Harry going to make a go of things do you think?' Ellen knew it was an impertinent question, but she wanted to know before she left.

Ingrid grinned. 'I hope so, in fact I think he's on the brink of asking me to marry him. I know I can't replace Maddie, but I think we can be reasonably happy.'

'I'm so pleased for you. Maddie was a very special friend to me and I'm sure she'd be pleased too.' Ellen then said goodbye and hurried back to the hotel, calling in to thank the shopkeeper and the butcher for all their help over the years. She sniffed back a tear, how she would miss Bothwell. It was as dear to her as Selborne had been. No, she thought nowhere could ever match up to Selborne, but Bothwell was a close second.

Later as she waited for the coach, the well-worn carpet bag containing their few clothes, Ellen felt her throat constrict. How she would miss The Falls of Clyde hotel and everyone in it. This felt so much like home, almost more than the tiny cottage where she'd lived happily for a while. It was the people who made it, she decided, especially Mrs Vale, Maura and Vera. They, together with dear Maddie, had been her family for so long; how was she ever going to manage without them? She smiled at John who was holding May in his arms. 'I'm trying not to cry, but it's hard to say goodbye to everyone.'

'I know my sweet, but you've said your goodbyes now, so don't look back. When the coach arrives, I'll let you follow our kindly gentleman into it, then I'll hop in at the last moment.'

She nodded, knowing that John was more worried about leaving Bothwell unseen than anything else; perhaps it's different for men, she mused.

Then she heard the sound of hoofbeats coming along the street and it wasn't long before another hotel guest had loaded his bags and was settling himself inside. Her grateful benefactor beckoned to Ellen and she carried William out into the autumn sunshine, glancing along the street as she made her way into the coach. 'Don't look,' she told herself, 'don't look.' Then, with a quick dash, John was in next to her, May giggling in his arms at being jogged about.

278

The other passengers smiled, but Ellen didn't see anything as her eyes misted with tears at the sight of her friends all standing at the window to watch her leave. She waved, and they all waved back: her last impression of Bothwell. It would be forever imprinted in her memory.

Many miles, and five days later, they arrived at New Ground. Ellen's first thought was that it was a rather flat and uninspiring landscape, until John pointed out that in one direction was a forest, and in the other the sea was not too far away. 'I'll take you back into Latrobe tomorrow so you can get to know the shopkeepers there, and you've yet to meet out neighbours. I must say they've tended my garden well, and look at the eggs they've collected for us. All from our own chickens, eh? What do you say about that?'

Their journey had been so trouble free that Ellen couldn't believe they had arrived so quickly. Although the coach had not come any further than Launceston, some of the money the gentleman had given Ellen was enough to pay for a lift on a cart coming to Latrobe and they had walked from there.

'What do you think of your new home, my sweet?' John broke into her reverie.

'What? Oh, I think it'll do us well, and the eggs will make us a good tea. I've bought some bread and a few bits to see us through today, so we'll be all right.' Ellen wandered from one room to the other, admiring John's handiwork. 'You've done well dear, you really have and I'll soon give it a few homely touches,' She went to him and planted a kiss on his cheek. 'Thank you, John. Thank you so much.'

'It's all for you and the children, my Ellen. I'll work hard and make us a better life, you'll see. It's what we deserve after all we've been through.'

A wide smile curved Ellen's lips. 'Yes, we do deserve it, don't we? It's taken us a while to get here, but now we can settle and bring our children up to be good hard-working citizens. We're the new generation of this island when you think of it. Nearly everyone here has been a convict, but now we're all law-abiding folk, just getting on with life.'

'It'll still be hard at times, I think, but we can manage it, can't we?'

'Yes, we can. Together we can do anything.' Then hearing children's voices outside, Ellen looked out to see their neighbours children playing with May, their squeals of delight filling the air.

She closed her eyes and her thoughts went back to earlier times, many, many years ago. In her minds eye she could see the cottage garden at Selborne where they'd all played as children.

And now the sound of different children's laughter brought back echoes of home and for a moment Ellen thought her heart would break. She would never again see her parents or brother's and sisters, never again walk along the dusty street lined with thatched cottages. Never again stand at the top of the Hanger and feel as though she were on top of the world…

Taking a deep gulp of air, she opened her eyes and looked at her husband. He, May and William were her world now and she would do her best for them.

Van Diemen's Land was their home. They would adopt it, and hopefully, their family would be only one of many to populate the beautiful island.

By the same author

Echoes of a Trumpet

After the labourers' riots of 1830, the village of Selborne was in turmoil.

Whole families were left without breadwinners when husbands and sons were transported to the other side of the world for their part in the uprising. But John Newland, the legendary ring-leader and *Trumpeter*, was released after only six months custody in Winchester gaol.

In this book his great-great-granddaughter serves us fact laced with supposition, to bring us a story of two young people caught up in the bitterness of a conflict which had happened before they were even born.

Only the strength of their love for each other can overcome such a legacy – the strained echoes of a trumpet, still stirring discontent after all those years

Published by John Owen Smith
ISBN 978-1-873855-30-0 (1-873855-30-3) November 1998

Other books from the same publisher

One Monday in November…and beyond—about the so-called Swing Riots of 1830—the last agricultural uprising in England. It gives the political and social background to the riots which swept across southern England and, as an example, details the particular manner in which it affected Selborne and Headley.
ISBN 978-1-873855-33-1 Aug 2002, paperback, 136pp, illustrations plus maps and a 'Rioters' Walk'.

A Parcel of Gold for Edith—*letters from Australia 1853–1875*
"Hidden in a tin that had once held Andies Candies, I found seven faded letters which revealed the life story of a remarkable woman, my great-great aunt." Joyce Stevens tells us the result of her 30-year search into the identity of one of Australia's Pioneer Women.
ISBN 978-1-873855-36-2 November 2001, paperback, 102pp, illustrated.

Heatherley—*by Flora Thompson*
Her sequel to the 'Lark Rise' trilogy
This is the book which Flora Thompson wrote about her time in Grayshott. It is the 'missing' fourth part to her *Lark Rise to Candleford* collection in which 'Laura Goes Further'. Illustrated with chapter-heading line drawings by Hester Whittle. Introduction by Ann Mallinson.
ISBN *978-1-873855-29-4 Sept 1998, paperback, 178pp, illus+maps.*

On the Trail of Flora Thompson—*beyond Candleford Green*
The author of *Lark Rise to Candleford* worked in Grayshott post office from 1898–1901. A local historian investigates the people and places she would have seen here at that time.
ISBN 978-1-873855-24-9 May 1997, paperback, 144pp, illus+maps.

Headley's Past in Pictures — *a tour of the parish in old photographs*
Headley as it was in the first half of the 20th century. In this book you are taken on an illustrated tour of the parish.
ISBN 978-1-873855-27-0 Dec 1999, updated 2003, paperback, 124pp, over 100 photographs, plus historical notes and maps of area.

John Owen Smith, publisher — www.johnowensmith.co.uk